J. A. (Joseph Archer) Crowe, G. B. (Giovanni Battista) Cavalcaselle

Raphael

His Life and Works

J. A. (Joseph Archer) Crowe, G. B. (Giovanni Battista) Cavalcaselle

Raphael
His Life and Works

ISBN/EAN: 9783744669863

Printed in Europe, USA, Canada, Australia, Japan

Cover: Foto ©Raphael Reischuk / pixelio.de

More available books at **www.hansebooks.com**

RAPHAEL:

HIS LIFE AND WORKS.

WITH PARTICULAR REFERENCE TO

RECENTLY DISCOVERED RECORDS,

AND

AN EXHAUSTIVE STUDY OF

EXTANT DRAWINGS AND PICTURES.

BY

J. A. CROWE AND G. B. CAVALCASELLE,

AUTHORS OF "THE HISTORY OF PAINTING IN NORTH ITALY,"
AND "TITIAN: HIS LIFE AND TIMES."

VOL. I.

LONDON:
JOHN MURRAY, ALBEMARLE STREET.
1882.

TO

His Royal Highness

THE PRINCE OF WALES,

THESE VOLUMES

ARE,

BY PERMISSION,

RESPECTFULLY DEDICATED

BY

THE AUTHORS.

PREFACE.

THE life of Raphael has been the subject of
countless biographies and essays in which admiration and praise were justly lavished on the greatest
painter of any age. From the days of Rumohr to
those of Passavant and Waagen, the master's works
were subjected to the minutest investigation; and
drawings, pictures, or frescos were examined, measured, and commented on with unwearying patience
and industry. Yet the outcome has not been commen-
surate with the labour expended; and we are still
without a life of Raphael which deals exhaustively
with his relations to the art and artists of his own or
previous centuries. Some have studied pictures to
discover and point out the influence of the antique
or contemporary craftsmen in Italy. Others have
looked at drawings to note their connection with
altar-pieces or frescos; Passavant alone devoted his
life to a catalogue of all Raphael's works. His

followers, amongst whom we shall note Springer and Grimm as pre-eminent, endeavoured to sift the errors of their predecessors, and, in numerous instances they succeeded in elucidating disputed points in Raphael's career. But no one, as yet, has convincingly traced the progress of the artist. Critics are divided into parties who fight, not without acrimony, over matters which remain obscure; and it is characteristic that even the intercourse of Raphael with Perugino has been left in considerable doubt.

The authors of these pages do not pretend to have solved the problems which vainly exercised the skill of so many inquirers; yet they hope to have done something to shed new light on Raphael's career. In the volume which they now offer to the public, they have shown how they ventured to explore and attempted to illustrate the period of Raphael's youth, which had hitherto been comparatively neglected. They have tried to prove how he was taught under his father and Perugino; and they have looked at every drawing as well as at every picture to trace the road which led him deviously to fame; they point out, it may be not unerringly, where he copied the antique, where his professional rivals or precursors; how he digested and assimilated after learning the lessons of all the masters of his country. Little or nothing, indeed, has been added to the documentary evidence which was stored since the days of Vasari; but all the materials in existence have been used, and neither time nor travel has been spared to study personally every example in whatever part of the world it was deposited.

The sources from which they quote, the Authors have invariably acknowledged. It is only necessary to add that where no express statement to the contrary has been made they have used Lemonnier's edition of "Vasari."

CONTENTS.

CHAPTER I.

Contemporary critics.—Origin of the Santi.—Frederick of Urbino.—Frederick as a patron of Art.—Giovanni Santi.—Guidubaldo of Montefeltro.—Raphael's infancy.—Giovanni Santi dies.—Santi and Raphael.—Raphael an orphan.—Perugino and Raphael.—Raphael's first master.—Perugino Raphaelesque.—Raphael Peruginesque.—Signorelli.—Timoteo Viti 1

CHAPTER II.

Perugian revolutions.—Art revival at Perugia.—Raphael's sketch-book.—Pinturicchio as a draughtsman.—Perugino's sketches.—Raphael learns drawing.—Copies of drawings from the Sixtine Frescos.—Other copies.—Their style.—He copies several masters, Signorelli, Mantegna.—He studies from monuments.—His school-fellows, and school work.—Visit to Urbino.—Library of Urbino, and copies by Raphael from pictures by Justus of Ghent.—Gallery of Urbino.—Raphael and the Cambio.—" Resurrection " of the Vatican.—Terni and Alnwick.—" Madonna Diotalevi " 45

CHAPTER III.

The Baglioni.—" Massacre of the Innocents," and other pen sketches.—The Solly " Madonna."—" Madonna with the Finch."—Practice at Perugia.—Connestabile predellas and Raphael's drawings for them.—Landscape sketches.—Invasion of Cesar Borgia.—The " Martyrs."—Raphael's " Crucifixion " based upon that of Perugino.—" Crucifixion " of Earl Dudley.—" Trinity " and " Creation of Eve."—Influence of Alunno, Signorelli, and Pinturicchio.—" Coronation of St. Nicholas of Tolentino."—" Coronation of the Virgin " and its predellas at the Vatican.—Imitation of the predellas of Fano . . 96

CHAPTER IV.

PAGE

The " Sposalizio " of Milan based on Perugino's predella at Fano and his " Sposalizio " at Cacu.—Raphael as an architect.—Bramante.— " Madonna " Connestabile.— Portrait of Herrenhausen.— Pinturicchio at Sienna, and his relations to Raphael.—Drawings for Pinturicchio's Frescos ; sketches for the same.—Design of the " Graces."—Eusebio da San Giorgio.—Guidubaldo, captain of the Church.—Raphael's sketches of the Palace and Fort of Urbino ; of other places in the Duchy.—His patrons at Urbino.—Alleged recommendation to Soderini at Florence.—Florentine influences on Raphael's style.—The " Knight's Vision."—" Cain and Abel."— " St. Michael " and " St. George."—The " Graces," and " Marsyas and Apollo."—Michael Angelo and Da Vinci.—Raphael's journey to Florence 163

CHAPTER V.

Return of Raphael from Florence to Perugia.—Completion of the altarpieces of Sant' Antonio and Ansidei and their predellas.— " Madonna " of Terranuova, and drawings for the pictures in the Venice sketch-book.—Influence of Michaelangelo.—Beginning of the fresco of San Severo.—Covenant with the nuns of Monteluce. —Alternate residence at Florence and Perugia.—Life and companionship with artists at Florence.—Perugino, Lionardo, and Michaelangelo.—Cartoons of Da Vinci and Buonarrotti.—Florentine patrons.—" Madonna del Gran' Duca," and " Madonna di Casa Tempi."—Precepts of Lionardo as applied by Raphael.—Madonnas " del Cardellino " and " in green."—Portraits of the Doni.—" Madonna di Casa Tempi."—Preparatory drawings in Lionardesque style 217

CHAPTER VI.

Raphael's practice at Florence and Perugia.—Guidubaldo and the Garter.—Raphael's " St. George " sent to England.—His portrait of himself and other alleged likenesses.—Stay at Urbino and Perugia. —" Madonnas " of Orleans and St. Petersburg.—" Madonna of the Palm."—Retrospect ; his style at Perugia, and changes which it underwent at Florence.—Study of Da Vinci, Fra Bartolommeo, Michaelangelo, and the antique.—Canigiani " Madonna."—" Holy Family " at Windsor.—Studies for the " Entombment."—Varieties of that composition, and its final completion.—Influence of Perugino, Mantegna, Signorelli, Fra Bartolommeo, and Michaelangelo. —Predella of the " Entombment."—" Trinity " of San Severo, and Raphael's practice as a fresco painter 277

CHAPTER VII.

PAGE

Raphael's visit to Urbino in 1507.—His relations with the Court of Duke Guidubaldo.—Portraits of the Duke of Urbino and Pietro Bembo.—Acquaintance with Francia.—"Holy Family with the Lamb," and designs connected with it.—Lionardesque influences.—The "St. Catherine" and "Madonna with the Pink."—Bridgewater and Colonna "Madonnas," and "Adoration of the Shepherds."—Varieties of the "Virgin with the Sleeping Christ and St. John."—Cowper "Madonna." "Bella Giardiniera," and "Madonna Esterhazy."—"Madonna del Baldacchino," and Raphael's friendship for Fra Bartolommeo.—Correspondence with Alfani at Perugia.—Raphael prepares to leave Florence.—Foundation of St. Peter at Rome, and effect of the rebuilding of that Basilica on Julius the Second and the Artists he employed.—Raphael goes to Rome .   . 331

RAPHAEL: HIS LIFE AND WORKS.

CHAPTER I.

Contemporary critics.—Origin of the Santi.—Frederick of Urbino.—
Frederick as a patron of Art.—Giovanni Santi.—Guidubaldo of
Montefeltro.—Raphael's infancy.—Giovanni Santi dies.—Santi and
Raphael.—Raphael an orphan.—Perugino and Raphael.—Raphael's
first master.—Perugino Raphaelesque.—Raphael Peruginesque.—
Signorelli.—Timoteo Viti.

RAPHAEL! At the mere whisper of this magic
name, our whole being seems spell-bound. Wonder,
delight, and awe, take possession of our souls, and
throw us into a whirl of contending emotions. Of
the cause it is hard to give a sufficient analysis. The
marvel is that whilst Raphael puts this thraldom upon
us, he remains, as a man, almost a stranger. We
know less of him than of Donatello, Michaelangelo,
Ghirlandaio, or da Vinci. What we feel in regard to
him is not due to any sufficient acquaintance with his
person, the details of his daily life, or the vicissitudes
of his career, but to a conviction that he who could
produce such masterpieces must have been a man of
uncommon mould, who infused into his creations not
only his own but that universal spirit which touches

each spectator as if it were stirring a part of his own being. He becomes familiar and an object of fondness to us because he moves by turns every fibre of our hearts. We are with him in his placid mood when the perfect sweetness and purity of his feeling imparts to us a sense of absolute harmony. We delight in the calm which rests on the brow of his Madonnas, the sublime love which he displays in their face and action, the innocence and joy which beam in the features of his infants. We feel that an artist who can combine such charms of shape and line with such loveliness of colour is gifted beyond expression. We seem to watch the working of his mind when composing those marvellous altarpieces in which devotion is so pure as to lift the worshippers above the sphere of humanity. We bow to him when he transfigures the Virgin into something akin to the heavenly. His passion when he depicts the grief of the Apostles and Mary, the subtleness of his thought, his inward grasp and potent delineation of all the motives which actuate and explain action, his versatility of means, and his power of rendering are all so varied and so true, they speak so straightforwardly to us, that we are always in commune with him.

It is hard to say whether in his own time Raphael was equally familiar to his countrymen. Some few could boast of having seen all his works. The majority of his admirers were probably not acquainted with more than one of the numerous phases into which his talent was subdivided as he passed from the Umbrian to the Tuscan and Roman styles. By this we may account for the narrow appreciation which his genius obtained from contemporary critics, some of whom indeed gave him credit for qualities which he did not possess. It was perhaps jealousy that made Benvenuto Cellini treat him with contempt. Ignorance may have prompted the neglect of Albertini. The same excuse could not be pleaded for Ariosto, who gave him rank after Sebastian del Piombo, or Sabba da Castiglione, who thought he "would have reached the pinnacle of fame had he but lived long enough." Paul Jove, who assigned to him the third place after Lionardo and Michaelangelo, admits his power of assimilation and rare creative faculty; but Michiel, the Venetian, alone said that though dead in the flesh, he would live in the memory of posterity to all time.

None, perhaps, appreciated Raphael in his own days more thoroughly than professional men. It was not Vasari alone who thought Raphael's art divine. There was not a master of the Umbrian or Florentine school at the beginning of the 16th century who would not have admitted his superiority. At that period Florence still held her place as the chief centre of every form of culture; she wielded undisputed sway in all matters pertaining to design. Yet so steady and universal had been the progress which art had made, that whilst Florentine painters were acknowledged as the ablest in all the world, there was hardly a state into which Italy was subdivided where rivals of almost equal eminence might not have been found ; nor would any one who chanced to visit Rome have been able to discern that the Florentines who laboured there had done more than claim for themselves a fair field and no favour. But art, high as it stood, was still capable of a higher impulse. That impulse came, and the master who gave it combined and embodied all the ideal elements which had been the outcome of earlier centuries. When Raphael appeared at Florence for the first time he was admitted to the brotherhood of his fellows as an equal. A few years later he was proclaimed their superior, and accepted as the chief who was to give its last perfection to Italian painting. At his death, which occurred prematurely, there was not a man of capacity to fathom the depth of his genius but might be ready to admit that the greatest master of modern times had been taken to his grave; nor would Italy have been ungrateful to confess that Raphael's like would never be seen again, or that the leading spirit whose presence all craftsmen had been willing to adore would never be replaced.

Raphael was born in a provincial city. He died at Rome, the political centre of the world in the papacy of Leo X. Between Urbino and Rome, the poles of his existence, he wandered with but one apparent purpose in life, the purpose—diligently pursued and never abandoned—of studying everything that had been done by others before him, of assimilating the good and eliminating the bad amongst the numerous examples which had come within his ken. From Urbino to Perugia, from thence to Città di Castello

and Sienna, from Sienna to Florence and thence to
Rome ;—throughout that wonderful journey which to
him was little else than a triumph, he studied one after
another, nature, the antique, and the Tuscan, and
when he finally broke the fetters of Umbrian tradition,
not a single one of the craftsmen then living would
have said that he copied any of them ; not one,
except, perhaps, Michaelangelo, would have denied
that he was the best and most perfect of them all.

He lived but thirty-seven years. But these years
witnessed a revolution which changed, without de-
stroying, Italian art, and firmly seated the new on the
foundations of the old ; a revolution which taught
with equal reverence the lessons of Giotto and
Masaccio, and those of Ghirlandaio and da Vinci ; and
gave at last a social position to painters.

The name of Santi which Raphael brought into
great repute was that of a lowly race settled as early
as the 15th century in the hills of the State of Urbino.
Travellers following the high road that leads from
Pesaro to Urbino may still see Colbordolo, a grey
conglomerate of farms and old walls, high up the dun
sides of the hills overlooking the valley of the
Foglia. It is long since these hills first lost their
clothing of oak and beech. Their weather-beaten
ridges now show more surface of stone than of leaves,
whilst on the lower grounds, and, as it were, in the
seams bordering the torrents that scour the country,
the loam is still dark and rich, and of great thickness ;
and the peasants who drive the plough creep slowly at
the side of their teams between the vine-clad trees,

as the patient and powerful oxen sink deep and wide furrows in the soil.

During the latter half of the 15th century this region enjoyed almost complete immunity from the troubles which disturbed the more open country near the great arteries of intercommunication. But previous to that time, before the Dukes of Urbino had permanently settled their state into a condition of well ordered government, the land was frequently harried by wild and revengeful neighbours; and in one of these expeditions, Colbordolo was fired and plundered by the followers of Sigismund Malatesta; and Raphael's great-grandfather Peruzzolo Santi fled—to avoid a recurrence of the disaster—to the comparative security of Urbino.

In the early days of Italian civilization Urbino may claim to have exercised to some extent a discriminating patronage of art. One of her political or ecclesiastical magnates asked Giotto to visit him, and the great master was not slow to accept the invitation.* Celebrated artists of all the sister professions received commissions from Urbinese patrons; and Tuscan annalists are found to have registered with reverent care the works of Flemish and Italian painters at Urbino. It would be a mistake indeed to think that the Montefeltros or della Roveres of Urbino, whose chief occupation was the hire of mercenaries for the more powerful states of the Peninsula, were either able or inclined to give permanent or effectual

---

* Vasari, ed. Lemonnier, i. 324.

patronage to artists. It has been said, indeed, by Raphael's friend, Baldassare Castiglione, that the palace of Urbino was the finest edifice of its kind in Italy—a palace conspicuous alike for its embellishments of furniture, arras, and silver plate, and its adornment with numerous statues, pictures, and books.* But this statement appears much over-wrought—as much, indeed, as that of later historians, who described Urbino as the Athens of Italy, and Frederick II. of Montefeltro as a prince who influenced Raphael's style.† If Urbino and its palace ever justified the praise which Castiglione and his successors gave it, they did so after Raphael had risen to the fulness of his fame; and if, in other paths than those of war, Frederick ever surpassed his neighbours, it was when he judiciously chose the architects and sculptors who built and adorned his palace, or when he employed the bookseller Vespasian to enrich his library with valuable manuscripts.

There were many reasons why Frederick should do what he did and no more. His profession had always been that of a soldier or trainer of soldiers, and at a very early period he had acquired the position of a contractor for men at arms and a teacher of the art of war. The palace which he built was planned so as to combine the comforts of a residence with the requirements of a military academy. Youths who

---

* Cortigiano, ed. of Padua, fol. 1766, p. 19.

† It is easy, but unnecessary, to enumerate the works which these artists executed for Urbino. But we should particularly remember that Piero della Francesca's treatise on perspective now preserved at the Vatican, was one of the MSS. in the library of Urbino.

meant to make fighting a profession came to drill and learn the military sciences at Urbino. The palace was a barrack, a riding-school and a college. In the first the students lived; in the second they were exercised; in the third they read. The rooms and halls contained few if any statues of any kind. What sculpture there was, with the exception of a few busts, was in the nature of friezes about the doors and windows, or on chimneys and staircases, and of these many are still extant to prove the skill of the ducal workmen. But even here the subjects represented were illustrative of the art of war. Of painting there was comparatively little,* and that little was confined to small spaces, because the Duke disliked fresco, and preferred painting in oil. Vespasian says that Frederick, "not finding masters to his liking in Italy, because they did not know how to colour panels in oil, sent to the Netherlands for a celebrated master, whom he settled at Urbino;" and this master "painted several pictures, in a study where the philosophers, poets, and doctors of the Greek and Latin churches were represented, and the Duke himself was portrayed from nature with such skill as to lack nothing but the spirit and the breath of life itself." †

---

* "Questo palazzo . . . di poche pitture . . e ornato . . . Delle statue parimente poche ivi se ne veggono." Baldi, Descrizione del Palazzo ducale d'Urbino, fol. Roma, MDCCXXIV., pp. 47 and 65.

† Vespasiano da Bisticci, Vite di Uomini illustri, ed. Cardinal Mai. Reprint of 1859, 8vo, Flor. Barbera, pp. 93–94. This evidence is the stronger as Vespasiano was a contemporary of Federigo, with whom he was personally acquainted. He was born 1421, and died at Florence 1498.

Federigo's taste for the works of the Flemings dates, no doubt, from the time when he purchased pictures by John Van Eyck, in which possibly he admired the portrait character as well as the technical finish, and a method of which Italians as yet had not the complete secret. He was apparently familiar with all the forms of artistic talent peculiar to the Netherlands; and well acquainted with the superior skill of the Flemings in weaving tapestry. Vespasian relates that he sent for Flemish workmen, who decorated one of his rooms at Urbino with arras.* The discovery of oil medium, which had been a subject of literary and artistic contention in Italy since 1450, had probably attracted his attention. He doubtless heard it discussed at Urbino. Vespasian omits to name "the celebrated master from Flanders" whom Federigo employed. But records and pictures tell that there was a Fleming at Urbino in Federigo's reign, and that "Justus of Ghent," who lived at the Feltrine court after 1464, was commissioned in 1474 to paint the "Communion of the Apostles," in which Federigo was represented with Zeno, the Venetian envoy of the Persian Shah. The presence of Justus at Urbino seems to have excited some commotion. The people of the ducal residence protested against foreign invasion. They sent for Paolo Uccelli and Piero della Francesca for the purpose of competing with Justus in the Brotherhood of Corpus Christi. By some freak of fortune, Uccelli's predella of the

---

* Vespasiano, *u. s.*

"Theft of the Pyx" came to adorn the base of Justus' "Communion," whilst Piero della Francesca, who had agreed to produce an altarpiece, withdrew from his contract or failed to complete it. But as if to prove that he too had learnt the secret of the Flemings, he was allowed to paint in oil the portraits of Federigo and his wife Battista Sforza, and thus he revealed the power of a highly gifted artist. But Piero's method was not exactly that of the Flemings; it had the opal flesh tinge peculiar to the practice of tempera. Federigo clung to his prejudices. Giovanni Santi did the honours of a host to his Tuscan colleagues, and caressed his dislike of strangers. Justus was employed by the Duke to paint his own portrait and the philosophers in the library of the palace, and Santi vented his spleen by singing the praise of Uccelli, Francesca, Van Eyck and Roger van der Weyden, whilst he ignored the merits of Justus altogether. A single Italian appears to have been treated with similar discourtesy. Francesco di Giorgio was never mentioned by Santi, though his talents as a painter were great and his skill in the sister arts was conspicuous.

During the wreck of the fortunes of the Rovere family, who inherited Urbino in the 16th century, the decorations of the library of Federigo were dispersed; but some of the pictures are still preserved in the Louvre, Windsor Castle, and the Barberini Palace at Rome, and the whole series of them reveals an artist or artists who combined the precision and realism of the Flemish schools with the higher art of the disciples of Melozzo and Piero della Francesca. Whether Justus was led to exchange some of the traditions of his countrymen for those of Italian masters is a question difficult to answer. About the time when the philosophers and fathers were finished, and after Federigo's appointment to a dukedom in 1474, another series was composed for a room of the palace of Urbino, and the seven sciences were represented on thrones, offering their emblems to various members of the families of Montefeltro and Sforza. Two panels of this series, now in the Museum of Berlin, and two more in the National Gallery, show so great an affinity to the style of Melozzo da Forlì that they have been assigned to him. But even here reminiscences of Flemish art are seen to linger, and it is questionable whether Justus may not have adapted himself to the manner of the disciples of Piero della Francesca, and by a great effort produced masterpieces which might otherwise not have been expected from the author of the "Communion of the Apostles." Raphael's father did not fail to give Melozzo a place amongst the artists whose celebrity was confined to Italy. He seems, indeed, to have had a near personal acquaintance with him; but he did not for this reason relent in his opinion of Justus. When he began the education of Raphael, he inculcated neither the maxims of Uccelli nor those of Piero della Francesca. He trusted entirely to his own, in which the Umbrian, not unmixed with reminiscences of Melozzo, preponderated. Raphael inherited from his father the art of the Umbrian, but he developed his manner under the tuition of Perugino; and from all the men who first adorned the palace of Urbino he learnt, we may confidently affirm, all but nothing. When in after years he visited Urbino, and, perhaps with awe, looked round the walls of the ducal studio, he thought the portraits of the philosophers worthy of attention; and taking out his pen and ink-horn, he sketched them in his book as we find them preserved in the gallery of Venice. We shall presently see that at this period of his career, Raphael was entirely under the influence of the Umbrian school to which his father belonged. The study of his works leads to the conclusion that he learnt the first elements of his profession from Giovanni Santi, but that his true and earliest master was Perugino.

When Peruzzolo Santi settled at Urbino in the 15th century, he laid the foundation of a family which prospered for several generations by the simple exercise of thrift. With patience, perseverance, and luck, the Santi accumulated money and possessions, and purchased household property, which in due course of time descended to Raphael and his relations. In the Contrada del Monte, which rises from the market-place of Urbino, the house bought by Sante in 1464 may still be found. The basement was a shop in which Sante kept a store, and Giovanni Santi ubiquitously represented a general dealer, or gold-smith and painter. Sante inhabited this house till his death on the 2nd of August, 1482. It then came by right of succession into his son's hands. Yet the death of his father does not seem to have wrought any change in Giovanni Santi's life. Under the patriarchal system which governed the family, children and grandchildren lived in common; and Giovanni, who had long been married to Magia Ciarla, the daughter of a tradesman of Urbino, had always been an inmate of Sante's dwelling. At the opening of Sante's will, it was found that Giovanni had inherited most of the paternal property in land and houses, but that his brother Don Bartolommeo, then in orders, had received a legacy in money and the freehold of a field, and his sisters Margherita Vagnini, and Santa Marini, each a dowry. Santa returned to Giovanni's house as a widow in 1490. Margaret's son, Girolamo Vagnini, lived to take the incumbency of the chapel founded by Raphael's will in the Pantheon at Rome, and Don Bartolommeo became Raphael's guardian after Giovanni Santi's death. Magia Ciarla's brother and sister, Lucia Zaccagna and Simone di Battista, were left out of Sante's will altogether.* In after years many of the members of Sante's family lived in common in the Contrada del Monte.

Giovanni Santi had scarcely administered to the will of his father when Federigo, Duke of Urbino, died and bequeathed the succession to his infant son Guidubaldo. The death of this prince was undoubtedly of serious moment to the state. When in his leisure hours Federigo came to rest in the castello

---

* See the records in Pungileone's Elogio Stor. di Gio. Santi. 8vo, Urb. 1822, and Passavant's Raphael, Paris ed., 8vo, 1860, i. pp. 357 and foll.

which he did so much to adorn, his time was not all spent in council, or teaching, or the pleasures of the chase. By profession a *condottiere*, he acquired in course of time both money and honour. His subjects, hardy sons of the hills, had learnt to love him as one who would take them, poor and martial as they were, to the wars, where they might indeed run the risk of losing their lives, but where success and luck might enrich adventurers with the plunder of cities or camps. Himself enriched by numerous victories, he had had the good sense to observe that people were never so happy as when they were lightly taxed. The booty which he carried home enabled him to found churches and monasteries, to build palaces, fortify places of strength, and inclose parks for the preservation of game; but it also gave him the power to dispense with heavy taxation. He was moderate, too, in the satisfaction of his tastes, and without any of those dangerous passions which marred the character of his neighbours, the Malatestas of Rimini or the Baglionis of Perugia. For this and other causes his popularity was immense.* Whenever he appeared in public the wayfarers, men and women, would kneel at his approach and cry " God keep you "; not because unreasoning awe taught them to bow to him as to an idol, but because they loved him personally. In his leisure moments Federigo was fond of bending his steps towards the market-place and visiting the shops of the tradespeople. He spoke familiarly to those

---

* Vespasiano, *u. s.*, p. 103.

whom he knew, and kindly to strangers.*   But a few
yards up the street that led from the market-place
lay the house of the Santi, and who knows but he
entered the store and chatted with the inmates.   His
sympathy for Giovanni Santi, who was a poet as well
as a painter, may have been small.   His preference
for strangers when competent artists were to be found
at home was no doubt known to Santi, who looked
with jealous eye on the favour accorded to these
intruders.†   But his person and fame were a theme
on which every one was fond of dwelling ; and Santi
once spent his time in composing a rhymed chronicle
in praise of his life and virtues, and though Federigo,
had he seen it, might not have wished to spend a
ducat on the purchase of this epic, his nature would
have led him certainly to think kindly of the writer.
The loss of such a prince at a time when his successor
was but an infant necessarily gave rise to great
anxiety.   But the regency under which Guidubaldo
was placed was not of long duration.   He courted
popularity with success, allied himself by marriage to
the politic family of the Gonzagas, and quickly
signalised himself as a leader of troops.   Walking in
the footsteps of his sire, he did more to patronize
national art than Federigo.   He finished the buildings
which his father had begun, and discarding the

---

* Ibid. 103—4.

† The evidence of this is but
circumstantial, yet still very
strong. Santi is silent as to Justus
of Ghent and the arras makers of
Federigo, yet he notices all the
contemporary Italian artists of
his time in the Rhyme chronicle.
His career became successful when
these strangers lost the patronage
of Federigo.

foreigners whose exclusive employment had been a source of jealousy to the Urbinese, he gave immense satisfaction to that class of his subjects who earned their livelihood by the practice of painting.* Giovanni Santi amongst others derived undoubted advantage from the change. After Guidubaldo's marriage with Elizabeth Gonzaga in 1489, he obtained the interest of two ducal families; he visited Mantua, and his death in 1494 elicited from the Duchess of Urbino kindly notice of his worth.† When Raphael succeeded to the paternal estate and profession, Guidubaldo's sister, Giovanna della Rovere, gave him her patronage; and it has even been thought that at a critical period of his fortunes she recommended him to the chief of the Florentine state.‡ Guidubaldo probably remembered that Santi's Life of Federigo was dedicated to himself, and he too promoted Raphael's fortunes at a very early period; nor is it too much to say that some of the success which attended the latter was due to the conduct of his sire.

Early in the period of his union with Magia Ciarla, Giovanni Santi had had the joys and cares of a father. Magia first gave birth to a boy, who died in 1485, next to a daughter who died in 1491.§ Raphael, the only child of his parents who lived to the age of manhood, was born in the old house in the

---

Contrada del Monte at Urbino in 1483; and all the world knows that when he died on Good Friday, the 6th of April, 1520,* his friends might have been meeting to celebrate the anniversary of his thirty-eighth birthday. Magia nursed the boy herself, not because it was the habit of all mothers to perform this duty, but because Giovanni Santi held that children throve better and enjoyed fairer prospects under the parental roof than in the cottages of hired "villeins and peasants."† So the boy lived and passed out of infancy, and learnt his primer, when he was not playing on his father's doorway or in the market-place. In daily contact with the tools of the painter, he watched the labours of Giovanni at his easel, and saw him send forth to admiring patrons those quaint but characteristic Umbrian altarpieces in which he depicted the majesty of the Virgin and Child and the admiration of attendant saints, or the meditative devotion of lay and churchmen kneeling at

---

* Vas. viii. p. 2, says, "nacque adunque R. in Urbino l'anno 1483 in Venerdi Santo a ore tre di notte," p. 59; "fini il corso della sua vita il giorno medesimo che nacque." Bembo's epitaph in the Pantheon of Rome runs so : "VIX. ANNOS XXXVII. INTEGER INTEGROS QVO DIE NATVS EST EO ESSE DESIIT VIII ID. APRILIS MDXX." The "same day on which Raphael was born and died" cannot apply if we assume, as Vasari has done, that the birth was on Good Friday, a moveable feast which fell on the 6th of April in 1520, and the 26th or 28th of March in 1483, according as we count by the astronomical tables or the Julian calendar. In MS. Chigi, ed. G. Cugnoni, 8vo, Roma, 1881, p. 30, this passage occurs : "Verum non admodum felici evento cessit id Raphaeli, frequentius enim, quam par erat venere (ferunt) illum utentem, obijsse constat anno MDXX. die vi. Aprilis, eadem qua natus erat septem supra triginta ante annos."

† Vas. viii. 2.

the Virgin's feet. He witnessed, though he would hardly notice, the deaths of his brothers and sisters, but he probably scanned with eager curiosity the ceremonies of Guidubaldo's marriage in 1489. His childish mind was doubtless more seriously affected by the death of Magia Ciarla, which occurred on the 7th of October, 1491.* He may unconsciously have witnessed the second marriage of his father, who shortly after Magia's death took to wife the daughter of a goldsmith, Bernardina Parte, whose age at the time would hardly enable her to feel the responsibilities of a parent. It would be easy to assume, yet presumptuous to affirm, that Bernardina Parte felt and gave way to the jealousy of a stepmother. She was very young when Magia Ciarla died, and still young when, six months after, she married Giovanni Santi. But she did not immediately give pledges of her own to her husband's affection ; and she might by seconding his love for Raphael have gained some ascendancy over her stepchild. Unfortunately the time meted out to her for this purpose proved to be very short, and the quarrels of a disputed succession soon produced a natural but inevitable estrangement.

Meanwhile the life of the inmates of Santi's house remained to all appearance comfortable and secure. Orders abounded at the store, and commissions came to the painter more rapidly than before. The Duchess of Urbino did Santi the honour of sitting to him for her likeness. She was satisfied of his abilities, and

---

* Pungileone, Elogio storico di Rafaello Santi. 8vo, Urbino, 1829, p. 3.

scut him to Mantua to take a portrait of Lodovico
Gonzaga.* But in summer 1494 Santi sickened, and,
feeling that his end was near, he asked for a notary
to whom he dictated his will, and in this instrument
he provided for all the members of his family. He
left to Bernardina her dowry, clothes, and a share of
his house, provided she remained a widow. With
special regard to her state at the time he reserved to
her daughters, should she have any, dowries of 150
florins apiece, to her sons under similar anticipations
a fair part of his property. He gave his sister Santa
board and lodging for life in the family dwelling, and
legacies to some other relations. The residue of his
property he divided in equal parts between his brother
Don Bartolommeo and Raphael his son by Magia
Ciarla. Don Bartolommeo was appointed guardian of
his children, and Pietro Parte his executor. One of
the testamentary clauses declares that Bernardina
shall live and dwell in the Contrada del Monte " with
the other heirs mentioned in the will."† It tends
to prove that Raphael was at Urbino at his father's
death ; and shows that Vasari too hastily assumed
that Raphael was apprenticed to Perugino in Giovanni's lifetime.‡

Santi's will was executed on the 26th of July. He
died on the 1st of August, 1494,§ leaving Raphael heir

* Campori, Notizie di Gio.
Santi e di Rafaello Santi. 4to,
Modena, 1870, pp. 4–5.
 † The will is in Passavant's
Raphael, i., pp. 361-2.

‡ Vas. iv. 316.
 § A second will, dated July 27,
1494, is printed in com. to Vas.
u. s., iv. p. 396. It contains
codicils of July 29, beneath which

to an estate under the guardianship of his uncle; and prospective successor to the property of his grandfather Ciarla.*

Brought up by a man of literary tastes, Raphael learnt to read and write whilst he studied the elements of painting under his father's roof; it was in keeping with the practice of the time that the boy should be taught when very young to mix pigments and handle the pen and the pencil.

Nineteen years before Santi's death Fra Bartolommeo had been apprenticed at eight years of age to Piero di Cosimo; and Raphael at the same age might have entered his father's workroom. It was not to be expected that he should progress much beyond the simplest elements during the short space of time that elapsed from his first initiation to the death of Santi. But in that short span, he received impressions which many years failed to obliterate, and it is curious to observe that as late as the opening of the 16th century his memory was still stored with typical forms inherited from his father.

If in the period of Raphael's infancy Santi fondly watched the babe asleep on its mother's lap, and

we read: Die 1 mensis Augusti decessit dictus testator. This will was annulled by the Court of Probate.

* The will of Battista quondam Nicolai Ciarla, dated Urbino, Aug. 8, 1494, bequeaths to Raphael, Magia's child, the sum of 150 florins. That of Camilla, Battista's wife, dated Oct. 8, leaves Raphael a nominal sum of 40 " bononenos." Pungileone, Elogio storico di Raffaello Santi, note to p. 12. See also Pass. *u. s.*, i. 41–2 and 361–3, and Pungileone, Elogio storico di Giovanni Santi, p. 136.

moulded the group into a picture on the wall of his own house,* we may still more easily understand his embodiment of Raphael's features in the angels of the "Resurrection" of Cagli.   One of the prettiest legends of Raphael's youth tells of this journey to Cagli, where his juvenile efforts are said to have contributed to the perfection of the maturer labours of Santi.†   Yet the boy may have travelled after his father's death, and visited the place hallowed by recollections of Santi's presence; and the reminiscences which afterwards appeared in his compositions may date from the period of these wanderings; for there is not the slightest doubt that the "Resurrection" of the Vatican has to some extent its counterpart in that of Cagli.

Amongst the numerous works which Santi left in the churches of Umbria, that of Gradara contains the germ of one of the graceful thoughts which Raphael afterwards expanded into something akin to the sublime.   The "Infant Christ on the Virgin's Knee" holds a captive bird, whilst it gives the benediction. This is a contrast quite foreign to the practice of Perugino, yet familiar to Raphael, who painted in his youth the "Virgin with the Finch," ‡ and in his manhood the "Madonna del Cardellino."   Nor is this all, for the "Virgin with the Finch," in grouping and movement of the Saviour, recalls Santi's "Virgin with the Pink," in the hospital of Fano.

The tenderness of Raphael is nowhere more con-

---

* See as to this the author's Italian Painting, ii. 594. The picture was long assigned to Raphael himself.

† Ibid. ibid. ; ii. p. 585.

‡ At the Berlin Museum.

spicuous than in the " Madonna di Casa Tempi " at
Munich, where the delight of the mother at the clinging of her son's cheek to her own is nobly expressed
in the faces of both. We look in vain for a similar
display of maternal affection in Perugino. But Santi,
in his rough honest way, tried to realise it in the
Mattarozzi altarpiece which now adorns the gallery of
Berlin.

The sleeping child in Santi's " Madonna " at the
National Gallery, or the sleeping boy in the wall
painting of Santi's house at Urbino, are natural pre-
cursors of those which impart so great a charm to the
" Brocca Madonna " at Milan, or the " Virgin of the
Diadem " at the Louvre. Another boy Christ in
Santi's altarpiece of Montefiorentino reminds us of
Raphael's Saviour in the altarpiece of the Ansidei
at Blenheim, whilst it similarly recalls the lovely
" Madonna Connestabile " in the shape and air of the
figure of Mary.

What Raphael did with these pictures of his father
was not to copy the composition or the outlines, but
to give fresh life to similar forms which he represented
afresh in a new and transfigured shape. The nearer
Raphael's study and view of his father's work, the
more frequent his recollection of it. The Buffi altar-
piece at Urbino clings to him with such tenacity, that
during his stay at Città di Castello, after leaving
Perugino and starting on his own way, he remembered it. Though his art was well formed in the
Peruginesque mould when he began the series of canvases with which he adorned the capital of the Vitelli,

yet the reappearance of Santi's type of the Eternal in the "Creation of Eve," becomes natural when we suppose that the Buffi altarpiece in which that type occurs was still lingering in Raphael's tenacious memory. The same mighty frame, the same wide forehead, the same cast of features, appear in both pictures, but refined in the masterpiece of Raphael by those powers of assimilation which of all others were those recognized by his contemporaries as characteristic of the great Urbinese. Nor is this a solitary instance, since elsewhere and in numerous examples, figures of angels, conspicuous in many altarpieces, flit past us in various compositions of Raphael's maturer time. As late as the period of the "Coronation of the Virgin" at the Vatican, when Raphael became so thoroughly saturated with the principles of Perugino and Pinturicchio as almost to deceive the craftsmen of the time, we still find the types of Santi commingled with those of Melozzo and Fiorenzo of Perugia, in wonderful shapes of seraphs, whose heads appear enframed in beautiful rows of spiral locks. Later still, when the "Votive Madonna" of Sant' Antonio of Perugia betrayed that Raphael had studied the greatest of the Florentines, and learnt something from Lionardo and Baccio della Porta, at the very moment when he paused on the confines of the Umbrian and Florentine styles, he still remembered the shapes which he had seen in the "Majesty of St. Jerome" at Pesaro,* the "Martyrdom of St. Se-

---

* Now at the Lateran Museum.

bastian" at Fano, and the "Resurrection" of Cagli. Santi's feeling, in its essence exquisite, yet in form and tint rude and imperfect, gushed exuberantly from the hand of Raphael, who combined with happy cunning the conceptions of his father and the colour or technical craft of Perugino. It can hardly be an accident that the art of Santi should thus have descended to his son. But remembering the youth of the one and the early death of the other, we are free to suppose, either that filial piety induced the youth to make a pilgrimage to the altars on which the works of his sire had been left, or that he inherited the drawings and sketches which Santi had collected and preserved. Vasari must have been wrong when he wrote that Santi took Raphael to Perugia to receive the lessons of Perugino.* He was right in saying that Raphael's master was his father. The chrysalis naturally yields the form of the parent moth.†

Shortly after the death of Giovanni Santi, his wife gave birth to a daughter, who took the name of

* Vas. iv. 316.

† If we should venture to acknowledge the genuineness of some drawings which collectors assign to Raphael, it would be solely because they display the form of Santi combined with some of the gentleness and delicacy of his son. Raphael may have copied his father's drawing in the angel in a cloud, praying, attributed to him in the Berlin print-room. Something like his own spirit may be found in two small rounds in the same collection, representing the Virgin and St. Peter (m. 0·8 in diameter). The Virgin in mantle and hood, her neck nun-like, swathed in cloth, the left hand raised, the right holding the dress, the face upraised and seen at three-quarters. St. Peter, full front, bare-headed, with a book and the keys in his hands, looking down. Yet these drawings can only date from a period subsequent to Raphael's departure from Urbino.

Elizabeth borne by the Duchess of Urbino.* Raphael
may still be supposed an inmate of the house in the
Contrada del Monte. He was joint heir to his
father's fortune with the infant Elizabeth, yet under
the guardianship of his uncle Bartolommeo, who
possibly grumbled at the prospect of paying the
dowry of his niece. Whether he pretended to feel
some difficulty in defraying the artistic education of
his nephew, who was now to learn his art amongst
strangers, or whether his nature was merely that of a
quarrelsome and selfish priest, Bartolommeo soon came
to open enmity with his brother's widow, and Raphael
might have blushed to hear that Bartolommeo, in his
own name and that of his ward, had been straining
the law to keep the heritage of Giovanni Santi in his
pocket. Though forced by a court of law in 1495 to
promise payment to Bernardina Santi of her dowry
and clothes, though sentenced by a civil court in the
same year to pay for the maintenance of his niece and
sister-in-law, Bartolommeo ventured to oppose by all
the means in his power the fulfilment of his obliga-
tions. For months and years he made the life of
every one in the Santi dwelling uncomfortable. Bernardina, in 1497, proposed an arbitration to ascertain
what sum she might reckon on for support, and the
bishop's court at Urbino made a reference in the
cause, and condemned Bartolommeo with costs. Two
years more elapsed before the slow forms of law

* The date of this child's birth   1499, June 3. Passavant, Raph. i.
is not known. She is mentioned   p. 365.
as alive in two records of 1495 and

allowed that Bernardina should receive an annual payment of 26 florins, and during that period of suspense she was forced to take refuge in her mother's house. It was not before May, 1500, that Bartolommeo and Raphael received discharge for the alimony, and litigation came to an end.*

We can only guess what life Raphael may have led if he remained at Urbino to witness these family feuds. The cool tone in which he writes of Bartolommeo at a later period, the loving terms in which he addresses his cousin Simone Ciarla,—that tender "carissimo quanto padre" which he scratches on one of his notes, lead us to believe that the time which he spent at Urbino was very much devoted to that relative. The records of the period are too scanty and incomplete to afford any precise information. They give no clue to Raphael's residence at Urbino or Perugia; they merely show that Raphael was absent when the last sentence in a long and tedious cause gave a tardy satisfaction to Santi's widow.†

The history of Raphael's youth from 1494 to 1504 is a blank so far as records are concerned, yet it is still possible to fill the void by circumstantial evidence. Vasari, it is admitted, erroneously assumed that Raphael was introduced to Perugino by Giovanni Santi, and he obviously based this statement on the fact that Raphael's style in 1504 was influenced

---

* The records of June 5, 1499, and May 13, 1500, are in the Jahrbuch der Kgl. Preuss. Sammlungen, 1882, Part ii.; others of earlier date in Pass. Raphael, i. 364-6.

* See the record of May 13, 1500, in Jahrbuch der Kgl. Preuss. Sammlungen, u. s.

by that of the Perugian master. Opinions differ as
to the period when this influence was felt. Some
have conjectured that Raphael settled early at Perugia; others, that he remained under the tuition of
masters at Urbino. We shall venture to affirm: I.
That he left home when still a child; II. That he
began to take lessons from Perugino as early as
1495.

A general, and apparently well founded, impression
prevailed till very recently that Perugino was a permanent resident at Florence from 1492 till 1498.*
It was well known that he frequently absented himself from Florence, but it was thought that, having a
painting room in the Tuscan capital, it was there that
his head-quarters were established. This, it appears,
is a mistake, and records now tell us that Perugino
was equally at home at Perugia, and at Florence;
but that he frequently resided at Perugia between
1495 and 1500.

Previous to 1492, Perugino's movements had been
capricious enough; after that date they were equally
if not more so. He was in Rome when Innocent the
VIIIth died; in Florence when he courted the daughter
of a sculptor of repute, whom he married in the autumn
of 1493.†   He afterwards completed a series of most
important works, the finest of which is undoubtedly
the " Crucifixion " of Santa Maria Maddalena dei

---

* See History of Italian Paint-
ing, vol. iii., Life of Perugino.
† The marriage took place at
Fiesole on September 1, 1493.

See Braghirolli (W.) in Giornale
di Erud. Tosc., 4to, Perugia, 1873,
vol. ii. pp. 73 and 143, and the
Sansoni ed. of Vasari, iii. p. 611.

Pazzi.* But before he had finished even this great commission, he transferred his household from Florence to Perugia, where we find him busily engaged in the first months of 1495.

On the 8th of March of that year he entered into a contract with the "Priori" of Perugia to paint an altarpiece, for the completion of which six months were allowed.

On the 8th of March he signed a second contract to execute within two years an "Ascension" at San Pietro of the Benedictines of Perugia.†

In January, 1496, Perugino was at work at the last of these pictures, when he received a visit from the auditors of the Cambio, who begged him to undertake the decoration of their Hall. Flattered by this attention, the painter accepted the commission, subject to the following conditions :—

He was to be permitted to finish the "Ascension."

He was to have leave to visit Venice, Fano, and Florence.‡

Convinced of the importance of securing the services of so great a painter, whose masterpieces adorned

---

* The frescos of this Florentine convent were begun in 1492 and delivered, finished, on the 20th of April, 1496. See Ulderico Medici's Dell' antica Chiesa dei Cisterciensi, oggi S. M. M. de' Pazzi. 8vo, Firenze, 1880, pp. 33-4.

† Perugia, San Pietro of the Benedictines. The picture is now at the Museum of Lyons. The contract of March 8, 1495, in Mezzanotte, Vita di P. Vannucci, 8vo, Perugia, 1836, pp. 295-6, has been transferred by the editors of the latest editions of Vasari (Sansoni, iii. 611) to the year 1496. But Rossi (Giorn. di Erud. Tosc. u. s. iii. p. 9) declares this to be a mistake, and the date of 1495 to be correct.

‡ Rossi (A.), Giornale di Erud. Tosc. u. s. iii. p. 9.

the Sixtine, the auditors accepted the delay and closed with the master's offer.*

On the 6th of April, 1496, Perugino appeared at Florence to deliver the frescos of Santa Maria de' Pazzi to the Cistercians who had ordered them. He invested some of his money in the purchase of land.†

On the 19th of January, 1497, he was again at Florence, where he met Benozzo Gozzoli, Cosimo Rosselli, and Filippino Lippi, and helped them to value the frescos of Alesso Baldovinetti.

In the course of the spring of 1497, the great altarpiece of Santa Maria Nuova of Fano, with its lovely predella of five pictures, was completed at Perugia, and taken in June to the altar for which it had been commissioned. We shall see how Raphael studied that predella and took it as a model for his own masterpieces.

February of 1498 is marked by the delivery of the "Virgin and Child," with angels and members of the brotherhood of Santa Maria Novella, to the church of San Pietro Martire in Perugia.

A few months later the "Madonna attended by six Saints" was displayed in Santa Maria delle Grazie at Sinigaglia. It had doubtless been painted at Perugia.

On the 26th of June, 1498, Perugino met the masters, who had been summoned to Florence to discuss the repairs of the lantern of Santa Maria

---

* Ibid. ibid. | † Ulderico Medici, *u. s.*

del Fiore; and on the 4th of September he bought a house in the Via Pinti.*

At the close of 1498 the frescos of the Cambio were begun.† But even this considerable cycle of paintings was not executed without interruption.

On September the 1st, 1499, Perugino was again in Florence, where he was sworn to keep the rules of the Florentine guild to which he was affiliated.‡

"In Florentia degens,"—a resident at Florence, the painter is called in the summons to appear at Santa Maria del Fiore. "Magister, pictor de Perugio,"—master and painter of Perugia, is his title when sworn of the Florentine guild.

Perugino, it is clear, had a domicile at Florence, and a domicile at Perugia. He was possessed of dwellings and painting-rooms at both places, and from 1492 to 1494 he lived exclusively in the first of these cities, but from 1495 to 1500, though he visited Florence occasionally, he resided chiefly at Perugia.

We shall have occasion to speculate on the influence which Perugino wielded during the period of tuition which preceded that of Raphael's independence. It may not be necessary to anticipate what the study of Raphael's masterpieces will necessarily divulge; yet it is but fair to state that one of the strongest arguments which can be adduced to prove

---

* Vas. ed. Sansoni, *u. s.* iii. 612.

† The first payment for the frescos of the Cambio was made on the 25th of February, 1499.

Rossi in Giorn. di Erud. *u. s.* iii. 14.

‡ Ibid., ibid., ibid.

the close connection of the two artists previous to
1500 is that Raphael, in composing the predellas of
the "Coronation" at the Vatican, used all the compositions and drawings which Perugino sketched in 1497
for the predellas of the altarpiece of Fano.   In other
respects the long dependence of Raphael on Perugino
is shown by evidence so clear that to rebut it would
require more than ordinary ingenuity.   And after the
altarpiece of Fano, there is no more pregnant example
to be cited than that of the Cambio frescos, a series
of masterpieces which, so far as Raphael's life is concerned, only gains or loses importance as we admit or
deny that Raphael was one of those who, from 1498
to 1500, contributed to their execution.*

No pursuit of more absorbing interest can be conceived than that of following what may be called the
trail of a great artist, when, knowing that he passed
that way, we still remain uncertain as to the age or
direction of the track.   At one time the trail looks
broad and worn, at other times it becomes a mere
scent or fades and vanishes altogether.   In Raphael's
case, as in that of Masaccio or Palmezzano, a great
source of difficulty lies in the frequent diversions
caused by deceptive cross scents.   Perugino is so like
Raphael at one place that we almost doubt the evidence of our senses.   Masaccio is so like Masolino
that we are lost in a maze of uncertainty.   The skill
of an expert would be tried to tell where Melozzo

---

* The date of 1500 is on the walls of the Cambio.

ends and Palmezzano begins. But though Raphael
and Perugino may at one period blend their forms to
confound us, there is a time when each of them has
his own prominent distinctness. They both ascend in
the orbits which nature has created for them. Those
orbits cross, and at the point of contact their bodies
seem lost in each other. But when they emerge a
curious phenomenon appears. Not only is Raphael
Peruginesque, but Perugino is Raphaelesque. The
work which Perugino accomplishes from 1499 to
1504 is indelibly stamped with the impress of
Raphael's genius. That of Raphael from 1502 to
1504 is equally influenced by Perugino's example.
Both reveal a constant interchange of thought. If,
however, Raphael was a master practising on his own
account in 1502, how did he rise to the eminence
from which he already then looked down on his contemporaries? If Perugino was Raphaelesque in
1500, how long had he been under this new spell?
We can trace Perugino's career from Perugia to
Rome and to Florence, and observe how steadily, but
how gradually, he was influenced by Tuscan example.
After 1496 a new element contributes to the manifestation of a change. Raphael's course is that of
a retentive and conservative mind, always intent on
steady and unbroken progress, ever acquiring, in-
wardly digesting and assimilating. Is it possible
that his nature before 1502 should have been in contrast with his nature afterwards? Is it not clear that
he enjoyed under Perugino a long and uninterrupted
course of artistic tending, and that he rose to the

station which he occupied in 1502 by measured steps ?

Let us suppose, for the sake of argument, that he began by forming a manner of his own, which took shape and grew into something unlike the manner of Perugino ; and then that he wandered to Perugia, where he proceeded to divest himself of that early habit in order to put on quite a new one. We should expect under these circumstances to find some trace of the first, and some evidence of progress to the complete transformation of the second. In the absence of all evidence of either kind, it is hardly to be conceived that Raphael should have joined Perugino as an assistant; it is natural to believe that he came as an apprentice. Vasari's statement that he took service with Perugino "as a boy"[*] has been accepted by some and contested by others. According as they differ they give him a master at Urbino or Perugia. One suggests Ingegno, another Timoteo Viti. In the first case, no evidence ; in the second, evidence of no conclusive force is adduced. It may be possible at some future time to find a certified example of Timoteo Viti's manner at the close of the 15th century, but his earliest style as now revealed appears based on the lessons of Francia, whose art had its roots in Bologna and Ferrara, to which Raphael at first was a stranger. But granted that Timoteo Viti was the master to whom Bartolommeo Santi entrusted his ward in 1495 at Urbino, for that is the latest con-

---

[*] Vas. u. s. iv. 317.

tention,* what is the deduction? The deduction is that Raphael remained at home till 1500, when his absence was expressly recorded. He then presented himself to Perugino, and settled down artistically and socially to a new life.

But if Raphael entered Perugino's service when the Cambio frescos were nearly finished, he can hardly have had a share in any part of them, since his method was not then Peruginesque. His time must have been spent in unlearning what he acquired under Viti, and acquiring what he had not yet learned from Perugino. But if this was his occupation in 1499 or 1500, how was it that Perugino became Raphaelesque at that period, and is it not more natural to conceive that that phase in Perugino's career, and the simultaneous phase of the Peruginesque in Raphael, were due to influences which acted reciprocally on both masters during a long period of years? Of all the theories which have been put forward during the last half century, none is more defensible than that which assigns to Raphael a share in the transformation of Perugino's manner to the sweet, luscious style of the " Assumption " of Vallombrosa, and the " Madonna " of Pavia. But we need not suppose that Raphael did more in these remarkable instances than infuse his own delicacy of sentiment into the mind of Perugino. We shall

---

* The latest biography of Raphael, a charming work by Mr. E. Muntz, 4to, Paris, 1881, puts as a " conjecture " that Raphael received lessons from Viti, but then Mr. Muntz adds, "Viti imitated the style of Raphael with rare perfection," pp. 23–25. See also Schmarsow in the Preussische Jahrbücher for 1880.

presently see that whilst his co-operation at first was
slight and formal, he afterwards progressed, so that we
are enabled to distinguish the pictures in which
Perugino's hand appears in the full plenitude of
mastery, but transfigured by feeling acquired from
Raphael, and those in which the design and composition of Perugino are carried out, as it seems, by the
very pencil of Raphael.

There is no more charming variety in Raphael's
easel-pieces than that of the converse which whiles
the hours of the Virgin as she tends the infant Christ
and the boy Baptist. His power of uniting symbol-
ism of the deepest and most mournful significance with
innocence and youth is so great, and it becomes so
intense in the calm solitude of expanded landscapes
that he throws us unconsciously into reverie and contemplation. Few will have looked at the "Bella
Giardiniera" or the "Madonna in Green" without
feeling some symptoms of this charm. Perugino was
no stranger to this mode of stirring the heart, at least
in the days of his connection with Raphael. Any one
acquainted with his "Holy Family" in the Museum
of Nancy, will observe how Perugino obtained this
result. He will see the infant Saviour stretching his
hand towards the reed cross which rests on the
Baptist's shoulder, the Virgin and John in prayer,
two angels in devotional attitudes. Thin leaved trees
dart upwards from the sides of a valley bounded by
hills and water; and grasses and wild flowers adorn a
meadow in front. Perugino's masterpiece is full of
the pathos which Raphael conveys. His colour is

almost as sweet, his landscape as calm.   The scene to which he takes us is in the heart of the Umbrian country at the edge of the lovely lake so dear to the youth of Sanzio.   His figures are innocent and playful as Raphael's.   Perugino deserves reproof when he transfers from one composition to another the same figure, the same attitude and gesture of hand and finger, but a single effort condones a number of these offences, and the " Madonna " of Nancy, in which the sentiment of Raphael is united to the precepts of Lionardo and Fra Bartolommeo shows how strong the influence was which a great master might fitly owe to a still greater disciple.

Nearer home, in the National Gallery, the " Madonna " of the Certosa of Pavia tells of an older but not less characteristic art.   We see the Virgin kneeling in adoration, guarded by archangels and lulled by the chaunt of seraphs in a morning sky.   An angel in extasy holds the infant on a saddle, suggesting the flight through the land of Egypt, when the humble animal that bore the mother of Christ was loosened of its burden and led away by the attendant Joseph. Here again are the lake, the hills, and the sparse leaved trees, the serene sky ; here, too, the Raphaelesque combination of beautiful grouping with youth and strength and delicacy of line, of dreamy depth and brilliant light, and soft luscious colour.   In the landscape is a stillness so profound that one listens for the hymn of the seraphs to come down. from the sky.   The whole picture is so redolent of Raphael, that his name involuntarily rises to our lips ; and. yet we are still far away from the time when Raphael could have shown such mastery. Perugino, inspired and perhaps helped in subordinate parts by Raphael is here a finished artist, old in years and skill, who takes of the freshness of his pupil whose age and comparative inexperience exclude any active or effective assertion of himself.

Of an earlier period, but closely related in style to the "Madonna" of the Certosa, the "Assumption" of Vallombrosa in the Academy of Florence claims on the same grounds an equal admiration. With all the grace of its later rival it shows perhaps a more manly genius, but every line and tone is stamped with the impress of Raphael's influence. When Perugino surrendered the altarpiece to the monks of Vallombrosa, he placed on his panel the date of 1500, without knowing what service he was doing to the historian of Raphael's life. It was, doubtless, about this time that he painted or caused to be painted the two profile portraits of Vallombrosan friars which modern criticism has so frequently assigned to Raphael.*

The conclusion to which this review inevitably

* Academy of Florence, No. 18. Wood oil. Busts under life-size. One inscribed "BALTASAR MONACO" in profile to the left is in the finest style of Perugino, and rivals those of Domenico Ghirlandaio in the Sassetti chapel at Florence. The other inscribed BLASIO, GEN. SERVO TVO SVCCVRRE in profile to the left has suffered more from retouching, yet appears to have been executed, with less freedom and power than the other, by a scholar still inexpert in the exercise of his art; not but the outlines are clean and precise, but the modelling is more timid, the colouring less bright. It may be that Perugino entrusted the portrait of Blasio to Raphael whilst he did the Baltasar himself.

leads is that during this period of his life, Perugino entered upon a new phase of pictorial development. Like the matron in the legend, he dipped into the *fons juventutis* to which Raphael invited him, and issued from it invigorated and young. Not that, before this, he had fallen into decrepitude. On the contrary, his artistic constitution had been fortified by the discipline of the Florentines. His power as a composer, and his long experience as an artist, enabled him to display the combined talents of a designer and colourist united to unrivalled technical skill in the use of pigments. But the key of tone in which he worked was low ; its harmony, if pure, was grave. His eye, attuned to the olive rather than the wheaten, had not as yet the ray of the bright Raphaelic lens. Towards the close of the century his work was chastened by an unexpected tenderness of feeling, and candour of expression, his drawing retained force yet improved in grace. His colour acquired an unaccustomed brightness and sweetness of modulation ; and this apparently because a boy who had come to him to be taught had wound himself round the master's heart and imparted to him some of his own being. Nor was the progress of this marvellous change either sudden or of set purpose, but rather constant, and all but imperceptible. From the altarpiece of Fano to the " Ascension " of Lyons, from the " Madonna " of San Pietro Martire to the " Madonna " of Sinigaglia, and thence to the " Assumption " of Vallombrosa and the " Virgin " of the Certosa, an uniform expansion is apparent from the beginning ; and Raphael is the guardian spirit whose beneficence is felt as that of the good genius in the fairy tale.

That Raphael, whilst he wielded this influence on Perugino, should also have received the impress of his master is too natural to create surprise. That he should have been so familiarized with Perugino's methods and feeling as to be fit to take part in some of the works which his chief executed between 1498 and 1502 is equally clear and an additional reason for believing that Raphael came to Perugia earlier: nor can it seem strange that he should be said to have had a share in the predella of the " Ascension " of Lyons or that of Munich, or that other predella in the Connestabile collection which we shall presently refer to, if Perugino had occasion to employ him at the time. As Peruginesque compositions, these delightful little pictures are admirable.*　But the co-operation of Raphael or other disciples in their production appears the more likely when we remember that Perugino's strength, in the opinion of his contemporaries, lay especially in life-size figures and not in small ones.†
Though Raphael is not proved to have executed the

---

* Rouen Mus. and Munich Gallery, No. 1173 and 1185. Assigned by Passavant, in the first edition of his Raphael (i. p. 64), to Raphael, but omitted in the second edition.

† In a letter addressed to Isabella, Marchioness of Mantua, in 1505 by her Florentine agent, Luigi Ciocca, the latter reports : "that he has employed Salai, a pupil of Lionardo, to judge of Perugino's work in the ' Combat of Chastity and Lasciviousness ' " (now at the Louvre). Salai reports that the work is good ; " but really it is not Perugino's business to execute small figures in which he is not clever, whereas he is clever in large ones." See Braghirolli in Giorn. di Erud. Tosc. u. s. ii. 247.

predellas of Munich and Rouen, his share in their production is too probable to be rejected altogether, even though he should have been confined to very subordinate duties. We shall soon have to observe how fond he was in his youth of miniature subjects thrown on miniature panels. The first to discover and apply his powers in that direction would naturally be Perugino. Later on he would be asked, as a matter of necessity, to cover Perugino's name entirely with work of his own.

After the death of Giovanni Santi, Raphael's guardians had abundant leisure to weigh the advantage and disadvantage of sending him to Perugia. If they were bent on giving him a master of celebrity they had but little choice. Bramante was probably away in a distant Lombard city, and Signorelli remained the only man whose repute could vie with that of Perugino. But Signorelli was not unknown to the people of Urbino; and the pictures which he had sent there would naturally suggest his name to persons conversant with Umbrian art. True, he resided in a small and comparatively obscure city. Yet, if we look at his works and consider the claims which might have been put forward in his favour as a tutor to Raphael, we must concede that he was second to no one that the Santi and Ciarlas could have kept in view. If Perugino was celebrated as a contributor to the decoration of the Sixtine Chapel at Rome, Signorelli was not without a title to similar. distinction. He was a favourite artist in every town of the Umbrian country, Perugia not excepted ; and Giovanni

Santi had not held him in less esteem than Perugino; yet, for some cause which historians have not ventured to point out, it did not occur to Raphael's guardians to entertain the idea of entrusting their charge to him, nor did a whisper of any relations between him and Raphael find its way into the pages of Vasari. Perhaps there were private reasons to be adduced for avoiding a nearer connection with him. There are passages in his life which throw some shadows on his character even now, and Don Bartolommeo or Simone Ciarla may have heard of earlier objections of the same kind, to which they attached a sufficient importance. But it is clear that had their decision been favourable to Signorelli, and had Raphael been entrusted to his care, the boy would probably have taken the guidance of the consummate master of Città di Castello with the same benefit as he derived from those of Perugino; and if we had not the evidence of the Venice sketch-book to prove how much Raphael looked at Signorelli's pictures we should find testimony of equal weight in other and perhaps more youthful works in which we recognise the graceful hand of Sanzio. We shall have occasion to note how some of the earliest drawings which Raphael produced at Perugia reveal some knowledge of Signorelli. But we shall observe at the same time that that influence was subordinate altogether to the influence of Perugino.

Where history and records fail, and even anecdote is silent, we hardly dare to venture on conjecture. Yet conjecture would scarcely be out of place in respect of one who practised the arts after Giovanni Santi's death at Urbino. If Timoteo Viti really lived as it is said that he did at the Court of Montefeltro when Raphael's future course was shaped by his guardians, the counsel, if not the lessons of such a man might have been thought worth having. His youth and want of acknowledged repute might make him personally unacceptable. But we may presume that his opinion would be listened to with respect. Timoteo, we are told, was still young when he turned from Bologna to seek an independent fortune elsewhere. Born about 1469 and trained to the profession of a goldsmith, which he was induced to exchange for that of a painter, his youth had been spent with Francia, whose house he abandoned in 1495. Vasari suggests that he reached Urbino immediately after his departure from Bologna. This was the critical time before midsummer, when Raphael's friends had to decide on his future movements. Fresh from the painting room of a master who loved him dearly, Viti might have spoken of Francia as a trusty and conscientious teacher. He would certainly not have suggested Signorelli, whose style was altogether in contrast with his own. The question still remains, was he consulted? And in answering this question we can only observe that there is more reason for thinking that he was, than that he was not. Viti may have formed an early or a late acquaintance with Raphael.* Raphael may

* Here again we may hazard a conjecture. Might not Viti have   accompanied Raphael to Perugia? There is a drawing of a storm

have met him as a boy in 1495, or as a man after 1500. But nothing is better certified than that Viti and Raphael were friends, and that Raphael afterwards invited Viti to Rome. Nor is it too much to presume that Francia owed his subsequent connection with Raphael to Viti's mediation. Whether Viti contributed to affect the decision of Bartolommeo Santi and Simone Ciarla or not, it is obvious that he might have urged conclusive arguments in favour of Perugino. Without being aware that Giovanni Santi had once expressed an honest admiration of the great Umbrian master, he probably knew of the genuine esteem in which Perugino was held by several members of the reigning family of Urbino. He was not, we may think, unaware that Giovanna, at that time regent of Fano and Sinigaglia, had been one of Perugino's most constant patrons, and still remained attached to him. He was in the way of knowing that the Roveres at Rome had befriended the master years before.* The friendship of the Roveres and Montefeltri might contribute to secure a favourable reception to Raphael. It is not unnecessary to set forth

---

against the walls of Perugia in the collection of the Louvre, which, though assigned to Raphael, is generally accepted as a work of Viti.

* Parlando . . . cum vostra Signoria de alcuni quadri de pictura che vanno nel studio nostro fra quali desyderavamo haverne uno de mano del Perosino : la S. V. se offerse de indurlo ad servirne *per esser suo domestico.*"

Isabella Gonzaga to Giovanna Prefetessa, Mantua, xxii. Sep. MD. in Giornale di Erud. Art. *u. s.* ii. 143–4. The Roveres, to whom Giovanna was related by marriage, were also patrons of Perugino, *i.e.*, Sixtus IV. and Giuliano, afterwards Julius the IId.; and Raphael himself, in a letter of 1508, calls himself an old "servitore et familiare" of Francesco Maria della Rovere (see *postea*).

all these reasons for believing or endeavouring to
show that Raphael was apprenticed to Perugino. But
putting them aside, the boy's career alone, as it comes
to be disclosed hereafter, proves conclusively that he
went, comparatively untaught, in the autumn of 1495,
to Perugia. What he found there in the way of art
and social or political relations is matter for a coming
chapter.*

* Pungileone and others have assigned frescos and pictures to Raphael of which they say that they were painted at Urbino before Raphael went to study under Perugino. A list of these and other pieces, falsely attributed to the master, will be found elsewhere.

CHAPTER II.

Perugian revolutions.—Art revival at Perugia.—Raphael's sketch-book.
—Pinturicchio as a draughtsman.—Perugino's sketches.—Raphael
learns drawing.—Copies of drawings from the Sixtine frescos.—
Other copies.—Their style.—He copies several masters, Signorelli,
Mantegna.—He studies from monuments.—His school-fellows, and
school work.—Visit to Urbino.—Library of Urbino, and copies by
Raphael from pictures by Justus of Ghent.—Gallery of Urbino.—
Raphael and the Cambio.—" Resurrection " of the Vatican.—Terni
and Alnwick.—Madonna Diotalevi.

THE natural longing for facts which distinguishes
our age is perhaps less conspicuous in the domain
of the arts than in that of the sciences. Yet it
would be inexcusable if we should neglect to acquire some knowledge of the place and people
in the midst of which Raphael began his artistic
career. It may not be useless to some readers to
know that Perugia is situated on a hill; in which it
resembles Orvieto, Cortona, or Assisi, but it is of
more interest to note that Perugia is high, and over-
looks twenty miles of country on every side except
one, and that Raphael might stand on its principal
eminence, and see the cradle of the genius of Giotto.
We may venture to fancy that when he first entered
those walls and took in at a glance the varied picture
of hill and plain and vale or castled height, and saw
the bulwark of the Franciscan order looming in the
distance, he vowed that he would one day rival the

great founder of the Tuscan school, whose youth had been spent at Assisi. The time in which, we think, he first entered Perugia was the time when the city ceased for a moment to be divided between the powerful factions of the Oddi and Baglioni. For years past one of these factions had encamped within or without the walls according as chance or treason, or force or cunning had expelled or invited them. In autumn of 1495, the last desperate effort of the Oddi to regain supremacy had been repulsed. A fearful massacre had taken place, and the Baglioni had remained masters of the place. Neither peace nor rest till then had been known to any one. Out of bowshot of Perugia, or beyond arrow flight of Assisi or Foligno there was no safety. Inside Perugia, Guido and Ridolfo Baglioni lay merciless and strong; outside, the exiled Oddi with friends in neighbouring villages and castles. Not a farmer or peasant on the hill sides or down the valleys far stretching to the banks of Thrasimene lake could venture to trim his vines or tend his olive trees without danger of being robbed or murdered. Every inch of ground was unsafe to men, women, or even children. Wolves and other savage beasts we are told ranged the country unpursued and fed on human bodies, where cultivation had been superseded by the wild growth of woods and coverts.* Banded together in companies of horse and foot the Perugian exiles

---

* Cronaca di Matarazzo. Archivio storico, tom. xvi. 8vo, Firenze, parte ii. pp. 15, 26, 53, 57, 59, may be consulted for this and other incidents in the above narrative.

harried the country up to the gates of Perugia, or the sons of Guido Baglioni sallied from the town which their father held and revenged the cruelties of the Oddi by cruelties equally bloody. For a time fortune seemed about to desert the Baglioni. The Republic of Sienna, offended at the loss of the Virgin's ring which had been stolen by a friar and deposited as a relic in the brotherhood of St. Joseph of Perugia, took part in favour of the Oddi, reinforcements were obtained secretly by the exiles from the Duke of Urbino, the prefect of Sinigaglia, and the lords of Pesaro and Camerino, and a strong force was collected for the storm of Perugia. On the 4th of September the Oddi and their allies gained access by a stratagem to one of the gates of the town, and pushed their forces within a single hour into the principal square. The Baglioni rose at the sound of arms and fought with desperation. By sheer courage they bore down their foremost opponents ; and as they gradually concentrated their partisans they worsted their foes and expelled them from the city, leaving the chiefs of the exiles dead or prisoners behind. It is needless to descant upon the use which the Baglioni made of their victory. Accustomed as despots to apply the hardest forms of tyrannical government, they hung and quartered their adversaries, and established a void in which they lived and prospered for a time. If, as history records, they sowed the wind to reap the whirlwind, and the sins of the fathers were visited on the children, the momentary calm which intervened gave an impulse to peaceful occupations, which was not to be despised; and painters, sculptors, and architects flocked in to repair the ruined palaces and restore the altars of which the churches had been deprived. Political retribution might afterwards disturb the prospect. The rest which preceded new storms was useful to art, and incomparably serviceable to Raphael.

A contemporary annalist has quaintly described the change from absolute misery to comparative prosperity. "Perugia," he says, "was distinguished for evil by men of infamous habits and iniquitous conduct. But she was not less distinguished for good by men of fair repute and honest lives. The victory of the Baglioni gave encouragement to much that was beneficial. Alms were freely distributed, and money was largely subscribed for the promotion of religion. The funds contributed by the piety of some and the repentance of others, served to build or rebuild numberless edifices. The convents of St. Columba, St. Mary Magdalen, and St. Mary of the Angels, were renovated; the foundations of the monastery of St. Jerome were laid; San Costanzo and Santa Maria de' Servi were restored; San Lorenzo, San Domenico, and San Francesco del Monte were enlarged. The Chapel of St. Joseph was prepared for the custody of the Virgin's ring; the hospital of the Misericordia received important additions, and the city gates were remodelled." Nor does the annalist neglect to name the masters who chiefly contributed to this wonderful revival. "It was at this time," he says, "that the altarpiece of San Pietro was executed by Piero di Castello della Pieve, an artist unsurpassed in any part of the inhabited globe ; second to whom, though in his rank equally famous, was Pinturicchio, commonly called Sordicchio, whose nicknames were equally due to deafness, a short stature, and a puny aspect." *

The gossip of a garrulous town chronicle has seldom been more fully confirmed by authentic records. In a letter addressed to Mariano Chigi in November, 1500, Agostino Chigi, afterwards known as the Magnificent, says, " Perugino is the best master in Italy, and except Paturicchio, his pupil, there are no masters worth speaking of." † Perugino's labours in 1495 and 1496 have been duly noticed. Pinturicchio, whose companionship with Perugino is proved by the frescos of the Sixtine and the testimony of Vasari, accompanied his partner to Perugia, where articles of association secured to him one-third of the profits, whilst two-thirds went to Perugino.‡ His contract to paint the " Holy Family " for Santa Maria fra Fossi, was sealed on the 13th February, 1496 ; his promise to furnish the Doctors of the Church for the Cathedral of Orvieto was signed in March of the same year. Both are evidence of great activity in the common painting room. The partners stood in the same relation to each other as Fra Bartolommeo and Mariotto Albertinelli in later years at Florence. Their friendship explains how it happened that Raphael became attached to both.

---

* Matarazzo, *u. s.* p. 7.

† Agostino to Mariano Chigi, in Cugnoni (G.), A. Chigi, 8vo, Rome, 1881, p. 77.

‡ Vas. *u. s.* vol. iii. p. 494.

Raphael would probably not have ventured, nor would his guardians have allowed him to undertake, a journey to Perugia during the active feud of the Baglioni and Oddi. But so soon as the fortune of arms gave preponderance to the victorious faction, the secret support hitherto given to the exiles by the court of Urbino ceased, and Raphael might travel to Perugia on roads that were comparatively secure. We shall consider him from this time forward an inmate of Perugino's house, " where he charmed old Pietro by cleverness of drawing, an amiable disposition, and polished manners." *

In one of the earliest Tuscan manuals, which treat of the rules of painting, Cennino Cennini distinguishes two classes of individuals, which he divides into pupils studying for gain and pupils choosing art as a profession for its own sake. He does not deny that some aspirants to fame may be actuated by both motives at once ; † but " assuredly," he says, " those persons are most to be commended who subordinate the first to the second." The rules which Cennini sets forth for the guidance of his readers are placed under the principal heads of drawing and colours ; but he distinctly asserts that drawing is the foundation of all knowledge.‡ Perugino's first inquiry seems to have been whether Raphael knew how to draw. Cennini

* Vas. iv. p. 317.

† Il libro dell' arte. Ed. G. & C. Milanesi, 8vo, Firenze, 1859, p. 3.

‡ Ibid., p. 17.

again recommends beginners to acquire the secret of preparing panels and drawing materials, and he gives special directions for making a portfolio or book of loose leaves for sketching at home or in churches and chapels. He then tells his disciples to learn the art of copying, first with the pencil or lead point, and then with the pen; and he concludes by recommending students to live in cities well supplied with works of art, in order that each according to his taste may choose one of the great masters for a model.

Raphael, if we judge by the evidence at our command, had overcome the difficulties of pen sketching when he became possessed of a book shaped according to Cennini's instructions, the remnants of which are preserved in the Academy of Venice. It is hard to say whether he began this book immediately after his arrival at Perugia, or later on in the days of his probation. But he showed a tendency to follow the precepts of Lionardo, who taught his Academy to study many masters, rather than those of Cennini, who would have confined him to one. Yet, at the outset, it may be said that he entirely devoted himself to Perugino, and it was only after acquiring the Peruginesque style that he thought of emulating the form of Signorelli. The leaves of the Venetian sketch-book, now reduced to fifty-three, are mostly drawn upon at both sides. They contain a great variety of sketches illustrating the different phases of Raphael's art from the period of his stay at Perugia to that of his departure from Florence. Here and there he allowed a friend to trespass on the page.

But this is but one more proof of his amiable disposition.*

Perugino's fame, in the eyes of his countrymen, was chiefly due to the decoration of the Sixtine Chapel, for which he composed a cycle of gospel subjects, in part executed by himself, in part entrusted to the hand of Pinturicchio. As junior partner and assistant in the firm of which Perugino was the chief, Pinturicchio worked on the designs and copied the sketches. of his great and accomplished master. The drawings of the Sixtine, like those of innumerable altarpieces and predellas completed for churches and palaces, were a part of Perugino's stock in trade, which he valued the more as they were suited for reproduction in different pictures, at various intervals and places. Their use as models for pupils studying " from the flat " was inestimable. When Perugino changed his abode in 1495, he took with him to Perugia the portfolios which contained these

---

* The sketch-book cannot be traced to the hand of any older collector than the painter Giuseppe Bossi of Milan, who purchased it, as alleged, from a lady at Parma. At Bossi's death, it was bought by the Abbate Cellotti, of Venice, from whom it was acquired in 1822 by the Austrian Government. It was a bound sketch-book, as three sides of each sheet bear marks of wear, which are not on the fourth side. Each sheet was a quarter of a folio, bearing as a water-mark a ladder in a circle, surmounted by a star, the same mark as that on other Raphael drawings. There were fifty-four sheets in all, of which fifty-three have been preserved, with 106 drawings upon them, part framed and exhibited, part in portfolios, at the Venice Academy. Most of them are patched at one edge with strips of paper, and some in this way have got to be larger than others. But the size of the sheets generally was m. 0·21 high by 0·16.

treasures, and Raphael's time was probably devoted at fixed hours to the labour of copying them.

It may often have been asked what became of these portfolios and their contents; and surprise may not unnaturally have been expressed at their total disappearance. But if we look back into the history of Italian painting to find that nothing remains even of the pictures executed by some men of great eminence; and if we remember that most of the cartoons which Raphael produced for the Vatican chambers have perished, we shall rather find cause to be thankful that some small portion of the wreck was preserved, than to complain that the wreck itself should have occurred. Perugino's drawings for the Sixtine frescos have perished; but it is pleasant to know that some sheets of sketches for other compositions have survived. The scarcity of similar creations by Pinturicchio might be explained by supposing that the master who trusted to Perugino as a draughtsman at the Sixtine, and to Raphael as a designer at Sienna, retained his habits of dependence to the last, and resigned to his journeymen the duties which he was unwilling or unable to perform. But Pinturicchio's powers as a draughtsman were those of a child as compared with those which distinguished Perugino. In the most brilliant period of his career at Rome, he was asked to paint an " Assumption of the Virgin " for Alexander the Sixth, and the drawing for that picture, which has been preserved, exhibits the style of an artist who grew old in the traditions of the Umbrian school. The Virgin in prayer in a Mandorla, the winged cherubs that cover the sky, the decrepid saints who witness the scene, St. Peter and St. Paul, who recommend the kneeling Borgia, are all creations that remind us of the minute and patient labours of a pedantic miniature painter.* No one who looks at this contribution to art at the close of the century which applauded the masterpieces of Ghirlandaio and Verrocchio can fail to perceive that the craftsman who produced it was a worshipper of worn-out forms, incapacitated by his early training to cope with the new current of thought which had set against him. It would have been folly in such a man not to avail himself of the superior genius of Perugino, or if Perugino failed, of that of the younger but still more powerfully gifted Raphael. Perugino was therefore necessarily accepted as the ruling spirit of the Perugian painting room, and Pinturicchio naturally occupied the post of second in command, which his patient habits and aptitude for work entitled him to fill.

In one respect Perugino's drawings, or rather the remnants of them which have been preserved, reveal the existence of a habit which afterwards clung to Raphael. His art, like Raphael's, was based on studies from nature, a single sheet of which might contain as many as a dozen or more figures thrown off at a sitting. Some of these sheets will be found to contain the first thought for portions of altar-pieces

---

* The drawing long assigned to Perugino, but now acknowledged to by Pinturicchio, is in the Albertina at Vienna.

executed at intervals of a quarter of a century. But as a single instance is worth pages of speculation, one example may be quoted to illustrate the rest. In the Gallery of the Uffizi is a sheet of Perugino's pen outlines of children, some of which are realistic enough to suit the sturdy naturalism of Titian, in close contiguity to others eminently fitted for use in sacred pictures. Amidst figures dancing or playing instruments we find one of a boy with his shoulders and head supported on a cushion—the infant Christ in the "Nativity" of 1491, in the Villa Albani at Rome. Lower down, a baby set in a leaning attitude against a saddle, and sucking the finger of its left hand, is the infant Saviour in the "Madonna" of the Certosa at the National Gallery.* Two little ones on the step of an altar, a third walking, are bodily represented in the family altar-piece of the "Root of Mary," at Marseilles. Perugino drew this sheet of sketches from his store six times at least in the course of his practice, repeating the infant Christ which he had used in the "Nativity" of the Albani Villa, first at the Cambio, next at S. Francesco del Monte, finally at Montefalco. He may have withheld these rapid and clever renderings of nature from his apprentices. Essentially his own, and groundwork of his labours, he probably looked on them as the pictorial capital at his sole disposal, the secret spring of his professional life, treasured out of sight as the merchant's private ledger

---

* With some slight variety in the position of the legs.

that divulges when seen the secrets of his mercantile transactions. He may have taught his disciples that sketches of this kind were the stock-in-trade of a large business, but he probably also told them that the time had not yet come when they should hope either to make or to use them. The models which he set before the youths in his painting-room were the finished drawings completed and cleaned for transfer to panel and fresco of which he had an almost inexhaustible supply ; and the frequency with which he gave them out for this purpose is proved by the numerous copies of the same design preserved in public and private collections. If in some cases we admire the cleverness and fidelity with which these copies were executed, others only give rise to a simple feeling of thankfulness that the feeble lines of a beginner should have handed down to us an humble imitation of a lost original. It is with some sentiment of this kind that we look at the group of St. Mary Salomè carrying the infant St. John, and her attendant, St. Joachim with St. James the Elder, a fragment taken from the lost cartoon of the altar-piece of Marseilles, which still bears the name of Tiberio d'Assisi in the Academy at Venice.* But there are cases in which the pupil transcribing his master's work imparted his own delicacy of feeling to the model before him ; and this applies in all particulars to the sketch-book at Venice, which perpetuates for our special

---

* Venice Acad. Frame XXVIII. No. 1. 0·26 h. by 0·14.

enjoyment the lost designs of Perugino's frescos in the Sixtine Chapel at Rome.*

One of the first drawings which Perugino seems to have set before his disciple was executed for the fresco of the "Baptism of Christ," in the Sixtine Chapel. In this vast composition, the foreground assigned to the holy rite is lined with spectators, whose forms and features are those of noted persons of Perugino's time; familiar, we should think, with the Arch of Constantine, the Pantheon, and other edifices which, under the semblance of Jerusalem, grace the site of mediæval Rome. In rear of the neophytes who wait on the ministration of John, the Baptist issues from the wilderness. On the left the Precursor discourses to an audience of men, women, and children partly seated on a bank, partly standing under the trees which gracefully spot the sky. From a spur of grass-grown rock to the right, the Saviour looks down upon the heads of his congregation and preaches the Sermon on the Mount. Of the people waiting on the Saviour two are turned to the right and present their backs to the spectator, looking up,—one calmly at rest, the other cloaked and helmeted with legs wide apart, and the back of one hand on his hip. The

---

* That it was the habit of the great masters to set their own drawings before their pupils as models to be copied, is shown in this passage of Vasari's Michael-angelo (xii. 161): "Avvenga che uno de' giovani, che imparava con Domenico (Ghirlandaio), avendo ritratto alcuni feminine di penna vestite, delle cose del Grillandaio, Michelagnolo prese quella carta," &c. &c.

Lomazzo in his Trattato, p. 320, describes it as a habit of Raphael to draw with the help of cross-lines, or, as he calls it, "fare le figure col telato."

drawing for these figures, originally conceived for level ground, shows the same individuals gazing forward and turned to the left; the palm of the foremost on his hip. A veil or net of squares which covers the paper suggests that the original from which the design was copied was lined for transfer to the wall, but the fresco differs in so many points from the drawing as to negative the supposition. The hardness of the contours, and the stiff action of the figures, betray the comparative inexperience of a beginner, whose first efforts are guided by mechanical appliances; and we can easily believe that he drew the net which covers the earliest of these pieces, with the firm intention of casting off this fetter in subsequent copies of a similar kind.*   As he progressed he gave up the net, and his later drawings exhibit greater freedom, though still taken from the Sixtine frescos.

The next model upon which the skill of the pupil was exercised is one of the sketches for the " Delivery of the Keys " at the Sixtine. This composition is so arranged that the Apostles are divided into couples behind the Saviour, who delivers the keys, and St. Peter who kneels to receive them. The grand figure on the left of the picture is that which was copied first ;—a fine massive form presenting its back to the spectator, the head in profile, the hand pointing with

---

* Ven. Acad. Frame XXIII. No. 11. Back of No. 5. Pass. ii. No. 3. This, like other drawings of the Venice sketch-book, is m. 0·21 h. by 0·16. We shall not repeat these figures except where the drawings of this collection appear to have formed no part of the sketch-book—or the size of the sketch-book leaves was altered by patching.

one forefinger as if to explain the mystery of the Saviour's mission.* Perugino considerately tempers the difficulties of his art to the rising talent of the apprentice and gives him the back view, which is easier than the front view of the human frame. Instead of being shown conversing with the man on his right, the Apostle is drawn looking up, whilst a second person, not in the fresco, bends his glance to the ground with look and action expressive of surprise.

Third in the series is an apostle in rear of the kneeling Peter, a fine grey-bearded man in a wide cloak, seen from behind,† and, fourth between Peter and him, a young apostle in full front with a scroll in his left hand, resting his right on his breast.‡ It would be easy to note varieties of these figures in the distances of the Sixtine frescos. But the points requiring elucidation here are not the notorious defects of Perugino's method or his tendency to repeat himself, but the course which Perugino followed in selecting models from his portfolios for the use of his apprentice. So far, the boy allows himself to be guided by the veil which artificially secures to him a faithful transcript. But the progress which he manifests from the stiffness of a first attempt to the comparative ease of a second, a third, and a fourth, is clear ; and we soon find a delicacy displayed which as much transcends that of Perugino as the

---

* Ven. Acad.   Frame XXIV. No. 5. Back of No. 3. Pass. No. 1.
† Ibid. Frame XXIII. No. 9.

Back of No. 7. Pass. No. 7.
‡ Ibid. Frame XXIII. No. 8. Back of No. 10. Pass. No. 5.

"Sposalizio" of Milan transcends the "Sposalizio" of Caen.

The first evidence of success in free-hand copying is given when the scholar transfers to his book the dame who sits amongst the listeners of the sermon of John in the "Baptism" of the Sixtine. The sketch, apparently designed for a barcheaded Magdalen in prayer, was changed in the fresco to a mother in a cap, holding her child on her lap.* The drawing was made without squares, and was but one of a series in which similar independence was shown. It was followed by a couple of sheets containing studies of drapery, the broad lines of which may be traced alike in the "Mother of Gershom" at the Sixtine and in Raphael's "Coronation of the Virgin" at the Vatican. Nothing proves more clearly the use which was made of these studies than their recurrence in the work of different hands. They were used by the disciples of Pinturicchio in drawings for the fresco of "Eneas Piccolomini kissing the Pope's Slipper," in the Library of Sienna.†

---

* Venice Acad. Frame XXIV. No. 3. Profile to the left. Back of No. 5. Pass. No. 2.

† Venice Acad. Frame XXIII. No. 10. Back of No. 8. Pass. No. 6. Four bits of drapery; the two lower ones being folds of figures seated in profile to the left. Same gallery. Frame XXIII. No. 4. Back of No. 14. Pass. No. 87. Five studies of drapery. The principal bits of each of these sheets have a general resemblance to the draperies of the Virgin and Christ in the "Coronation of the Virgin" at the Vatican. The first is like a copy from a study by Perugino, for the skirt of the mother of Gershom in the Sixtine fresco. The second is not so clearly traceable to Perugino's frescos. But its use by the disciples of Pinturicchio is shown in a silver-point drawing for the left side of the fresco of "Eneas kissing the Pope's Slipper" at the

In a similar spirit and with equal success, the same hand has copied a beautiful " St. John Evangelist," standing bareheaded with his hand on his breast, and looping up the gathers of his cloak,* and a Virgin kneeling in prayer,† that may have belonged to the " Nativity " of the Sixtine before it was sacrificed to the " Last Judgment " of Michaelangelo. The Virgin, often repeated by Perugino and Pinturicchio, had an early origin, as we find it alike in Perugino's " Nativity " of 1491, at the Albani Villa, near Rome, in his " Nativity " of 1500 at the Cambio of Perugia, and in Pinturicchio's " Nativity " in the Rovere chapel at Santa Maria del Popolo at Rome. The feeling with which this creation has been repeated is very charming, but relatively weak when compared with that which elevates the transcript of another figure designed for the " Zipporah " of the Sixtine. In the right-hand foreground of this composition a lovely girl kneels in graceful action before the mother of Gershom. This beautiful apparition is carefully reproduced, and the perfect candour of a face of rounded line, with the additional beauty of a drapery unsurpassed in Perugino's practice, are transfigured into

---

Piccolomini library of Sienna, in possession of Mr. Malcolm, a drawing which after it was made, appears to have been rejected by the master. In this piece the five bits of which Sheet XXIII. 4, at Venice, is composed, have been used. The sheet was in the Wellesley collection. It is on pale blue-grey paper with prepared ground, and the lights are laid in with white. Size, 10 inches h. by 7½, ascribed to Pinturicchio, but probably by Eusebio da San Giorgio.

* Ibid. Frame XXIII. No. 5 Back of No. 11. Pass. No. 4.

† Ibid. Frame XXIII. No. 7. Back of No. 9. Pass. No. 8

something so lovely as to leave an impression far more intense than the great original from which it is taken.[*]

But Perugino did not confine his pupil to one form of lesson, he taught him to draw heads; and two sheets of outlines of that kind designed for the Sixtine are amongst those which are done with the most admirable purity. In the lower left-hand corner of one of them the face of Gershom's mother is shown. On the right-hand corner is that of the woman leading a child behind Moses. Above these, two busts of females offer types of similar mould, but with varied expression, and different ornaments of ribbands and veils.[†] Three out of four of these outlines are repeated in the "Sposalizio" of Caen. Two female heads in the second sheet—the upper one to the right and the lower one to the left—are taken from the model who sat for the series in the first sheet. A third head in the upper left-hand corner, with a pretty draped cap and profuse waving hair, suggests Peruginesque reminiscences of Donatello, Pollaiuolo, or Mino da Fiesole.[‡] In his Tuscan wanderings Perugino necessarily studied the masterpieces of Florentine sculpture, and the author of the Venice Sketch Book did not fail to copy more than one of these studies, a noble specimen of which we shall

---

[*] Ibid. Frame XXIV. No. 2. Back of No. 8. Pass. No. 42. The figure in the drawing as well as in the fresco is in profile to the right.

[†] Ven. Acad. Frame XXIII. No. 6. Back of No. 12. Pass. No. 60.

[‡] Ven. Acad. Frame XXV. No. 2. Back of XXV. No. 20. Pass. No. 50.

find in the sibylline look and attitude of a beautiful woman in the collection of the Venice Academy.*

Turning from women to children, and reverting to Perugino's sketches for the Sixtine Chapel, we find the scholar eagerly and cleverly imitating Perugino's figures of boys; and conspicuous amongst those imitations is the undressed child who re-appears dressed in the fresco of "Moses and Zipporah."†

Nor did Perugino exclusively choose the models which he set before his disciples from the designs of frescos. He also looked out drawings of single saints, from which the torso, the legs, and the head of the martyred St. Sebastian were copied in a series of leaves.‡ In previous efforts, the boy had been confined to the easy imitation of draped figures, naked

---

* Ven. Acad. Frame XXVI. No. 8. Pass. No. 9. Back of XXVI. No. 18.

† Ven. Acad. Frame XXVII. No. 1. Pass. 51. Back of XXVII. No. 24, represents a Corinthian capital. Besides the boy mentioned in the text, there is a figure of another boy, with his back to the spectator, and a head modelled in relief by help of white body colour.

‡ Three sheets, viz., Ven. Acad. Frame XXIV. No. 7. Back of XXIV. No. 1. Pass. No. 79 (the legs). Ibid. Frame XXV. No. 6. Back of 16. Pass. No. 77. (Torso and head). Ibid. XXV. No. 16. Back of No. 6. Pass. No. 78. In the gallery of Lille, No. 725, is another study of a Peruginesque St. Sebastian exhibited under Raphael's name. The saint is represented with the right arm above the head, the right behind the back. The face looks downward. Round the loins is a hip cloth. The paper is much torn and patched and crumpled, so that an opinion as to the genuineness of the work is difficult. But the execution is like that of Raphael copying Perugino. One rent disfigures the left breast. Two others are in the thighs. Pen sketch. Size, m. 0·278 h. by 0·132. Wicar's catalogue tells us that this is the original sketch for a small picture which in 1807 was at Turin, but which came later into the collection of Mr. Migneron, a mining engineer in Paris (not seen by the authors).

infants, or heads. Now he was called upon to face the difficulties of the full-grown nude. His task is to give the outline of frame and limbs, to indicate with slight but accurate strokes the projection of bones and muscles, and the working of articulations. The head, which forms a separate study, is thrown upwards to show the throat and the cavities of the nose and brows: and the intricate modelling is brought out by hatching carefully directed to second the appearance of rounding in the parts, and the vanishing of one surface into the other. Though he labours at this lesson and barely escapes hardness his work is earnest, conscientious, and correct. A couple of admirable copies follow, which are taken with such fidelity from the "Studies for Prophets" in the framework of some altar-piece that we almost think the draughtsman is Perugino himself. A foot in a corner of one sheet, a hand in another, add to the interest with which we follow the progress of the youthful artist.* A draped Saint of genuine Peruginesque character comes next,† then a profile of a man looking up,‡ finally a couple of lions, rampant and couchant, sketched perhaps

---

* Ven. Acad. Frame XXIII. No. 3. Back of No. 13. Pass. No. 75. Ibid. Frame XXVI. No. 7. Back of No. 19. Pass. No. 73. Both pen sketches.

† Ibid. Frame XXVI. No. 14. Back of No. 2. Pass. No. 32. This drawing is also known by a copy in the Albertina of Vienna, which shows that it was set before more than one pupil of Perugino. Much in the same spirit and of the same time is the figure of a youth playing a mandoline, No. 1 in the Oxford collection, which, if genuine, is a feeble effort of Raphael's early time.

‡ Ven. Acad. Frame XXVII. No. 25. Back of No. 22. A man with a small pointed beard and light curly locks, looking up and turned to the right.

from a captive beast in possession of the Baglioni, one
of which is found in Perugino's " Penitence of St.
Jerome " in the Museum of Caen.*

The form of Raphael as a man looms so mighty and
grand before most of us that we hardly realise the
picture of the youth who prepares himself for the
stage upon which he acquired fame.   Hercules fighting the Hydra is familiar, but Hercules in his cradle
is not equally so.   Yet Raphael, too, seems to have
drunk of the milk of Juno.   He is not less a marvel
as a boy than his prototype is a prodigy as an infant.
We feel the truth of Vasari's contention when he says
that Raphael's imitations of Perugino were so remarkable that they were not to be distinguished from the
originals, but we cannot doubt that the peculiar
feeling which betrays the disciple was discernible to
the subtle glance of his biographer.†   Yet it may
happen that some persons will still venture to hold
that the drawings of the Venice sketch-book are the
originals prepared by Perugino or his partner Pinturicchio for the frescos of Rome.   To those who
should cherish this opinion we may ask whether the
Venice drawings can really have been used at the
Sixtine Chapel, or whether the hand and outline are
truly characteristic of either Pinturicchio or Perugino.

---

* Ven. Acad.   Frame XXIV.
No. 8.   Back of No. 2.   Pass. 41.
Couchant lion, outline turned to
the right.   Ibid.   Frame XXVI.
No. 12.   Back of No. 4.   Pass. No.
40.   This is a lion walking, the
counterpart exactly of that in Perugino's " St. Jerome," No. 2 of the
Museum of Caen, but reversed.
The lion might have been studied
in Perugia, as the Baglioni kept a
large one in their palace.   Mataranzo, Cronaca, *u. s.* ii. 104.

† Vas. iv. 317.

At the period of the decoration of the Sixtine Chapel, when both these masters were at the zenith of their fame, their designs must have borne the stamp of an art altogether mature. With all respect for the genius of Raphael, that is not the impression which the Venice transcripts of the Sixtine frescos produce. They are the unequal creations of a youth who starts with modest powers and gathers skill and confidence as he proceeds. The net of squares which he uses is not the guiding tracery of the painter, since the figures in the drawings vary from those on the walls. The contour is not always that of an old and experienced hand, since the tentative efforts of a disciple, striving to imitate the models of his master, are frequently apparent. Perugino's art in extant sketches is that of a man full of the freedom and vigour of experience and command. But freedom and vigour are the two qualities which are most conspicuously absent in the earlier numbers of the Venetian series. It might be said, indeed, that the lines which are too feeble for Perugino are still good enough for Pinturicchio. But Pinturicchio's style of drawing is now very well known; and he was not the master who conceived and composed the frescos of the Vatican. Years have elapsed since it was shown that he might have taken part and probably did take part in the decoration of the Sixtine,* and any one conversant with his style can point out even now his share in the work of Perugino. But no

---

* History of Italian Painting, vol. iii. pp. 178-9.

evidence can be adduced to show that he did more than perform the humble and suitable duty of carrying out the designs of his partner. The drawings of the Venice sketch-book do not exclusively reveal the tentative efforts of an unskilled hand. They display, in sensible gradations, the progress of a youth of peculiar gifts. The earlier transcripts from the Sixtine are below the powers of Perugino. The later ones far transcend in elegance and purity anything that Perugino could by any possibility have produced.

Raphael, however, was not a copyist of Perugino alone. He was equally capable of reproducing with fidelity the drawings of Gio. Santi, Signorelli, Filippino Lippi, Mantegna, Justus of Ghent, Donatello, Pollaiuolo, and Ghirlandaio, and no one as yet has been bold enough to say that reproductions of this kind in the Venice sketch-book are original works of those potent masters. It is impossible to predict how far the spirit of unbelief which is now abroad may be carried, but it is not unlikely that some generation of critics will arise which shall signalize its perspicacity by denying that Raphael copied the drawings of his contemporaries. But we must not forget that there is one test which can always be applied when the question arises, whether Raphael did or did not copy the contemporaries of Perugino. Possessed as he was of all the peculiarities which mark that master's manner, his outlines and workmanship were eminently calculated to deceive. But this very faculty naturally tended to betray him in imitations of the

works of other painters, and it is undoubtedly notice-
able in his copies of Santi, Signorelli, and Mantegna.
Thus, when we look at the Venice sketch-book and
pause before the aged St. Andrew holding the beam of
the Cross which, we can hardly doubt, was conceived
originally by Giovanni Santi, the spirit of Perugino
seems to linger in the form and loop of the gnarled
drapery.*   The man-at-arms who presents his back
to us whilst he holds the staff of his lance and plants
his hand on his hip, the naked man blowing a trumpet,
or the mailed soldier striking at the infant in its
mother's arms, every one of them is impressed with
the general features of Signorelli's style, tempered in
their ruggedness and strength by something mild that
modifies the asperity of the master of Città di Castello.
Nothing indeed would be more pardonable than to
say that the Venice sketch-book contains drawings by
Signorelli.   It would be difficult to find anything
much more marked than the accent of the contour
and muscular development of the man-at-arms, whose
tight-fitting shoulder-plates and jacket seem to merge
inperceptibly into flesh as we descend to the detail of
the legs and feet.†   The lean muscularity of the
trumpeter and his wiry strength as he sounds the horn,

---

* Ven. Acad. Frame XXVI.
No. 1.   Pass. 13.   St. Andrew
turned to the left, and bearded,
with locks falling to the shoulders,
the right arm and hand supporting
the cross.   A scroll on the handle
of a stick in the left.   Here is a
positive reminiscence of Santi and
something of Pinturicchio.   The
drawing is modelled in body colour.

† Ibid. Frame XXVII. No. 15.
Back of No. 12.   Pass. No. 16.
Pen and umber.   A figure of this
character appears in one of Signorelli's frescos at Montoliveto.

with his head thrown back and his cheeks blown out,
are as truly characteristic of Signorelli as the coarse
breadth and bony scantling of the feet.* The dip
and waving line of the limbs in the mailed soldier,
and the masculine breadth of shape in the mother
who defends her child, are unmistakeable; † yet in all
these figures the hand of Perugino's disciple is not
concealed. We shall see how Raphael, later on,
copied Signorelli with a clear impress of his own
identity, and yet without losing the character of the
great original. Equally distinct in its combination of
the Raphaelesque with the Florentine and Umbrian
styles is the drawing in the Venice sketch-book of an
old man kneeling in prayer and dressed in a long
cloak, in which a study by Filippino is copied with
drapery lined in the fashion of Perugino.‡ But the
most curious evidence of unwillingness to deny the
Umbrian nature is conveyed by a transcript of Mantegna's "Entombment." It would be equally interesting and important to investigate how the designs and

* Ven. Acad. Frame XXVI. No.
5. Back of XXVI. No. 11. Pass.
No. 29. Nude, turned to the left.
Pen and umber. This sketch looks
as if it might have been intended for
a last judgment, like that of Signorelli at Orvieto.

† Ibid. Frame XXIII. No. 2.
Back of No. 16. Pass. No. 23.
Pen and umber.

In the spirit of Perugino and
Signorelli, but somewhat akin to
the drawings just described, is a
sketch of a saint in an ample
cloak, bending forward and supporting himself with both hands
on a pole. This drawing, a pen
and umber sketch rather dimmed
by time, is catalogued at Oxford
and numbered No. 3, size 7¾ inches
h. by 3½, and comes from the Alva
and Lawrence collections. It represents St. Joseph, and is on
brown tinted paper.

‡ Ibid. Frame XXVII. No. 5.
Back of 21, which contains a drawing of a Corinthian capital (Pass.
No. 71). Pen and umber. Figures
turned to the right.

prints of contemporary masters found their way out of
the hands of those who produced them into the portfolios of men desirous of studying the art of the
numerous schools into which Italy was divided.
Perugino, who was familiar with almost every city
that lay between Venice and Rome, had invaluable
opportunities of collecting drawings, for which he
might easily exchange sketches of his own.   It is not
too much to presume that he was a collector whose
store of examples was naturally open to the inspection
of his pupils.   We can ,thus explain how Raphael
would be able to copy the models of Umbrians and Florentines, whose principal masterpieces were unknown
at Perugia.   The purchase and sale of prints on the
other hand was a regular business in the capitals
frequented by artists, and though little is known of
the trade in the 15th century, its extent is very
clearly proved in the 16th, when Albert Dürer
quarrelled with Marc-Antonio for pirating his plates
of the " Passion."   Michaelangelo seems to have been
equally acquainted with engravings by Schön and by
Dürer, and there is no reason why Raphael should
not have been familiar with works of the same class,
when we recollect that he might have inherited them
from his father, or obtained them from Perugino.
Mantegna's engravings could hardly have been unknown to either of these masters since one of them had
visited Mantua, and the other Venice.   But Perugino
had special cause to know Mantegna and his works,
and there is no difficulty in explaining how his pupil
might have seen a copy of the " Entombment " when

staying with the master at Perugia. A short time before his return to that city, Perugino had taken a young beauty named Chiara Fancelli to wife, and signalized his admiration and affection by transferring her features to numerous altar-pieces. The fond old man used to dress her hair in ribbands and veils with his own hand, that he might feast his eyes, and perhaps those of Raphael with her charms. Chiara came of a family of artists. Her father, Luca, who had made his name as a sculptor in Florence, was transferred when at the height of his practice to Mantua, where he enjoyed the patronage of the Gonzaga and the friendship of Mantegna. He gave his daughter to Perugino with a large dowry, and she, perhaps, took the " Entombment " of the Mantuan painter from her father's collection to that of her husband.* Be this as it may, Mantegna's " Entombment " came to be known in the painting-room at Perugia, and bits of it were transferred to the Venetian sketch-book, including on one side of a leaf the figure of Joseph of Arimathea holding the winding-sheet ;† on the other side Christ on the winding-sheet carried by Nicodemus and the Virgin, and bewailed by St. John the Evangelist.‡ We all know Mantegna's

---

* See *antea*, p. 27, and Braghirolli, in Giornale di Erud. Tosc.
ii. 73, *et seq.*

† Ven. Acad. Frame XXIII.
No. 15. Back of No. 1. Pass.
No. 82. Full length. Pen and
umber. To the right of the left
foot of the figure, which is turned
to the left, is a repetition of the
first and second toes, important as
showing Raphael's study of cor-
rections.

‡ Ibid. Frame XXIII. No. 1.
Back of the foregoing. Pass. No.
81. Pen and umber.

print and its contrasts of grim death with agonizing
shrieks ; we have all studied those metallic forms and
drapery which strike us as of kin to the works of the
Greeks in their classical correctness. No one who
has once seen them can forget the moving groups in
which grief is represented with such intense realistic
passion ; or the capricious arrangement of dresses,
tightly fitting or loose in the wind, and searching
alike the deepest fold or the shallowest depression in
stuffs. At the first blush the copy looks like a
Paduan replica of an original drawing for the print.
But a closer inspection reveals an Umbrian in Lombard disguise. The run of the lines, the rendering of
feet, hands, fingers, nails, and articulations is no longer
wholly Mantegna's, and the looped strokes indicating
breaks in the drapery are as clearly Umbrian, as the
toning down of Mantegna's bitter hardness, which
seems to indicate that the student's kindly feeling
rebelled and diluted the concentrated essence in the
original to something softer and more suggestive of
pathos. It is difficult to conceive anything at once
more true and more false than this copy, and yet how
clever and bold it is ; what knowledge and will, what
practice of hand it reveals ? Raphael realized the
higher laws of composition and arrangement which
distinguish the " Entombment " when a similar subject was entrusted to him by one of the noblest and
most bitterly tried ladies that lived at the time in
Perugia. His duty as a copyist, would simply
consist in a trial of patience and skill. But the task
of a pupil in Perugino's painting-room would not be

complete when he rose from his desk. Taking his book in his hand, he would sally forth into the street, and entering some church or chapel, copy the details of architecture and ornament which struck his fancy; here the frieze of a pilaster which might not be allowed to remain unused as years went by, and independent practice succeeded to lesson and study;* then a Corinthian capital which might adorn the perspective of a portico,† or, the griffin, cognizance of Perugia, a grand relief in bronze, which to this day shows the fabulous hybrid, rampant with heraldic wings and claws, and mane and paws and grotesque tail above the gate of the Town Hall.‡

From the days of Vasari to those of Passavant, three centuries and a half have been spent in repeated efforts to celebrate worthily the genius of Raphael. A copious literature in every language has been devoted to the sole purpose of praising his masterpieces; and pictures early and late have been examined and dissected to detect and divulge, if possible, the master's thoughts and feelings in the act of composing and executing them. No biographer has faced the difficulty of studying or endeavouring

---

* Ven. Acad. Frame XXVII. No. 17. Back of No. 14. Omitted in Pass.'s list. The ornament begins at top with the bust of a child, with an arabesque ornament about the head, and strings of beads, the whole resting on a scolloped tray. The tray rests on two griffins; and these again on the back of a heraldic bird. An ornament of this kind will be found on a pilaster of Raphael's predella of the Annunciation at the Vatican.

† Ibid., ibid. Frame XXVII. No. 21. Back of No. 5. Acanthus leaf from a Corinthian capital. Pass. No. 71. Pen sketch.

‡ Ibid., ibid. Frame XXVII. No. 2. Back of No. 25. Pen sketch. The griffin in profile to the left.

to show where or how he spent his time during the period which intervened between his childhood and adolescence. If the sketch which has just been made can lay claim to any correctness it will have established that some pupil of Perugino was engaged at Perugia for years in studying the art of the painter who was then acknowleged as the greatest artist of his time in that country ; and that that pupil's labours have been preserved. If it should be denied that the person so favoured was the master of Urbino, we must assume that Raphael only left home after acquiring an art of his own. He must of necessity have lived at Urbino long enough to form his manner, and as it is conceded on all sides that he ultimately came to labour under Perugino's orders in Umbria, and there acquired a style deceptively like that of his teacher, he must inevitably have gone through stages of development of most unusual diversity. Coming into Perugino's service as a journeyman, yet a stranger to his style, he must not only have had the genius to divest himself at once of the manner acquired at Urbino, but the genius also of throwing off the characteristics of that manner so completely that no trace of it remains.

One of the most amiable and natural traits in Vasari's character is the love of anecdote which leads him to make us acquainted with the personal relations of celebrated artists. Unhappily there is nothing so utterly untrustworthy as the notices which he gives of the youth of great men. Genuine poetry may be found in his tale of Giotto tending his father's flock in the pastures of Vespignano, and drawing a lamb on a stone whilst Cimabue passes and divines the future greatness of the Florentine master. True pathos lurks in the scene where Santi takes Raphael from his weeping mother and carries him off to Perugia. The picture of the truant Giotto neglecting school to spend his stolen hours in the dwelling of Cimabue, is not more sober in reality than that of Raphael taking leave of a stepmother for whom he had no apparent affection. When Vasari has to deal with men of humble name he seldom condescends even to anecdote; and whilst in the one case he does something to mislead, in the other he disdains altogether to enlighten our ignorance. To his guidance or neglect we owe it alike that nothing positive is known of Raphael's school-days, or his connection with the companions who frequented the city of his residence, or the painting-room of Perugino. Ample leisure will be given to us to study his relations with Pinturicchio when we contemplate their joint labours at Sienna. Of Spagna we know generally that he was one of Perugino's disciples who would never have left the city of his choice, but that the jealousy of foreigners which characterised Italian painters, drove him away to the comparative solitude of Todi. He is named amongst the apprentices of Perugino in March, 1502,* and Vasari

---

* Giovanni *charson* (garzone) who receives payments in kind for Perugino in 1502, we may take to be Spagna, who elsewhere is called Giovanni detto Hyspano. See Rossi, Giornale di Erud. Tosc. iii. 25.

has numbered him amongst the companions of Raphael's youth. But Spagna owed less to his originality than to imitative skill, and Raphael's style, as well as his friendship, clung to the solitary master in after years at Rome. Domenico Alfani, whose attachment is revealed in Raphael's correspondence, lived to feed, artistically speaking, on the creations of his comrade, and Raphael's love survived even the trial of a distant separation. Manni, Eusebio da San Giorgio, Ibi, and Berto, began to practise as masters at Perugia, before Raphael's probation. Roberto, or Uberto Montevarchi, was his obscure successor as an apprentice in the painting-room of Perugino.* More important than the natives, the Florentines who frequented Perugia may have contributed to foster Raphael's wish to visit the most celebrated city of Tuscany, and Domenico del Tasso, who once carved the woodwork of the Cambio Hall, was doubtless no stranger to his younger contemporary, whilst Baccio d'Agnolo, who began the stalls of Sant' Agostino in 1501, might repay the early services of Raphael by hospitable welcome in the Florentine dwelling in which Michaelangelo, Cronaca, Perugino, Filippino, and Granacci, were occasional visitors. During Perugino's journeys to Florence, Venice, Fano, and Sinigaglia, Raphael cannot have remained an idle spectator in the painting-room over which Pinturicchio presided. It is natural to presume that his labour was

* In 1502. See the records in Rossi, Giornale di Erud. Tosc. iii. 25. Montevarchi is called Luberto in these records. Vasari (iii. 591) speaks of him as "Pietro il Montevarchi."

not without material advantage to his employer; yet
we cannot forget that there were times when Raphael
performed no other duties than those which might
justify Perugino in claiming for himself the produce
of his disciple's industry. Predellas at Rouen and
Munich bear Raphael's name, but they chiefly owe
that distinction to the fondness of the world for high-
sounding nomenclature. We may not deny that
Raphael had a share in these beautiful panels, but
impartial criticism bids us to confine his co-operation
to a modest and limited portion. We may note by
the way, that the predellas are stock-pieces which
hardly vary from each other except in the number of
figures which Perugino designed. The group of the
" Saviour and John the Baptist " is repeated with
slight varieties from that of the Sixtine Chapel. But
the solemn attendance of four kneeling seraphs and
four attendant saints at Rouen is simplified to that
of two angels at Munich.* The Epiphany has no
counterpart in continental galleries, though it was the
groundwork of masterpieces produced under new conditions by Raphael.† But the " Resurrection " of
Rouen is enlivened with seven, that of Munich with
but three guards.‡ The style in which these five
pieces are executed is that of Perugino, yet the
reasons which might lead us to believe in Raphael's
co-operation are not based on the mere belief that he
was naturally employed on such labours. The com-

---

* Rouen Museum, No. 270.   ‡ Munich Pinak. No. 1185;
Munich Pinakoth, No. 1173.   Rouen Museum, No. 271.

† Rouen, No. 269.

positions left a strong impression on Raphael's memory; he copied Perugino's original drawing of the group of the "Baptist and Christ with two Attendant Angels," which had probably served for the altar-piece of Sant' Agostino of Perugia, as well as for the predella of Munich; and on the back of the sheet, in obedience to the rigid laws of economy which dictated his conduct at this period, he drew a charming group of "St. Martin Dividing his Cloak," which has the signal merit of being at once the earliest original study that Raphael ever made, and a proof of the double influence which swayed his pencil in those earliest of his days. St. Martin sits on horseback, and holds the skirt of his cloak with his left hand, whilst his right grasps the reins and the sword with which he divides the cloth. The horse would not have satisfied Perugino, nor, indeed, would Raphael himself have looked back on this attempt at equine delineation with any satisfaction. But youth and earnestness beam in the face and action of the saint, whose kindly simplicity is unsurpassed in later creations of the master; whilst the beggar, a horned Satan, scantily covered with a hip-cloth, displays a patient, if not quite masterly study, of the nude. More remarkable, however, than this contrast, the Saint exhibits Raphael's dependence on the models of Perugino, whilst the beggar equally reveals his admiration for the stern and effective strength of Signorelli.*

---

* Stædel collection at Frankfort on the Main.   Pen and umber sketch.

The various and minute occupations of painters' apprentices have been defined with tedious accuracy by more than one of the craftsmen of Tuscany; but the holidays or pastimes which varied their intervals of toil have not been thought worthy of record. Raphael appears to us in the pages of history as a person whose business it was to work and not to play. But youth has its moments of relaxation for the high and the lowly, and Raphael was probably no exception to the rule which everyone obeyed. Festivals at Perugia were not confined to Sunday; and Easter was particularly devoted to religious pomp and social relaxation. Yet holidays at Perugia may not have had the same charm for Raphael as holidays at Urbino, and he may frequently have sighed for the lanes of his native city, and wished that he could revisit the scenes of his childhood. The long eighty miles which separated him from home and the uncertainties of a road not always secure may have been sufficient reasons for not undertaking in ordinary times a journey of great length and possible danger. But if business called and leave could be had, there was no reason why the trip should not be made, and there came a time when the quarrels of Bartolommeo Santi with Bernardina Parte may have required his presence at home. The lawsuit between these litigious relatives had dragged its slow way through the courts without producing anything but costs, till it occurred to both sides, in 1499, that a compromise would be the very best settlement that could be effected. It was therefore agreed that a payment of a sum of money in quarterly instalments should be accepted by Santi's widow as an equivalent for her rights of alimony; and in a deed bearing date at Urbino in June, the conditions of this agreement were ratified by Bartolommeo Santi and Piero Parte on behalf of Raphael and Bernardina. Though Raphael was not present at the solemnity, as the deed of compromise expressly implies,* it is not improbable that he had been summoned to Urbino to sanction it. The time was not unfavourable for a journey to the Feltrine capital. Guidobaldo had just recovered from the gout, brought on by his defeat near Florence in 1498. A favourable treaty had secured to him honours and pay from the Venetian Senate, and the adoption of Francesco Maria della Rovere had given new hopes to the people of the Duchy. Raphael was therefore in a position to enjoy the sight of happy faces, and leisurely to revisit the churches and monuments of his native place, or the rooms of the palace to which the Duke and Duchess would probably grant him access. It is the more likely that the visit took place about this time, because Raphael, under the influence of Perugino's lessons, now probably copied the " doctors and philosophers " whose likenesses had been painted there by Justus of Ghent. Federigo of Montefeltro, when ordering these pictures, intended to celebrate the glory of his ancestors by contrasting their qualities with those of the heroes of antiquity whose names had

* See the record, dated June 5, 1499, in Jahrbuch der Kgl. Preuss. Sammlungen, Part ii. 1882, together with that of May 13, 1500, in which Raphael's absence is distinctly recorded.

been handed down to posterity as possessors of all mortal
gifts. The seven virtues which crowned the effigies
of the Montefeltros and Sforzas in one of the halls
might be naturally supposed to dwell in the doctors
and statesmen who filled the first reading room of the
ducal library ; * nor, we may think, was it without a
secret wish to rival the beauty of similar illustrations
elsewhere that Federigo had entered upon this great
pictorial enterprise. Raphael, fresh from a residence
at Perugia, would have had occasion to see the portraits of chieftains and doctors with which Domenico
Veniziano filled the palace of the Baglioni ; † and a
pardonable ambition might lead him to take and show
to his master the outlines of figures which exhibited
the skill of a Fleming in the very subjects upon
which Perugino himself was at that moment busy in
the hall of the Cambio. Happily the originals which
adorned the palace of Urbino were preserved, and the
sketches of Raphael are easily compared with the
panels in Paris and Rome to show how well an
Umbrian scholar might imitate the masterpieces of a
Fleming. In every line we are conscious of Raphael's

---

* " Besides the library, there is
a reading room, round which
wooden arm-chairs are placed, all
carefully worked in tarsia and in-
taglio. The wainscotted walls are
broken into recesses in each of
which is the portrait of some celebrated writer, with a short eulogy."
Baldi, Descrizione, *u. s.*, p. 57.

† The palace of the Baglioni
and Domenico Veniziano's pictures
in it are mentioned by Vasari, who
says, however, they had already
perished (ii. 674). The legends
beneath the pictures were written
by Mataranzo, who describes the
palace in his Chronicle (*u. s.* 104).
See also Giornale di Erud. Toscana,
iii. p. 10.

wish to make a faithful transcript; in every line he leaves the impress of the school of Perugino.

It is doubtful whether all the portraits of Urbino are preserved.   But of the fourteen panels at the Louvre and an equal number at Rome, Raphael certainly copied eleven, and these are the "Aristotle," "Boethius," "Cicero," "Homer," "Piero d'Abano," "Plato," "Ptolemy," "Seneca," "Solon," "Virgil," and "Vittorino da Feltre."   A nameless "Doctor," the original of which has not been handed down to us, may serve to fill a gap in the index of paintings attributable to Justus of Ghent.   It has been said of these pictures that they alternately display Italian and Transalpine character,—a mixture of the schools of the Netherlands and Central Italy.   The genius of Raphael has noted and reproduced these features with surprising fidelity.   He draws the flow and curl of hair in the spirit of Melozzo, the rough working hands with the realistic truth of Justus, the dresses with Germanic breaks.   He follows the master as he oscillates between the two extremes of the models of Bruges and Forlì.   But Umbrian feeling invariably elevates his copy to the level of nature, and the drapery and outline, or the handling of the pen, remind us of the lessons of Perugino.   The mask of a Homer or Virgil is but the ruder precursor of nobler effigies in the Parnassus of the Vatican.*

---

* *Aristotle.*—Ven. Acad. Frame XXV. No. 19. Back of No. 1. Pass. 61. Pen and ink sketch, as are all the following, to the knees, the body turned to the left, the face three-quarters to the right,

At the close of the 14th century, the palace of Urbino had been improved and enlarged by Guidu-

the right hand raised, palm downwards, the left on a clasped volume. The beard is waved, in the fashion of the Assyrian sculptures; the hair long but wavy, issues from a cloth cap. Reminiscence here of Melozzo. At the top "ARISTO-TELI[S]TA," below, in more modern characters, " ARISTOTELI . STAGI-RITAE." The original is No. 512 at the Louvre.

Boethius and Ptolemy, on one sheet, Ven. Acad. Frame XXVI. No. 17. Back of No. 9, Pass. 69, erroneously places on the back of this sheet a figure of Quintus Curtius. In reality the back is a study of drapery. Boethius, to the left, in a hooded Flemish cap, counts on his fingers. Under his left elbow a book. Opposite to him Ptolemy to the right, with a frame-globe in his left hand, a skull-cap and turban round his forehead. The shaven face of Boethius contrasts with that of the hairy bearded Ptolemy. The first is Flemish, the second recalls Melozzo. Below " C. I. PTOLEMAEO ALEX . FI . BOETIO. The original of Ptolemy is now No. 513 at the Louvre.

Cicero.—Ven. Acad. Frame XXV. No. 9. Back of No. 11. Pass. 65. The figure is seated, in profile to the right, supporting a ponderous folio, a Roman skull-cap is on the head, a fur cape on the shoulders, a very fine classic profile of Italian type. Below " M . TVLIO . CICER.

Homer.—Ven. Acad. Frame

XXV. No. 11. Back of No. 9. Pass. 66. The poet is seated, to the right, the right hand on his knee; the fingers of the right drum upon the cover of a book. A laurel wreath binds the hair. The eyes are closed, the beard short, the frame inclosed in a cloak with a collar. To the right of the head a less finished copy of the same. The Flemish character of the drapery is marked, though the line is Umbrian. Below " HOMERO SMYRNAEO."

Plato.—Ven. Acad. Frame XXV. No. 5. Back of No. 15. Pass. 64. Seated with an open book on his lap. Plato is bearded, with long hair waved after the fashion of Melozzo. His face is in full front, and he expounds a text. The hands are coarse and bony. In cursive to the right the words, " AL MOLTO MAG." Below " PLA-TONI." The original is No. 511 at the Louvre.

Seneca.—Ven. Acad. Frame XXV. No. 1. Back of 19. Pass. 62. In a hooded cape to the left, supporting a book on his knee with his right, which is not seen. As in all these drawings the drapery is Peruginesque. Below " ANNAEO SENECÆ CORDVE." The original is now No. 510 at the Louvre.

Virgil.—Ven. Acad. Frame XXV. No. 7. Back blank. Pass. 67. Turned to the left looking down. Laurels in his frizzled hair, a book in his left hand. Italian rather than Flemish in

baldo. But the rich and valuable collection of pictures which Castiglione so highly prized had not been formed.* What part of the treasures laboriously brought together by princes of the house of Montefeltro was then displayed is as hard to distinguish as the masterpieces which the cupidity of Cesar Borgia removed in 1503.† The canvases and panels which gave celebrity to the palace in after ages were not as yet created. When the ducal establishment was broken up in 1631, the heirlooms of the Montefeltri and

character. Below "P . VERG . MARONI . MANTVANO." The original is No. 508 at the Louvre.

Pietro d'Abano.—Ven. Acad. Frame XXV. No. 3. Back of 17. Pass. 70. Turned to the left a book supported with both hands, in conical cap. Close vest and cloak. The hair is short, the face shaven. Quite in the Umbrian style. Below in cursive " QUINTUS CURTIUS," a forged inscription, the picture, No. 503, at the Louvre bearing the name," PETRO APONIO."

Nameless.—Ven. Acad. Frame XXV. No. 15. Back of XXV. No. 5. Pass. 63. Bearded man with long hair and short beard to the right, with a book flat on his lap, and the right hand gesticulating. On the head a cap with a raised scolloped brim. A mantle with a collar fastened at the neck and opening to show the vest below.

Solon.—Ven. Acad. Frame XXXV. No. 3. Pass. 68. This drawing bears the forged inscription at foot of a folio of " ANAXAGORA." It is a copy of the Solon, No. 509, at the Louvre with unfinished hair. The drawing is similar in execution to the others of the series. A figure in a mantle to the right turning the pages of a folio, a peaked cap on the head.

Vittorino da Feltre, on the back of the foregoing, is a copy of No. 502 at the Louvre. Ven. Acad. Frame XXXV. No. 3. A profile to the left of a man with a book, and wearing a high cap.

Passavant's belief that these drawings were made in 1504 is clearly erroneous. Raphael drew in quite another style at that period—the period, we may recollect, of the Sposalizio of Milan. Pass. i. p. 66.

* Di poche pitture, e stucchi e ornato il Palazzo, posto mente alla grandezza sua ; il che forse è nato del non avere quel principe (Federigo da Montefeltro) avuto l'occhio ad altro che all' eternità... ovvero dall' aver lasciato le dette cose a tempo più opportuno. Delle statue parimente poco se ne veggono forse per la medesima ragione. Baldi, Descrizione, *u. s.* p. 53.

† Ibid. p. 56.

Rovere were removed to Florence and to Rome. But a copious inventory drawn up in 1623 enables us to discern that great and important changes had been made in the decoration of the place.* The library had apparently been stripped of its old adornments, and the portraits of the sages had been impartially transferred to the obscurity of distant deposits or the light of a spacious hall. In a large and sumptuous gallery the effigy of Francesca Maria the IInd presided over an assembly of dukes, princes, chieftains, orators, and saints; and Aristotle, Boethius, Dante, Plato, Seneca, Scotus, Sixtus the IVth, and Thomas Aquinas, transferred perhaps from the panels of the library, ennobled the walls with their presence. Two hundred views of cities and provinces represented the localities illustrated by the deeds of heroes. In other rooms the pictorial riches of many centuries were accumulated,—a various selection of 283 portraits and 452 compositions by numerous painters. Unhappily the diligence of an illiterate scribe, who wasted his time on velvet curtains and gilt frames, forgot the authors of the pictures. But we discover, after a microscopic search, seven panels by Raphael, including a " Madonna and Holy Family," which are probably the " Madonna of Orleans " and the "Madonna with the Palm," Giorgione's " Uguccione della Faggiola," the " Martyrdom of St. Agatha " by Sebastian del Piombo, and eighteen or twenty canvases of Titian, each one

---

* Inventario di Guardarobba MS. in the Oliveriana of Pesaro. No. 386, entire in Appendix.

of which would be worth a fortune in our day. Lesser masters form a small contingent, in which Bassano, Baroccio, Francia, Palma Vecchio, and Tintoretto are prominent figures. Amongst the nameless creations of Italian skill we dimly trace the likeness of Frederick and Guidubaldo attending a lecture, a panel by Piero della Francesca, which fell to the ignoble station of a table in a labourer's cottage, where it was found in our day and restored to honour at Windsor Castle. Countless medals, miniatures, gems, and bas-reliefs were stored away from sight. Twenty-one statuettes filled odd corners, and twenty-three marble busts, including one by Donatello, adorned various consoles; but of statues there were less than a dozen, and of these one half were dubious antiques.* It was once thought desirable that we should know what the specimens of sculpture were which migrated with the ducal library to Rome; and a hope was entertained that the knowledge thus acquired might throw light on the studies of Raphael. But as the palace of Urbino clearly contained no valuable examples of the classic period, it was impossible that Raphael should thus improve the art which he had acquired from Perugino. If he showed himself sensible at all of the forms illustrated in the palace of his lieges, his taste was directed to the works of a Justus, Melozzo, or Piero della Francesca.

---

* We notice a female torso without arms and legs or head, a Venus, &c., which it is now impossible to trace. Donatello's "head" in the "Guardaroba" of Urbino is mentioned by Vasari, iii. p. 264.

We shall decline the temptation of describing the places which Raphael may have visited on a journey from Perugia to the city of his birth and back to the painting-room of his master. We need only to recollect that when Raphael was reconciled with his step-mother he may have been busy with Perugino, in the completion of the frescos of the Cambio.

The hall of the Cambio deserves to be admired as an illustration of the fervid piety of an age of blood, ennobled by the genius of Perugino. We may smile at the changers who thought to adorn their place of meeting with the holy pictures of the "Nativity" and "Transfiguration," or the prophets and sibyls who foretold the coming of Christ, forgetting that they had once been driven from the temple. The semblance of the virtues may well embody the qualities required of men of their profession, but it seems high-flown or far-fetched to prefigure *their* prudence by that of Cato, Fabius, or Socrates; *their* justice by that of Camillus, Pittacus, and Trajan, or *their* temperance and fortitude (?) under losses—by those of Sicinius, Leonidas, Horatius Cocles, Scipio, Pericles, or Cincinnatus. But the public which applauded Gozzoli and Signorelli when they decorated chapels with scenes from Dante's "Inferno," or figures of Petrarch, Dante, and Giotto, might well accept the hallowing influence of Gospel subjects in a place devoted to the sordid pursuit of wealth. It had long been the fashion to pit against each other the faults of the Middle Ages, and the virtues of ancient Greece and Rome, or modern *condottieri* and classic heroes; and Perugia

itself might wish silently to contrast the forms of
Leonidas and Cocles with those of the "soldiers"
and "sages" whose likenesses were painted by
Domenico Veniziano in the porticos of the Baglioni
Palace.*   The Signs of the Zodiac in the ceiling of
the Cambio were familiar to the readers of the Astro-
labe, before the changers made them known to a more
numerous, if less select, circle at Perugia.   The voice
of rumour has proclaimed that they were painted by
Raphael after taking the heart of Perugino by storm.
Since the 17th century, when this rumour was abroad,
no document has been found to prove or to disprove
its truth.   Yet we may trust in some things to the
evidence of our senses; and we cannot look at the
beautiful impersonations of the planets on the Cambio
ceiling without concluding that they were finished by
Raphael and Spagna, or by Raphael alone.   The composition and design of these masterpieces have been too
often described to require further illustration.   It may
suffice to say that nothing can efface the impression
which they produce except a certified denial of the
authorship of Raphael.   In the absence of any such
record, we may believe that a man whose skill enabled
him thus early to work on the lines of Perugino must
have felt the will and learned the lessons of the master
years before.

The shades of style which distinguish the frescos of
the Cambio are sufficiently marked to bear definition
in words.   The full Peruginesque form in the Gospel

---

* See *antea*, note to p. 82.

subjects and the nascent Peruginesque art in the "Planets," contrast like the manhood and youth of two persons of one stock. The practised skill of the one is shown in unwavering boldness of execution, the youth of the other in timid handling and minute but copious detail. Yet the comparative inexperience of the disciple is counterbalanced by qualities of a high order. Excessive thinness of shape and dryness of figure are redeemed by classic grace in heads, winning candour in faces, and surprising delicacy of structure in limbs and extremities. The poetry of youth and the experience of age are pitted against each other; and youth wins by its inevitable charm.

The daily task of painters since Giotto's time had been to find some new and genial way of composing a narrow cycle of subjects invariably recurring as the demand for pictures extended. Raphael was trained to this task in a school in which variety was perhaps unduly contemned. But the superiority of his genius displayed itself in numerous early examples, and his first attempts are ennobled by diversity, whilst their form preserves the mould of Perugino. So great a gift combined with the feeling and grace peculiar to Raphael must have led Perugino to trust his pupil at a very early period with the composition as well as the execution of pictures. But it is natural to suppose that previous to this Raphael carried out the whole labour of altar-pieces of which Perugino merely furnished the design. A general consent of opinion may embolden us to affirm that the young disciple produced, under these conditions, at least one altar-piece of importance. On the neutral ground upon which two such names as those of Perugino and Raphael are found to meet, it might seem incumbent on us to weigh the evidence in favour of one or the other. Yet we may perhaps dispense with the cumbrous apparatus of criticism and venture to state on the strength of tried arguments that Raphael received a sketch of the " Resurrection," from which he worked out every part of the altar-piece of the Vatican with his own hand. There are signs in two sheets of sketches at Oxford that Raphael once indulged the thought of giving to a composition of this class the form as well as the handling of an original. Equally superior in practical knowledge to early school copies and in experience of the difficulties of nude to the " Charity of St. Martin," these sketches might once have justified Raphael's desire to start on his own path to independence. But if any such idea temporarily swayed his will he speedily surrendered it to the stronger will of Perugino,* and it is enough to point out that the " Resurrection " of the Vatican betrays the inexperience of youth in imperfect design and feeble foreshortening, whilst sweetness of colour and freshness of feeling give us a foretaste of the perfection, which we admire in their fulness in other

---

* Oxford collection, No. 12, from the collection of the Duke of Alva and Sir T. Lawrence. Silver-point on grey paper. 12¾ in. h. by 8¾. A guard seated on his shield. Higher up the flying guard.

No. 13. Same collection and size. Below a recumbent soldier, looking up; above, a kneeling figure, with a staff in the right hand, and something like a cup in the left, perhaps a study for an angel. Rudiments of a head are on the paper, in front of the kneeling figure. The lights on both sheets are laid on with white.

and more authentic pictures of a later time. Nothing
is more characteristic than the simplicity of Raphael's
outline or the delicate mechanism of his drawing in
articulations. The hands are always plump, the
fingers short, and the nails cut down to the pink of
the skin. The modelling is soft and rounded in flesh,
but equally rich and flat in dress textures. In all
these points the "Resurrection" of the Vatican displays the hand of Raphael, whilst the slender nude
of the Saviour rising from the tomb reveals the type
of Perugino hardened to something of the bony
leanness of Pinturicchio. The quaint mixture of
classic draperies in the sacred figures and modern
dress in the guards of the sepulchre shows how
Raphael improved the occasion to contrast the gayest
hues of a rich and variegated pallet. In the days of
the bitterest feuds of Perugia, every child could
distinguish the parti-coloured black, or red and white
of the Oddi, from the blue and red and green of the
Baglioni. There were picturesque and gaudy contrasts
between the right and left side of one limb, or between
one limb and the other in the tight-fitting dress of the
partisans on both sides. Raphael carefully avoided
an exact copy of either, a prudent resolve in one who
might be bounden to each in turn. But he rang
a true note of gay harmony in the dresses of his
guards, and contrasted with inborn skill a green with
a pink and an orange, a ruby and yellow, or steel with
brass or bronze.*

---

* Rome, Gallery of the Vatican, | cesco of Perugia, afterwards trans-
No. XXIV. Once in S. Fran- | ferred to Paris (1797), and restored

With equal care, and, perhaps, more complete success, Raphael gave shape to simpler conceptions of his master, and the date of a contract for a triptych in San Fortunato of Perugia is revealed by the share which Raphael took in its execution. It seems to have been part of the covenant that the central panel should represent the Virgin and Child, and the side panels St. Mary Magdalen and St. Catherine of Alexandria. A diffident opinion may be put forward that the first is a small half-length assigned to Raphael in the house of the Countess Fabrizi at Terni, the second and third are heirlooms in the collection of the Duke of Northumberland at Alnwick. It was not uncommon that painters of name in the days of Perugino and Signorelli should be asked to pledge themselves to paint some of the heads, if not the whole figures of an altar-piece. But if a clause of this kind was inserted in Perugino's agreement on this occasion, he treated it with unusual neglect. We fail to discern even the hand of Perugino in the " Virgin " of Terni, which is little more than a reduction of a well-known group familiar to us in the Madonnas of the Vatican or of Sinigaglia. The Infant Christ stands on the lap of His mother and clings to the veil which encircles her form. Her head and His are sentimentally bent and turned in opposite directions. The finish of the

---

in 1815 to the Vatican. It had been restored before its departure for France by Francesco Romero. See Giorn. di Erud. *n. s.* v. p. 235. Another version of the Resurrec- tion, ascribed to Raphael, is noted, as we are kindly informed by Dr. Bode, in the collection of Rossie Priory. But it has not been seen by the Authors.

parts in which the lights are heightened with gold, is as careful as it is minute, but these qualities scarcely compensate for marked feebleness of design and heaviness of proportions; and we seek in vain for the beauties of tint and modelling which mark the handling of Raphael. A drawing of St. Catherine at the Uffizi, might invite us to pause in attributing the saints at Alnwick to any one but Perugino.*   Yet the treatment is graceful enough to be worthy of Raphael, and the picture which was taken from the drawing is so full of sweetness, and so rich in colour, that the presumption is very strong in favour of Raphael. The soft tenderness of expression and the easy simplicity of attitude which the saint displays as she stands holding a book in her left hand, and resting her right on the instrument of her martyrdom, are quite as much within the compass of Raphael's skill at this period as the beautiful landscapes that form the backgrounds; and though we should concede less brightness and loveliness to the " Magdalen " than to the " St. Catherine," both might be classed amongst the early productions of the master of Urbino.†

---

* *Uffizi*, No. 408.—The saint is turned to the left, with a palm in her left hand. Her right is on the broken wheel, which rests on the ground. The veil, curling in the wind behind her, is very graceful, as are likewise the rising ground and trees on the left.

† *Alnwick*, from the Cammuccini collection.—*Terni*, House of Countess Fabrizi, from the Alfani Palace at Perugia. The Virgin and Child is on panel 18½ in. h. by 12¼ in. On the back we read : " Questo quadro la fatto mastro Piero da Castello della Pieve anco Perugino, e Lornamento l'ha fatto Antonio Tedesco M. . . ." Yet Rumohr (Forschungen, iii. p. 74) and Passavant (Raphael, i. 55, and ii. 11) assign it to Raphael.

Quatremère de Quincy (note to p. 197 of Bogue's edition of the Life of Raphael—1846) assigns the

Last on the list of pieces which might be assigned to the period of Raphael's dependence on Perugino's designs, the "Diotalevi Madonna" at Berlin, claims attention as combining the traditions of the Peruginesque school with the handling of its most graceful disciple. A tall, slender, long-necked Virgin supports the Infant, sitting on her lap—one hand round the waist of the Saviour, the other on the shoulder of the worshipping Baptist; Christ is in benediction, John receiving the blessing with the cross in his grasp. The Virgin's oval face shows the arched eyelid, the pursed mouth and small chin, peculiar to Raphael, combined with an expression of resignation, and a shade of *smorfia*, that recall the type of the earlier Umbrians. The lean and bony hands, the cramped fingers, are as distinctly Peruginesque as the pot-belly or masculine feet and limbs of the Infant Christ, and the stout shape of the boy Baptist. We recollect the "Madonna" of San Pietro Martire, which Perugino executed in 1498, and vague reminiscences of Santi's "Buffi" altar-piece cross our mind as we look at the picture. But the way in which the forms are transcribed is Raphael's, though it may be that the transcript is imperfect. Something,

---

Magdalen and St. Catherine to Raphael, which had then passed from San Fortunato of Perugia (Guida di Perugia by Constantini, p. 134) to the Cammuccini collection at Rome. Passavant (i. 55) also acknowledges the authorship of Raphael, whereas Waagen (Treasures, Sup.) assumes that of Spagna. The Magdalen is turned to the right, the St. Catherine to the left, each on a diminutive panel. The former wears a lake-coloured dress and blue mantle, and her hands are joined in prayer. The latter wears a blue dress and a mantle, with crimson shadows and yellow lights.

too, is apparent of Raphael's wheaten tones, his careful, tender handling and sweetness of colour, and we note the starting-point from which we arrive at the perfection of the "Virgin" of Terranuova, and the "Sposalizio" of Milan.*

* Berlin Museum. No. 147, on poplar. M. 0.69 h. by 0.50. Bought in 1841–2 of Marquis Diotalevi, at Rimini, in whose family the picture had been an heirloom, assigned to Perugino. Price 980 thal.=£147. The Baptist holds his arms reverently crossed on his breast. The sky, with a low horizon of distant landscape, recalls that of the "Madonna" of Pavia at the National Gallery. The panel has been injured, the outlines are enfeebled by scaling and mending, and some abrasions weaken the modelling. The latter applies particularly to the left eye of the Virgin and the contour of the cheek of the infant Christ; the former to spots about the head of the Baptist, and the body and leg of the Saviour. The blues have degenerated. The draperies are of high surface against low surface flesh. The nimbus form is old fashioned Umbrian. Compare Perugino's "Madonna" of 1498, No. 35 in the Gallery of Perugia.

CHAPTER III.

The Baglioni.—"Massacre of the Innocents," and other pen sketches.—The Solly "Madonna."—"Madonna with the Finch."—Practice at Perugia.—Connestabile predellas and Raphael's drawings for them.—Landscape sketches.—Invasion of Cesar Borgia.—The "Martyrs."—Raphael's "Crucifixion" based on that of Perugino.—"Crucifixion" of Earl Dudley.—"Trinity" and "Creation of Eve."—Influence of Alunno, Signorelli, and Pinturicchio.—"Coronation of St. Nicholas of Tolentino."—"Coronation of the Virgin" and its predellas at the Vatican.—Imitation of the predellas of Fano.

During the first years of Raphael's residence at Perugia the faction of the Baglioni ruled the city without opposition. Guido and his five children, Astorre, Morgante, Gismondo, Marc Antonio, and Gentile, shared the sweets of power with Ridolfo and his sons, Troilo, Giovan-Paulo, and Simonetto. But Guido was the chief of the clan, though his influence was secretly opposed by a wild gang of relatives, who acknowledged the lead of his nephew Grifone. To govern this overgrown family of chieftains was not easy; and Guido's authority in the main reposed on no safer foundation than that of fear. The child who led a squadron of lances and learnt to count its strength by the number of its years, the youth whose days were spent in raids, the man who sold his services to the highest bidder, and fought one day for those whom he opposed the next, were not to be awed by any law than that of force or interest; and Guido commanded because he had interest, and was ruthless, as well as rich and strong. Yet with all the advantages which his age and position gave him, Guido knew that no ties of relationship or blood would avail to keep the dagger of the son from the throat of his father, or the sword of one child from the side of his brother, if profit were to be expected from crime.

It was under this state of things that the 16th century opened in Perugia. The people of the city fawned on those who oppressed them and celebrated with eagerness all occasions of rejoicing. The money changers of the town called on heaven to protect them at the opening of the Cambio hall. They proudly showed to an admiring public the masterpieces of Perugino.* Astorre Baglioni, betrothed to Lavinia Colonna, made preparations for a wedding which gave important employment to painters and architects.† But far away on the political horizon a cloud was rising which soon gathered in a raging storm; and days of feasting and pleasure were followed by hours of massacre and plunder.

The preparations for Astorre's marriage were entirely worthy of the occasion. A triumphal arch was erected in the square of Perugia, and hung with the victories of Astorre, designed by skilful hands on

---

* Journals of the Changers of Perugia, 1500. "Propitius esto nella revolutione Yesu a noie del millecinquecento che incarnasti a nostra redemptione." Giornale di Erud. Artistica, *n. s.* iii. p. 32.

† 1500, 28 Giugno, magnificus Dom. Astor de balleonibus uxorem duxit. 1, 2, 3 Luglio. "Per le splendide nozze non se sedde Dastor baglione, et ut brevibus utar. Tanto apparato a Proscia mai se vedde." Ibid. ibid. ibid.

appropriate canvas. To shelter the wedding guests
from the rays of a burning sun, a veil of cloth was
stretched over the piazza, and the solemn entry of
the bride was celebrated by cavalcades, and the marriage by feasting, dancing, and a passage of arms.*
Raphael enjoyed, we may think, the chance which
was then offered to him, of signalising his talents as
a painter. The scanty annals of the time refuse to
connect his name with any, even the smallest events
of this pageant. But, assuredly, if he had leisure,
he witnessed the occurrence. The chiefs of the
Baglioni were vaguely informed of a conspiracy
during the progress of the festivities; and their spies
told them that the danger had only been postponed.
Yet when the outbreak came, and Grifone, with a
band of conspirators, rudely interrupted Astorre's
honeymoon, and cruelly proceeded to massacre his
relatives, they were unaccountably taken by surprise.†
Astorre was killed as he rose from his bed, vainly
protected from the blows that were aimed at him by
the devotion of his wife. Guido, Gismondo, and
Simonetto all fell in turn. The bodies of the slain
were stripped and dragged into the streets, where
they lay on stretchers, Astorre "as an old Roman in
his blood," Simonetto "scornful and proud in death
as in life." Grifone's mother, Atalanta, and his wife
Zenobia, fled to a country-house, where he vainly
clamoured for pardon, which they denied, and speech
which they refused. With the ring of their curses in

---

* Matarazzo Cronaca, u. s.   † This massacre occurred July
15, 1500. See Matarazzo, u. s.

his cars, he withdrew to command the burial of his victims. But retribution was neither slow nor long deferred. Giovan Paulo, flying for safety through the night, gathered adherents as he ran, secured some aid from Vitelozzo of Città di Castello, and marched with a troop of 800 men to Perugia, where he quickly found an entrance. His form is compared as he rode and forced the gate of the Due Porte to that of St. George, armed in proof and galloping on his charger. He was met by Grifone at the corner of a street, but he disdained to face the murderer of his kinsmen, and preferred to see him cut down by his followers. A general massacre purged the city of the conspirators and deluged the market-place with blood. At the sound of arms, Atalanta and Zenobia, the mother and wife of Grifone, left the asylum in which they had taken refuge, and threaded their way through the streets, where they found their son and husband bleeding from numberless wounds. Atalanta stooped over the body of her son and prayed to him to forgive the authors of his death. A word of pardon issued from his lips, a silent pressure of his hand, and he expired. Next day Giovan Paulo took possession of the Baglioni Palace, which had belonged to Grifone. The desecrated cathedral of San Lorenzo was cleansed with wine, and Atalanta made a vow, perhaps even then, that she would dedicate an altar to the memory of her son and adorn it with an entombment, which was to be a masterpiece by Raphael. The scenes which Raphael may have witnessed were perhaps embodied in the Heliodorus of the Vatican chambers.

We recognise St. George at the Hermitage prefigured by Giovan Paulo, storming cap-à-pie through the gates of Perugia. But the memories of these tragic days must have clung to Raphael in other and more dramatic forms. He might remember Astorre, "grand as an old Roman," as he lay stripped on the ground, when he drew the rigid shape of a dead man in the gallery of Oxford,* or Astorre taken down into the street, as he sketched the flexible body removed from the cross in the Albertina of Vienna.† He might recollect the wailing of Atalanta and Zenobia as Grifone was carried away to burial, when he designed the numerous varieties of the "Entombment" which were all compressed into the masterpiece of the Palazzo Borghese. The very figures of the dead are recalled in the splendid drawing of the Birchall collection, where a soldier deposits a corpse on the ground by the side of others that rest in their shrouds.‡ Every one of these sketches and designs has a direct connection with the tragedy of Perugia, the person of Atalanta, who ordered, and Raphael, who painted the "Entombment."

The impressions left by extraordinary events on those who have witnessed them vary with the capacity of individuals to seize or to realize their scope. A young painter might recollect or brood over many incidents that occurred during the feud of the

---

* Oxford University Gallery, No. 38.

† Vienna, Albertina. Drawing at the back of a Charity designed on lines similar to those of the predella of the Borghese Entombment.

‡ Rogers and Birchall collection—exhibited at Manchester. Pass. No. 453. 9½ in. h. by 11 in.

Baglioni, and yet be powerless to give them a con-
crete form. That Raphael at eighteen should have
been incapable of delineating the scenes which his
memory retained, and matured skill enabled him to
reproduce, need not create surprise. The limited
experience of his student years would suggest to him
a host of insuperable obstacles. But in the measure
of his power he may have found vent for his feelings;
and the "Massacre of the Innocents," with which he
adorned the Venice sketch-book, seems to reflect the
workings of his mind at this time. We feel when we
look at Raphael's drawings that his store of amiability
is almost inexhaustible, yet we hardly expect the simplicity which he conveys in this composition. The
least complex forms of passion are those which he
first displays. A soldier stoops to thrust his dagger
into the heart of a nurseling that lies unconscious of
danger on its mother's lap. She sits on the ground
without an effort to avert the stroke; and her fear
is expressed by stopping her ears. Another soldier
points his sword at a woman whom he has caught by
the hair. The babe in her arms rends the air with
its cries, but she walks leisurely away; whilst a
third mother throws her slipper at the soldier's head.
It has been well said "that innocence *equally* dwells
in the victims and their executioners, and that swords
and daggers are drawn as if they were not meant
to strike.* It is evident that Raphael's youthful

* Charles Blanc in the Gazette des Beaux Arts, vol. iv. of 1859,
p. 202.

mind can hardly realize the deadliness of a murderous purpose. Yet in the action of the guards a germ of momentary action may be discerned which expands at a later period into the noble form of Marcantonio's print. Nothing can be more charming than the purity of the line, or the cleverness of the pen stroke in shading, except, perhaps, the simplicity which betrays the artist's tenderness of soul.*

The very same spirit leads Raphael to similar results in episodes of another kind. If we could suppose that the lion who was kept in a den at the Baglioni palace had escaped during the troubles and fled to the hills overhanging the valley of the Tiber, we might fancy that the hungry beast attacked a man in his way, whilst an unconscious shepherd played a bagpipe on the brow of a declivity. Raphael takes an incident of this kind as his subject. He draws the lion growling at the man who lies on the ground, and shrieks as he feels the breath of the animal and the weight of its paws on his breast; a faithful dog vainly barks for help. The piper plays, and his flock browses unconcerned on the grass of the neighbouring slope. Raphael never drew anything more natural or true than the busy shepherd and his charge. He never conceived anything more untrue than the lion and his prey. His mind cannot yet fathom the depths of terror which such a situation should convey. Fear is depicted in the contraction of

---

* Venice Acad. Frame XXVII. No. 14. Back of No. 17. Pen and umber drawing. Pass. No. 24.

the features and hand, belied in the strange repose of
the legs and body. The symptoms of instant paralysis
which an attack of this kind would produce, are neither
suggested nor conveyed, and still. the drawing is one
of the most beautiful that Raphael produced in the
days of his probation.*

Meanwhile Raphael's versatility was shown in
other drawings of the most surprising diversity. A
lovely figure of a winged angel, floating in gossamer
dress and ribbands on a cloud, and casting flowers,
reminds us of the graceful allegories of the Cambio.†
An angel in adoration, holding a circlet with both
hands, seems to foreshadow the heavenly beings
that cover the sky in the " Standard " of Città di
Castello.‡ Winged centaurs with dolphins' tails, a
decorative swan, a turtle, and arabesques of snakes
at the side of a mask of Medusa, recall at once the
ceiling of the Goldsmiths' Hall at Perugia, and the
Chambers of the Vatican.§

---

* Ven. Acad. Frame XXVII.
No. 13. Back of No. 16. Pass. No.
33.   Pen and umber sketch.

† Berlin Museum ; from the
Pocetti collection. Pen and umber
sketch washed with yellowish
shading. The figure is entire and
turns to the left, with wings and
arms outstretched, and sprays of
leaves in both hands. The same
thought is in a later drawing of
the Venice sketch-book realized at
last in the Holy Family of 1518
at the Louvre. In the lower
corner to the left a winged cherub
sits on a cloud.

‡ Venice Acad. Frame XXIV.
No. 4. Back of XXIV. No. 6. Pass.
No. 26. Pen sketch slightly washed
with umber. The drapery here is
not so light as in the foregoing.
The handling is so bold that it
suggests a later period than that
of the Standard at Città di Castello.
But practice tells us that the boldness and freedom of a sketch is
partially lost in the finished picture.

§ Venice Acad. Frame XXIV.
No. 6. Back of XXIV. No. 4. Pass.
21.   Pen sketch ; the head of
Medusa to the right.

A "Bacchus" at the Uffizi, drawn by Raphael in the Peruginesque form, displays more than Raphael's usual grace, and renders with antique simplicity the full length nude of a youthful god, looking down and balancing a vase on his head.* Leaves from the Venice Sketch-book are filled with academic studies as true to nature as the "Bacchus" is true to the ideal type of the Greeks. A man in upward stride, with his back to the spectator, glances round as he walks to the sound of the pipes;† another man, similarly occupied, dances past in rapid motion;‡ a shepherd in ragged shirt and hose plays the bagpipes.§ Samson, with the grip of an athlete, breaks the lion's jaw; ‖ a muscular nude stands pensive and stern with

---

* Florence, Uffizi.   No. 531. Black chalk washed with flake white. Full length in profile to the left.

† Venice Acad. Frame XXIII. No. 13. Back of XXIII. No. 3. Pass. No. 76. An outline of an arm at the side of the figure might suggest doubts as to its being by the draughtsman of the piper. But the line is Raphaelesque. The foreshortening of the right leg is as masterly as the definition of the muscles is searching and clean. Compare the piper in Signorelli's Pan, Berlin Museum. No. 79A.

‡ Venice Acad.   Frame XXVI. No. 2. Back of XXVI. No. 14. Pass. No. 31. The head here is concealed by the raised left arm. The lean muscularity of the frame is rendered with the strength of Signorelli, whilst a study of a foot

on the right side of the paper shows more of the Peruginesque style. The detail in every part is minute and correct, in the same way as the detail of a hand (small life size), the palm being shown with all its wrinkles and folds. Ven. Acad. Frame XXIII. No. 14. Back of XXIII. No. 4.   Pass. 86.

§ Venice Acad. Frame XXV. No. 12.   Back of XXV. No. 10. Pass. 27. Profile to the left. Here again is a study of an arm and hand on the right side of the shepherd, which looks almost too feeble for Raphael. A copy of this drawing, assigned to Raphael, is numbered 2 in the Oxford Gallery.

‖ Venice Acad. Frame XXVI. 3. Back of XXVI. No. 13. Pass. 35. Samson, turned to the left, has the right knee on the lion's back and opens his jaw with both hands.

his arms across his breast. The models vary in each case. Many of them recall Signorelli, and particularly his piper in the "Triumph of Pan" at Berlin. Samson is a mixture of Signorelli and Pollaiuolo, the nude with his arms across seems a copy from Pollaiuolo himself.* All the drawings exhibit the power and facility of a youthful genius whose training has been Umbrian, yet who studies to acquire the strength of the greater Florentines. His sketches are outlined and modelled with the pen in the Peruginesque style. The life which they display, the mastery of form which they reveal, and the flexibility of pen-stroke by which they are characterized, are proofs of an immense range of observation and retentiveness of memory. But the Peruginesque style is but a medium in which we still trace the influence of Tuscan masters, whose designs no doubt were in Perugino's store.

Whilst Raphael thus devoted his time to close study, he was still under the orders of the superiors to whose commands he was subject by duty as well as by habit. He had no dispensation assuredly to neglect the work of an assistant when his master presided in

---

This magnificent drawing, in the style of Pollaiuolo, looks like the design of an old cameo, to which new life has been given by an appeal to nature. There is no trace here of Umbrian tenderness. The line is Peruginesque, but the model is Florentine. Hence the probability that Perugino gave Raphael Tuscan drawings to copy.

* Venice Acad. Frame XXVI.

13. Back of XXVI. No. 3. Pass. 36. Bald man in profile to the right, outline like one of Lionardo's illustrations to the "Proportion." But the style is very like that of Pollaiuolo, in his celebrated drawing of the Louvre (three nudes), signed "Antonij Jacobi," &c., &c., and we might presume that it was copied from Pollaiuolo at Perugia.

the painting-room. At such hours as he laboured for himself or for his own instruction, he was free to do what he pleased. At other hours he was bound to think exclusively of the subjects which Perugino was commissioned to execute. But this constraint naturally produced a mental thraldom which caused the circle of ideas in which he moved to become identical, so to speak, with that of the artist who directed him. Once in early days his mind had been filled with the beauties of the subjects which Perugino transferred to the predellas of Fano. Now he dwelt with reverent fondness on the compositions which in numberless instances engrossed the time of his chief. Was he aware that Perugino recollected the " Sposalizio " of Orcagna when he composed the same episode for the brotherhood of St. Joseph at Perugia ? His lively recollection of this masterpiece was certainly shown in the later development of the same theme at Città di Castello. When Perugino consented to depict the " Coronation of the Virgin " for San Francesco of Perugia, Raphael brooded over the legend preparatory to its repetition in the altar-piece of the Vatican. He thought out the " Trinity " and " Crucifixion " of Città di Castello after seeing Perugino's earlier sketches and cartoons. Yet in the ordinary forms which painting took in these days, Raphael, though mindful of Perugino's bidding, seems always to have tried to improve on the conceptions of his master.

None of Raphael's early creations more thoroughly embodies Perugino's feeling than that of the Solly

"Madonna" in the Museum of Berlin. The Virgin sits in a landscape and reads from a missal, whilst the naked Christ on her lap divides his attention between the pages of the book and a captive finch. The broad oval of the Virgin's face circumscribing features of excessive smallness, a large hand with the nails worn down to the quick, are cast as truly in the mould of Perugino as the plump frame, and the fore-shortened bullet head of the infant Saviour. The lack as yet of that fulness of tender grace in action and expression which peculiarly mark the master-pieces of Raphael is not inexplicable. The technical execution of the pupil is displayed in something like an approach to those enamelled tones which may be called distinctly Raphaelesque; which we see indeed in the bright sky and the soft slopes of a distance delicately touched to show the trees relieved on the brownish ground or the heaven beyond it; but which we miss to some extent in the filmy flesh tints that lie in hollows beside the high surface pigments of the dress shadows. Something, too, that reveals Raphael, is the minute application of gold lights, and a reminiscence of Santi, which lingers in the picture in spite of its general likeness to Perugino's earlier creations.*

* Berlin Mus. No. 141. Half length, on poplar, m. 0·52 h. by 0·38. Known as the "Madonna Solly," having been acquired with the Solly collection in 1821. We may note the absence of taper in the hands, the liquid substance of flesh tints in which the pigments refuse to second absolutely the efforts of the artist. The star on the bright blue mantle, the blanket texture of the red lining, the contrasts of black and gold in the missal are all reminiscences of the older schools, as are likewise the thin veils on the Virgin's head and the child's body. The infant Christ holds in his right hand the string

As a test of his own powers and his capacity to set aside tradition, Raphael afterwards watched a couple of children, and in a sketch, now preserved at the Louvre, caught their outline and movement as one of them, creeping on all fours, struck his companion on the head. The injured boy sits despairingly on the ground and cries as he thrusts his tiny fingers into his eye. On the back of the sketch Raphael transformed the pouting child into an infant Christ on its mother's knee. Tears and lamentation are turned into stillness and prayer. But the attitude and the forms are preserved, whilst the features and shape of the Virgin are repeated from those of the picture at Berlin, and transfigured into something more graceful and tender than was ever imagined by Perugino.

More purely Raphaelesque and bolder than the Solly "Madonna," its counterpart in the sketch at the Louvre is much more gracefully conceived. The Virgin's head is more pensively inclined and turns from full to three-quarters. The child looks down instead of looking up at the missal.* The landscape is wider and more simple. We need not assume that Raphael expressed all this at the very moment when he worked at the "Madonna" with the finch, but the close relationship of the Louvre sketch, which was never translated into a picture, with the "Madonna" Connestabile and other varieties in which the book is

---

that ensures the captivity of the finch in his left. Time has been unkind to the picture, the gold lights of which are all but abraded. The picture by Perugino, of which we are here reminded, is the altarpiece of 1494 at Cremona.

* Louvre. Pen and umber sketches on two sides of one sheet.

a leading feature shows how long and how constantly
Raphael meditated over themes, the originals of which
he had found in the painting-room of Perugino.

Internal evidence might suggest that Raphael
modelled the Virgin with the finch from a design by
Perugino, but the probability of the circumstance is
diminished by the knowledge that his next creation of
the same kind was derived from a drawing of his own.
In the collection of the Albertina at Vienna, a sketch
is preserved in which the style of Raphael is curiously
engrafted on that of Perugino and Pinturicchio. St.
Jerome, and St. Francis are drawn in attendance on the
Virgin, who watches the Child on her lap as it reads
from a label scroll.* Raphael transferred the subject to
a panel in the Berlin Museum, and merely altered the
child's attitude and action to one of benediction. A bald
bare-headed friar represents St. Francis; St. Jerome
wears a beard and a cardinal's hat and lappets. Two
churches in the distance symbolize the mission of the
Saints, whose names are engraved in half abraded
nimbs on the sky. The mildness of their faces, the
peculiar shape of the Virgin's hands, and the broad form
of the child are all typical of Perugino's art, but the

* Vienna, Albertina. The Virgin is seen to the knees. St.
Jerome to the left, St. Francis to
the right. The drawing is catalogued under the name of Perugino. Like much of Raphael's
work at the time it recalls Pinturicchio as much as Perugino, and
it reminds us most of Pinturicchio
in the outline of the infant Christ's
head, and the frizzle of hair which
gives it a peculiar character. But
there is something too in the whole
drawing which makes one suspect that Raphael had seen a print
by Martin Schön. Under no circumstances can the drawing be assigned to Perugio or Pinturicchio.
See Lippmann's clever criticism,
Raffael's Entwurf zur Madonna del
Duca di Terranuova. 4to. Berlin,
1880, p. 2.

tender air and gentle features of the Virgin, which equal in sweetness, as they do in line, those of the "Coronation" of the Vatican, the speckled cushion or gilded ornament which betray the influence of Pinturicchio, and vague reminiscences of Giovanni Santi, which characterise the group, reveal the disciple of all three.*

During the progress of these juvenile productions, we may presume that most of Raphael's time was spent in the rooms of Perugino, situated within the precincts of the Hospital of the Misericordia at Perugia.† We have to picture to ourselves the daily greeting with the great Umbrian master. We shall fancy that Raphael witnessed the coming of Baccio d'Agnolo, who persuaded Perugino to stand surety for a contract and furnish him with drawings for the stalls of St. Lorenzo.‡ We see him watching the

* Berlin Museum. No. 145. Half length, on poplar. m. 0·34 h. by 0·29. From the Borghese collection, sold in 1829 to the King of Prussia by Count von der Ropp. The bad state to which the panel has been reduced (patches of restoring are visible on the face and beard of St. Jerome and the right leg and left foot of the infant Christ), might induce a severe critic to doubt the originality of the picture. The surface has no longer the perfect modelling of Raphael, but still there is much in favour of Raphael's name. The child recalls that of Santi, in the "Madonna" in Santa Croce of Fano.

A black chalk drawing of the head of St. Jerome, exhibited (No. 709) in the Museum of Lille, is catalogued as an original study by Raphael for this picture, but it has no claim to genuineness.

† "Adi primo de marzo, 1504, fior. cinque . . . a lo spedale de la miserichordia che so (no) per achonto de fior. octo pegione." Perugino had a lease for twelve years of two large rooms in the hospital of the Misericordia—from the 1st of January, 1501. Archivio del Cambio in Giornale di Erud. Tosc. vol. iii. p. 25. For that period the tradition that his painting-room was in the Via Deliciosa is therefore baseless.

‡ The date of these events is

progress of the "Sposalizio" of Caen, and the "Madonna" of Pavia, both of which were finished about this time. Nor can we doubt that he was allowed to vary his daily avocations by leave to accompany Perugino or his partner on some of their distant peregrinations. Perugino and Pinturicchio were both summoned to Sienna in the summer of 1502, Pinturicchio to paint the Library of Andrea Piccolomini, Perugino to paint an altar-piece for Mariano Chigi. Pinturicchio pledged himself on the 29th of June to decorate the ceiling and the walls of the Library with frescos of which the *cartoons* were to be executed, the *heads* to be finished in fresco by himself. Two hundred ducats were paid down, one hundred more were promised at Perugia, when Pinturicchio should go home to prepare materials and engage assistants.* Perugino signed his contract on the 4th of August in the presence of Antonio Barile the sculptor and Brancatio di Gherardo a painter, to complete a "Crucifixion" within a year. The picture was to adorn the Chigi Chapel in Sant' Agostino of Sienna, and represent the crucified Saviour and eight Saints. A predella was to contain subjects appropriate to the principal scene, and a sketch delivered before the signature of the covenant was accepted, subject to

1501-2. Mariotti (Lettere Pittoriche, pp. 167-8), says 1502. But the contracts are really dated Perugia, March 27, 1501, and October 1, 1502. (Rossi, in Giornale di Erud. Tosc. *u. s.* i. p. 121.)

* Covenant of Pinturicchio, dated June 29, 1502, at Sienna, in G. Milanesi's Documenti Senesi, iii. pp. 9 and 111. It is important to bear in mind these words of the contract: "Sia (Pinturicchio)

later revision, by the Chigi.* Both contracts were drawn up and witnessed at Sienna, and Perugino remained there till the close of the first week in September, when he returned to Perugia. He may have employed the time at his disposal in painting some principal parts of the altar-piece entrusted to his charge. On his arrival at Perugia about the 10th of September, he took a commission for a double altar-piece at San Francesco del Monte, and he accepted the obligation of painting several figures at the feet of a Christ in relief on one side, and a " Coronation of the Virgin " on the other side of the picture. Here, also, preliminary studies were presented to the approbation of the patrons of the altar, and directions were given for the painter's guidance.† But instead of proceeding with his task, Perugino retired after an interval of three weeks to Florence, where he arrived about the beginning of October, and for upwards of a year he remained in the Tuscan capital.‡ Whether the design of the " Crucifixion " at Sienna was furnished by Raphael or not is uncertain. It is equally doubtful whether Raphael was deputed to finish the picture

tenuto fare li disegni delle istorie di sua mano *in cartoni et in muro.*" He was bound to draw the cartoons and transfer them to the walls. He was not bound to make the designs for the cartoons himself.|

* Contract dated Sienna, Aug. 4, 1502, in C. Cugnoni's Agostino Chigi il Magnifico. 8vo, Rome, 1878, pp. 78-9.

† Mariotti, Lett. *u. s.* p. 164.

‡ See the contract of Oct. 1,

1502, in which Perugino accepts the duty of furnishing Baccio d'Agnolo with designs of the stalls at St. Lorenzo of Perugia. Mariotti, Lett. Pit. *u. s.* 168 ; see also the letter of F. Malatesta to Isabella Gonzaga in Braghirolli's contributions to the Giorn. di Erud. Tosc. ii. p. 160, where the presence of Perugino at Florence on the 24th of Oct., 1502, is established.

of Mariano Chigi. But nothing in the altar-piece
itself excludes the co-operation of Perugino's disciple,
whether we consider the colouring which is pure and
beautiful, or the features and shapes of the Saints,
which recur with varieties in the " Crucifixion " of
Città di Castello.*

The finished cartoon for the coronation of San
Francesco del Monte, when last seen in the collection
of Dr. Wellesley at Oxford, fully bore out the opinion
that its execution was due to Raphael,† whereas in
respect of drawing, form, and colour, the altar-piece
now in the gallery of Perugia, betrays a feebler hand
than that of the cleverer disciples of Perugino, Raphael
not excepted. Many of the single parts still suggest
the help of Perugino's best assistants, and some
figures are reminiscent of the " Sposalizio " of Milan,
whilst others have their counterparts in the " Crucifixion " of Earl Dudley.‡

Perugino's contract with Mariano Chigi specially

---

* It is remarkable that the face
of St. Monica, the hands of the
Magdalen, and the head of the
Evangelist, in the altar-piece of
Sienna, have almost their counter-
parts in the face of the Virgin, and
the hands and the head of the
Virgin in the " Crucifixion " of
Città di Castello (Earl Dudley).

† Ex Wellesley collection at
Oxford. Cartoon 15½ in. h. by 11½.
Pen and bistre, heightened with
white, much injured and abraded,
but still revealing the hand of a
youthful artist, remarkable for the
carefulness and, at the same time,

for the timidity that we recognize
at this time in Raphael.

‡ This picture is now in the
Gallery of Perugia. Its execution
may be due to the joint efforts of
Raphael, Spagna, and others. A
great disadvantage from which the
altar-piece suffers is the distemper
medium in which it is carried out.
The figures are life size. The
Magdalen in the two crucifixions
are almost identical, but reversed ;
there is also much similarity in
the figures of the Virgin and
Evangelist in each picture.

treats of a predella which unfortunately no longer survives. But predellas were not kept as carefully as the altar-pieces to which they belonged, and we vainly look for those appendages to the "Sposalizio" at Caen, the "Crucifixion" and "Coronation" of San Francesco del Monte. Yet the preservation of several isolated predellas by Perugino may prepare us at any time for discoveries in this direction; and amongst other small works of this kind, one or two of special interest for the history of Raphael exist in the palace of Count Connestabile Staffa at Perugia. The first represents the "Epiphany," the second the "Nativity," and both are painted in distemper. In the "Epiphany" the Virgin is seated to the right, under the porch of a temple, with the Child in benediction, standing on her knee. Joseph, in attendance on Mary, leans on his staff, whilst the senior of the Magi kneels on the foreground of a landscape and presents his offering. To the left the second and third kings and three persons of their suite, in the tight-fitting Umbrian dress, form a pretty and appropriate group.

In the "Nativity" the Virgin kneels before the infant Saviour, whose naked form is supported by a winged angel on a pack-saddle, whilst Joseph and two shepherds kneel in prayer to the left; an ox and an ass are resting to the right; and a landscape of low hills, with trees of a sparse leafage, form the background of the picture. Both panels are by an artist who clearly displays a tenderness of feeling akin to that of Raphael. There is an evident tendency to

ignore the masculine developments of the full grown
nude; to cling to juvenile models conspicuous for
leanness and slenderness of shape. Large extremities
and articulations contrast with smallness of facial
features. A certain stiffness and timidity is manifest
in the definition of movement or the realization of
momentary action. But these peculiarities from
which Raphael is not free in the "Sposalizio" of
Milan, are counterbalanced by serenity, simplicity,
and graceful thought, the more charming as the
small figures of the predellas display their inherent
defects less strongly than the large ones of the Perugian "Coronation."*

Once only in the course of his practice Perugino
introduced the pack-saddle into an altar-piece, and it
is noteworthy that he should have done so in the
"Madonna" of Pavia, the masterpiece of all others
which modern criticism has connected with the name
of Raphael. But whilst he hesitated to set the child
on the seat, and merely leaned its form against the
saddle, he completely realized the rest of the composition in the form of the Connestabile predella. He
placed the angel in rear of the child, at its side the
kneeling Virgin. The master's design is carried out
with all the skill of matured talent; that of the pupil
is more playful and graceful, but less perfect in execution. Which of the two was first created? We

---

* Perugia. Palazzo Connestabile Staffa. Small panels, in distemper. The "Epiphany" is better
executed than the "Nativity." In
the former the pure and lovely
face of the Virgin is disfigured by
an abrasion of the cheek.

possess but one drawing for the "Madonna" of
Pavia, and that is unmistakeably by Perugino.*
Raphael's sketches at Oxford comprise the first
thought and the finished cartoon for the Connestabile predella.   In a sheet of miniature studies,
thrown at random on different parts of the paper—
the Virgin adores the infant on her knee, whilst a
third person moves forward as if in the act of making
an offering; higher up is a fragment of a figure, the
head of a man, a woman looking round, a shepherd
kneeling near a cushion, against which an infant
Christ reposes.   In the upper corner to the left a
church is depicted, with its tall steeple and cupola,
within the circuit of a crenelated wall, flanked by
towers, to which access is obtained by a flight of
steps, reminding us even now of the picturesque site
of Castel Durante.   At the bottom of the page are
the words, in Raphael's hand: "Carissimo" and
"Carissimo quanto fratelo."   Just above these lines a
boy Baptist gently supports the infant Christ on the
pack-saddle.†   Another drawing of the same collection represents the infant Saviour on the saddle,
attended, though not supported, by the Baptist,

---

* British Museum. See Hist.
of Italian Painting, vol. iii. p. 224.
Another version of the same group,
with separate studies, for the head
of Tobias and the hands of both
figures is catalogued, No. 16,
under the name of Raphael at
Oxford. We can only repeat what
has already been written before on
the subject of this drawing, viz.,
that it is not to our mind a clear
production of Raphael.

† Oxford Gall. No. 5. Pen
drawing in bistre. $10\frac{3}{8}$ in. h. by
$8\frac{1}{4}$. From the Antaldi and Lawrence collections.

whose duty has been taken by the Virgin, who kneels to the right, and rests her right hand on Christ's shoulder.* The prettiest thought in the first conception of the group is thus set aside, probably because it was difficult to imagine the boy Baptist in a scene immediately connected with the flight into Egypt. The final expansion of the subject is displayed in a small cartoon pricked for use in the Connestabile predella—a charming outline, in which a lovely angel, with frizzled locks, supports the foot and shoulder of a beautiful infant, and looks devotionally at the Virgin kneeling in prayer before him, whilst Joseph and two shepherds, on their knees to the left, make the lamb-offering in a landscape of rounded hills, and the ox and the ass rest within the pent-house, of which one beam is seen to rise behind the figure of the angel.† Further on in his pictorial career, Raphael tried other forms of the composition, and his efforts in that direction are still apparent in a sketch in which the infant Saviour, no longer on the saddle, but on his mother's knee, is adored by the Virgin, and supported as she prays by the boy Baptist. This was an attempt to reconcile the first thought of the Connestabile predella with a new grouping of the "Virgin and Child;" but if ever the

---

* Oxford Gall. No. 6. Drawn in silver-point on lavender paper. 7¾ in. h. by 9. From the Antaldi and Lawrence collections. The Virgin here is undraped. Some of the outlines seem to have been retouched.

† Oxford Gall. No. 7. Pen and bistre drawing, pricked for use. 7¼ in. h. by 10¼. From the Ottley, Lawrence, King of Holland's, and Chambers Hall collections.

intention of carrying out this idea was entertained, it was speedily and finally abandoned.*

Jotting down these rapid sketches at random, Raphael seems to have been equally at home in the painting-room of Perugino and in the churches and palaces of neighbouring towns. On the reverse of the sheet, which contains the words: "Carissimo quanto fratelo," we notice two figures, one of which wears a hat and stoops to span a crossbow, whilst the other, in the tight-fitting dress of the period, raises a similar crossbow and takes a deliberate aim with it. The same figure recurs in a Raphaelesque drawing at Lille, on one side of which a variety of the "Virgin and Child with the Book" is designed.† There is nothing to distinguish the Oxford sketch from the series of those which imitate the forms of Signorelli in the collection at Venice except that the figures are unfinished, most of the contours being slightly indicated with black chalk and one leg of the archer shooting being finished with a pen.‡ But whilst we

---

* Ex Wellesley collection at Oxford. 8 in. h. by 8⅝th. The Virgin sits to the right and in profile to the left. She adores the child, who sits in benediction on her right knee. A winged angel to the left kneels and supports the infant Christ by grasping his body with both hands. The distance is a flat landscape. This drawing, of the Florentine period, is rapid and skilful, like that called the "Death of Adonis" at Oxford.

† Lille Museum. No. 705. Pen and bistre drawing, very careful and even feeble, so that doubts might be suggested as to its genuineness. Yet it is too like some of the drawings for the coronation of the Vatican to be excluded from the catalogue of Raphael's works. Size m. 0·250 h. by 0·178. Near the archer in the act of shooting is a spectator pointing upwards.

‡ Oxford Gall. No. 5. Pen drawing in bistre and black chalk. 10⅜ in. h. by 8¾. From the Antaldi and Lawrence collections.

fail to discover the originals from which Raphael took
his figures in the Venice sketch-book, we recollect
that the archers at Oxford are copied with faithful
accuracy from Signorelli's "Martyrdom of St. Sebastian" at Città di Castello. We recollect, or rather
we shall presently see, that Raphael went to Città di
Castello to contract with the patrons of a chapel in
San Domenico for the "Crucifixion" of Earl Dudley,
and as the "Martyrdom of St. Sebastian" by Signorelli
is still in S. Domenico, where it has rested for well
nigh four hundred years, Raphael must have copied
it, whilst he excogitated one of the most ambitious
of his early pictures. Yet, before or after this, he
seems to have paid one of his occasional visits to
Urbino, since we find an outline of the inner court of
the palace of the Montefeltri in the drawing of Lille,
which represents the lost altar-piece of St. Nicholas of
Tolentino, once an ornament of Sant' Agostino of Città
di Castello.*

At two different periods, yet at no great interval
of time, another city of the duchy of Urbino received the visit of Raphael, who made two drawings
of it in the Venice sketch-book and in a sheet at
Oxford. On one side of the latter a country church,
which reminds us of Assisi, and a group of the
"Virgin and Child," are rapidly thrown off with a pen
dipped in bistre; on the other, a town on an eminence
covers a hill sloping in front to a river bank guarded
by towers. These towers cast reflections into the

---

* Lille Mus. No. 737. See *postea*.

stream.   A bridge on the left leads to a fortified gate, and thence to a street that straggles up to an eminence crowned with palaces and churches.   In the Venice sketch-book the same town is depicted with its towers entire.   At Oxford the aspect of the place is somewhat changed, and a square keep on the water side is battered at the top and covered with a temporary wooden roof.   Beyond, to the right, a stretch of hills vanishes to a flat horizon suggestive of the vicinity of the sea.*   Though very much changed, the site of Fossombrone on the Metaurus still invites recognition, and it would seem as if Raphael had first sketched the city when it flourished peacefully under the sway of its archbishop, and then revisited it later when it had undergone a siege.   The foreground of the Oxford sketch contains a figure of the penitent St. Jerome, kneeling with the stone in his right hand and preparing to beat his breast.   His shaven crown and lean face, bending heavenwards with inspired longing, reminds us of Perugino's St. Jerome in the " Crucifixion " of Sienna.   The repetition of the same head in a pencil

---

* Oxford Coll. No. 17. Pen and bistre drawing. 10 in. h. by 8¾. From the Antaldi and Lawrence and Woodburne collections. Pass. thinks the town is Perugia. The Venice catalogue suggests Urbino. Both opinions are evidently wrong. Fossombrone, though much altered, offers the same site, the same prospect of hills, the road, the stream, and a bridge. But the houses on the water's edge are now all new. The replica at Venice without the figure of St. Jerome is in Frame XXVII. No. 16, and also a pen and umber sketch with a bit of a striped sail in the sky to the right. The two drawings are similar in style and execution, the figure of St. Jerome, Peruginesque, and in an early form of the Peruginesque in Raphael. The Virgin and Child on the back of the Oxford drawing looks like a spurious work.

study at Lille tells how carefully Raphael prepared
himself, by appealing to nature, for the arduous
labour of pictures executed under the superintendence of his master.*   But the Venice and Oxford
drawings are not solitary examples of Raphael's fondness for landscape sketching.   There is another view
of a city in the Oxford collection, which is so picturesque that it has been considered an ideal composition.   Yet the road and bridge, the citadel, church,
and palaces, and the river sweeping round the base of
turrets, commanded by a battlemented keep;—the
whole town nestling in a valley commanded by
sparely wooded hills, has still some resemblance to
Urbania, the modern substitute for the old fortress of
Castel Durante.†   The round towers and palace that
now belong to the family of Albani, the bridge by
which they are approached, and the course of the
Metaurus, which flows half round the town, all suggest
that the Oxford sketch was a view of an actual city;
and not an ideal composition.

We might fancy from all these indications that
Raphael made frequent excursions from Perugia to

---

* Lille Mus. No. 688. On
greenish paper, a drawing in silver-
point. m. 0·130 h. by 0·105. Very
careful, and in the Peruginesque
style of Raphael's early time.

† Urbania has still much of the
character of Raphael's sketch. But
identification is difficult, as the
keep and many of the towers are
not to be found there now. Yet
the castle, now Palazzo Albani,
shows remnants of mediæval forti-
fications, and two round towers,
near a bridge, through which the
Metaurus flows, are built in the
same style as those in the Oxford
sketch. This sketch, by the way,
is a pen and bistre drawing, No.
175, in the catalogue, which classes
it improperly in our opinion,
amongst the works of the school
of Perugino. Size 6¼ in. h. by 9¼.
From the Antaldi and Lawrence
collections.

various parts of his native duchy. Yet anyone who studies the troubled period of Italian history which includes the struggles of Perugia and the Baglioni, or of Urbino and the Montefeltri with Cesar Borgia, will feel how difficult it is to give a chronological sequence to these artistic holidays. Early in January, 1502, Lucretia Borgia left Rome on her wedding trip to Ferrara. She was met on the road by Guidubaldo, who gave her a night's lodging at Urbino, and escorted her to Pesaro. Elizabeth Gonzaga, Guidubaldo's consort, joined her suite and graced the solemnities of the marriage with her presence. On the 13th of June, Cesar Borgia left Rome, and within a week he appeared with an army at Cagli. On the night of the 20th, Guidubaldo fled through the hills into Lombardy, and on the 21st Cesar occupied Urbino. It was just after this and in that very summer that Perugino and Pinturicchio signed their covenants with the Chigi and Piccolomini at Sienna. Castel Durante, Fossombrone, even San Leo, the strongest place in the Duchy, fell into the hands of Borgia. No wonder that Perugino should have thought it advisable to exchange the residence of Perugia for that of Florence. There was no knowing what would happen to the Baglioni or the petty chieftains who governed Umbrian cities. Hardly had Perugino left Perugia in the first days of October when the partisans of Guidubaldo rose. San Leo was taken by stratagem, Fossombrone by storm from the lieutenants of Cesar Borgia, Urbino revolted, and Guidubaldo returned on the 18th of October to comfort its inhabitants. But winter had scarcely set in when a revulsion took place. Cesar Borgia bribed the Umbrian *condottieri*, and Guidubaldo was forced to bend before the storm and surrender all but the strong places of San Leo, Majole, St. Agata, and San Marino. On the 8th December, he rode without stopping to Città di Castello, but only to find Vitellozzo its chief in parley with the enemy. With perfidious wiles Cesar enticed all the captains of bands to a meeting. With their assistance he captured Sinigaglia on the 31st December, and the same night witnessed the murder of them all. At the news of the massacre Giovan Paulo and his clan despaired of being able to hold their own, and as Cesar appeared before Città di Castello and forced the Vitelli and Guidubaldo to run into Pitigliano, he drew his forces together, and rode from Perugia, which fell into the hands of Carlo Baglioni. Guidubaldo, feeling insecure, fled a second time to Venice, and left the field to his enemies. Cesar Borgia, now master of a great part of Central Italy, prepared to keep what he had gained, but in five months the situation changed. Alexander the VIth died. On the 28th of August, 1503, Guidubaldo was again master of his duchy. In September, Città di Castello recalled the Vitelli, and Perugia was re-occupied by Giovan Paulo Baglioni. Raphael may have visited Città di Castello before December, 1502. He may have seen Castel Durante, Urbino and other cities of the Duchy in summer of the same year, and revisited Fossombrone after the restoration of Guidubaldo in August, 1503, or he may have lain quietly at Perugia during the whole of 1502, and witnessed the voluntary departure of Giovan Paulo Baglioni on the 6th of January, 1503. The fact recorded by Vasari that Maddalena Degli Oddi gave him an order for a "Coronation of the Virgin," would countenance that belief. But what became of him when Carlo Baglioni was again expelled in September, 1503, or was it then that he wandered from Perugia, and revisited Urbino? There are but one or two certainties to which we can cling in the attempt to elucidate these obscure points in Raphael's history. Raphael completed all the pictures which he undertook for Città di Castello by the beginning of 1504. His presence at Città di Castello before the close of December, 1502, would not preclude a second visit after September, 1503, when the government of the Vitelli was restored, but these visits may have been short, and made for the purpose of looking at the site of the altars on which the pictures were to be placed; and there is nothing to prevent us from assuming that the masterpieces which Raphael created were executed at Perugia. Being at Città di Castello, he might be tempted to extend his wanderings and visit Urbino, Cagli, Castel Durante or Fossombrone, remaining a day or a few days only at each of these places.

It is not easy to discover how often Raphael honoured the capital of the Vitelli with his presence, but sketches made at different stages of his practice, and numbers of commissions which he obtained from the patrons of its churches, might lead to the inference that he was often summoned by its wealthiest magnates. The successive delivery of three altar-pieces and a processional standard to four different religious bodies, would justify the assumption of at least four journeys to Città di Castello. The question most difficult to solve is in what order the delivery was made. Meanwhile, Raphael may have busied himself with the composition of smaller pictures ; and one which might lay claim to consideration as an original shall here find a place.

About the beginning of this century the princely collection of the Borghese family comprised a little panel traditionally assigned to Raphael, and representing a martyrdom. Like many other treasures of a similar kind it was sold to a foreigner, and exported to England, where it long remained in the hands of a single owner. "The Martyrs," as the picture was called, remained comparatively unknown ; but it was once exhibited in London, and on that occasion it left the impression on many minds that it was a genuine work of the master to whom it was ascribed.

A legend of ancient date connects the name of St. Nicholas of Bari with the performance of a miracle. A consul had been bribed to accuse some guiltless youths of a capital offence. The sentence had been passed, and the innocent victims were about to suffer, when St. Nicholas appeared and arrested the hand of the executioner. Some subject of this kind seems to have been proposed to the author of "The Martyrs." He accordingly represents one of four youths already sacrificed to the cupidity of the consul, whilst the executioner is about to decapitate a second, and the third and fourth kneel in expectation of death. At the moment of dealing the blow, the swordsman's hand is stayed by a saint, who appears in cardinal's dress on a cloud, and puts the guards to flight in terror and dismay. The scene is laid in a landscape varied with hills and lakes, and trees thrown lightly against the sky. The body and head of the first victim lie prostrate on the foreground to the right; the second kneels in prayer awaiting the stroke, and the third and fourth are also on their knees expecting their fate. But as the executioner raises his sword to strike, the cardinal appears in the air and grips his arm. Three guards to the left take to their heels, and the consul in his robes strides quickly away. The same subject, treated by one of the ablest of the Giottesques in San Francesco of Assisi strikes us by the severity of its lines and the simplicity of its distribution.* But two centuries intervene, and an artist of modest experience but inborn genius, multiplies its incidents and enriches it with complex thoughts. His conception is full of animation; the lines of his composition cleverly combine with those of his landscape. A reminiscence of Signorelli in the soldier who runs away and presents his back to the spectator seems natural to the boy who copied the Archers of the St. Sebastian of Città di Castello. Peruginesque form, equally conspicuous in the figure of the consul, looks natural again in a disciple of the great Umbrian of Perugia. Raphael's hand seems revealed in the shape of the executioner, who recalls the small

---

* S. Francesco of Assisi, Cappella di San Niccolo.

"St. Michael" at the Louvre, whilst the flying
soldier who turns as he runs repeats the fugitive
guard of the "Resurrection" at the Vatican. The
graceful attitudes and true action of the youths awaiting death, the feeling which they embody, the careful
unaffected contour of the drawing, and the brilliant
surface of bright, fresh colour which meet us at every
glance, all are evidence of the skilful yet still modest
hand which produced the predellas of Sant' Antonio
and Ansidei, though style as yet exclusively Peruginesque takes us back to the time when Raphael was
wholly under the bann of Perugino.*

We may resist the temptation of connecting this
pretty illustration of a legend akin to that of St.
Nicholas of Bari with that of "St. Nicholas of
Tolentino," which Raphael executed in his youth, the
more as it is not handed down to us that the miracu-
lous interposition of Nicholas of Bari took place after
one of the victims had been sacrificed; the more, too,
as we cannot say that St. Nicholas was ever represented in cardinal's dress in any Italian picture.

It is curious that of the two earliest altar-pieces
which Raphael executed at Città di Castello, no
annalist should have told us at what time they were

---

* "The Martyrs" was bought
in 1801 by Mr. Young Ottley for
£116. It had been previously in
the Palazzo Borghese at Rome.
It belonged till quite lately to
Mr. W. Stuart, of 36, Hill Street,
Berkeley Square, by whom it
was sold for £186 at Christie's,
on the 19th of March, 1875, under
the name of the "Martyrdom of
St. Placida," to Mr. Waters, of 15,
Buckingham Palace Road. It was
exhibited in 1857 at the British
Institution by Mr. Stuart. It is
painted in oil, on wood, and is 9½
in. h. by 1 ft. 4½ in.

ordered.   The same obscurity covers the origin of the
" Crucifixion " of Lord Dudley, the " Trinity " and
" Creation of Eve," the " Coronation of St. Nicholas
of Tolentino," and the " Coronation of the Virgin " at
the Vatican.   Yet we can scarcely doubt that the
" Crucifixion " of Lord Dudley was the earliest
picture which Raphael composed on a large scale at
the opening of his career; and the presumption is that
when he completed it he had served his time with
Perugino and acquired the freedom which enabled
him to sign his name.

The " Crucifixion " is a subject which Raphael
painted twice before he was twenty, and never
attempted afterwards.   It was quite natural that, so
long as he felt the constraint of the school in which
he was bred, Raphael should have treated that episode
as a display of the highest form of resignation rather
than as an exhibition of demonstrative wailing.

The grave thought of Giotto, which strove to
combine the highest ideal of shape with the utmost
grandeur of expression, was as foreign to Raphael,
notwithstanding his vicinity to Assisi, as the vehement passion which Signorelli exhibited in the frescos
of Orvieto.   Perugino in the " Crucifixion " had
never ventured beyond the traditional rules of composition familiar to the Umbrians.   The utmost that
he had sought to attain was rhythm and regularity of
distribution.   Compared with Perugino's masterpiece
at Sienna, the " Crucifixions " of Città di Castello do
not manifest any desire to stray from the bounds fixed
by the Umbro-Tuscan master.   The symmetry of

Perugino at Sienna is faultless; that of Raphael at Città di Castello without a blemish. In all, the picture is vertically divided into equal parts by the limb of the cross. At Sienna the sky line runs almost through the middle of the panel. Winged seraphs, the sun, the moon, the pelican are placed at the angles of a pentagon, of which the centre is the Saviour's head. The light is concentrated in the middle of the furthest horizon. On the foreground two groups are set in gentle upward and downward curves; the symmetry is that of a pattern. In the "Crucifixion" of Lord Dudley, with a similar distribution of light, an elliptical arrangement is preferred. The foreground is occupied by two kneeling and two standing saints in a perfect semicircle. The mastery of Raphael is shown in the cleverness with which he has raised the position of the standing figures in relation to that of the kneeling ones. The angels are compactly placed to fill the spaces beneath the Redeemer's arms, and if there be a fault it is that one of these angels should hold two cups to the wounds in the Saviour's hand and side.

The "Trinity" is pyramidal. Two saints at each side of the cross form the base of the figure, of which the Eternal in a Mandorla is the apex, but a reversed triangle is skilfully inscribed by means of the crucifix itself. To disturb this symmetry, or break the lines by tragic action, might suit the powers of dramatists like Giotto or Signorelli, but would have run counter to Peruginesque teaching. But if the tragic were excluded, ineffable serenity and supreme resignation might all the more be indulged, and this Perugino and Raphael both tried to accomplish. But it was the special gift of Raphael, with the inexhaustible fund of feeling and tenderness which he possessed, to produce moving pictures which embodied more guile-less simplicity, and more grace and purity than any artist before or since was enabled to convey, and within these lines we feel and enjoy the charm of Raphael's conception.

The "Crucifixion" of Lord Dudley was executed for a chapel at San Domenico of Città di Castello, the patrons of which were of the Gavari family. As late as 1693 it adorned an altar beneath the organ. The wants of the Gavari, or of the Dominicans who inherited the Gavari chapel, subsequently became pressing, and the picture passed through the hands of several owners before it came finally to England. Vasari thought that but for Raphael's name the "Crucifixion" would have been assigned to Perugino, and in this he is nearer the mark than those who point out the mere dependence of the pupil on the models of his master.* Throughout the whole of his career Raphael was careless to conceal that his own conception was grafted on that of his predecessors. It was indifferent to him whether he wandered into an Umbrian or a Florentine garden. He took the flowers as they came, and extracted the honey. But when he began to wander, his experience was neces-sarily limited, and the "Crucifixion" is naturally an Umbrian product. Perugino communicated to Raphael

---

* Vas. viii. p. 4.

not only his figures but his style and system of repli-
cation. From 1491, when he painted the "Crucifixion" of the Villa Albani, till 1502–3 when he
composed the "Crucifixion" of the Chigi, he followed
an invariable groove of thought. The "Christ" of
1491, at Rome, and that of 1494–5, at the Poverino
of Florence; that of 1492–6 at Santa Maria Magdalena de' Pazzi, or of 1502–3, at Sienna, were executed
with more or less distinction from the same model.
But in the course of years, and especially up to 1496,
Perugino brought the type of the suffering Redeemer
to a great perfection, in respect of correctness of proportion, dignity of aspect, propriety of movement, and
purity of contour. In the setting and distribution of
figures he created mere varieties with surprising
regularity, and we, who now so easily compare the
qualities of his numerous pictures, are well able
to point out where he asserts his own powers, and
where he falls into the defect of iteration. We can
see that the "Virgin" at the Pazzi and the "Virgin"
of San Girolamo delle Poverino are the same; that
the "St. John" of the former and the "St. Jerome"
of the latter are only varied by dress or a change in
the position of a head, and that the "Magdalen" at
the Pazzi reappears with slight alteration at Sienna.
Raphael only differs from Perugino so far that the
"Crucifixion" of Città di Castello, instead of repeating
the earlier creations of his own pencil, reproduces the
earlier creations of Perugino, Signorelli, or Alunno.
The "Christ" of Città di Castello is that of the
Pazzi, Poverino, or Sienna. The same model seems to

have sat for master and disciple, and Raphael's chair and easel were placed a little to one side. The right foot is nailed a little over the left, the knee of the right leg is necessarily raised above the level of the left knee. The difference, if there be any, lies in the experience which long years have given to the one, and the want of practice which is natural to the tender years of the other. Raphael has to contend with difficulties which Perugino had overcome. The carved work of the "Redeemer" in San Francesco del Monte was in close proximity when he studied the action of the figure in his own altar-piece. His memory might take him in fancy to the chapel of San Spirito, where Signorelli had painted one of his best versions of the subject in 1494, or, whilst thinking over the difficulties which surrounded him, he chanced to visit Foligno, and cast his eye on the "Crucifixion" which Alunno had composed for the church of St. Nicholas in 1492. In his general rendering of the frame and extremities of the "Christ" of Earl Dudley, Raphael embodies distinct reminiscences of Signorelli and Alunno, without being able to forget that he is Perugino's disciple; he even takes from Alunno the idea of one angel holding two cups to the Saviour's wounds.* His skill is sorely tried, in spite of his

---

* Alunno's Predella of 1492, with the "Crucifixion" as one of its subjects, is now No. 31 at the Louvre.

It is curious that there should once have existed, but that we should now be unable to find, a "Crucifixion" assigned to Raphael, which a century ago was preserved in St. Domenico of San Gimignano. The history of this piece is that it was given to the Dominicans of San Gimignano by F. Bartolommeo di Bartolo, a brother of the

cleverness, by the complexity of the movement of the Saviour's limbs. The curves of the bony legs, and their dry articulations are very searching, but lack the simple outline of Perugino. Modulation, or flexible rendering of flesh, correctness of proportion, and forcible expression are gifts with which Raphael is not yet as abundantly supplied as Perugino. Nor is it fortunate for him that he should have chosen distemper as a medium, because the hard contours of sinewy nude, or the breadth of egg-shaped heads, affected in bend and foreshortening, are not ennobled by Perugino's velvet tones, or those sweet colours which mark Raphael's own practice in oil. Harmonious in scale, the tints are still without that richness of enamel which enchants us in later creations of the same pencil, and landscape of melancholy serenity has less of effective charm than the varied and lovely views which form the backgrounds of similar compositions by Perugino.

If we turn from the "Redeemer" to the attendant

order who had been confessor to Alexander the VIth. It represented Christ crucified, in the same attitude (reversed) as the "Christ" of Earl Dudley. At the foot of the cross were the Virgin (right) and (left) the Evangelist. The picture was on the altar " del nome di Dio," at St. Domenico of San Gimignano till the close of last century, when, the French invasion having taken place, it passed into private hands. Bought by a surgeon named Buzzi, who had it cleaned by the painter Fèbre, the picture came into the hands of a Prince Galitzin at Rome, who allowed Rosini, the author of the History of Painting, to make an outline of it. (See Plate LXX. of Rosini's Atlas.) There is something Raphaelesque in the scheme of this picture, the landscape of which is like that in Raphael's cartoon of the "Meeting of the Emperor and his Affianced Bride" in Casa Baldeschi at Perugia. See Rosini's History, iv. 21 and 26, and Pecori's San Gimignano, pp. 420 and 521.

Saints in the " Crucifixion " of Earl Dudley, the same remarks are applicable. The "Virgin" which Perugino turned into a Monica at Sienna, and Raphael or his comrades restored to her original character at San Francesco del Monte, reappears with unimportant alterations in the " Crucifixion " of Lord Dudley. " St. John Evangelist," who comes to us again and again in Perugino's masterpieces at the Pazzi, the Poverine or Sienna, recurs in Raphael's conceptions. We know him again though changed to some extent by varied setting of the head or inception of stride. Raphael only changes the dress of the Magdalen, as she appears in the replicas of Perugino. Diversity is obtained by transferring the head of the Evangelist at Sienna to the Magdalen's shoulders at Lord Dudley's. The kneeling " Mariano Chigi," a noble portrait at Sienna, becomes a St. Jerome at Città di Castello. The angels in both are reproductions of the same designs with very slight modifications, their Umbrian character being marked in Raphael, as well as in Perugino by similarity of vestments,—tight, slashed sleeves, and tunics girded up at the hips with bands; the superfluous lengths of which are flying in circlets in the wind. What charm there is beyond extreme delicacy and gesture Raphael owes to simplicity and tenderness of feeling. It is because of the youth of these impersonations and their serenity that we find them so winning. A breath of new life re-animates old forms. The cleverness with which a rhythmical cadence is obtained is beautifully exemplified in the movement of the Saints at opposite sides of the cross. The Virgin and Evangelist at the two extremes look pensively into space, whilst the Magdalen and St. Jerome glance with upward longing into the face of the lifeless Redeemer.[*]

But the source from which Raphael was inspired, is fed by other springs than those of Alunno, Signorelli, and Perugino. The head of his "Evangelist," with its pretty trickery of ringlets, recalls the typical ones of Pinturicchio, whilst the beautiful lines of the undulating landscape, broken by cliffs and enlivened with trees, remind us of the same features in Pinturicchio's contemporary altar-pieces. The tendency to lean on Perugino was so irresistible, that, whilst that artist lived at Perugia, his partner's influence on Raphael was evanescent. But when Perugino went to Florence and failed to return, Raphael soon learnt to look upon Pinturicchio as a second chief, whom he was neither loth to accept as a guide nor disinclined to serve as an assistant.

The "Trinity" and "Creation of Eve" were

---

[*] London, Dudley House. Wood, arched. 8 ft. 6 in. h. by 5 ft. 5 in., or m. 2·57 h. by 1·64. The panel is somewhat retouched in the foreground. It is injured by two longitudinal splits, one of which runs down the figure of St. Jerome, the other down the figure of St. John. Vasari saw this picture on its altar (viii. 4), and Francesco Lazzari in Serie de' Vescovi di Città di Castello. Foligno, 1693, p. 285, describes it. It was sold (? when) to a French-man for 4000 scudi, figured in the Fesch collection, was bought at the Fesch sale by Prince Canino for 10,000 scudi, and sold in 1847 to Earl Dudley, then Lord Ward. At the bottom of the cross are the words in four lines, "RAPHAEL . URBIN . AS . P. Passavant registers a drawing of the torso of Christ. A figure of the Virgin is noted by Bartsch, in the Albertina at Vienna. But we are unacquainted with either of these pieces.

executed after the "Crucifixion" of Earl Dudley, for
the Brotherhood of the Santissima Trinita, at Città
di Castello. They were painted for a processional
standard, and were doubtless frequently displayed in
the streets of that city. But in the course of their
wanderings they were seriously injured, and in 1638,
it was found necessary to frame them on an altar of
the church to which they belonged. In the middle of
the present century they showed such symptoms of
decay that an attempt was made to restore them which
proved altogether unsuccessful. The remnants now
preserved in the gallery of Città di Castello, are little
more than half of the original work. But they still
suffice to show that when Raphael finished them he
had made some progress in mastering the difficulties
of his art. One of the canvases represents the
"Eternal" in an almond-shaped glory supporting the
beam of the cross. The dove sheds its rays on
the Redeemer, whose head is encircled with a crown
of thorns. Two winged cherubs appear at the
Eternal's side ; and St. Sebastian and St. Roch kneel
in prayerful attitudes in the foreground. Behind
them a landscape of simple lines shows the gentle
curves of a low range of hills sinking to the horizon,
and slight trees thrown against the sky. A walled
town covers one of the slopes to the right, and a
road shows its windings in the distance. Cast in a
mould half reminiscent of Perugino and Pinturicchio,
the head of the Eternal is youthful, manly, and purely
Raphaelesque. The Saviour on the cross surpasses
in contour and modelling that of the "Crucifixion"

of Lord Dudley, yet it is formed in the same traditional shape. The cherubs are natural precursors of those in the coronation of the Virgin at the Vatican, but if possible, younger and more innocent. Reverence and mourning characterise the attitude and face of St. Sebastian kneeling to the left with his hands crossed on his breast. Intense feeling dwells in the upward glance and turn of the head of St. Roch to the right, who kneels with his hands joined in prayer. Copious substance and rich tone characterize the colour; drapery cleverly encircles the shapes, and the outlines are careful and correct.

The "Creation of Eve" takes us back to one of the subjects which Giotto designed with unrivalled skill in the campanile of the Florentine cathedral. But Raphael instead of showing the figure of Eve rising slowly, at the bidding of the Creator, from the side of the prostrate and sleeping Adam, chooses the earlier phase, when the Eternal, striding (hastily and un-couthly) towards Adam, feels for the rib out of which Eve was fashioned. Two angels in air look down, with something of the grace that charms us in the sketches at Venice. Adam, in noble repose, unites the classicism of an antique with the realism of nature in its fleshy elasticity. Recumbent with his head to the left, he lies unconscious on the ground with a belt of leaves round his hips; one leg rests upon the other, and the head with its spacious forehead, pursed lips, and small chiselled nose, affects the same rotundity as the angels of Lord Dudley's "Crucifixion." But the Eternal, bearded, square in skull, and herculean in shape, reminds us of

those types which Raphael inherited from his father
Santi. The redeeming quality in this double picture
is the tenderness of feeling which abounds in the
figures of the angels, the richness of the blended colour,
and the beauty of the distance.*

It is particularly unfortunate that the "Coronation
of St. Nicholas of Tolentino," which is the third large
composition that Raphael painted for a church at Città
di Castello, should have been dismembered and lost in
1789, equally unfortunate that historians from Vasari
downward, should have neglected to describe it.†
Happily a free copy of its principal group was made
at the beginning of last century for an Augustinian
nunnery, and the transfer of this picture to the gallery
of Città di Castello enables us to perceive that St.

---

* Città di Castello. Municipal
Gallery. No. 32. "The Trinity,"
No. 16. "The Creation of Eve."
Canvas. Each picture m. 1·675 h.
by 0·96. At the suppression of
the convents in 1857-8, these
canvases were removed to the
palace, and placed under the care
of Count Carlo della Porta of Città
di Castello, who, being himself an
artist, tried to remove the crust of
ages, and the repaints of a restorer
named Caratoli. But after an attempt to clean the heads of the
two kneeling saints in the "Trinity," he wisely abandoned his
purpose. Half the colour in the
"Trinity" is gone, and particularly
the shadows of the legs and torso
of the Christ, the face of the Eternal,
and heads of the cherubs. Otto
Mündler, in 1857, could see the

contours in black chalk under the
scaled colours. The whole is now
very dim and injured by restoring.
The Greek meander and ornament
round the pictures date from 1589.
The frame was made in 1638, when
the standard was placed on the
high altar of the church of the
Trinity. Of all the drawings by
Raphael which now exist, but
one recalls these masterpieces—an
outline in silver-point at the Oxford Gall. No. 25, on creamy paper.
10 in. h. by 7¼ in. A kneeling
model in a gaberdine and tights,
looking up and showing the palms
of his hands. But this might be a
first idea for the St. Jerome of the
Dudley "Crucifixion" as well as
for the St. Roch of the "Trinity."

† Vasari, viii. 3.

Nicholas of Tolentino was represented in the frock of a monk, bearing the book and crucifix, and standing with both feet on the body of Satan, whilst four angels at his side bore scrolls with inscriptions in his praise.* The upper part, there is reason to think, was composed of three principal figures, all bearing crowns in honour of the titular saint, one of which is described by Lanzi and Pungileone from hearsay, as the first person of the Trinity in a halo of cherubim, the second as the Virgin Mary, and the third as St. Augustine, or St. Nicholas of Bari.

This version is confirmed by two most interesting drawings by Raphael in the galleries of Oxford and Lille. At Oxford, St. Nicholas of Tolentino stands with his left arm raised in a menacing attitude, and looks down, whilst an angel at his side holds a scroll. On the same sheet a study of a hand and arm, on the back of it four studies of hands and arms, one for a mitred Saint in the drawing of Lille, another for St. Nicholas of Tolentino with the book; and besides, the head of the angel and two slight outlines of stand-

---

* Città di Castello. Municipal collection. Altar-piece on canvas, with figures of life size. St. Nicholas of Tolentino, in a monk's frock, holding the crucifix in his right hand and an open book in his left, stands on the body of Satan, who writhes and grips with both hands at the dress of the saint. The figure of the Evil One lies with the head to the right and not to the left, as it is in the Lille drawing. To the left one angel, to the right two angels hold long scrolls with inscriptions. Above the Saint is a cherub's head with five wings. The background is a landscape seen through an arch-way. This altar-piece appears to have been executed at the beginning of the eighteenth century. It was found in the nunnery of the Augustinians, now Oblate Sale-siane.

ing figures.* At Lille, St. Nicholas of Tolentino stands in the dress of a model, but in a different attitude from that of the Oxford drawing, as if in the action of holding the cross, whilst Satan, on whose prostrate body his feet are resting, lies motionless on the ground. To the left, near Satan's head, an angel like that of Oxford is placed. Above this group and within the panelled vaulting of an arch, St. Nicholas, a model in a close skull-cap and tight vest and hose, looks down and holds a crown with both hands; his shape is seen to the hips in a mandorla. At the sides, but lower down in the sheet, yet still above St. Nicholas of Tolentino, a bishop with mitre and crosier, and a female resting to the waist on clouds, are set in profile to the right and left. On the other side of the sheet is a study in black chalk of the figure in the mandorla, a fragment of the drapery of the angel, four pen sketches of swans, with an outline of the inner court of the Palace of Urbino.†

By means of these sketches, as well as of the copy at Città di Castello, the " Coronation of St. Nicholas " is revealed in its original simplicity. It contained but one mitred saint whose form had any call to appear in connection with St. Nicholas of Tolentino, and this is St. Nicholas of Bari.‡ Like all that Raphael

---

* Oxford Gallery. No. 4. Black chalk. 14¾ in. h. by 9½. From the Alva and Lawrence collections.

† Lille Museum. Nos. 737 and 738. On white paper. m. 0·338 h. by 0·240. The first with six figures, very faint, in black chalk.

The latter less faint and very highly finished.

‡ According to Pungileone the picture was sold in 1789 to Pius the VIth, through the agency of the "Painter Ponfreni," who cut it in pieces and made one picture

did between 1502 and 1504, the sketches of Oxford and Lille are Peruginesque in character, but they are drawn with such freedom and fine perception of modulation in surface, and with such mastery of the intricacies of movement, as to indicate a perceptible gain of power in the author of them. They also show that Raphael was bold enough to sacrifice some of the customs of the school to novelty of distribution.

Contemporary with these pictures Raphael produced others in which traditional arrangement was more completely preserved; and conspicuous amongst these is the "Coronation" of the Vatican, which was executed for a member of the Oddi family at Perugia. The Oddi had suffered much from the persecution of the Baglioni, and they had never recovered the power which their ancestors wielded in the 15th century. But the Baglioni, if they were too politic to permit the return of the chiefs from exile, were not so inhuman as to exclude their ladies; and during the civil wars Maddalena degli Oddi enjoyed the use of the chapel which her ancestors had founded in San Francesco of Perugia. At what period she entered into the covenant which gave her the "Coronation" of Raphael is unknown.* It is not even proved that

---

of the "Eternal." The fragments remained in the Vatican, whence they disappeared at the French invasion. Wicar in his Inventory says on the contrary that the picture was bought for Pope Pius VI. by J. B. Soncino Ridolfi for 1000 scudi and divided. The lower group remained entire and the upper part was divided into three. See Pungileone, Elogio stor. di R. Santi, u. s. pp. 35-7, and the catalogue of Lille printed in 1856.

* Consult Vas. viii. p. 3, and Mariotti Lett. u. s. p. 238-9.

Raphael was the artist with whom the contract was made. But the work is certainly his; and the style in which it was composed and painted points to the time when Raphael was under the joint control of Perugino and Pinturicchio, and a resident at Perugia. We may therefore presume that when Raphael was employed by his patrons at Città di Castello, he was labouring also for Maddalena degli Oddi; though we cannot say whether the picture was undertaken on Raphael's sole account, or on that of the partnership of which Perugino and Pinturicchio were the heads.

It was clearly the intention of Maddalena degli Oddi, when she ordered the altar-piece, to obtain an "Assumption of the Virgin," for which Raphael's first drawing has been preserved. But the causes which led to the change from an "Assumption" to a "Coronation" have not been revealed. We only know that the painter having made a sketch of the first, was induced to change his plan, and by an easy, though not unexceptional transition, led to the production of the second. The studies which had been made for the one were found suitable for the other, and in both the boy models who sat in their jerkins and hose were made to display their fair faces and modest airs with advantage. It is difficult to realize how the painter whose figures are more nearly ideal than those of any artist of the 15th century, breathed into his creations the purity and innocence for which they are conspicuous. It is a fact that the studies for the principal figures of the "Coronation" were made from boys who sat in the necessary attitudes and action, dressed in the tight jackets and leggings, and the round hats which they wore in the streets of Perugia. Having set these boys to hold crowns, or play the viol, the tambourine, or the harp, Raphael first drew them in outline; then, giving play to his imagination, transformed them into winged inmates of heaven, and swathed their slender shapes in becoming drapery; their youth and boyish features were serviceable alike for embodiments of Christ, of Mary, or of angels.

In sketching the "Assumption" which was first designed for Maddalena degli Oddi, Raphael might have trusted entirely to his memory or to his skill as a copyist. Close by in San Pietro lay the altar-piece of Perugino, where the Virgin, in the midst of the apostles, looks up to the Redeemer who ascends in a glory of Seraphim. He had seen that altar-piece, we may think, growing under Perugino's hand, but he might have studied it later in the church for which it was composed. Two years or little more had elapsed since Perugino had finished another picture of a similar kind, the "Assumption" of 1500 in the convent of Vallombrosa. That also Raphael had seen, but he was not confined even to these masterpieces, and he might be prompted to avoid ancient errors if allowed to study the sketches of Pinturicchio's "Assumption" in the Rovere chapel or the Borgia chambers at Rome. Of all these models, Raphael's sketch of the "Virgin attended by Angels" at Pesth, is a reminiscence, if not something more. The Virgin stands on a cloud in an almond-shaped glory, the tips of her fingers brought together in prayer; from her drooping head a hood falls in gentle folds to the shoulders, unites with the mantle which is fastened at the throat with a brooch, and opens to show the arms, and closes again at the waist from whence it falls in folds to the ground. The eyes are turned heavenwards, the face is benign. The head of the Eternal in the apex of the Mandorla, between two winged seraphs, boy cherubs supporting the clouds out of which two other cherubs look up in adoration, complete the centre of the picture.* To the left an angel stands and plays the violin, half concealing a second, who rubs a tambourine; to the right an angel in profile with a pocket-viol, and in rear of him a fourth angel with a harp.† Of all the instruments which make up this celestial concert, the violin and harp are familiar to us in the works of Perugino. The tambourine is the favourite of Angelico and his pupils, which Raphael may have seen in Benozzo's " Assumption " at Montefalco.

If the original sketch for the " Assumption " had been carried out, Raphael would soon have transformed the superficial imitation of Perugino and Pinturicchio which marks the conventional drapery of the Virgin, into something more refined. He was not content to trust for his angels to any source but nature. He therefore set his country models of boys in the necessary attitudes, and these first studies for the

---

* One of these angels—that to the right with his arms raised—recalls the similar figure by Perugino in the "Madonna" of the Bologna Gallery. No. 197.

† Pesth Museum. Esterhazy collection. Pen and umber sketch, arched at top. The left side of the drawing much stained.

"Assumption" are still preserved in the museum of Lille.
One of the boys, in his hat and week-day clothes, plays
the tambourine, and details of the hands are carefully
made out on separate parts of the sheet. Another
pose of the same youth yields an angel playing a
pocket-viol. But instead of looking up with a foreshortened face as we find him in the Pesth design, he
looks down musingly, and the slight interval which
parts the two drawings in date of execution indicates the
moment when the idea of an "Assumption" was given up,
and that of a " Coronation of the Virgin" was adopted,
for in the "Coronation," the tambourine-player bends
his face towards the ground and not towards the sky.*
Hardly had the original design been put aside when
Raphael recomposed the whole of it. He lightly
threw on a sheet, now at Lille, two contours of boys,
one of whom sits and prays with joined hands, whilst
the other likewise sits and holds a crown over his
neighbour's head. Hastily drawn with a pen this
sketch scarcely looks as good as Raphael should have
made it, but there was a necessity perhaps for haste,
and assuredly the figures coincide with those of
the group in the picture.† Better, yet also from the
model, and with very rapid strokes, Raphael outlined
a boy touching the strings of a mandoline, which he
put aside for one playing a violin, on the skeleton of

* Oxford Gallery. No. 9. Two
silver-point drawings, on pale grey
green paper, heightened with
white. Two separate sheets on
one mount. Each 7½ in. h. by 4⅞.

From the Ottley and Lawrence
Collections.

† Lille Museum. No. 701. Pen
drawing, with retouched outlines, on
white paper. m. 0·246 h. by 0·179.

whose frame the drapery hangs in folds, flapping in the wind.   Both sketches on the same paper are exhibited at Lille.*   Even these efforts did not prove entirely suitable ; the head of the boy had been bent to the left; a better effect might be got if it were turned to the right.   A model now sat, but only for the head and the hand, with the bow.   The type of the face, in itself lovely, is realized with marvellous skill, locks of the finest curly hair float about the cheeks and neck, and this perfect and inimitable study adorns the British Museum.†   To the left of the Virgin and Christ in the " Coronation," the studies for the tambourine and viol players at Lille do service, but in this wise, that whereas the latter stands to the left, and the former to the right in the design, their position is reversed in the picture, the viol is turned into a harp, and both figures are clothed in ample drapery.

Groups of the apostles necessarily pertain to the subject of the Assumption, but the natural adjunct is the tomb from which the Virgin has risen.   It is an accident attributable to the change in the upper part of the original arrangement that brings the tomb in connection with Raphael's " Coronation."   At San

---

* Lille Museum.   No. 707. Silver-point drawing on grey prepared paper. m. 0·200 h. by 0·222. On the reverse (No. 708) are fragments of the decoration of a room, washed in bistre.

† British Museum. Silver-point drawing, one-eighth of life size. The head turned to the right. Below, the arm and hand hold the bow.   On prepared grey paper. From the Payne Knight Collection. 11 in. h. by 7$\frac{9}{12}$.

Francesco del Monte he had drawn the apostles, watching the Redeemer from the ground as he set the crown on the temples of His mother; the sepulchre and its flowers were not thought of.   Here the tomb had been introduced in connection with the Assumption, and, after that idea was abandoned, the tomb was preserved, yet we have no complete design for the twelve; the magnificent silver point head and hands of St. Thomas now preserved at Lille, is but a study of detail at the back of the pen and ink outline of the Virgin and Saviour.*   The first thought for the uplifted head of St. James the elder, at the right side of the picture, is also at Lille accompanied at the back by two fragments of the drapery of that figure,† whilst varieties of the foreshortened face of the same saint are found in the Oxford Gallery and the sketch-book at Venice.‡

Raphael tried with great ingenuity to cover the principal defect of the " Coronation " of the Vatican

---

* Lille Museum. No. 700. Silver-point drawing, on prepared vellum paper. The head looking up, is foreshortened and seen to the throat. Long rich locks fall at both sides. Below, the right hand, showing the back, the left showing the palm. 0·266 h. by 200. Back of No. 701, *antea*. Another replica of the head is in the Malcolm Collection.

† Lille Museum. No. 702. m. 0·337 h. by 0·192. On white paper. The head is not unlike that of St. Thomas, but seen at three-quarters to the left, and down to the throat. Copious locks fall to the shoulders and back.

No. 703. Two details of the drapery of the left leg. m. 0·358 h. by 0·208. The head in the picture is more foreshortened and more completely turned to the left than that in the drawing. But query is the drawing genuine? It is certainly feeble.

‡ Oxford Museum. No. 10. Pen drawing in bistre. 3¼ in. h. by 2⅜. One of several studies on a single mount. The head turned to the left as it is in the picture. Venice Acad. Frame XXV. No. 4. Back of XXV. No. 18. One of four heads reverse of that at Oxford. Very finely lined with pen and bistre.

by artifices which hardly effect their purpose. Built
up in two divisions, each part of the composition is in
itself a picture. Below, the tomb, at an angle to the
plane of delineation, allows of an advantageous distribution of the apostles in a circle. Four of the
twelve peer into the grave, and are conscious of a
miracle. Five are attracted by the scene above them,
and the rest commune amongst themselves. St.
Thomas, gazing heavenward with the Virgin's girdle
in his hands, is the chief connecting link between the
lower and the upper part of the altar-piece. It is a
weak connecting link, neutralized besides by the
horizontal streak of sky which parts like a ribband
the hills of the distance and the clouds of the coronation group. The landscape of undulating hills, with
its saplings and flecks of verdure, varies with curves,
the line of the apostles' heads. The tomb, beautifully
decorated with lilies and roses, swells the chord of
harmony in the variegated dresses near it. Yet the
fact remains. There are two pictures independent of
each other, and this impression clings to us in spite
of Raphael's art.*

---

* Vatican Museum, No. XXVII.
Wood, arched at the top. 9 ft. 2 in.
h. by 5 ft. 2 in., or m. 2·67 by 1·63.
Taken to Paris in 1797, it was
there transferred to canvas. When
carried away in April of the year
above named from the Oddi chapel
in S. Francesco of Perugia, it was
valued 1200 scudi, and it was
stated that the panel had been repaired a few years before by Francesco Romero. See Giorn. di
Erudi. Tosc. u. s. v. 235–242. From
the various operations of restoring
the picture has suffered abrasion,
especially in the fine gildings, and
parts of it have very much darkened.
A copy marked MDXVIII . MEN .
JVLII, is on the high altar of the
church of Civitella Bernazzone, not
far from Perugia.

Apart from this the charm of the "Coronation" is due to exquisite finish, copious but never obtrusive detail, drapery of great simplicity of line, yet of balanced mass and appropriate fall, admirable youthfulness of features and a wonderful purity of air and expression.   Archness in the angels, timidity in the apostles are consequences inseparable from the tenderness of the artist's years.   Perugino, no doubt, would have created something more manly and more powerful, but the archness and timidity of his disciple are united to so much delicacy of feeling and such pure taste in colour, that the loss on one side is amply compensated by corresponding gain on the other.   Characteristic of the heads is an elliptic contour of great breadth at the cheeks; equally characteristic is the wide separation of the ciliary arches, leaving a broad base to the nose, which fines down suddenly to a delicate point and thin nostrils.   The pursed lips are like those of a child about to suck.   The necks that support these heads are often as broad as the head itself.

Some of the finest work in the whole picture is concentrated on the Saviour, whose features are serene and youthful, and the Virgin, whose downcast head and eyes are angelic.   Eight winged seraphs about the sky give a sweet vibration to the air, and two boy angels peeping out of the clouds at the feet of the Virgin and Christ, are precursors in attitude and face of those in Raphael's greatest masterpiece, the "Madonna" of San Sisto.

Looking back at the works of Perugino and Pinturicchio in connection with those of Fiorenzo, Melozzo, and Santi, we are struck by the individualism of the first in a set form of extremities. Short fat hands, and equally short fingers and nails are the rule. Pinturicchio's style, akin in this to the style of Santi and Melozzo, is marked by roundness and shortness of heads. Angels are drawn with affected slenderness and daintiness; male saints with feeble frames and decrepid features. Copious locks enframe the faces and tumble in frizzles or in rows and bunches of twisted curls. Gilding and surface ornament are gaudily effective. But landscape detail, at once rich and minute, is lavished on grasses, weeds, flowers, and stones. In all these peculiarities the "Coronation" of the Vatican betrays the influence on Raphael of Perugino and Pinturicchio. But the latter is the master whose influence most clearly predominates; and we rise from the contemplation of this most interesting work with the conviction that it was conceived on the lines of Perugino's "Ascension" of 1496 or of the "Assumption" of 1500;—that its fundamental idea was altered by circumstances which induced the painter to modify his first intentions;— and that, during the progress of his labours, Raphael lost the control of Perugino and fell under the supervision of Pinturicchio.

But an altar-piece was not necessarily perfect when its chief incident was complete. The predellas were important adjuncts which required equal thought in their composition and execution. Raphael had promised to furnish an "Annunciation," an "Epiphany," and a "Presentation in the Temple," and it was natural that he should study examples of the same subjects in the works of his master. As early as 1497, Perugino had painted for Santa Maria of Fano a predella, which comprised the "Birth of the Saviour," the "Presentation in the Temple," the "Marriage of the Virgin," the "Annunciation," and the "Gift of the Girdle to St. Thomas." Raphael probably remembered that he had witnessed the origin of these predellas. He recollected that, in the very first of these subjects, Perugino had ingeniously adapted some of the figures with which the Sixtine frescos had been adorned. With his own pen he had copied the girl on her knees before Gershom, and with his own eyes he had seen that figure do duty before the infant Christ in the predella of Fano. He had watched the transfer of the girl bearing a vase on her head from the fresco of Zipporah to the cottage of Mary at Fano. Here was a road of which he knew the windings. It was quite natural that he should follow it. But with that insight into the propriety of things, and that delicate taste which distinguished him, he saw where Perugino's art was capable of improvement, and he then remodelled his design, or acknowledging Perugino's capacity, he adopted his arrangement and refined it. In the predella of Fano, the Virgin annuntiate kneels under an open colonnade, receiving the blessing of the Eternal, who appears in the sky, and the message of the angel, who kneels in a side portico. Without changing his style, he repeated the architecture in a purer and more chastened form. He altered the time and the action, imagined the Virgin sitting, yet conscious of the coming of the angel. He kept the figure of the Eternal, and the dove flying down from the sky. Perugino had arranged the "Presentation" in the choir of a temple, the high priest behind the table, Joseph and Mary at the sides, the male and female witnesses in couples in the aisles. Raphael was content to take the central group as it stood. He chose for the attendants what he thought the best of those invented by Perugino. Though it was not one of the subjects at Fano, the "Epiphany" was an episode which Raphael had studied and thought over for the Connestabile predella. He took it bodily from thence, and enriched the composition with fresh incidents.

Yet the predellas of the "Coronation" of the Vatican cannot be dismissed without some further examination of the time and the influences under which they were completed. There are studies for them which convey the impression that they were not finished uninterruptedly; and the question arises whether the interval which separates the inception from the completion of these delightful pieces was not broken by a journey to Florence. It may also be asked, was Raphael's acquaintance with the predellas of Fano made at the period of their production in 1497 ? Did he derive his knowledge of those works from cartoons in Perugino's painting-room, or did he visit Fano himself ? To all these inquiries the answer must be dubious, but in balancing probabilities un-biassed observers will perhaps agree that Raphael saw, and probably helped Perugino when the altar-piece of Fano was created. That altar-piece was carried out when Perugino's power was at its highest. It combines dignity with grace, richness of colour with the purest harmony. Its technical handling is perfect. It displays absolute mastery of the noblest forms of composition and perspective. It embodies much of the charm of tints, and atmosphere; much of the brilliancy which Raphael gradually acquired; and but for the existence of masterpieces of this kind, and our knowledge that the disciple must have seen and studied them, we should be unable to explain why, or to understand how, Raphael's genius expanded.

The cartoon from which the " Annunciation " of the Vatican was pricked off is now in the Louvre collection; and it is our privilege after the lapse of more than three centuries to see the very lines which Raphael drew and transferred to panel. The scene is laid in a double portico, through the arches of which we glance at a landscape with a church enclosed by walls, and two flanking towers approached by a road and bridge. How dearly Raphael loved that landscape, how affectionately he dwelt on those towers and spires, is shown by the way in which he repeated them in the sketch of the boy on the pack-saddle, or the Virgin with the missal, at Oxford, or the panel of " Marsyas and Apollo " at Rome.*

---

* See *antea*, Oxford Gall. No. 5, and *postea*, Oxford Gall. Nos. 23 and 24.

The double portico and its round Corinthian columns alternating with square pillars akin to those in the "Homage of Æneas Sylvius" at Chatsworth, the arabesques adorning the faces of the pillars, for which a kindred study is seen in the Venice sketch-book,—every line and every detail of them prove what care and thought were concentrated on every portion of a picture, however small. In the sky to the left the Eternal, with the orb in benediction, preserves the traditions of the Umbrian school, takes us back to the days of Bonfigli at Perugia, of Giovanni Santi at Sinigaglia, or Perugino at Fano. The angel running in with outstretched-wings, eagerly giving the blessing as he grasps the lily, is a picture of rapid motion; enhanced by a bird-like length of limb combined with some shortness of body. The Virgin, on a chair to the right, modestly looks down, surprised, as the gesture of her right hand suggests, yet she still holds the book with her left; her form in part concealed by draping of the mantle, is a delightful manifestation of the purest feeling.*

On the same scale as the cartoon, but with the additional charm of colour, the Vatican predella exhibits the master's skill in working out effects of atmosphere and light. The figures project against the clear brown of the columns and pillars, or the partitioned squares and stripes of the tesselated floor, and the twilight of the colonnade contrasts with the

---

* Louvre. Cartoon, pricked for use. m. 0·30 h. by 0·43. Pen drawing washed with bistre. From the collections of Mr. Ottley, Sir Th. Lawrence, and the King of Holland.

sun-lit slopes of the vale beyond. Peruginesque in spirit and handling, yet technically beneath the level of Perugino, the picture is not free from dryness or affectation; but these and other imperfections are compensated by qualities upon which to descant anew would be but to repeat what hardly bears repeating.*

The "Presentation of Christ in the Temple," more closely following the model of Perugino than the "Annunciation," was chiefly copied from Perugino's predella at Fano, as the cartoon, now at Oxford, shows.† In picture and sketch, as well as in the final rendering at the Vatican, the High Priest stands behind the font, leaning over to receive the Child from the Virgin, whilst Joseph, to the left, twitches the folds of his mantle with one hand, and rests the other on the font cover. The Child, turning in alarm to seek its mother's bosom, is nature caught in action and eternalized. But the very form of the pillar on which the table rests is copied faithfully from Perugino.

Of the women attending the presentation, but one is taken from the Fano predella, and transported from right to left of the group. She looks at one of her

---

* Vatican Gallery. No. X. m. 0.39 h. Framed with the "Epiphany" and "Presentation." Transferred to canvas when taken to Paris at the close of last century (1797). A copy of half the original size by Sassoferrato is in San Pietro of Perugia.

† Oxford Gallery. No. 11. Pen drawing, pricked for transfer. 8 in. h. by 7¾ (m. 0·204 h. by 0·196). Bequeathed by Mr. Chambers Hall. Previously in the Lawrence, Woodburn, and King of Holland's collections.

companions, who carries a pair of doves, whilst a third female is partly seen at the edge of the picture. But if not in the Fano predella, these two last figures are not the less Perugino's, since they are copied or adapted from the " Sposalizio " of Caen.*

The two men nearest Joseph are the same in the predellas of Fano and the Vatican. The third in Perugino's group, resting his hands on a stick, was not to Raphael's taste. He substituted a man in a cap and pelisse, showing his back and the profile of his cheek. But this, too, is an adaptation of the man nearest the edge of the picture in the " Sposalizio " of Caen.

Raphael here lays himself open to the charge of intellectual theft. But if he copies, he also ennobles. The beautiful trait of the child shrinking from the high priest, the spirit, the expression, and tenderness of Raphael, are all foreign to his master, who could never have conceived, much less have rendered, the half smile of the Virgin, and the busy kindliness of Simeon. Beyond all, the clear and beautiful colour, and the grand effect of the central group thrown into light by the gloom of the niche, surpass in beauty anything that Perugino achieved, though Perugino's

---

* Vatican Gall., No. X. See *antea*. The head of the woman nearest the Virgin is slightly injured and abraded. A careful copy of this picture is in the Palazzo Meniconi at Perugia. Passavant notes another copy on canvas in the Ricci Collection at Rieti (ii. pp. 14–15). Copies of some of the figures are in a predella by Eusebio da San Giorgio in San Francesco of Matelica. Two other copies of the "Presentation," one of them very rude, are in the gallery of Perugia. The best of the two seems painted by Eusebio.

figures might be less affected or less attenuated in frame than those of his disciple. But, after all, is it theft in a young artist to follow the lines and repeat the groups of pictures in which he had himself a share? and what if the commission for the Oddi altar-piece was given to Perugino, who entrusted it to Raphael? Nothing is more probable than that Raphael took part in the execution of the predellas of Fano. The traces of his hand are not easily detected in the panels; but they are visible in one of the cartoons from which the panels were painted. Two of these cartoons are in the Albertina at Vienna; one is the "Marriage of the Virgin," and appears to have been executed by Perugino; the other represents the "Delivery of the Girdle to St. Thomas;"* and Raphael's style of drawing, the type of face which he models into a Virgin or a saint, are easily discoverable in this remarkable sketch, which combines, as no other sketch of the kind has done, his peculiar hatching and outline with the characteristic umber modelling of Perugino. The Virgin sits in a cloud above an undulating landscape. The apostles below are divided into two equal groups of standing men. St. Thomas below kneels to receive the girdle. The feebleness betrayed in extremities, the sameness of movement apparent in the hands, the poorness of draperies taken from lay figures, and a general absence of balance in action might be traced

* Vienna, Albertina. The Sposalizio. m. 0·215 h. by 0·430. Pen and umber, washed with umber and heightened with white. "St. Thomas receiving the Girdle." m. 0·275 h. by 0·455. Pen and bistre, and the figure of St. Thomas washed with umber.

to Raphael, but most distinctive as revealing his presence are the type, outline, and filling, of some figures, and more particularly of those figures which represent the Virgin and St. John. One can only say that if Raphael did not execute this drawing, it was done in the form which his drawing assumed, the form which we recognise as his in perfectly genuine designs of this and earlier periods.*

When Raphael had the will, even now, he was not too modest to exhibit originality. His picture of the "Epiphany" unites the pomp and state of a royal procession, as it was understood by the Umbrians, with all the life and movement and variety of incident which characterizes the Florentines. Impelled by a wish to leave the Umbrian groove, he successfully tried to strike out something novel and complex for himself, and he expanded the old combination of the "Nativity" and "Epiphany" into one composition, with a spirit quite beyond his years. The Virgin seated to the right in front of the pent-house, the Infant Christ on her knees receiving the homage of the kneeling King, St. Joseph attending, and the rest of the Magi with their suite witnessing the ceremony, these are the time-honoured incidents which Raphael had seen a hundred times, and not less happily than cleverly expressed in the "Adoration" of Fiorenzo di Lorenzo at Santa Maria Nuova of Perugia, nor did he hesitate to acknowledge the skill of the old Umbrian in the principal group of the Monarch kneeling before Mary.

---

* We note the same style of drawing in the studies of drapery at Venice marked Frame XXIII. Nos. 4, 7, and 10.

But there is genius in the way in which he gave nature to the *dramatis personæ*, and the contrasts which he drew between the magnificent apparel and state of the kings and their followers, and the humble devotion of the shepherds of Bethlehem. On the knee of the Virgin, who sits in purple on a raised *podium*, the Infant Christ is seated, but His bearing is not that of the Divinity who approves and imparts a blessing. The boy shrinks from the sheen of the gold cup, and turns to his mother's bosom. The king not only presents the gift, but looks as if he would overcome the child's timidity. His bearing is humbled by devotion. The crown lies at his feet near a gold cup which stands on the ground. To the right of the Virgin a kneeling shepherd looks eagerly at the pretty struggle; another leans forward and stretches his neck to catch a sight of the Saviour, and a third, as if dumb-struck, holds his lamb offering. In rear, between the Virgin and the King in genuflexion, St. Joseph rests on his staff, and raises his left hand in wonder, looking round as if surprised by the rich apparel and magnificent attendance of the bearded monarch next him, and his younger companion, a prince of youthful aspect, with all the engaging charms which Raphael knew so well how to convey. Further to the left the horses, led or ridden, are prettily massed in front of a screen of trees which partly conceals the sky and landscape.*

---

* Vatican Gallery, No. X. *u. s.* The whole predella, including the three compositions transferred from panel to canvas, measures m. 1·89 in length.

In the gallery of Copenhagen,

Had no other studies for this predella picture been preserved than the figures of two youths on horseback, or the heads of two young men in hats, which cover sheets of the Venice Sketch-book, we might fancy that Raphael had never left the Umbrian country when he composed the " Epiphany ; " but the profile of an old man, which is cleverly sketched on one of the same sheets, and the profile of the bald shepherd in profile, on another drawing of the Venice collection, reveals the painter's acquaintance with Florentine models, and suggests the question, whether Raphael, even at this period, had not been asked by Perugino to pay a flying visit to the Tuscan capital, where he might see the masterpieces, or at least some drawings of Lionardo da Vinci.*   The whole of this predella, as

---

No. 60, a copy is exhibited, 11½ Danish inches h. by 18¾ in. Wood. Though assigned to Sassoferrato it is gaudy in tone, feeble in perspective, and wanting in feeling.

In the British Museum a drawing of a young king, turned to the right, holding a cup (Payne Knight collection, No. 62), is assigned to Raphael. It does not correspond to the figure of the young king in the Vatican predella, nor is it by Raphael, but by Eusebio da San Giorgio or Tiberio d'Assisi.

In the British Museum likewise is a drawing of the suite in an " Epiphany," with several men on horseback (Payne Knight Collection, No. 163). This design in silver-point, heightened with white, is much injured, and described as a study for the " Adoration of the Magi " at S. Pietro, now Gallery of Perugia. The picture is now attributed to Dono Doni. The drawing is like the foregoing by an Umbrian of the school of Perugino and Pinturicchio, imitating Raphael.

* Venice Acad.   Frame XXVI. No. 4. Back of XXVI. No. 12. Two men on horseback, one turned to the right, the other in full front. Pen drawing. A copy of the right-hand figure in pen and umber is assigned to Raphael in the Teyler Collection at Harlem.   Venice Acad. Frame XXV. No. 4. Back of XXV. No. 18. Two heads of youths, seen at three-quarters, facing each other in hats. That to the left is the seventh head (reversed) from the left side of the Epiphany. On the lower part of

well as the series of sketches which belong to it, bear the stamp of Raphael's art, when he made the drawings for Pinturicchio's frescos in the Library of Sienna, and nothing seems more natural than that having gone so far north of Perugia, he should extend the journey, and satisfy a legitimate curiosity by visiting Florence. But apart from this, it is of interest to note the coincidences which occur in the "Epiphany" and Raphael's Siennese designs.

The led horses are similar in character and build in the "Epiphany," the Venice Sketch-book, and the "Bridal Meeting," in Casa Baldeschi at Perugia.*

The young attendant, with his hand on his hip, and his back to the spectator in the "Epiphany," is much in the same action and attitude as the man leaning on a stick in the foreground of the "Coronation of Æneas Sylvius," at Sienna.

The kneeling King and the soldier, with a partisan, in the "Epiphany," are quite in the spirit of the Emperor and guards in the Baldeschi drawing. The latter at the same time recalls the figures of Signorelli in the neighbouring monastery of Mont' Oliveto.

The Cartoon for the "Epiphany" in the Gallery at Stockholm, though shorn of a portion of the left

---

the sheet to the right of the study of an apostle for the "Coronation," is a profile to the left of an old man, wearing a cap, which quite suggests the study of Lionardo. The head of the bald shepherd, also very Lionardesque, is in the Venice Acad., Frame XXXV. No. 2—a drawing 0·23 h. by 0·17, not belonging to the Sketch-book.

* See previous note.

side of the composition, is drawn in the same style as
the sketches for the Library at Sienna.*

* Stockholm Museum. Royal
folio. Sketched with point, then
finished with the pen, pricked for
use. The three horses and two
riders on the left side of the picture are not in this sketch.

In the Palazzo Donnini at Perugia a small cartoon of the whole
composition challenges attention,
but has suggested to some critics
serious doubts as to its originality.

CHAPTER IV.

The "Sposalizio" of Milan based on Perugino's predella at Fano and his "Sposalizio" at Caen.—Raphael as an architect.—Bramante.—"Madonna" Connestabile.—Portrait of Herrenhausen.—Pinturicchio at Sienna and his relations to Raphael.—Drawings for Pinturicchio's frescos; sketches for the same.—Design of the "Graces."—Eusebio da San Giorgio.—Guidubaldo, captain of the church.—Raphael's sketches of the palace and fort of Urbino ;—of other places in the Duchy.—His patrons at Urbino.—Alleged recommendation to Soderini at Florence.—Florentine influences on Raphael's style.—The "Knight's Vision."—"Cain and Abel."—"St. Michael" and "St. George."—The "Graces," and "Marsyas and Apollo."—Michael Angelo and Da Vinci.—Raphael's journey to Florence.

PREVIOUS to the completion of the predellas of the Vatican, previous, therefore, to Raphael's probable visit to Florence, the "Sposalizio" was exhibited in San Francesco of Città di Castello, for which it was originally intended, and on the portal of the temple in the background of the picture the painter himself inscribed the words: "Raphael Urbinas, MDIIII."

According to Vasari, Raphael had ceased at this period to imitate, in order to refine on, the manner of Perugino.* In the spring of 1504 he came of age, and the time arrived when he might fully assert himself, and show of what wood he was shaped. The display which he makes in the "Sposalizio" truly reveals a capacity for refinement, but coincident with

---

* Vas. viii. pp. 3 and 4.

that an absolute disinclination to forget the lessons of
Perugino. It would be difficult indeed to name a
single picture in which Raphael more thoroughly put
his master under contribution than the " Sposalizio."
Too independent to give way to the mere impulse of
copying, it was not his will to affect originality if
observation convinced him that existing models could
be used for his purpose. He therefore took from the
" Sposalizios" of Caen and of Fano, the genesis of which
he had seen, the shell of a new composition ; and the
charm which his masterpiece produced is attributable
alike to refinement and imitation, to which he added
his own peculiar gift of subtle and delicate grace.

The " Sposalizio " of Milan has a threefold interest :
first, as illustrating the political event of the theft of
the ring at Sienna ; next, as showing the religious importance of the sacrament of marriage ; and last, as displaying the peculiar form of Raphael's talent in 1504.
The centre of attraction in the composition is the ring
which Joseph presents to Mary. Subordinate to that
is the shape of the temple, which fitly represents the
majesty of Rome. The skill with which the whole is
put together clearly manifests the genius of Raphael.

The ceremony is performed in the court fronting
the church, where the High Priest, in state dress,
unites the Virgin and St. Joseph. A striking resemblance shows the connection of this group with that
of Raphael's own in the " Presentation " of the Vatican predella. At a distance a decent sprinkling
of spectators look on. The scheme of distribution
is that of Perugino in the " Sposalizio " of Caen,

except that Raphael, in defiance of tradition, places the males to the right and the females to the left of the officiating priest. It differs from that of Perugino at Fano so far that the bridal pair is united under the canopy of heaven, and not at the altar. Raphael, in fact, takes the scenery from the altar-piece of Cacu, and the grouping from the predella of Fano, and with subtle gallantry he gives the place of honour to the fair sex.

Nothing can be more graceful than the attitude and action of the priest in the Milan altar-piece, who by taking the wrists of each of the couple, brings the fingers of Joseph in contact with those of Mary. His fine bearded face is gently inclined, his eyes are directed to the ring, and his whole being is wrapt in the duty which he is performing. Mary, almost as tall as Joseph, looks bashfully down. The veil which covers her head winds round her shoulders, and forms a knot on her bosom. Her mantle is raised by a pretty movement from the ground. Joseph, bashful too, though past the meridian of years, stands in one of those artificial attitudes of which Perugino was so fond. He carries the flowering wand, and, near him, the disappointed suitor angrily breaks the barren one across his knee. Various moods of jealousy and displeasure are depicted in the faces of the remaining company. The noblest of the bridesmaids—a girl at the Virgin's side—recalls the grand creations of Lionardo. Her figure and face beautifully express sympathy and friendship, and do so with singular distinction. The women near her look variously at the spectator or at the ceremony. They are all magnificently dressed in veils and cloths, according as youth allows them to indulge, or age forbids them to assume youthful fashions. Compared with the bridesmaids of Perugino, they seem made of purer clay than the rest of mankind. They tell of a very early acquaintance in Raphael with ladies of a high social sphere. The men, on the other hand, are comparatively feeble. Yet if we admit a certain affectedness of movement and attitude, combined with lack of manliness—if the heads are too small, the frames too long, the faces too regular, and the knees and feet too large, something winning still remains in the gentleness which everyone concerned displays. Tallness and slenderness are not unpleasantly exaggerated; drapery is becomingly set, and not without advantage to the shapes which it adorns. Flesh of good modelling, and fair, if not searching burnish is carefully balanced in light and shade of moderate contrast; and a great sweetness comes from the mellow enamel tones of the faces and the bright tints of dress, adorned with delicate gilding. Yet, after all has been said to interpret the charm of the " Sposalizio," experience will temper praise with the thought that Raphael is only adapting, though ennobling, the conceptions of his master. If the outlines of the predella of Fano, or the cartoon for it in the Albertina at Vienna, could be seen in a mirror, the " Sposalizio " of Milan would be found, and with it replicas, slightly varied, of four of the most important figures in Perugino's masterpiece.

In the process of inversion which Raphael himself

applied, a natural difficulty arose from the necessity
of altering the movements of the arms and hands in
the principal personages.   In the ordinary course the
bridegroom gives the ring, and the bride receives it,
with the right hand.   If a figure in action is inverted,
it becomes left-handed.   To restore the balance the
arms and hands must be changed.   Raphael accomplished this with graceful ease in his rendering of the
" Virgin," but he did not make the trial in respect of the
bridegroom.   Perugino's conception of " Joseph " at
Fano, is weak.   It shows the head in profile, and the
loins and shoulders from behind.   A quick stride has
brought him to the altar, whilst the priest with solemn
measure, holds Mary's elbow and gives the blessing,
with uplifted hand.   Raphael had seen the advantage
of changing the action and air of the clerk.   He also felt
the necessity of recasting that of the bridegroom.   But
instead of trusting to his own creative powers, he fell
back on Perugino.   The best man with the flowering
wand, and the suitor next him breaking the barren
rod, were taken from the predella of Fano, and set in
reverse in the "Sposalizio" of Milan, and the best man
now became Joseph himself.   But the result was so far
unfortunate, that undue prominence was given to the
disappointed suitor, whose action had been judiciously
thrown into the background in the "Sposalizio" of Caen.

There is no evidence that Perugino or Raphael
were architects in the true sense of the word, but like
most men of their profession, in central Italy, they
perfectly understood perspective, and the broad rules
of architectural structure.   They were both equally

fond of decorating their pictures with buildings and landscapes. But Perugino and Raphael started from different goals. The first acquired from the Florentines the traditions of Brunelleschi, the second was guided, we should think, by the lessons of Bramante. When Perugino was asked to illustrate the triumph of the Church in the "Delivery of the Keys" at the Sixtine, he copied the "Baptistery" of Florence, to which he added a domed roof and Tuscan porches. In the "Sposalizio" of Caen, he planned an octagon with domed porticos. Raphael, who had followed his master in so many other things, broke from him in the matter of architecture. He doubled the octagon into a sixteen-sided polygon, which he fringed with a sixteen-sided colonnade, and covered with a low cupola. His design is more florid, his taste less pure than that of his master. Little is known of Raphael's relations with Bramante. But it is highly probable that they began early, since Vasari tells us that it was Bramante's interest which pushed the fortunes of his kinsman at the papal court. The church in the "Sposalizio" at Milan, recalls that which Bramante built in 1502, in the court of San Pietro in Montorio, at Rome. It embodies reminiscences of the temple of Neptune, which has been preserved in effigy in the plates of Bartoli. Bramante alone could have managed so complete a combination of both edifices as Raphael's masterpiece presents.* If there be a fault in Raphael's

* The Tempietto of Bramante was built in the court of San Pietro in Montorio in 1502. The Temple of Neptune is given with other sacred buildings of the same character in Santi Bartoli's Liber Romanæ Magnitudinis, fol. Rome, 1699.

conception of the distance for the "Sposalizio," it is that the centre of vision is too high above the heads of the figures in the foreground. The buildings and *dramatis personæ* are seen from different points. But the landscape at the edge of the temple is lovely. In the plain to the left, a man rides away, perhaps with the news of the wedding. A church, a domed tower and spire nestle in the slope of a wooded hill, backed by higher and more distant ridges. To the right the spurs of bare and wooded declivities give outlines of great beauty.*

* Milan, Brera. No. 35. Panel arched at top. M. 1·69 h. by 1·14. Till June 28, 1798, the picture remained in S. Francesco of Città di Castello, for which it was executed, and where Vasari had seen it (viii. p. 4, and Pungileone's Raphael, p. 282). It was given up by the municipal authorities to General Giuseppe Lecchi at the above date, he being in command of a French brigade in the town at the time. Lecchi sold it, December 9, 1801, to Giacomo Sannazaro of Milan, from whom the Hospital of Milan inherited it on June 8, 1804. On the 8th of March, 1806, a viceregal decree ordered the purchase of it for the State, at the price of 53,000 fr. On the cornice of the temple, above the entrance, are the words "RAPHAEL VRBINAS," and in the spandrels below "MDIIII." The picture was restored at Milan by Mr. Molteni, who flattened the battens, and stopped the wormholes with quicksilver. But the cleaning to which he or earlier restorers subjected the panel injured the patina of the picture and threw the colours out of focus. The most discoloured part is the flagged pavement behind the principal figures. A copy of the "Sposalizio," signed "RAPHAEL INVENTOR," by Andrea Urbani, is in the sacristy of San Giuseppe at Urbino (An. 1506). Another copy is said to exist in the Augustinian convent at Città di Castello.

Amongst the drawings of the Venice Sketch-book, which Raphael probably had before him at the time of the "Sposalizio," is one containing four heads, copied from originals which Perugino had used for the "Sposalizio" of Caen. (Ven. Acad. Frame XXIII. No. 6.) One of these heads at the bottom of the sheet to the left is very like the girl immediately behind the Virgin. In another sheet of the same collection (Ven. Acad. Frame XXV. No. 2), a head of a woman with light frizzled hair, resembles the girl at the left side of the "Sposa-

Almost contemporary with the "Spozalizio," the "Madonna" Connestabile, its rival in fame, was completed by Raphael for one of his Perugian friends.

Nothing has been more admired than the subtle diversity with which Raphael repeats a single theme in endless varieties. It is hardly possible to describe in a manageable compass the least complex of them. In the very earliest of his days, Raphael had embodied

lizio." Passavant assigns to Raphael and describes as a study for the Virgin of the "Sposalizio," a female head in black chalk, with a slight turn to the left, No. 675 in the Museum of Lille. But the drawing is not genuine in the first place, and in the second the movement of the head is not that of the Virgin at Milan. The style of the drawing justifies its being assigned to Timoteo Viti, its character being Lionardesque and Florentine. Another drawing in the Lille collection, No. 680, represents a female with tresses escaping from a striped cap, looking to the right, at three-quarters. This fine silver-point head (m. 0·30 h. by 0·22), approximates somewhat to that of the girl immediately behind the Virgin. It is a genuine Raphael drawing, yet seems to have been executed at Florence, and therefore after the "Sposalizio." A study of heads and figures in the Academy of Düsseldorf, ascribed to Raphael, and mentioned by Passavant, ii. No. 285, as work of Raphael at the time of the "Sposalizio," leaves the impression upon us of work by Perugino for the "Sposalizio" of Caen. Similarly we should

notice a bust of a youth in a fanciful hat, black chalk drawing on grey paper, once in the Wellesley collection at Oxford, which recalls the figure of a suitor in the "Sposalizio" of Milan, who breaks the rod. This drawing now belongs to Mr. Locker, is 0·10 h. by 0·22, and seems the work of a Peruginesque, but not of Raphael. On the other hand, we notice in the Oxford collection, No. 36, a study of a head with curly locks, turned three-quarters to the left, and to the left of the head a study of a hand. The head is very like those of the "Sposalizio;" the hand likewise, though not exactly traceable to that picture. But this part of the drawing has been altered for the worse in the finishing, the first and third fingers being better in the silver-point line which underlies the pen contour. The shadows of the hand are washed with umber, which is not the case with the hand. From the Antaldi and Lawrence collections. 8¾ in. h. by 9⅜. A profile of the Virgin's head for the "Sposalizio" of Caen, is properly assigned to Perugino in the Museum of Caen.

the idea of prayer in the Virgin reading a book. Later on he rang surprising changes on this chord. Sometimes the infant Christ was conceived playing with a bird or picking at a pomegranate, yet invited to look at the pages of the book. He might be fancied watching the gambols of the boy Baptist, yet the prayer-book was his companion on the Virgin's knee.

Another form is that of the infant Saviour looking at an apple which the Virgin holds, whilst the babe in her arms unconsciously plays with it. In course of time, Raphael had portfolios of designs with varieties of this kind, and as the practice of his master had taught him, so his own now told him to fashion the thought of a morning into a picture, or put it by for subsequent use, reviving, years after, that which had first struck him whilst transfusing into the subject all the charm of increased power and advanced technical skill. Sometimes again he began by embodying in a picture an idea which he afterwards abandoned or transformed; and of this kind the "Madonna" Connestabile, one of the most lovely of his early pieces, is an example. The cartoon for this Madonna in the Berlin Museum is quite a youthful Peruginesque creation. It represents the Virgin standing in a landscape with a mantle drawn over a veil that covers her hair and forehead. On her left hand the naked infant Christ is resting, whilst her right holds the apple with which he is playing. A touching dependence on Perugino is still displayed in the form and fold of the drapery, but the purity of the outlines, the graceful oblong face, the tender and melancholy expression are all truly Raphaelesque.* When the subject was transferred to panel, Raphael merely ran the graver over the lines, and the Connestabile "Madonna" passed into existence. Yet after the transcript had been made, something occurred to alter the master's purpose, and the infant playing with the fruit was now imagined looking at the leaves of a missal. The picture not the less became a charming and delightful one to look at. It is one of the purest, most delicate little pieces of workmanship that can be conceived, exquisitely handled, of the sweetest tone and softest modelling. Full of feeling in expression and in line, the pretty group of Mother and Child is set in a landscape so clear and bright with all its minuteness, that it is hardly possible to think that a higher degree of perfection could be allied to such smallness of proportions.† What led Raphael to substitute the missal

---

* Berlin Mus. Pen and umber drawing, with traces at the bottom of Raphael's intention to compose a round. About the infant Christ's head is a line halo and traces of a similar one are round the Virgin's head. A few lines to the left indicate a distance of hills and trees. At the back of the sheet (a brownish white paper) is the original drawing for the " Madonna " di Terranuova. The drapery fold is given quite conventionally with perforations for the eyes of the folds. The stuff too is double. The drawing once belonged to Don José Madrazo at Madrid. It is of the same size as the picture, and measures m. 0·155 h. by 0·120.

† Petersburg, Imperial Palace. The picture was sold by Count Scipione Connestabile of Perugia, on the 21st of April, 1871, to the Empress of Russia for 330,000 fr. The picture is a round, in a square of m. 0·160, the panel being all of one piece with the frame, which was carved before the round was painted, and the corners were ornamented with a yellow meander on blue ground. When the picture was transferred to canvas at Petersburg, the damage threatened by a vertical crack running down the neck and bosom of the Virgin was averted. As the picture has been withdrawn from public gaze, it may be well to describe some

for the apple, is hard to say. For the final shape which the composition took, he had a model in the very hospital of the Misericordia, in which the painting room of Perugino was situated. There, in a more archaic form, the Virgin may be seen holding the book, and the child in her arms turning the leaves, and the scene is laid in a landscape of valley and hills. All that was required to improve on this picture was to preserve the composition, but correct its outlines. If the Virgin was overweighted and heavy in head, the child puny in frame ; if the drawing was incorrect and the figures were ill-proportioned, all that Raphael required was to search out the contours and restore the lost balance of the lines. Tradition suggests, that, if he did so he was merely revising his own work, for both versions of the Virgin with the book are assigned to the same hand. Yet this much only is certain,

---

parts of it which may otherwise escape attention. The landscape distance to the left shows a pretty tree growing on a rising ground, near a road, on which a man rides a white horse. To the right the distant hills are capped with snow, a rare sight in Italian pictures, and a boat swims on the waters of a lake. The substitution of the book for the apple was discovered when the picture was taken off the panel, and the original outline of the hand and the apple was found. The background to the left is a little abraded. From records published by Professor Adamo Rossi, it would appear that the picture originally belonged to

Alfano di Diamante, uncle of Raphael's friend, Domenico di Paris Alfani, from whom it descended at last to the collateral branch of Connestabile Staffa. See Giornale di Erud. Artistica, vol. vi. pp. 322–336.

Of several copies noticed by Passavant, one in the Casa Oggione at Milan is old and therefore valuable as being almost of the time of the original ; another, on copper, in the Penna Palace at Perugia, is careful but more recent, others have been described in Casa Baglioni at Perugia, in possession of Alex. von Humboldt, in Granada Cathedral (Spain), &c., &c.

that the Connestabile "Madonna" is justly acknowledged as a genuine and almost priceless masterpiece,
whilst its counterpart of the "Misericordia," now in the
gallery of Perugia, can at best but claim to be one of
the feeblest attempts of Raphael's tenderest youth.*

If the mental struggles of these days and their outcome in artistic work could be realized, we should
probably find that about this period Raphael also
designed a picture of the "Virgin and Child" with
the book, which fills a sheet in the Albertina at Vienna.
Christ's mother with her hand on the open missal
stands behind a parapet on which the book is resting.
The naked cross-legged child sits on a cushion before
her and picks at the pomegranate which she offers to
him.   A muslin veil, over which a mantle is thrown,
enframes a face of a long and graceful oval, the eyes of
which are lovingly cast down; simple lines of hills and
bushy trees suggest a landscape distance.   Peruginesque in Raphael's later Perugian form the drawing
is finished, and ready for transfer to a panel, and yet
seems never to have been used for any practical
purpose whatever.†

---

* Perugia Gallery. Wood. From
the hospital of the Misericordia.
The figures are one-third of life
size.   The outlines are wiry.   The
colour a little dry and hard.   The
blue cloak has turned to black,
and the surface generally has been
injured by restoring.   The large
heavy form of the Virgin's head
and the disproportionate smallness
of the infant Christ remind us of
the work of Eusebio da S. Giorgio.

There is some difference between
this and the Connestabile "Madonna" in the position of the
child's arms and legs.   The latter
are crossed, the former both busy
with the book.   Size, m. 0·575 h.
by 0·470.   But compare Pass. ii.
p. 16.

† Vienna, Albertina.   Black
chalk drawing, half length. m. 0·39
h. by 0·29.   From the collection of
Julian of Parma and Prince de

The same period which gave Raphael claims to public admiration for these and other pictures of devotion, witnessed his first attempt as a painter of portraits. His likeness of a man of middle age now in the Herrenhausen collection at Hanover has not extorted praise from critics of many generations, since it remained till now in comparative obscurity,* yet it deserves attention as a proof that the talents of the master were equal even now to every form of delineation. The man who sat was about fifty years of age. His head is covered with a wide soft hat, from which long and abundant hair escapes. A sallow, beardless face, with a regular nose and mouth, and prominent cheek-bone, and small eyes closely set against the barrel of the nose, are characteristic features, which to some extent recall the self-made likeness of Pinturicchio in the frescos of the church of Spello. If to these we add a heavy neck and drooping shoulders suggestive of a certain ungainliness, we have the picture of an Umbrian of Raphael's early time. The great firmness with which the forms are defined and

---

Ligne. The heads of "Virgin and Child" are turned to the left. The legs of the Infant are crossed. A tear in the paper at the level of the Virgin's shoulders disfigures the drawing.

* Hanover. Haussmann collection. Now at the Palace of Herrenhausen. No. 7. Wood. m. 0·55 h. by 0·41. Bust of a man, three-quarters to the left, in a black cap and long hair and black coat, closed at the neck, where the edge of a white shirt appears. This picture was long assigned to Giovanni Bellini, but is now properly called Raphael. It has suffered from cleaning and restoring, and the hair has been brought into curls, which possibly did not exist before. The right hand, which is half seen, holds a scrap of paper. The background is a dark blue grey. A vertical split runs down the picture to the left of the face.

modelled, the wheaten tone merging into white in the
lights and dying into liquid brown on the shadows, are
all distinctive marks of Raphael's hand at the time of
the " Sposalizio."

In summing up the evidence which Raphael's pictures afford, we found that a study of the "Sposalizio"
and the predellas of the " Coronation " of the Vatican
favoured the belief that they were executed about the
same time. The comparison of all these pieces with
Perugino's predellas at Fano, manifested Raphael's
continued dependence on the models of his master.
But we also saw that between the " Epiphany " of the
Vatican and the studies which Raphael made for
Pinturicchio's frescos in the library of Sienna, there
was a remarkable coincidence of matter as well as of
manner. The questions which upon this immediately
arise, are whether Raphael's visit to Sienna, which this
coincidence suggests, was short and casual, or protracted and planned.

We must remember that as far back as June, 1502,
Pinturicchio had covenanted with Cardinal Piccolomini
to decorate the library at Sienna with frescos, that he
had received a sum of money in advance to return to
Perugia, and that after engaging the necessary assistants he had settled at Sienna, where according to
all probability he painted the ceiling of the library in
1503, and began the frescos of the walls in the autumn
of 1504. Vasari says that one of Pinturicchio's assistants was Raphael, who went with his friend to Sienna,
and then made sketches and designs and drew cartoons for the frescos. In confirmation of this state-

ment some evidence historical and circumstantial may
be adduced, and yet an opinion seems to be widely
held that Raphael never laboured at Sienna and never
assisted Pinturicchio at all.

Strangely enough the grounds for this opinion are
chiefly derived from the text of Vasari himself, who,
speaking of Raphael's work at Sienna, variously
asserts :—

I. That he made all the sketches and cartoons;

II. That he made the cartoons from the sketches;

III. That he made some of the designs and cartoons
for the library frescos.

To these statements which attribute the sketches, the
designs, and the cartoons of the Sienna library to
Raphael, some historians demur because they exclude the
designs of the Piccolomini frescos from the catalogue
of Raphael's works; others again demur because
Pinturicchio's contract with Cardinal Francesco
Piccolomini contains a clause in which he pledges
himself to make all the designs of the stories with his
own hand in cartoons and on the wall; and it is
thought that Pinturicchio's covenant and Vasari's
statements can only be reconciled by a moral condem-
nation of Pinturicchio. Vasari defines a sketch as a
first slight drawing hastily put together to
determine the movement and general form of a composition. He says that a "design" is a clean and
finished version of the sketch, and a "cartoon"
an enlargement of the design.* Had Raphael exe-

---

* Vas. i. 154.

cuted all three, the labour of Pinturicchio would have been confined to the painting of the subjects on the wall, but it is not necessary to take Vasari's statements as correct to the letter. His interpretation of artistic words is at times extremely loose, and he frequently confounds under the general name of sketches and designs, the slightest scratchings of a pencil, and elaborate studies or drawings for whole compositions. Some of the finished designs for the Piccolomini frescos have been preserved, and with these a number of studies for groups or single figures; and there is no denying that these are works of Raphael's hand, but it has not been possible to discover the original sketches or the cartoons; and in the absence of these we shall charitably believe that Vasari's lines and Pinturicchio's contract are reconcileable, and assent to the proposition that Pinturicchio was only bound to furnish the rough drafts which Raphael afterwards worked off into finished drawings with the help of occasional appeals to nature.*   It would be difficult to find anything more interesting in connection with Raphael's life than the designs for the three principal compositions at Florence, Perugia, and Chatsworth, or

---

* It may be also that the contract between Pinturicchio and Cardinal F. Piccolomini, which declared that the former was bound to make all the "designs of the stories with his own hand," lapsed at the death of the latter, and that a subsequent contract did not contain that clause. One of the conditions of the contract besides the foregoing was that Pinturicchio was not to paint frescos or altar-pieces anywhere so as to delay the completion of the library. Yet it is certain that after the signature of the covenant and before the completion of the library he painted the chapel of St. John at Sienna. See the contract, *u. s.* Doc. Sen. iii. 9.

the studies for separate groups and figures in the galleries of Florence, Oxford, and Venice; and it is important as confirmatory of Vasari's statement to note, not only that all the sheets bear marks of Raphael's style in air, outline and shading, but that the legend and the names of men and places in one of them are in Raphael's handwriting, whilst the background contains a view of the towers of Urbino, which it is quite improbable that Pinturicchio should either have seen or sketched.

It is hardly necessary to add that the frescos of the Piccolomini Library were intended to perpetuate in colours certain important incidents in the life of Æneas Sylvius, who ascended the papal throne in 1458. Pinturicchio received the subjects from Cardinal Francesco Piccolomini when that prelate made the contract with him, a few months before his promotion to the chair of St. Peter.* The most important drawing which Raphael made for the series is a finished sheet at the Uffizi, squared for transfer to a cartoon, on which the following legend in the painter's hand is inscribed.

"The story is this, that Messer Enea was in the suite of Messer Domenico da Capranica, who had been made a cardinal, though his election had not been published, when he went to Bâle to the council, and having embarked at the port of Talamone, and being about to enter the port of Genoa, he was caught by a tempest and driven to the mouth of the Tiber."†

---

* See contract in Documenti Senesi, *u. s.* iii. p. 9.

† Talamone was the port of Sienna.

Raphael's conception of this subject is a cavalcade of cardinals and officials, with mounted servants and runners on a rising ground near the sea shore. Behind a grove of trees to the right is the entrance to a port, with long wooden piers defended by two high battlemented towers. On a promontory beyond lies a town, and bounding the horizon to the left a string of islands; vessels are sailing in the offing; and a large galley lies at moorings by the nearest pier, upon which a busy troup of porters is carrying luggage. On the sky above the islands Raphael wrote the words " Sardinia " and " Corsicha." The town to the right, over which a storm cloud lingers, is " Genova," and on the nearest tower the word " Talamone " is inscribed. But the whole scene is imaginary, and the towers at the entrance to the port are those which still overlook the Castle of Urbino.

Domenico da Capranica, distinguished from the crowd of cardinals by the inscription of his name and the absence of the cardinal's hat, " because his election had not been published," rides to the right an ambling palfrey led by a liveried servant, whilst two armed runners head the escort on each side. In rear is a cardinal ; in front a youth in a plumed hat heads the cardinal's suite, behind which a group of prelates and followers is closed by a young bareheaded captain on a prancing charger.*

---

* Florence, Uffizi. Frame 143, No. 520. Pen, bistre and white drawing.   26 in. h. by 15½, arched at top and squared for transfer to the cartoon.   Much stained, torn and pieced.   Passavant falsely read *Libia* for Tiber. See Raphael, ii. p. 222.

The masterly execution of this composition, with its clever contrasts of light and shade, umber washes, and flake-white hatchings, shows with what care Pinturicchio had selected his assistant. Yet when it came to his turn to transfer the design to the wall,—for that duty was not performed by Raphael,—he made the most unfortunate changes in its arrangement, bringing the party nearer to the water side, expunging the piers, substituting Sienna for Urbino, and imagining a storm cloud discharging its showers by the light of a rainbow on the roads of Genoa. His gaudy style hardened the elegant creation of his pupil into an artificial composition which jarred the more, as that which Raphael had brought to completion, was already less spirited and bold than his own original study for the picture. When we contemplate the fresco of Pinturicchio, the design of his disciple and the study at the Uffizi on which the design was based, we observe that they all depend on each other. The study is slighter and more rapidly executed than its companion drawing in the same collection, but it only displays the more life and spirit on that account. It deals with the escort and not with the cardinals, but the escort is in rapid motion, cantering and showing the paces of its horses, and displaying its helmets and plumes. One of the runners, all but naked, races, with dishevelled hair, and ready shield, to the front; near him, the youth on the prancing charger. The difference between the study and the finished design lies in the more instantaneous action which characterises the first, and the staidness which marks the second. Both equally bear the impress of Raphael's hand, but the study more than the design, betrays that elementary knowledge of equine delineation which already marks a similar outline for the " Epiphany " of the Vatican in the sketch-book of Venice.*

The second design at Chatsworth represents Æneas kissing the foot of Eugenius the IVth, before a large company of prelates and cardinals, whilst in the distance to the left, the consecration of Æneas to the bishopric of Sienna is depicted. More remarkable for careful balance and symmetry than for any exceptional graces, this composition shows the Pope in a marble chair under a canopy of stone, extending his slippered foot to be kissed by the kneeling churchman in front of him, whilst the prelates at the sides are standing near the pontiff, and the stalls in front of the throne are occupied by the Sacred College. The tesselated floor, the nave and aisles, the pillars and archings, through which we see on the one hand the Pope give the mitre ; on the other a landscape in the foreground of which spectators are grouped,—all this reminds us greatly of the " Annunciation " designed by Raphael for the predella of the Vatican, recalls not only the form of architecture pictured in that composition, but its simplicity of outline, and its delicacy in the rendering of drapery and extremities,

---

* Uffizi. Frame 153. No. 537. Pen and umber drawing with five figures on horseback and one on foot ; on the back a male figure, a head of a child, and a lion. This drawing strangely enough escaped the attention of Passavant.

and a feeling of youthfulness in the features and
expression of the *dramatis personæ.*[*]   But here, too,
as in the cavalcade, the finished design was not
brought to perfection without elaborate studies; and
the fine group of four cardinals, a silver-point drawing
in the Malcolm Collection, in Raphael's most finished
early style, reveals the trouble which was taken in
preparing the materials for the Piccolomini frescos.[†]

The third design in the Baldeschi Collection at
Perugia is the meeting of the Emperor Frederick
with Eleanor of Portugal, where not only a charming
display is made of the Emperor taking the hand of
his bride, as she stops before him, and Æneas as the
best friend of both appears to unite and encourage
them; but a fine distribution of courtiers and dames
adds to the splendour of the occasion.   The scene is
made still more imposing by the addition of knights
on their chargers and men-at-arms drawn up at the
sides of a pillar, intended to carry the scutcheons of
the Kaiser and his bride.   In rear of this courtly
array, Raphael gives a view of a distance in the
neighbourhood of Perugia, which is not in accord
with history.[‡]   The legend and the necessities of the
subject required, that he should set the scene in the

---

[*] Chatsworth Collection.   Pen
and umber drawing, shaded with
sepia.

[†] Malcolm Collection, from the
collection of Dr. Wellesley at Oxford.   Silver-point drawing of four
seated full length figures of
cardinals in a row, and turned to
the left.   Size 8⅝ in. h. by 5⅝.

[‡] Casa Baldeschi at Perugia.
Pen, bistre and white.   21 in. h.
by 15.   Inscribed in Raphael's
hand, with the words " Questa e
la quinta," and in almost illegible
letters, " di papa pio."   The drawing is folded in four places and
much torn and ill repaired.

suburbs facing the Camollia gate at Sienna, and Pinturicchio has repaired the omission in the fresco by introducing the gate and some of the square towers of the city behind it.

But these three designs were evidently not the whole of those which Raphael delivered for the occasion. There are studies of men-at-arms which appear to have been used for the composition of the meeting of the Emperor and princess Eleanor, and at the same time for another subject. In one of the frescos, Æneas is shown at the court of the Emperor kneeling to receive the poet's crown, which it was the privilege of the monarch in those days to confer. Here again the artist has imagined a royal pageant. The great officers of the crown, the knights, the men-at-arms, and pages stand around as the Emperor on his throne holds the laurel wreath above the head of the kneeling Æneas. The studies of three of the guards, with halberts and caps, and one chamberlain, with the stick of office, by Raphael in the Oxford Collection, though not reproduced with absolute fidelity in Pinturicchio's fresco, were evidently outlines made from models for the drawing which once existed of this beautiful composition.*

One peculiarity deserves mention in respect of all

---

* Oxford Museum. No. 14. Four standing figures. Silverpoint on slate-coloured ground. 8¾ in. h. by 9 in. From the Ottley and Lawrence collections. A drawing much in the spirit of this one but of six heads in various positions, is in the Venice sketch-book. No. XXV. 10. A pen drawing, at the bottom of which are the front face and profile of a child.

these preliminary works, which is, that none of them absolutely reveal the presence of the artist at Sienna. The very existence of so many studies from models in the day dress of the Perugian people, the absence of any feature peculiar to Sienna, the towers of Urbino in one design, the lake country of Perugia in another, all this might show, that Raphael's preparations for Pinturicchio's frescos in the Piccolomini library were made at a distance from the place of their destination; and this might appear all the more credible because the form in which Raphael draws, the feeling which pervades his compositions, and the Peruginesque dryness which his outline displays, all point to Perugian influences, as much as the fact, that some of the studies for the Piccolomini designs are interchangeable with those for the predella of the Vatican.* And yet there is some evidence that Raphael and Pinturicchio were at Sienna together in these days, since one of the drawings in the Venice sketch-book shows that at a very early time, and probably about 1504, he had occasion to notice a masterpiece which could only then have been seen at Sienna. The celebrated group of the "Graces," which Cardinal Francesco Piccolomini once put up in his palace at Rome, had been taken to the cathedral of Sienna, preparatory to its exhibition in the library, and there it was copied by Raphael and admired by Vasari.† In respect of Raphael's drawing, as well as in respect of others

---

* See this point explained in Hist. of Italian Painting, iii. . . . Romæ, Lib. iii. p. 14; Faluschi, Guida di Siena, 1784, p. 17;

† See Albertini, De Mirabilibus Vas. v. p. 267.

equally genuine, doubts have been expressed whether Raphael really produced it or not; yet it would be difficult to point to any study more characteristic of his style in the Peruginesque days, and we can only suppose that the doubts which have been expressed were suggested by the damage done to a drawing injured by neglect and the efflux of time. The tendency of Raphael to give Umbrian character and Peruginesque contour to form, even when copied from different masters, naturally showed itself in studying from the antique. There stood before him a piece of sculpture apparently copied by some Roman craftsman from a masterpiece of the Greek time. The group was in a mutilated state, the head of the central figure was gone, one of its legs broken below the knee, the arms of all three were ruptured at the shoulder. The spare classic shapes, suggestive of extreme youth, Raphael copied with their mutilations; but his want of experience of the antique, his tendency to reduce everything to the Umbrian standard, led him to give more fulness and rounding to the forms, and more realism to the parts, than a true copy required; and when he came at a later period to paint a picture of the " Graces," he still retained the belief that more nature and realism were required than he had seen in masterpieces of ancient art.* But it seems doubtful

---

* Venice Acad. Frame XXVI. No. 18. Back of XXVI. No. 8. This drawing in pen and umber is a copy of two of the " Graces " at Sienna, viz., the central one with her back to the spectator, and her left leg broken, and that seen in front to the left. In the original group, now removed to the Sienna Academy, the central Grace has

whether he would have thought of such a subject as the "Graces," had he not previously seen and copied the group in the cathedral of Sienna: and this, in conjunction with the Venice drawing, and the picture in London, warrants the belief that Raphael really did visit Sienna at the period mentioned by Vasari.

Still the mere copy of a couple of figures from an antique in the cathedral of Sienna would not of itself establish more than a stay of a few hours in that city; and Raphael might have made the journey for the sole purpose of delivering to Pinturicchio the designs of the Piccolomini frescos. But his name is traditionally connected with commissions which Pinturicchio had to execute at Sienna; and this, again, presupposes a stay of the two masters in company. When Pius III. died, in 1503, the decoration of the Piccolomini library was interrupted, and Pinturicchio painted the chapel of St. John in the cathedral, and altarpieces for the Piccolomini and Sergardi chapels in San Francesco, of Sienna. There is a tradition—and some historians say a record—to prove that Raphael designed the predella of Pinturicchio's "Nativity" in the Sergardi chapel, and various studies by Raphael in the Oxford collection seem intended for a predella

lost the left arm, but a fragment of it and the hand on the shoulder of the Grace to the left remain. Raphael's sketch only indicates the place of the arm, the hand is omitted. The sheet is injured and discoloured, the lines and modelling being much enfeebled. But Professor Springer's opinion that much good will is required to acknowledge the genuineness of the drawing is to us incomprehensible. The line, the modelling, and hatching are all Raphael's. Compare A. Springer's Raphael and Michaelangelo, fol. 1877, p. 88.

of this period.* But as tradition alone survives, whilst the pictures and records have perished, the point remains in doubt, and will probably continue to baffle investigation. Something, however, might still be told to confirm the companionship of Raphael and Pinturicchio at Sienna in 1504, if we could identify the Herrenhausen portrait, described in an earlier page, as that of Pinturicchio in his fiftieth year. Meanwhile it should be remembered that, however much the relations between Raphael and Pinturicchio at Sienna may remain obscure, and however much the annalists of Sienna may urge that the two masters painted together in the library of Cardinal Piccolomini, the frescos abundantly prove that not a line or a pencil-stroke in them can by any possibility be assigned to Raphael.

The treatment which we observe in these frescos is that of Pinturicchio, varied with that of assistants

---

* Compare Della Valle to Cardinal Ghelini in Bottari Lett. ed. Ticozzi, 12mo, Milan, 1822, vi. p. 393 ; Pungileone, Raphael, *u. s.*, note to p. 55, and annot. ; Vas. note to p. 274, and compare Oxford Coll. No. 12 ; sheet of two soldiers, No. 13 ; a soldier and an angel also Oxford Coll. No. 8. Black chalk drawing, 12¼ in. h. by 7¾ in. wide. From the Alva and Lawrence collections, representing a youth erect, with his right arm raised, his left holding a fragment of a reed. No. 15. Two studies in black chalk, same size as the foregoing, and from the same collections. One of the studies represents a youth turned to the right, looking to the left, the right hand on the hip, the left resting on a stick. The other on the back of the sheet represents a youth in the same position as the last, but with the left hand on the hip and a cup raised in the right. These drawings are in the same character as those of the group of four already noticed, and Passavant even thought that one of them, that of a man resting his left hand on a stick, had been used in the fresco of the "Coronation" of Æneas (see Pass. ii. No. 531). But all three figures seem intended for an "Epiphany."

engaged by Pinturicchio in the school of Perugia. Of
these assistants one, we imagine, may be traced with
more certainty than the rest—Eusebio da San Giorgio,
a modestly-gifted craftsman of the Peruginesque school,
to whom Pinturicchio paid as much as 100 ducats for
arrears of wages at Sienna in 1506, probably did
much to assist the master; * and there is the more
cause for thinking that he was one of the chief exe-
cutants of the wall paintings of the library of Sienna,
because he seems to have been engaged in some respects
in the same task as Raphael. He produced designs
for some of the frescos, one of which, in the Malcolm
Collection, represents a row of churchmen and spectators for the picture of " Æneas kissing the Pope's
Foot." This drawing was elaborately finished, and has
been assigned to the hand of Pinturicchio himself.
But its inferior character is apparent, not only because
it was not applied to the wall painting for which it
was executed, but superseded by that of Raphael, but
also because it bears the impress of the manner of a
third-rate Peruginesque, who copied the same models
in Perugino's workshop as were copied by Raphael
when he made the drawings of the Venice sketch-
book.†

But almost at the period when the Connestabile

---

* Vas. vi. p. 56.

† Malcolm Coll. No. 827 of
the Grosvenor Gallery Exhib.
of 1877-8. It represents in a
silver-point drawing, 10 in. h. by
7½ in., six seated figures of doctors
or prelates in oriental dress, with
eight other figures standing behind
in the background. The draperies
of several of those figures are
adapted from the studies copied by
Raphael in that sheet of the Venice
sketch-book, which has already
been noticed as a set of draperies
in the Venice Acad. Frame XXIII.
No. 10.

" Madonna " was produced, Raphael also completed
silently pictures which connect him with patrons and
places distant from Perugia ; nor is it without interest
to explore, for the purpose of discovery, what the
master's movements at the time may have been.   It
is difficult, no doubt, to determine when Raphael
finished the Connestabile " Madonna," but if we
assume that he did so when the " Sposalizio " was
exhibited, it may be inferred that he then had leisure
to visit Urbino.   We saw with what spirit and grace
he composed " The Ride of Æneas and Cardinal Capranica " for the Library at Sienna.   Had he witnessed
some incident of the kind, by which the picture was
suggested ?   A glance at the history of .he time will
show that this was not impossible.   In September,
1504, a ceremony of great significance was performed
in honour of the two houses of Montefeltro and della
Rovere.   Guidubaldo, having spent the autumn of
1503 in establishing his authority at home, had been
summoned to Rome, where Julius II. conferred on him
the rank of captain-general.   From January to May,
1504, the whole family was living at the Vatican,
with the exception of the duchess, who governed her
husband's state.   Francesco Maria had been ordered
home from France, to plight his troth to Eleanor
Gonzaga.   His mother, Giovanna, accompanied the
Pope's sister, Lucchina, to the capital.   In June the
whole party came trooping northward.   Forlì was
recovered and reorganized in summer, and September
saw a splendid cavalcade winding its way through the
mountains to Urbino.   At the head of a brilliant

suite the Pope's Nuncio rode with the baton of command and the banner of the Church in his charge. It was a stately procession, of which Raphael would probably hear as it passed by way of Perugia to Gubbio and Cagli. It entered Urbino with great pomp and solemnity, and the ceremony of the benediction, with the delivery of the briefs of Francesco Maria's adoption, was magnificently performed in the cathedral. Nothing more natural than that Raphael, having witnessed, and perhaps accompanied, this pageant, should then have sketched the ride of Æneas, and transformed the castle of Urbino, which he had just seen, into the port of Talamone. It is but a presumption that matters occurred in this wise, yet there is some corroborative evidence of the pre‧sumption in the Venetian sketch-book, which contains at least two drawings indicating a stay in the Feltrine capital. We have not forgotten how Raphael in early years had been allowed to copy the sages in the library of the ducal palace. We now discover him in a later phase of his practice sketching the walls of the palace itself.

To modern travellers the familiar features of Urbino are the approach by the road from Pesaro, the gradual ascent to the summit, from which the sweep of the Umbrian hills is seen, the view of the town as a turn in the highway discloses it, and shows the palace with one of the fronts supported by pointed towers. The road becomes a street running beneath the towers on the one hand, and skirting on the other a line of houses on arcades. Past the castle and cathedral it divides into branches in various directions. In Raphael's time the prospect was very different. The road from Pesaro was that which came direct over the hill to the great court of the palace. A less frequented path led to the face defended by the towers, and from thence it struggled up a battle-mented causeway to an arched gate that separated the palace from the cathedral. The causeway was built on stone buttresses rising out of the sluggish waters of a moat; and the cathedral walls, reposing on solid rock, stood inaccessible from that side on a bank over-grown with grass and trees. Rainwater was artificially supplied to the moat by a dam. There rose at the side of the cathedral a square campanile, and in rear of it a low cupola.

Raphael sketched the cathedral and the castle with the moat and causeway from a place to the north of the palace. The campanile, as he drew it, is cut square at the top and loopholed for musketry. The building looks as if it had undergone a siege. The loopholes run along the length of the walls of the cathedral, and battlements defend the towers as well as the causeway. Far away over the high ground to the right are the windings of the Pesaro road. On the back of the sheet Raphael takes an equally characteristic view. To the north-east of Urbino the hills are steep and precipitous. Here (beneath the old citadel) the defences followed the rugged outlines of the hills; and towers round and square overlooked the giddy depths of rocky precipices and long curtains united one to another in picturesque succession.

Raphael sat out on a spur and drew the serpentine windings of the wall and its supports.* When he transferred the tower of the castle to an imaginary port of Talamone, he neither forgot the battlements of the platforms nor the conical caps that make them like oriental minarets.

But the sketch-book is not exclusively supplied with views of the palace and walls of Urbino; it comprises views of other places, and one of its sheets contains outlines of a church in the form of a Greek cross, with a tall steeple and spire, on a mound half way up a hill. At the foot of the mound, and skirting a wooded ravine, there runs a line of defences with walls and towers, inside of which are some edifices of ecclesiastical and secular architecture.† Of the same period as that of Urbino, this drawing acquires a date when we find, that Raphael reversed its contours to form the distance of the "Madonna" of Terranuova.‡ On the back of the sketch a fine study of rock and boulders is rapidly thrown off.

---

* Venice Academy, not exhibited, Pass. 92. To the left trees on the foreground, and on the bank above them the campanile of three storeys, leaning against the cathedral, the apsis of which rises against the end of the church. To the right of that the archway between cathedral and castle, to which the causeway leads, which is built on arches with their buttresses resting in the moat. Rising inside the causeway is the flank of the palace, showing the eastern turret. Beyond this the Pesaro road on some high ground, behind which a view of the Umbrian hills, at the waterside, on the extreme right, a flight of steps leading to the water. On the back of the sheet to the left, a tower with a conic cover, behind it the precipitous hill, with the wall along it, broken at intervals by three more towers. In the distance, ranges of hills.

† Venice Acad., not exhibited, Pass. 95.

‡ Venice Acad., not exhibited, Pass. No. 96. In the sky of this

This too, has been reversed by Raphael, and forms the right hand side of the background to the "Madonna" of Terranuova. But the "Madonna" of Terranuova is one of the masterpieces of 1505, in which the genius of Raphael may be seen struggling between the lessons of the Umbrian and Florentine schools.*

From September to the middle of December, 1504, the Feltrine Court resided at Urbino, and the duke and duchess lived there in state with Giovanna and her son, attended by their courtiers; and had Raphael been there as we should think, it might appear that he then made the acquaintance of Baldassare Castiglione, who had joined Guidubaldo from Rome. He would have known Ottaviano Fregoso, and Morello di Ortona who were councillors of the duke, and he would have met Cesare Gonzaga and others, whom the dialogue of the Cortigiano has made familiar to the present age. He might have become sufficiently intimate with Francesco Maria della Rovere, to justify those passages of his letters in which he speaks of his

---

sketch is a head with long curls and an eagle, with a serpent, apparently a modern addition, to the original drawing. The outline of the hills covers not only this sheet but a section of the next one, at the side of which we also find a modern hand, cherub, and head of an aged man (Pass. 94). The juxtaposition of these two drawings shows that the book in which they were was a bound book. The old No. 38 on the

upper part of the last sheet shows that the drawing of boulders was on page 37, on the reverse of which we find the view transferred to the Terranuova "Madonna."

* Similar sketches are on another sheet, No. 97 and 98 of Passavant's work, shewing on one side a view of a Cyclopean wall and a rapid drawing of churches and steeples and houses in a landscape. This sheet is in the Venice Academy.

old and familiar devotion to that prince;* and he could have painted the portrait of Guidubaldo, of which Cardinal Bembo declared in 1516, that it was surpassed by the later portrait of Tebaldeo.† It is the more to be credited that all this occurred at Urbino, because Raphael would hardly have come there later without finding the Feltrine court dispersed. After December, 1504, Guidubaldo was again called to Rome, and broke up his establishment in order to reside at the Vatican. His stay at Rome extended to March, 1506, after which, and between that date and his death in 1508, Raphael would have less time to cultivate the patronage which manifests itself in various ways and particularly in the delivery of many pictures.‡ No doubt none of the masterpieces which Raphael now produced have been traced directly to Urbino, but the "Vision of the Knight" at the National Gallery, the "St. Michael" and "St. George" at the Louvre, and the "Three Graces" in the Dudley collection in London, are all more likely to have been ordered by patrons at Urbino, than by patrons at Perugia.

We may regret at this juncture the doubts which have necessarily been thrown upon the genuineness of a letter, said to have been written in Raphael's favour by Giovanna della Rovere, to Piero Soderini, the chief of the Florentine state. Unfortunately the printed

---

* See *postea*, Raphael's letter of 1508, in fac-simile in Longhena and Pass. i. 497.

† Bembo, Opere. vol. v. pp. 48–9. Letter dated Rome, April 19, 1516.

‡ For the chronology here and *antea*, see the diary of Paris de Grassis MS., Munich Library, Baldi's Guidubaldo, &c., &c.

version of this letter mentions Giovanni Santi as being alive on the 1st of October, 1504; and the difficulty of correcting a mistake of this magnitude without reference to the original is so great, as to leave the historian no alternative but to ignore the document altogether.* Yet it would have been most desirable to establish the genuineness of this letter, as it would afford a direct proof not only that Raphael was connected with the Feltrine court in 1504, but that he purposed at that time to visit the Tuscan capital. In the absence of such evidence, we can only urge in favour of a Florentine journey, that various circumstances make it extremely probable. We saw that the " Epiphany " of the Vatican predella suggested the painter's acquaintance with Florentine models. The marked similitude of style between the drawings for the predella and the designs for the frescos at Sienna, and the near relation of both to the " Sposalizio " of Milan, which all point to a common period of production, would likewise pre-suppose a journey to Florence at the close of 1504. At the same time the Venice sketch-book seems to have been furnished with designs, in which more than one proof is afforded that Raphael's mind was then subject to new and most potent influences,—influences, which can only be explained if we assume that they were

---

* In full in Bottari, Lettere, _u. s._ i. pp. 1 and 2. Originally in the Gaddi Collection at Florence (1757). The letter has passed through many hands. It was sold at the Salle Sylvestre in Paris in Jan., 1856, for 200 fr. But the present owner is not known. See E. Müntz's Raphael, _u. s._ note to p. 128, and Passavant's Raphael, i. 496.

coincident with efforts to exchange the provincial Umbrian manner, for the more skilled and intelligent style of the greater Florentines. We may fancy that any one acquainted with Raphaelesque art would be able to put his finger upon those emanations of Raphael's pencil which illustrate the struggles above alluded to. In one of the pages a powerful drawing of the "Infant Christ in Benediction" takes us back in fancy to the "Epiphany" of the Vatican, revealing a new method of studying nature, without an absolute surrender of the old current of Peruginesque thought.* In other outlines of boys, the weight and squareness of Perugino's types, are found in juxtaposition with forms of a more lithesome character, which tell of the effort made by Raphael to exchange memories of the school for direct studies from life. Four children on one sheet, to some of whom Raphael has given wings, illustrate this moment in his career.† Equally suggestive in the same sense, is the charming group in the sketch-book of four infants playing with a dead sucking-pig. The naked babe close by, the leg, the shading of a foot, and diagrams displaying projections of shadows on globes, recall those lessons of the school of Lionardo, which the youthful master

---

* Venice Acad. Frame XXIV. 1. Back of XXIV. 7. Pass. 80. Pen and umber. The earnest gaze of the eye has already something of the supernatural which strikes us in the child of the Orleans "Madonna."

† Venice Acad. No. XXV. 14.

Back of XXV. 8. Pass. 56. To the left a winged child running, to the right, meeting him, a child playing with a flower, then one presenting his back, and a fourth, winged, and running towards the left. Pen and umber sketch.

would more easily take at Florence than elsewhere.* Increased boldness and freedom is shown in another sketch of an angel-like boy playing with his own foot, whilst the head of a child above it, exhibits the system of modelling in neutral tint and flake white, which essentially pertains to the Florentine school of da Vinci.† A seraph in dancing motion with outstretched arms and fluttering wings, floats on a cloud in the act of shedding flowers. Our memory reverts to a beautiful early version of the same figure in a Peruginesque drawing at Berlin, and an equally beautiful, but later version of it in an altar-piece at the Louvre.‡ The contrast which we realise is startling, the contrast between Umbrian feeling in the first days of the master's practice and Tuscan feeling in his later Roman period. We measure in a moment the

* Venice Acad. Frame XXV. 20. Back of XXV. 2. Pass. 49. Pen and umber.

† Venice Acad. Frame XXVII. 1. Back of XXVII. No. 24. There are two figures of boys, one to the left running, one to the right, showing his back and looking round to the left. Above him the round head, described in the text, three-quarters to the left looking up.

‡ Berlin Museum. Print room. m. 0·15 h. by 0·19. From the Poccetti Collection. This is a beautiful little drawing in pen and umber, washed with umber. The angel is turned to the left, whereas at Venice he is turned in the opposite direction. The figure, slender and tall, is draped in the Umbrian fashion, with the girdle flying outwards in circlets. To the left a cherub sits on a cloud. The angel seems to be dropping over him the sprays of leaves in his hand.

Venice Acad. Frame XXVI. 10. Back of XXVI. No. 16. Pass. 11. Here the angel is stepping down from one cloudlet to the other. The flowers drop from his hands. Beneath sits a figure of a man, in a cap and robes, on the ground. His hands are joined over one knee, and he looks down moodily. A copy of this drawing by Viti is in the D'Aumale collection at Chantilly (Reiset). The altar-piece at the Louvre, to which allusion is made in the text, is the "Holy Family" of 1518.

distance that separates the art of Raphael at the two
extremes of his career, whilst we observe that the
sentiment which dwells in the angel of the sketch-
book, seems suggested by the graceful creations of
Sandro Botticelli.

More characteristic even than this, the sheet which
contains the heads of the riders in the "Epiphany"
and the upturned face of St. James in the "Coronation" of the Vatican, comprises a profile of an old
man which represents quite the Florentine system of
searching in the study of detail,* whilst another sheet
in which the aged shepherd of the "Epiphany" is
drawn with a plastic force almost unknown as yet to
Raphael is accompanied by an outline of a head in the
spirit of Donatello and a profile like that of a Greek
medal, striking as an approach to that which recurs
transfigured in the Oxford studies for the fresco of
San Severo at Perugia.†

Turning from the pages of the sketch-book to the
pictures which Raphael produced after finishing the
design at Sienna, we trace with ease the progress of
the master as he shakes off the old Umbrian habit to
gird himself for that of the nobler Tuscan in such
works as the St. Michael and St. George, the Graces,
or the Marsyas and Apollo. Preceding these the
"Vision of the Knight" at the National Gallery merely

---

* Ven. Acad. Frame XXV. 4.
See *antea*, p. 147.

Venice Acad. Frame XXXV. 2.
At the back four studies of arms.
Pass. 83. There are three heads. The
upper one turned to the right, the
lower one (to the right) turned to
the left. The third, a profile to
the right, is furnished with bushes
of hair, whilst the two others are
bald.   Pen and umber drawing.
† Oxford, No. 28.

combines Peruginesque style with a more delicate strain of Raphaelesque thought. It hardly leads us beyond the walls of Perugia, though the subject, in the spirit of the fables dictated to Perugino and Costa by a princess of the house of Gonzaga, points more surely to the Roveres and Montefeltros than to any of the patrons traceable to the vicinity of Raphael's residence. No sooner had the duchess of Urbino returned from exile than she held her court in the time-honoured fashion. The castle was again enlivened with the presence of young people who studied to become soldiers and statesmen. But Guidubaldo had aged during the troubles of the previous years, and his sickly habit confined him after dinner to his couch. The young people leaving him to his repose, met in the rooms of the duchess, and many a courtly conversation took place, we are told, in which lectures were given for the conduct of true lovers, polished courtiers, and accomplished soldiers. This amiable, but perhaps not very efficacious antidote to the practical lessons of the time as taught by Cesar Borgia, the Baglioni, Vitelli, or Sforza, might be appropriately illustrated by an artist of Raphael's type, and it would scarcely have been possible, one should think, to find a man better fitted to depict, as he did, a youthful knight asleep on his shield dreaming, but encouraged to fortitude, expectant of glory, and cheered to the prospect of happiness by love and beauty. The knight in his armour differs but little from a sleeping guard at the sepulchre;* and allegory as yet seems very much

* See *antea*, the "Resurrection" of the Vatican.

akin to sacred art, but the charming thing about this little picture is its graceful straightforwardness and the total absence of any affectation of the supernatural. The knight takes his rest and leans upon his shield at the foot of a laurel tree. A lovely girl stands near his head with a sword in one hand and a book in the other; a maid equally lovely watches at his feet and presents a myrtle blossom, whilst far away the landscape recedes and the eye wanders over rocks and fields to a village and a lake and a hill crowned with a mighty boulder, a spire, and a fortress. Raphael was not without feeling for contrasts of female beauty. The girl with the sword is not less charming than her companion, but more sedate and less festively clad, the maid with the flower wears a twisted veil, an ornament of corals, and a light tunic over her skirt, her shape and face were matter of much thought to Raphael, and a study which he made from nature preparatory to painting the picture is one of the prettiest things in his Venice sketch-book.* The drawing, or rather the full cartoon, pricked for pouncing on the panel, displays in every part the faultless treatment of a hand trained to every finesse of pen drawing. Yet the chief attraction of the composition is the softness and velvet texture of its colours, which are of that peculiar depth inherited by Raphael from Perugino. The mere description of the tints suggests harmony. The knight's steel greaves contrast with orange brown

---

* Venice Acad. Frame XXV. No. 8. Back of XXV. No. 14. Bust of a girl with copious hair, partly plaited, partly in curls on her shoulders. Pen and umber sketch.

hose, a green mantle, armour inlaid with lapis lazuli, a blue and green coat, and a red shield. The girl to the left wears a blue dress and skirt bordered with red, yellow sleeves with a green lining, a sword in a green sheath, and a book with red edges and a blue binding. The maid to the right with corals in her hair, across her bosom and round her waist, a yellow-brown veil, a sky-blue tunic with deep blue borders and golden lights, cherry sleeves and red petticoat, all these colours, set in proper quantity and juxta-position, form a radiant chord such as only Raphael in the Peruginesque time could produce. Behind the sleeping knight the slender trunk of the laurel with its few leaves rears itself against the clouded sky which changes to a yellow haze, where it meets the distant hills of the Perugian lake district. The touch, the tone, the graceful lines, the youth of the knight and his companions are all reminiscent of the period when Raphael finished the predella of the " Coronation " at the Vatican; the maid with the myrtle blossom is cast in the same mould as the Virgin of the " Annunciation," the " Presentation," or the " Epiphany."*

At the period when Raphael composed " The Dream of the Knight " he probably also painted " The Sacrifice of Cain and Abel." It seemed as if the patrons

---

* London National Gallery. No. 213. Wood. 7 in. square. This little picture was long in the Borghese collection, from which it successively came into the hands of W. Y. Ottley, Sir T. Lawrence, Lady Sykes, and the Rev. Thomas Egerton. Sir M. Sykes paid £470 for it. Mr. Egerton sold it for £1,050, in 1847.

The cartoon, till quite lately framed with the picture itself, is stained, and has a tear about the head of the girl with the flowers.

who visited his painting-rooms were all anxious for some miniature subject in the form so successfully applied to predellas. "The Sacrifice of Cain and Abel" is twice as large as "The Dream," though it does not exceed a square foot in surface. Yet the artist has gathered into this small space some subtle varieties of thought. An altar of square stones is built on the brow of a hill, partly rising, partly falling to the sky, and showing at both edges a rich vegetation and slender branchings of trees, through which the sky shines clear. Abel kneels on the sward to the left, a curly-headed, long-locked youth in a blue gaberdine, whose hands are joined in prayer, and eyes are turned to heaven, as he sees a flame descending to fire the green wood that blazes and sends a pillar of smoke into the air. Cain, at the opposite side, has gathered the wood and set fire to it; his hands are on the edge of the altar, and he blows with all his might at the cinder, which seems unwilling to do more than create a smoke, which curls back into his eyes, and threatens to encircle his head. There are fine contrasts in this little picture between the quiet fervour of Abel and the angry energy of Cain—between the simple beauty of the first and the coarse type of the second, whose violence and strength are shown in muscular development and short hair and beard. The colours of the sky, the clouds, and the varied smokes are very cleverly harmonized; the club on the foreground prefigures the fratricide. Sweet richness of tone, warm colours, and Raphaelesque burnish are only less perfect than they might be, because time and accidents have variously injured the surface of the panel.*

Whilst Guidubaldo lay at Rome, in the winter of 1504, concerting measures with Julius for the pacification of the Romagna, the duchess spent the carnival in festivity at home, and put upon the stage "the comedy of Cæsar Borgia and Pope Alexander; the progress of Lucretia Borgia to Ferrara, when the duchess was invited to the wedding, and the state was invaded; Guidubaldo's return and forced departure; the massacre of Vitelozzo and his companions; the Pope's death, and the duke restored to his estate." † The gladness which found vent in these proceedings might, and perhaps did, suggest other illustrations of rejoicing; and it seems quite appropriate to the occasion, that Raphael should design "St Michael Encountering the Demon" and "St. George Overcoming the Dragon." Both these little pictures have come, we hardly know how, into the collection of the Louvre. St. Michael, on foot, treads on the neck of the evil one; he is armed in proof, and winged. With the red cross on his shield, he raises on high the sword with which he threatens to despatch the monster, but kindred monsters stalk about the ground;

---

* Rome. Signor Enrico Baseggio. Small panel. 8¼ in. h. by 13¾ in. Said to have been once in the Aldobrandini collection, in Rome, but subsequently (in this century) in possession of Mr. Emerson, in London. (See Pass. Raphael, ii. p. 315.) The panel has been injured in various ways, least in the foreground of grasses and weeds—most in the flesh tones; especially, of the figure of Cain.

† Baldi's Guidubaldo, *u. s.* ii. 165, and Ugolini, *u. s.* ii. 128-9. The play was played on Feb. 19, in the Ducal Palace.

serpents twist their folds about the people in the distance; a tomb opens in the background; and penitents are pursued by devils. The heavens are red and black with the smoke and fire of a burning castle. It is probable that Dante's Inferno was the source of Raphael's inspiration. One of his patrons no doubt had read to him the proper chaunts of the poem, but for himself we think he looked at a print of one of Jerome Bosch's "Temptations," in which wizards perform their incantations, animals of quaint structure strut about regions fitfully lighted by fires burning in hideous caverns, and the sky is dark and lurid with many-coloured smoke. But on this, as on all occasions when Raphael took ideas from his neighbours, he transformed and gave a peculiar effectiveness to them; and all the paraphernalia of the necromancer of the sixteenth century is cast in shade, and made fitly subordinate to the principal action in the picture, which is that of " The Archangel," whose bright form, encased in golden armour, adorned with a blue skirt and green wings, is brilliantly relieved, either against the sky, into which the smoke is rising, or against the dusky ground upon which the monsters show their many-coloured horns, and impossible beaks and tongues. It is an exquisitely-finished piece, in which colour again produces a rich effect, enhanced by strong contrast of light and shade.*

---

* Paris, Louvre. No. 380. Panel. 0·31 h. by 0·27. According to the records of the Louvre this picture was one of two which belonged to Mazarin, and was bought of Maza- rin's heirs for Louis the XIVth. It is stated in one of the latest lives of Raphael (E. Müntz, *u. s.* p. 121), that Lomazzo speaks of this picture as having been executed for Guidu-

But beautiful as it is, the "St. Michael" is less so than the "St. George," whose figure is singularly graceful, yet full of power. The grim dragon transfixed with a spear, the point of which is in his breast, whilst the broken fragments are lying on the ground, hardly looks more dangerous than the young and active Saint, whose strength seems all husbanded for the stroke of the sword which is about to fall. The grey on which he rides gallops into the foreground, and sends the mantle and plume of the knight a-flying in the breeze. In a beautiful landscape of trees and rock, which more than all else gives evidence of the superiority which Raphael had gained over Perugino, the Queen is made to start in flight with arms thrown forward, and curling locks blowing away from under the crown on her brow. The scene is one of full daylight, compared with which that of the fighting "St. Michael" is but a gleam in murky clouds. The one picture all dark, the other gay and full of that spirit which Raphael caught as he sketched the cantering horseman for the coming of Æneas at Tala-mone.* Nor did the master in this instance create

---

baldo of Urbino. But Lomazzo on the contrary speaks of a "St. George" as having been done for the Duke, and says of the "St. Michael" that "it is in France at Fontainebleau," *i.e.*, in the collection of the Kings of France. (Trattato, p. 48.) It is characteristic of this piece that the colours are thin, and the texture delicate; whilst the Connestabile "Madonna" and the "Dream" are

of strong impast with evidence of copious use of a fat vehicle.

* Louvre. No. 381. Wood. 0·32 h. by 0·27. This too, was in the collection of Cardinal Mazarin. (Villot's Cat. Louvre. 1863.) Horse and rider here are turned to the right. In the distance in the same direction is the figure of the Queen. On the foreground, fragments of the lance, coloured red and white spirally. Passavant quotes Lomazzo

without studied preparation. He probably felt more fully than ever before the impulse of instant action, when he penned the beautiful drawing at the Uffizi in which the group of man and horse and monster is thrown upon the paper with so much truth and energy. Raphael's progress, which at this time appears to have been surprisingly rapid, cannot be studied more fitly than in this preparatory sketch for the "St. George," which, for mastery and quickness of execution, favourably compares with the designs of the frescos at Sienna. Such, indeed, is the advance which the comparison of these works makes manifest, that the conclusion seems inevitable that Raphael by this time had enlarged his experience by a journey to Tuscany, and a stay in the capital of Florence.*

As he lingered at Sienna on his way to the north or on the road from Florence to Perugia, he may have found some Siennese patron, who suggested to him that since he had seen the group of the "Graces," it might be a grateful task to him to paint a picture of

---

(ii. 22), to show that this picture was painted by Raphael for the Duke of Urbino, but Lomazzo's text (Trattato, p. 48) does not enable us to decide whether he is alluding to the "St. George" of the Louvre or the later "St. George" of the Hermitage at St. Petersburg, and the probability is that he means to speak of the latter. Passavant (ii. 22) also says that Lomazzo describes a copy in the church of S. Vittorio of Milan of a "St. George" which Raphael painted for the Duke of Urbino. But

Lomazzo makes no allusion to the Duke of Urbino in reference to the copy in question. It may be that the copy of the "St. George" is that which hangs with one of "St. Michael" in the Leuchtemberg palace at St. Petersburg. Both are poor and dry imitations.

* Florence, Uffizi. No. 530. Pen and umber study of horse and rider and dragon; the horse without harness or bridle. On the ground, instead of the fragments of the lance, a skull, a jaw-bone, and a femur. Size 0·26 h. by 0·21.

that fable. Certainly "The Three Graces," as they now
appear in the Dudley Collection, form a composition,
the feeling and technical execution of which recalls,
whilst it shows an advance upon, the predellas of the
" Coronation " of the Vatican and the " Vision of the
Knight" at the National Gallery. Raphael, indeed,
need not have trusted to memories of the marble at
Sienna for a design of a subject which, from the
oldest classic times to the period of the revival, had
been repeated in wall paintings, bas-reliefs, and
gems. Still it cannot be forgotten, that he had been
struck by the group in the library and had drawn a
portion of it; and that when he began his labours
he made what may be called a pictorial restoration
of that classical masterpiece. He conceived the
Graces locked together as the Greek sculptor had
conceived them. The central one, with her back to
the spectator, resting her hand on the shoulder of
her sister on the left, she supporting the hand of
her sister to the right, each holding one of the
apples of the Hesperides. All are bound together
by a common feeling, they have a similar occupation, their faces, their naked shapes are all taken
from a single model, a graceful, young, fleshy girl of
Umbrian type. Raphael it is clear had not evolved
out of his own consciousness an ideal of perfect
female beauty, or, if he had, it was not seconded by
his hand. There are parts of " The Three Graces "
which are not faultless ; there are outlines and
articulations that are awkward or defective ; and yet
the youth and elegance of these rounded forms are

fascinating, and their flesh is modelled and blended with so much delicacy, that we · forget the imperfections or lose them in the dreamy atmosphere which covers the distance of rolling ground against which they are seen. One detail connects the picture with that of the "Vision of the Knight;" the same corals which enliven the head-dress of the girl with the myrtle blossoms decorate the hair of each of the Graces.*

"Marsyas and Apollo," a picture long in possession of Mr. Morris Moore, at Rome, probably represents a more advanced stage of Raphael's practice than the classic picture of Earl Dudley. It illustrates in a striking manner the rapidity with which Raphael acquired the guiding principles of the ancient art of the Greeks. In the Graces he disregarded the laws of selection familiar to the pagan schools, and yielded to a clear tendency to realism. In the "Marsyas and Apollo" he worked almost entirely in the spirit of the antique. As a composition nothing can be

---

* London, Earl Dudley. Wood. 6¼ in. h. by 4¾ in., or m. 0·17 by 0·12. From the Borghese collection, having passed through the hands of the Woodburns and thence into the collection of Sir Thomas Lawrence. This picture is well preserved, and has only lost its patina in some slight parts. The Grace to the right wears a veil round the hips. Raphael cannot well have seen the "Graces" of Pompeii, of which two examples, with ears of corn and flowers, are in the Naples Museum. But he might have seen such examples as the lamp, of which there is an engraving in Bellori's Lucerne Antiche, or the bas-relief of the time of Marcus Aurelius in the Mus. of the Capitol, or the original, wherever it may have been, of Marcantonio's print. But clearly the origin of his picture is the group at Sienna. A faulty part o Raphael's picture is the right leg of the Grace to the right.

simpler than the design of this picture, which contains but two figures in a landscape. To the right Apollo, with one hand resting on his hip, stands on the foreground near the lyre, the quiver, and the bow, which are his special attributes. He listens haughtily, but intently to the strains of a pipe which Marsyas plays as he sits on an opposite bank. The lyre hangs on the stump of a tree. Behind it, and behind Marsyas' seat, a sapling rises into the sky and mingles its branches with those of a tree on a further projection of the ground. In rear of these a river flows through a valley, a road lines the bank, and further on a bridge is defended by a fort and polygonal tower; beyond this again the valley opens, and a lake bathes the foot of a range of hills. In the pure sky overhead a hawk is darting downwards to strike at its prey.*

As usual, this picture was preceded by studies and a finished design. One example of the first seems preserved in the sketch-book at Venice, where a naked man in gentle stride is represented with one arm pendent and the other raised, as if to support a vase.

---

* Rome, Mr. Morris Moore. This picture is on a panel, m. 0·392 h. by 0·292, or 15⅜ in. by 11⅓ in. It was bought in England, and seems from the initials, J. B., on the back to have belonged to John Barnard, whose collection was dispersed about the year 1770. The genuineness of the work was not at first acknowledged. It was even denied by Dr. Waagen, by Passa-vant, and Mündler (see Pass. Raphael, ii. 415, and Zeitschrift für b. K. ii. p. 198); but their opinion is not now considered acceptable. The letters R. V., or signs like those letters, are on the quiver at Apollo's feet. But the genuineness of the picture does not depend in any way on these signs.

Though originally drawn, one might think, for an Epiphany, this study is with some slight exceptions the counterpart of the "Apollo" in reverse. It is certainly one of the most cleverly modelled pen-drawings that Raphael had as yet produced.[*] The cartoon, in pen and umber, and umber and white shading, reveals at the first glance that Raphael had not only seen, but determined to put forth the ideal qualities of the antique. Though much injured by abrasion, the figure of Apollo could scarcely have been produced in greater perfection. It is a model of manly beauty trained down to the slenderest shape compatible with strength. The head enwreathed in leaves and rushes is quite Olympian, when compared with that of the busy Marsyas, whose face and form in the mould peculiar to Perugino is altogether of the earth, earthy. The landscape alone is imperfect, being a mere wash of white and grey divided by a trunk of a tree, lopped of its branches.[*] The contrast of the god with the churl is less striking in the sketch than in the picture, where the head of Apollo, now adorned with Ambrosian locks, attains a great serenity, and the body and limbs are chiselled with extreme delicacy. Con-

---

[*] Venice Acad. Frame XXIII. No. 16. Back of XXIII. No. 2. Pass. 22. The figure is turned to the right. In the right hand corner is a study of a foot and kneeling leg.

[†] Venice Acad. Frame XXXV. No. 7. M. 0·28 h. by 0·33. This drawing has been lopped at the right side so as to show but a part of the hand and arm with the wand of Apollo. The legs are imperfect from the wear of the paper, which has been patched and repaired. At one time the drawing was catalogued under the name of Bartolommeo Montagna. Pass. ii. p. 415, assigns it to Francesco (!) Viti. The head of the Marsyas is very like that of the rejected suitor and other similar types in Perugino's predella of Fano.

scious superiority has seldom been expressed with more power and severity, whilst in Marsyas the lowly herd is betrayed by rude features, corpulence, splay feet and cropped hair ; and one feels a touch of pity and sympathy for the deluded wretch who bends to his work with the eagerness of one unconscious of defeat and unprepared for death. It is perhaps a chance ; at the feet of Marsyas grows the deadly belladonna.   For the rest, the landscape, in its freshness, recalls many a sketch of Raphael's youth, repeats the distances of the " Standard " of Città di Castello or of the " St. George " at the Louvre, whilst it foreshadows that of the " Madonna del Cardellino." Precision of contour, delicacy of modelling, clean, bright burnish of flesh, but above all richness and harmony of tone distinguish this admirably finished masterpiece, which in truth combines so much more than Raphael as yet had achieved, that we feel he must have seen Florence before he completed it.

The question, where the " Marsyas and Apollo," or the " Graces," or the " St. Michael " and " St. George " were painted, is difficult to answer, but after duly weighing probabilities we may presume that they were executed at Perugia, under the influence of a temporary visit to the Tuscan capital ; and Vasari's narrative enables us to believe that, when Raphael first went to Florence, he did so without intending to give up his residence at Perugia.   The charm which the works of the great masters produced, led him to repeat his visits ; he found friends at Florence, whose interest was perhaps greater to him than that of his friends at Perugia, and, taught by the experience of Perugino, he established a painting room in the Florentine capital, without giving up the workshop which he had inherited from his master at Perugia.

About the time when Raphael may be thought to have first become acquainted with Florence, Tuscan artists acknowledged the professional superiority of two principal masters in art, Michaelangelo, who had recently finished the bronze "David" on the public square of the city, and Lionardo da Vinci, who had composed "The Last Supper" at Milan, and accepted the office of military engineer to the Florentines. The rivalry of these two giants rapidly became the theme of a legend. Da Vinci had been commissioned to paint "The Battle of Anghiari," in the town hall of Florence. In autumn, 1503, he received the keys of the Pope's quarters at Santa Maria Novella, where scaffoldings were put up to enable him to work at his cartoon. No such undertaking, no cartoon of such magnitude had ever been seen in Tuscany. It was made up of one ream and twenty-nine quires or about 288 square feet of royal folio paper,* the mere pasting of which necessitated a consumption of 88 pounds of flour, the mere lining of which required three pieces of Florentine linen.† Whilst Lionardo was employed on these labours, Piero

---

* This calculation is based on the measure of the quarter folio of Raphael's Venice sketch-book, which is 0·16 by 0·21. Eighty quires are counted to one ream, six sheets to the quire.

† See the account in notes to Vas. Sansoni ed. iv. p. 44.

Soderini gave Michaelangelo commission to fill in
the opposite side of the hall, and he too had a
scaffolding erected in the hospital of the Dyers, at
Sant' Onofrio, in August, 1504.   According to the
story preserved by Vasari, and current amongst
Florentine craftsmen, the news of a close encounter
and bitter competition between Da Vinci and Michaelangelo was soon carried beyond the limits of the
city.   It came to be known at Sienna that Da Vinci
had designed an admirable group of horsemen, to
rival which Michaelangelo had imagined a group of
equally fine, if not finer foot soldiers.   Raphael heard
of this competition, and putting aside all other
concerns, set out for Florence, saw the cartoons, and
was so struck by the perfection of the art, as well as
by the beauty of the city, that he protracted his stay
for an indefinite period.*

  * The dates which we gather from official records
prove that Da Vinci designed his cartoon between
January and December, 1504, and that Michaelangelo drew the first lines of his in August, 1504.
In March, 1505, Da Vinci began to paint from his
cartoon in the Town Hall.   In August, 1505, Michaelangelo was ready to do the same.   It is therefore
clear from Vasari's narrative, that Raphael may have
heard of the great Florentine competition after August,
1504, and that he may have heard of it from persons
intimately acquainted with both the Florentine masters.   In that very autumn of 1504, Michaelangelo

---

* Vas. viii. pp. 5, 6.

renewed his contract with the Piccolomini, to furnish the statues for their chapel in the cathedral of Sienna. Early in the same year, Perugino, who had known Da Vinci in the work-room of Verocchio, who must indeed have met him at the selection of the site for Michael-angelo's "David," and doubtless knew that he had begun the cartoon, came down from Florence to Perugia to spend his summer in the Umbrian province. It is hardly conceivable that Raphael should not have seen his old tutor on this occasion, a man to whom he was bound by ties of a special affection; it may have happened that Perugino on his way back to Florence in September, took the road which passed through Sienna instead of that which led through Arezzo, and induced Raphael to join him in his journey. We can fancy that matters occurred so that Perugino on his return to Florence told Raphael of the magnificent cartoons which Da Vinci had all but finished at Santa Maria Novella, and of a similar cartoon begun by Michaelangelo at Sant' Onofrio, and that Raphael was induced to visit the Tuscan capital under the guidance of his own teacher.

If Raphael, at the time, was under a covenant to assist Pinturicchio at Sienna, Perugino, who had been master to both, would easily settle the conditions of his departure; Eusebio would naturally come in as a substitute for Raphael in carrying out the frescos of the library, and Raphael would leave Sienna without difficulty to enjoy the pictorial feast in store for him at Florence. At Florence, it would be his fortune to meet Da Vinci, who would probably join with Perugino in advising a visit to the principal churches and monuments of the capital. That Raphael, during his first short stay at Florence, studied the works of the older Tuscans as well as those of his contemporaries is apparent, not only from the influence which those masterpieces produced upon his style generally, but from the effects which became immediately manifest in the small pictures of St. Michael, St. George, and the Graces. On his return to Perugia, Raphael undertook the composition of the " Madonna di Terranuova," he completed the altar-piece and predellas of Sant' Antonio, and began the frescos of San Severo, and in all of these he displayed his acquaintance with the style and the works of Lionardo, Michaelangelo, and Baccio della Porta.

CHAPTER V.

Return of Raphael from Florence to Perugia.—Completion of the altar-pieces of Sant' Antonio and Ansidei and their predellas.—"Madonna" of Terranuova, and drawings for the pictures in the Venice sketch-book.—Influence of Michaelangelo.—Beginning of the fresco of San Severo.—Covenant with the nuns of Monteluce.—Alternate residence at Florence and Perugia.—Life and companionship with artists at Florence.—Perugino, Lionardo, and Michaelangelo.—Cartoons of Da Vinci and Buonarrotti.—Florentine patrons.—"Madonna del Gran' Duca," and "Madonna di Casa Tempi."—Precepts of Lionardo as applied by Raphael.—Madonnas "del Cardellino" and "in green."—Portraits of the Doni.—"Madonna di Casa Tempi."—Preparatory drawings in Lionardesque style.

RAPHAEL probably left Perugia in 1504 with half-done work awaiting his return. Before he started, we may presume that he had orders from the nuns of Sant' Antonio for an altar-piece, and from the family of the Ansidei for a "Mother and Child with saints"; and it is more than likely that before he set out on the journey which ended with his visit to Florence, he had actually begun both those compositions. Deep in the secrets of the Peruginesque style, surrounded by a public which more than any other in Italy clung to time-honoured models, Raphael, we should imagine, had begun both of those pictures in obedience to the canons of a taste confined within the limits of Umbrian tradition, and subject to stringent orders from patrons claiming to have opinions of their own. We can, indeed, fancy that when he returned to his painting-room and recollected the marvels of Florentine art, the frescos of Masaccio and Ghirlandaio, and the "Last Judgment" of Baccio della Porta, he may have been surprised at the immobility of Umbrian painting, and astonished that his own work should have been so long under the ban of a narrow and provincial schooling. Vasari says, "it soon became apparent that Raphael had been at Florence, since, thanks to having seen so many things by first-rate masters, he so varied and embellished his manner that his second style seemed to have had no connection with the first." *   As he came and saw the half-finished altar-pieces, it must have occurred to him that he would have designed them on other lines if he had had to compose them afresh; but being above all a practical man, and having to consider the covenants which he had made, he changed his style so far only as was compatible with the form which his work had already assumed; and this is probably the true explanation of that which gives interest to the "Madonna" of Sant' Antonio: the union in one picture of the best of the Peruginesque time with the earliest of the Florentine period.

Not the least, probably, that Raphael would have done, had it been possible to begin the altar-piece of Sant' Antonio anew, would have been to modify the relation of the lunette to the central picture. There is hardly a later example in Raphael's practice of that Umbrian form of arrangement which connects, yet keeps apart, the Virgin enthroned and the attendance of saints from the vision of the Eternal and his accompaniment of seraphs.   In the "Madonna"

* Vas. viii. p. 9.

of Sant' Antonio the lunette is a separate picture.
The Heavenly Father is depicted as an aged man
with a bald head and dark forked beard, with a
golden globe in his left hand, and his right hand
raised in the act of benediction. Two seraphs float in
the blue ether behind him, and two winged angels,
one on the left with his fingers joined in prayer, one
on the right with his arms across his breast, are
poised in the heaven at his side. Beneath this the
Virgin is seen seated on an elaborate throne, a wide
chair of stone on ornamental plinths backed with
cloth of crimson and gold, and protected by green
hangings and a circular canopy. On her knee the
infant Saviour sits clothed in a white tunic, edged
with blue, the parti-coloured scapular of St. Anthony
of Padua embroidered on his shoulder, and a brown
belt and cloak of blue over his limbs. In the words
of an old record, " amiculis indutum," he was clothed
because the nuns, as Vasari tells us, were not to
look at the nakedness of little children. Hence, too,
the boy Baptist to the right, who presses forward
under the guidance of the Virgin's hand, is also
dressed, though an infant, in the shirt of camel's hair
and robes of green and gold and purple. He looks up
lovingly at the infant Christ, who answers him with
a blessing. At the sides, to the right St. Margaret
and St. Paul, to the left St. Catherine and St. Peter,
in front of a landscape of hills under a clear sky.

It is strange at a period which we know to have
produced the " St. George," the " St. Michael," and
the " Graces," to see the pure Raphaelesque art,

which reveals itself in the faultless head and oval
face of a Virgin modelled in the form of the Connestabile "Madonna," disguised, so to speak, in old
Umbrian costume—a tunic of which the seams are
embossed with golden ornaments, a blue mantle
sprinkled with golden spangles, after the fashion of
Pinturicchio. The quaintness of these vestments, the
old-fashioned air of the infant Christ and Baptist, must
have struck Raphael when he came home as something that he would have avoided if he had been in
Florence earlier; but it was done and it was there;
and such relief as he could give by richness of tone
and purity of harmony, he now imparted to the best
of his power. The Eternal in the lunette might
strike him as reminiscent of that which his father had
created in the Buffi altar-piece at Urbino, or Perugino
had designed for the " Baptism " at the Sixtine, or
the " Ascension of San Pietro " of Perugia; he might
even think the face reminiscent of the Father in the
" Creation of Eve " at Città di Castello, but here, too,
it was late to make a change. The seraphs and the
left-hand angel might appear to him too like those of
the " Coronation." But these also he resolved not
to change; the angel to the right, whose shape
recalls Perugino and Santi, he animated with a new
breath of the life of the Florentines. But where
the influence of Tuscan art is most sensible, is in
the Saints attending on the Virgin, because apparently more had been left to be done to them than to
the rest of the picture. The profile of St. Catherine
with her palm and wheel was made to combine the

guileless forms of the "Coronation" angels, and the more conscious ones of Baccio della Porta, whilst the "St. Margaret" united similar elements with something of Lionardesque grace in dimpled smile, pretty ribbons, a tasteful trim of hair, and wreaths of pure white roses. St. Peter looking out of the picture will still suggest memories of Perugino and even of Giovanni Santi, but the sternness of the head, the studied drawing of the feet, the subtle rendering of natural movement in the hand, of which a finger is lost in the leaves of the book, and the broad sweep of the drapery, tell as clearly of Florentine elements commingled with Umbrian teaching as the grand severity of air or the pose and expression of St. Paul, leaning on the sword, whose shape foreshadows the still more perfect one of that in the "St. Cecilia" of Bologna. In short, the monumental attitudes, the breadth of the forms, the grace and beauty of the females, and the grand style of the draperies prove absolutely Raphael's study of the works of Da Vinci and Della Porta.*

---

* This altar-piece is now in London, on wood, 8 Roman palms square. The only documents relative to it are those which refer to its sale. In May, 1677, the nuns of S. Antonio begged permission to sell it "to pay their debts, and because the surface in some parts was flaking away." On the 7th of May the central panel and lunette were valued at 1,800 scudi. They were sold on the following day for 2,000 scudi to Antonio Bigazzini, a Perugian noble, who bound himself to substitute a copy for the original. Shortly after this the picture came into the hands of the Colonna family at Rome, and thence to the royal palace at Naples, where it remained till the expulsion of the Bourbons. It came into the hands of the Duke of Ripalda, who leaves it in store in the National Gallery. The sale price is said to be £40,000. The scaling which

The altar-piece of the Ansidei, designed for a chapel in the Church of San Fiorenzo, probably struck Raphael in the same way as the "Madonna" of Sant' Antonio. It doubtless struck him as a model suggestive of old and provincial fashion.

The Virgin enthroned, seems enshrouded in drapery, the mantle on her head covering all but her waist and right knee. Like a hood edged with gold, it frames the face, the throat and waist, leaving bare the thin veil that protects the fair hair and the fresh young countenance with its dignified look and drooping eyelids. Opening at the neck it shows the upper hem of the red dress wrought with an embroidered monogram. It is a youthful mother who looks down

---

was apparent in 1677 was probably due to a horizontal split in the panel which runs along the eyes of the two female saints, and has given occasion for some unfortunate patching. Besides this the surface has been unequally cleaned and retouched on more than one occasion, whence a worn and washed out appearance. (See Giornale di Erud. Tosc. *u. s.* iii. pp. 310–15.) It has been said that the principal group of the Virgin, Child, and Baptist was copied from an *older* altar-piece of 1498, by Bernardino di Perugia (Paliard in Gaz. des Beaux Arts, vol. xvi. anno 1877, p. 259), now in the Gallery of Perugia. There is no doubt the central group is almost the same in both pictures. But there is no proof that Bernardinus painted his version in 1498. On the contrary, the pic-

ture which he did paint in that year, a Virgin and Child with two angels, in the church of La Bastia near Fabriano, inscribed "BELARDINVS DE PERVSIA PINSIT, 1498," snows by its elementary execution that the painter's skill was not then equal to the production of the altar-pieces resembling Raphael's. This must have been done later and probably after the completion of Raphael's at Sant' Antonio; and this is the more likely as there is also a "Coronation" by the same Bernardinus in the Gallery of Perugia, which imitates that of Perugino from S. Francesco del Monte. Bernardino of Perugia, who is not to be confounded with Pinturicchio, is therefore the copyist and not the precursor of Raphael in the case before us.

at the book that lies on the folds of the cloak on her
knee; her hands and fingers are curved over the
leaves, whilst the right reposes on the shoulders of the
pensive child that sits cross-legged on her lap and
holds in its fingers the blue and gold-striped sash
which winds round its arm and body. St. Nicholas,
in a white jewelled mitre, stands reading below,
bending to the book in his left hand, a splendid
crozier in his right, his neck muffled in a white cloth,
over which a deep green pivial with an orange lining
and gilt borders is fastened with a bishop's brooch.
Under the folds of this ample vestment pleats of a
white surplice are visible, itself falling short of a
black robe beneath which the saint's red shoes appear.
Three metal balls on the floor are the emblem of the
bishop's sanctity. John the Baptist, steadily planted
on the right foot, the left leg forward, bare-armed
and bare-legged, in camel's-hair tunic, and a blood-
red mantle edged with gold, holds a crystal cross in
his left hand.

The picture appears to have been conceived with
the trust of one who thought to be true to Umbrian
form for ever. In accordance with Perugian tradition, the arched porch enframes a view of sky and
hills, a stone plinth forms the throne, to which carved
steps lead, the throne supports being edged with
Greek borders, in harmony with the ornament of the
niche and dossal, the green canopy and its scolloped.
fringe and festoons of hanging corals. The Virgin,
high on the throne, the saints on the floor below, all
this is variegated with gay tints of vestments and

accessories and much gilding of phylacteries and
borders. Here, again, as in the "Madonna" of Sant'
Antonio, Raphael had but to strive by dint of ingenuity to deck the old lines with new surroundings.
He therefore kept only so much gold as might give
light and sparkle to the locks of the Virgin and
Child, or relief to the borders of their dresses; he
surrendered embossments and spangles, and to the
blanket texture of lined and double stuffs he imparted
a better sweep, which to some extent concealed the
old Perugian system of drapery fold. This, with rich
and intense colours and hatchings of shadowed flesh,
carefully tempered by scumbles and glazes which
damped the glare of strong and variegated tones, gave
to the altar-piece that brightness and gloss and light
which, notwithstanding its old form, still make the
altar-piece of the Ansidei the object of a constant
pilgrimage to the Palace of Blenheim.*

The current of Raphael's thought and his art, when

---

* Blenheim. Wood. 9 ft. h.
by 5 ft. Bought by Lord Robert
Spenser through Gavin Hamilton
in 1764, from the church of San
Fiorenzo on condition of furnishing
a copy (which still exists in the
place of the original) by Niccola
Monti. Lord R. Spenser gave the
picture to his brother, the Duke
of Marlborough. On the frieze
beneath the canopy are the words
SALVE MATER CHRISTI." On the
border of the Virgin's mantle near
the left hand is the date MDVI,
and not as stated by Passavant
(Raph. ii. p. 31) and Waagen
(Treasures, iii. 127–8), MDV. This
picture is very fairly preserved, but
the sky and the porch, and particularly that part of the porch to the
right, is made cold by rubbing down.
The pavement of warm reddish
yellow is likewise somewhat
cleaned off, and the whole is thus
in some measure out of focus, the
less cleaned parts being darker
than the rest. The drapery of the
Virgin's mantle is not a good
specimen of Raphael's art, and is
probably due to the inferior hand
of a disciple.

he composed the "Madonna Ansidei," may be guessed in part from the picture, in part from the drawings which preceded it. The time in which the altar-piece was finished, as shown by the cyphers of 1505 or 6 on the hem of the Virgin's mantle and the Peruginesque character of the contour as displayed in some designs, indicate the interval which elapsed between the beginning and completion of the work. If the Umbrian craftsman stands revealed in the distribution or the architecture and accessories, and sometimes in poor and addled folds of drapery, he betrays himself equally in the attitude and faces of one at least of the attendant saints. Raphael had a tendency, of which he was long in divesting himself, to produce female hands short of finger and nail. His habit of making vanishing foreshortenings in heads recurs as late as the period of the "St. Catherine" of the National Gallery, and both these characteristics are found at Blenheim. But when Raphael gives to masculine extremities a coarse and unrefined shape, we know that he is not yet far on the way towards freeing himself from Umbrian influences. His "St. Nicholas" at Blenheim has a certain likeness to the suitors in the "Sposalizio" of Milan, but his figure of the Baptist is brought out in strong Peruginesque feeling, and with those peculiarly ungentle projections of hand and foot which also disfigured the older practice of Perugino.

There is a shade of the Florentine in the larger and more powerful scantling of the frame, and evidence of the later progress of the work is also apparent in the brighter colouring and its more perfect blending. In the greater freedom and more ideal rendering of the Virgin's head, and a broader sweep of form generally, we discern that, however early the first touches may have been put in, the later touches were given after the production of the "Madonna di Terranuova" and the "Eternal" of San Severo.

One of the first thoughts for the " Madonna Ansidei," a pen drawing at Frankfort, represents the Virgin and Child enthroned and St. Nicholas of Tolentino in attendance. A throne and canopy with strings of corals, an arched porch and carved plinths, are clearly contemporary with those which we observe at Blenheim.* But other preparatory sheets prove that the composition had been engaging his thoughts at the very time when he composed the subjects for the Sienna Library and the predellas of the Vatican. The Virgin bending to a book in her left hand in the Lille Collection,† almost as early as the angels of the Vatican "Coronation," was drawn from a male model, even to the hand which forms a separate study on the

---

* Frankfort. Stædel Collection. 10 in. h. by 6½. Pen and umber drawing, arched at top. The Virgin is turned in the same direction as the Virgin of Blenheim. But her fingers play with one foot of the pretty Infant Christ, who gives the benediction. To the left the saint holds an open book in his left and a crucifix in his right. From the Lankrink, Dawson-Turner, Lawrence and King of Holland's collections.

† Lille Mus. No. 704. Silverpoint drawing from a model in hose and jerkin. The head at three-quarters to the left. The left hand raised and holding the book. The figure is seen to the knees, below which is a study of the hand with the book. M. 0·26 h. by 0·17½. Passavant (ii. No. 375) calls this a study for the "Madonna del Cardellino," but it is much earlier in date and not in the movement of that figure.

lower part of the sheet.   But on the shoulders of the model a female head was set, and for this a separate design was also completed, which reveals the same advance upon the figure as a whole as the Virgin's face in the picture reveals an advance on the rest of the altar-piece. Yet neither of these outlines came to be the exact counterpart of the "Madonna Ansidei," because the master finally set the hand and book in a different way, and turned the Virgin's face in the contrary direction.   Yet there is still a distinct connection between these pieces and the bust of a girl—that lovely silver-point drawing of a maiden with down-cast eyes in the Malcolm Collection, which seems clearly to have been the concluding effort to realise the features of the Madonna in the outline of Lille.* Later on in the Florentine period the same leaves were collected to form the beautiful version of a "Virgin and Child with a Book," which, with its two little fragments of landscape and separate study for the Infant Christ, form one of the treasures of the Oxford Gallery.†   It is interesting to trace similar features of water, walls, and towers, both in the sketch and the Blenheim altar-piece.

---

* Malcolm Coll. Bust of a young girl, in silver-point on pre- pared paper. $10\frac{1}{4}$ in. h. by $7\frac{3}{4}$. From the Ottley, Lawrence, Wood- burne, King of Holland, and Wellesley collections. The head is at three-quarters to the left, in veil and hood, showing the hair twisted off the temples, the left ear, and the throat. The hood fastened at the bosom with a jewelled brooch, highly finished and shaded. On the obverse of this drawing is a sketch of a youth.

† Oxford Gall. No. 23. Pen and ink sketch of the Virgin seen to the knees, seated, with the naked infant on her knees. She holds the book, with the leaves of which the infant plays. In the

But the connection of all these drawings is not with the "Ansidei Madonna" alone. The Virgin of the Malcolm Collection in its type and features recalls "The Virgin" of Terranuova, and the children in that picture are cast, as we shall see, in the mould of those at the Eternal's side in "The Trinity" of San Severo, whilst the studies for the Eternal are similar to each other, whether intended for the fresco or the lunette of Sant' Antonio.

As in the composition of the "Ansidei Madonna," so in that of other contemporary masterpieces we have a set of progressive studies which reveals the gradual expansion of Raphael's mind. There are sketches for the altar-piece of Sant' Antonio and the frescos of San Severo which enable us to track the master's way in the gradual development of his art. The fine silver-point figure at Oxford, which shows "God the Father" in half-length, with open palms, looking down from a cloud, seems but a variety of a pen outline at Lille, in which the head is turned another way and one hand is raised in the act of benediction.*

distance a bridge, buildings, hills. On the back of the sheet a repetition of the child in larger size. From the Lagoy, Dimsdale and Lawrence collections. 4⅖ in. h. by 5⅜ in.

Oxford Gall. No. 24. Study in pen and ink for the landscape of the foregoing. Same size. From the same collections.

The drawing of a head and legs. Pen sketch. 0·45 h. by 0·16 in the Lille Coll. is described as a study for the Baptist of the Blenheim altar-piece, but differs from it in turn and action of the head and legs, and differs from it in this, that the handling is that of a later period. Yet the art is that of Raphael.

The authors fail to recollect the study of "St. Nicholas" described as being in the Gallery of Stockholm by Pass. ii. No. 312.

* Oxford Gall. No. 30. Study for the figure of a young man looking down from the clouds.

Neither of these leaves differ in style from the full length at Oxford apparently conceived to represent the first person of the Trinity.*   Yet not one of these pieces seems exactly to have suited the purpose for which it was intended, as Raphael did not use them in any of the works with which we are acquainted.

For the Terranuova "Madonna" the period of fruition may be traced much further and much longer.   As far back in his career as the time of the Connestabile "Madonna," Raphael had imagined a group of the Virgin and Child with the Infant John and two male Saints, of which a finished drawing was made on the back of the very sheet on which the cartoon of the Connestabile "Madonna" was thrown.†   When he finished this

---

Silver-point on pale cream-coloured prepared ground. 9½ in. h. by 7½. From the Wicar and Lawrence collections. Slight study, partly shaded. On the reverse is a slight design of a church or portico.

Lille Mus. No. 697. Pen sketch, very rapid. From the Fedi collection ; also seen to the waist. The hand in benediction is retouched. Size 0·11 h. by 0·10.

* Oxford Gall. No. 31. Silverpoint, on pale cream-coloured prepared ground. 8⅛ in. h. by 5¾. From the Antaldi and Woodburne collections. Squared for transfer to a cartoon, but, so far as we know, never used. It is the figure of a youth in hose and jerkin, seated, looking to the right.

† Berlin. Print-room. 0·160 h. by 0·125. On whity-grey paper. Pen and umber drawing. To the left the boy Baptist, in a coat and mantle, at the Virgin's knee, holding with the left hand the end of the scroll, of which the other end is held by the Infant Christ on the Virgin's lap. She has hold of the Boy with her right, and her left is stretched out with a gesture of surprise which assists the look of wonder with which she glances down at the two children. Behind to the left a young saint, three-quarters to the right. To the left an aged saint with a forked beard, whose hands are joined in prayer. This beautiful drawing is not without awkward defects in the bundled drapery, and the curious accident of the Virgin's hand and the hands of the saint to the right all coming together. But the delicacy of the drawing, the grace of the movement and expression

composition, Raphael found no occasion for transferring it to a picture. Later on, as his skill improved, he repeated the subject in a bolder though slighter shape in a sheet which is now at Lille.* But even then the subject remained unused. The journey to Florence occurred and in his wanderings through the collections of Florentine patricians, it almost seems as if Raphael caught a new inspiration from one of the masterpieces of Michelangelo. It had been Buonarotti's chance to paint a picture of the Virgin for Agnolo Doni which had given rise to a quarrel with which Florence might have been full at the very time of Raphael's visit. Agnolo Doni and his wife Magdalena were amongst the noblest of Raphael's sitters. Nothing so likely, as that Raphael should have been one of the first to see in the rooms of the Doni that celebrated round of the Holy Family which now forms one of the choicest ornaments of the collection of the Uffizi. Under the influence of the impression which that picture produced, Raphael may have recast the subject of which he had already made two versions and produced the " Madonna " of Terranuova which embodies all the sweetness of his older style with a boldness, and strength and freedom of mani-

---

are lovely and purely Raphaelesque. From the Madrazo Collection at Madrid. At the back the cartoon of the Connestabile " Madonna," *u.s.*

* Lille Mus. No. 686. Pen and umber, on white paper. 0·18 h. by 0·16. The same group, in a bolder hand, of more rapid line, arched at top. But this drawing is disfigured by a patch, which has been put in and drawn upon, so that the Virgin's left hand seems to rest on the hip of the Infant Christ. This and the whole of the lower part of the infant, as well as the arms and hand of the old saint to the right, is modern.

pulation, and an effective poise of light and shade, hitherto unprecedented in his practice. In the two drafts of the " Madonna " of Terranuova, which only differ from each other so far as they were drawn at different times and with a certain variety in the handling, the principal group is that of the Virgin seated with the Infant Christ on her lap, showing the scroll to the boy Baptist at his side. The Virgin expresses surprise alike by her glance and downward bend of head, and a gesture of the left hand. The setting of the group is one-sided, but this is ingeniously corrected by making the bearded saint to the right behind the Virgin larger and more important than the angel to the left. The later origin of the Lille drawing seems indicated by the arching of the upper part, from which it may be inferred that Raphael was studying to change the picture from its original form of a square to that of a round. It was apparently not till he had seen the circular panel of Michaelangelo, or some masterpiece of a similar kind at Florence, that he imagined the group of the Virgin and Child and Baptist in a round without attendant saints, relieved against the low wall of a court, and thrown with an effect hitherto untried against a strongly shadowed landscape. To balance the composition, which now required some sort of counterpoise to the figure of the Baptist, that of the infant saint to the right was introduced, who looks so beautifully and so archly at the tender commune of the Saviour and St. John. Fruit of the journeys on the way to Florence had been, as before observed, the wonderful boulder, and the walled city and spires in the distance of this splendid composition.*

There is reason to think, though time has dealt hardly with the drapery of this picture, that it combined quite a Florentine massiveness of light and shade with a glow of colour intense beyond anything previously achieved. The way in which the shadowing of the background and that of the right side of the figures is made to contrast with the lighting of the hills and sky and that of the left side of the figures, the cleverness with which the group is thrown into focus in front of the dark grey wall which separates the Virgin from the landscape, is a masterpiece of pictorial arrangement only to be explained by new and very powerful influences ; and to these we must equally attribute the broader and more certain modelling of the flesh, the more successful transparency of the shadows, and the greater fairness of the wheaten flesh tints. Peruginesque drapery, with its blanket texture and loops and branches, remind us still of an earlier time to which also we are banned by the well-known features of the children, whilst the breadth of the cast of folds and the loveliness of the saints, combined with the greater beauty of the Virgin, show that Raphael's style was being divested more and more of that Umbrian leaven which from this time onward gradually tended to disappear altogether from his practice.†

---

* *Antea*, pp. 193–4.

† Berlin Museum. No. 247A. Wood. 2 ft. 9¾, or m. 0·87 in diameter. Originally in possession of the Dukes of Terranuova, first at Genoa, then at

In the fresco of San Severo, which apparently was ordered about the same moment as the Terranuova "Madonna," two periods are distinctly marked : the earlier, pointing to the time of Raphael's first visit to Florence, the later, to a more intimate acquaintance with the Florentine masterpieces of the 16th century. Nor is anything in the inscriptions with which the fresco is furnished or in the state of the painting itself to run counter to this belief. The monks of San Severo had, it would seem, made a covenant with Raphael to paint the "Trinity" and "Fathers of the Church" in a lunette, and saints on the wall below. Raphael at intervals finished different parts of the subject. He first composed the Eternal in clouds, attended by two cherubs with scrolls, then the Saviour in glory between two angels in a company of saints. But having got thus far he stopped, and after Raphael's death Perugino completed the imperfect decoration. It was then and not till then that inscrip-

---

Naples. Bought at Naples in 1854 for 30,000 scudi. Fairly preserved. The blue mantle of the Virgin, bleached to grey-blue. Some light cleaned off the face of the Infant Christ. Something abraded from the cheek of the Baptist. Some changes in the outlines of the left hand of the Virgin. But for this the picture untouched. In the picture the gesture of the hand of the Virgin and the drapery are given with much more skill than in the Berlin drawing, and the arrange-

ment of the hands of the Baptist is altered, so that he takes the scroll with his right instead of his left, and so is enabled to hold a little cross which is not in the sketch. The boulder on the right side of the picture is the same as that in the Venice sketch-book, and the same in its principal features as the rock in the landscape of the "Vision of the Knight."

The study for the Infant Christ in the collection of the Uffizi, noted in Pass. ii. No. 115, is not a study for the "Madonna di Terranuova."

tions were placed on the wall expressing the fact that Raphael painted the "Trinity" in 1505, and Perugino the attendant saints in 1521.* We can only see in the terms of this inscription, which was written after Raphael's death, a general statement of the fact that Raphael undertook in 1505 a contract which he failed to carry out in its integrity, which indeed was only completed with the help of the master, then aged and decrepit, who had guided Raphael in his leading-strings. It is difficult to judge at the present time of the original beauty of Raphael's work at San Severo, or even to discern what the aspect of the Eternal may have been, as he sat with his hand on the book imparting the blessing. The remnants of this all-important figure are now little more than the hand on the book with spot-like bits of a red dress and a portion of the head and nimbus, whilst of the cherub to the right the hips and legs alone remain. But the fragment which has been preserved will serve to demonstrate that it was the first part of the composition, to which Raphael applied himself; and the large and fleshy forms of the cherubs show by their type and the way in which they are drawn, that the models from which these children were taken were

---

* San Severo, Perugia. To the right, beneath the frescos of the wall, are the words in capital letters, "Raphael de Urbino Domino Octaviano Stephani. Volaterrano Priore Sanctam Trinitatem. Angelos astantes Sanctosq. Pinxit, A.D. MDV." To the left, "Petrus de Castro plebis Perusinus tempore Domini Silvestri Stephani Volaterrani a dextris et a Sinistris div. Christopheræ Sanctos sanctasque pinxit, A.D. MDXXI." Other remarks as to the condition of this fresco, *postea*.

the same as those that served for the boys in the
" Madonna " of Terranuova.

That Raphael, having finished the altar-piece of
Sant' Antonio and the " Madonna " di Terranuova,
should have made no further progress than this with
the fresco of San Severo, need scarcely create surprise.
He was probably pressed enough for time, having
to finish the " Madonna Ansidei " and its predellas ;
the predellas, too, of Sant' Antonio, and the " Pax
Vobis " which about this time was delivered to a
friend at Pesaro.   A record of the period shows what
a busy artist he must have been.   At the close of
December, 1505, the nuns of the Perugian convent
of Monte Luce were casting about for an artist to
paint a " Coronation of the Virgin," and they seem
to have asked their lay friends as well as their
spiritual advisers to point out to them what artist
they had best employ.   The journals of the convent
state that Raphael appeared in the parlour of the
nuns on the 29th of December and signed a covenant
upon which he received an advance of thirty ducats,
which he never succeeded in earning.   The epithets
which grace Raphael's name in these documents are
flattering to his skill and position at Perugia.   He
was " the best painter known to the citizens of
Perugia," the best also in the opinion of the Fran-
ciscans who had seen his works.*   But to be the
best he must also have been the busiest, and of this

---

* See the extracts from the journals in Pungileone's Raphael,
u. s., pp. 192–3, and Pass. ii. 311.

we shall see that there is abundant proof. When he painted the " Virgin and Saints " of Sant' Antonio, he was not a solitary artist slowly working his way into celebrity, he was a master with plenty of work before him, and a number of assistants to help him. Such at least is the impression which his labours at this time produce.

The predella of Sant' Antonio, divided into five pictures representing " The Road to Golgotha," " The Agony on the Mount," the " Pietà," " St. Francis," and " St. Anthony of Padua," were dispersed two centuries ago to different collections; they are now, as it were, isolated pictures;—claiming attention for themselves instead of being modestly lost in the framings of a large altar-piece.* We must fancy them in their original places, if we desire to be fairly critical respecting them. It is hardly right to judge of Raphael's quality by the labour which he gave to the panels of a predella. On rare occasions it might be all his own. More frequently he would share it with a disciple, in some instances he would only be answerable for the sketch.

As Raphaelesque designs carried out by Raphael's disciples, the " St. Francis " and " St. Anthony " at Dulwich may once have been attractive. Time, accident, and restoring have deprived them of almost

* The records of the sale to the representatives of Christina, Queen of Sweden, on the 7th of June, 1663, for 600 scudi, are in Giorn. di Erud. Toscana, iii. p. 305 and ff.   See also the catalogue of her collection in Campori, Raccolta di Cataloghi, p. 359, and the catalogue of the Orleans collection in Waagen's Treasures, ii. 194.

all charm.* Better preserved, yet not originally without conspicuous defects, the "Agony in the Garden" at Lady Burdett Coutts' represents a scene from the "Passion" in quite a prosaic form. Whilst the Saviour kneels on the Mount to receive the cup, the three Apostles lie sleeping on the ground. The level of a very ordinary realism has been hardly attained by one who probably followed Raphael's lines, but who, as he painted, overran or fell short of the contours set forth by his chief.† The subject nobly carried out by Perugino in a celebrated altarpiece at Florence, had already been better designed by another disciple of the master in a small picture at Urbino which was afterwards honoured, though with

---

* Dulwich Gallery. No. 306. Wood. 9½ in. h. by 6⅚ in. St. Anthony turned to the left, the head to the right, with the book and lily (new). The head has been abraded and restored. A piece was added to the left side of the panel.

No. 307. S. Francis with the cross and book. Head and body turned to the right. The lower part of the face injured and re-touched.

† London. Lady Burdett Coutts. From the collections, Queen Christine, Orleans, Bryant, and Lord Eldin (Edinburgh). Purchased at the sale of the poet Rogers. Wood. 9½ in. h. by 11. A copy of this piece, obviously made from the same cartoon as the original, belongs to Professor Aus'm Weerth at Bonn, who bought it for 400 thalers.

A copy of old date, very thick in the pigment, and pallid in the flesh tints. Like its counterpart it contains short muscular figures of coarse mould, copied without selection from ordinary models. The Christ especially is without elevation, of burly person and quaintly furnished with copious chough of hair. Some retouching, *ex. gr.*, in the hands of the Saviour, and some cleaning generally have injured the picture. Of this and the two other panels of the Sant' Antonio predella, there is a copy of the year 1663, by Claudio Inglesio Gallo, in the church of S. Antonio at Perugia. It tells us that the picture of the "Agony" was on the left, that of the "Pietà" on the right of the "Golgotha." See also Giornale di Erud. Tosc. iii. 309-10.

slight regard to truth, with the name of Raphael himself.* But in spite of all defects, the "Christ on the Mount" still charms by sweetness of tone and that indescribable quality which makes everything Raphaelesque fair to look upon.

More skilfully treated, more moving and less servilely on Perugino's lines, the "Pietà" of Mr. Dawson attracts not the less that the usual architectural surroundings familiar to the Umbrians, are replaced by a landscape and trees. As in Perugino's version of the same subject at the Florentine Academy, the Virgin mourns over the body of the dead Christ, whose form is supported on her lap by the Evangelist. The Magdalen lies prostrate at the feet which she kisses, and Nicodemus and Joseph of Arimathea grieving look on at each side of the composition.† Here Raphael's work excels in delicacy of religious feeling and melody of tone.

"The Road to Golgotha" in the collection of Leigh Court takes the form of an antique frieze reproducing

---

* This picture once belonged to Mr. Fuller Maitland, and is now catalogued without a name in the National Gallery. See reasons for assigning it to Spagna in History of Italian Painting, iii. 308. A copy of this picture fairly old in date was exhibited at Rome in 1870, in the convent of S. M. degli Angeli, as the property of Signor Ignazio del Frate.

† Mr. M. H. Dawson. Wood. 9½in. h. by 11 in. From the Christine, Orleans, collection. Sold for £60 at the Bryant sale in 1798.

Passed into the collections of Bonnemaison, Rechberg (Munich), Sir Th. Lawrence, and M. A. Whyte, of Barron Hill. Nicodemus to the left holds the nails. To the right Joseph of Arimathea, in a turban, clasps his hands and looks at the dead Christ. Compare Perugino's Pietà, of 1493-4, No. 58, in the Academy of Arts at Florence. The head and nude of the Saviour are fine ; the colour rich and harmonious, and the whole fairly preserved.

the various incidents of a procession. Foremost to
the right two riders in Eastern dress, one in a turban
with a lance and pennon, pacing forward and looking
back ; the other, also turbaned, firmly seated and with
strong grip curbing the fire of his charger. In the
centre, Christ with the cross on his shoulder, dragged
by an executioner, who hauls at him with a rope, is
saved from sinking by the help of Joseph of Arimathea. The ground is kept at the sides by four
characteristic figures of guards. In rear of the cross
the Virgin drops into the arms of the Maries, and
John the Evangelist wrings his hands as he sees her
fainting. We note the study of horses and horsemen,
which served to produce the suite of "Æneas Sylvius"
and the " St. George " of the Louvre. Such faults as
squareness of shape or excess of stride in the Christ, or
strained action in the executioner, due no doubt to
the hand of a disciple, are counterbalanced by study
of nature in the fainting Virgin and grieving John,
by ease in the sit and movement of the riders and
energetic impulse in the gesture of the Evangelist.
But here again the picture attracts chiefly by sweetness and richness of colour and a delightful combination of harmonious tones in the variegated dresses of
the soldiers and guards, and a landscape of plain and
hill and towers. Unless we fancy that Raphael
found the design for the fainting Virgin in his
master's portfolio, as he may well have done in
Florence in 1504, we must assume that he painted
the central panel of the predella of Sant' Antonio
after August, 1505, since Perugino introduced the

same group, of which he indeed was the originator, into the "Descent from the Cross," which he completed after it had been left unfinished by Fra Filippo, in 1504, at Santa Maria de' Servi at Florence.*

It is to this period of Raphael's striving that we should ascribe the "Pax Vobis" at Brescia, a miniature half-length of Christ, in which the modelled flesh, covering a large superstructure of bone, betrays a desire to adopt the naturalism of the Florentines. It is not unpleasant to see some of the tenderness of the Umbrians and some of the conventionalisms of the Perugian school still clinging to the master whose charm is kept up as of old by handling of very subtle workmanship and colouring of great delicacy.†

---

* Leigh Court. Wood. 9½ in. h. by 2 ft. 9½ in. From the Orleans Collection. This panel was sold to Mr. Hibbert for £150, then to Mr., late Sir W. Miles. Here too we notice short, thick-set models of fleshy character, with large and coarse extremities. The picture is fairly preserved, but somewhat enfeebled by cleaning in the group of the Virgin and Maries. Compare the "Descent from the Cross," by Lippi and Perugino, at the Servi in Florence, for which the contract was made by the latter on the 5th of Aug., 1505, and who finished it in 1506. (Vas. Sansoni, ed. iii. p. 586.) Passavant notices (ii. 29) a Christ similar to that of Leigh Court in the Bridgewater collection in London, and says it is ascribed to Raphael. But this statement contains several errors. The picture

is in the Stafford Gallery. Christ carries the cross on the right shoulder and not on the left as at Leigh Court, and the name of the painter is not Raphael but Spagna.

A fair old copy of the predella of Leigh Court is in the Pianciatichi collection at Florence.

A pen drawing, copied from the picture in reverse is No. 519 in the Uffizi at Florence. It came from the Santarelli collection.

A drawing of two horsemen, at a gallop, riding to the right, washed in umber, in the Ambrosiana at Milan, might be taken for a study for this picture, but that it is not by Raphael.

† Brescia. Tosi Collection. From the Mosca family at Pesaro. Wood. 11½ in. h. by 9¼. The grey-blue sky fades down into the horizon, which is bounded by a screen of

Passing from this to the predella of the "Madonna Ansidei" at Bowood, we shall see that Peruginesque tradition still lingers in the artist's mind, though Florentine lessons are slowly working to permeate and change his style. St. John to the right, stands cross in hand, on a grassy elevation preaching to a crowd of listeners. Three in front are seated and one is standing, all heedless of two naked children playing at their feet. Next to these on the left are three men, one seen from behind, one in profile, the third in full front. To the extreme left are dignitaries in various attitudes, one of them obese, with his thumbs in his belt. Between the two last groups a servant waits on horseback, and as a background to the whole the landscape of sky and hills is partly veiled by clumps of dark-leaved trees.

The Baptist would remind us most of Perugino, but that in form and build he displays a larger scantling than the Umbrian, and a weight of bone similar to that which characterizes the figures of Ghirlandaio in the "Sermon of John" at Santa Maria Novella at Florence. Quaint bits of headgear like that of the man in a violet conical cap in the centre of the picture are distinctly traceable to the painting-room at Perugia. The vanishing of the foreshortenings of some heads is Umbrian, but amongst the foremost figures in the first and last rows of listeners,

---

trees and brown ground. Long hair is covered with a crown of green thorns. A small beard grows about the chin and lips.

The red hip-cloth is wound round the body and falls over the arm which is raised in the act of bene-diction.

some are distinguishable whose grand repose and picturesque vestments recall the models of Masaccio at the Brancacci, whilst others exhibit the natural freedom of the Florentines contrasted with the traditional attitudes of the Perugians. It is curious, indeed, to find combinations of two styles in one picture ;—superabundance of dress and broken folds in some figures, and moderation coupled with monumental grandeur of drapery in others. The line of hills forming the distance, the grove that intercepts the sky and the rich velvety texture of varied colours are Umbrian and Raphaelesque. The playfulness of the two boys who struggle for a seat at the feet of the foremost sitters charmingly commingles the innocent and grave. We remember the studies of the Venice sketch-book in which Raphael catches a group of children pulling at a dead sucking-pig.[*]

We see Raphael's connection with the Tuscan capital becoming closer as we look into the pictures which he painted in these days. Pity that history and records should fail to give evidence of that which pictures so convincingly prove. But if we should venture to theorize on a matter so difficult, we might presume that after having been at Florence for a time at the close of 1504, Raphael temporarily, but at

---

[*] Bowood, but once the property of Lord R. Spencer. Wood. 1 ft. 8½ in. long by 10½ in. h. A sweetly coloured picture, not free from injury from unequal cleaning and partial restoring. Conspicuously in the spirit of Masaccio is the foreground standing figure to the left, and the foreground sitting figure to the right. Florentine in movement are the two hindermost listeners next to St. John.

repeated intervals, absented himself from that city in order to revisit the place of his early adoption. We recollect that in December, 1505, he took the contract from the nuns of Monte Luce. He may have been at Perugia fitfully at other moments during which he finished the altar-pieces and predellas of Sant' Antonio and Ansidei. It would be the duty of his pupils and assistants to labour at the subordinate parts of these compositions, leaving it to himself to give the final masterstrokes. We should think there is evidence of this not merely in considerable parts of the predellas which have been described, but in the whole design and execution of portions of the "Madonna" Ansidei, since we cannot attribute to the master himself any part of the defective work which disfigures the drapery of the Virgin's cloak in that otherwise beautiful altar-piece. Yet we may still believe that whilst Raphael came inspecting, correcting, and directing to his painting-room at Perugia, he left behind another similar painting-room at Florence, whither, after his journeys to the South, he would return to perform exactly the same duties as those he had performed at Perugia.

There is no practical difficulty in supposing that the Terranuova "Madonna" was executed at least in part at Florence, but then the upper portion of the fresco of San Severo was undertaken almost at the same time at Perugia. The moment came when the "Madonna del Gran' Duca," and the small "Madonna" of Lord Cowper were composed, both of which appear to have been amongst the earliest works that were begun and completely finished in the Tuscan capital.

In order to understand Raphael's course at Florence we must ask ourselves, who the artists were whose company he frequented. Perugino seems to be the artist, Perugino's the practice to which Raphael and his practice seem in these days to have most resemblance. Perugino had left the Umbrian country in autumn, 1504, perhaps had even taken Raphael with him to Florence. In November and December, then in January and February, 1505, we find him wrangling with the agents of the Marchioness of Mantua about a picture which he seemed unwilling or unable to compose. In the midst of this wrangle Perugino disappeared, and it was not without surprise that those who wanted him found the Patriarch, as he was called, on his way to Perugia. Whilst Isabel Gonzaga thought he was finishing her "Triumph of Chastity," he was covering a wall of twenty-two feet square with an "Epiphany" at Città della Pieve, and composing a "Martyrdom of St. Sebastian" in the Church of Panicale. Six weeks sufficed to perform the journey and paint the pictures, and the patriarch was home at the end of April and ready to deliver the "Triumph of Chastity." At the close of June, with Lorenzo di Credi, and Giovanni delle Corgniole, to value the mosaics of Monte di Giovanni, for a chapel in the cathedral, was but the business of a day.

We can fancy that Raphael's life was very like Perugino's at this period. Unsettled, active, he was a travelling and travelled painter; but in the intervals, when he remained at Florence, he had the advantage of old relations with Perugino, and if he should have to suffer from the enmities, he was fairly sure to profit by the friendships, which the patriarch enjoyed. That meeting which we just saw Perugino hold with Lorenzo di Credi, might have been witnessed by Raphael, who surely would try his utmost to become acquainted with all the masters, who had been fellow disciples with Perugino in the workshop of Verrocchio. Lionardo, another of these disciples, was seriously busy, beginning to paint on the walls of the public palace, from the great cartoon, which he had finished at Santa Maria Novella. As early as February, 1505, the scaffoldings and ladders for this great enterprise had been set up in the town-hall. At no great distance, in the church of the Servi, Perugino himself was about to finish the "Entombment" which Filippino had left a fragment, and Da Vinci had neglected to complete. What fell to Raphael's own share to do, is not so certainly on record, but he was not idle, we may be sure, and when his labours were over in the painting-room, he doubtless wandered into the Brancacci chapel to study Masaccio; past Orsanmichele to look at the statues of Donatello, into Santa Maria Nuova to admire the "Last Judgment" of Baccio della Porta, or into Santa Maria Novella to wonder at the grand creations of Domenico Ghirlandaio. Baccio d'Agnolo, the friend and crony of Perugino, whom he had known at Perugia, kept a shop in one of the Florentine streets, and there Michaelangelo or the lesser masters of the artistic guilds would come and exchange greetings. It was here, we may believe, that the greatest of Florentine sculptors first heard of the rising talents of the Umbrian youth, who was to be his rival at Rome. Here Raphael came to take counsel from the large experience of the architects Cronaca, Giuliano, and Antonio da San Gallo, the three masters who had just succeeded in transporting Michaelangelo's "David" into the public square of the city. Andrea Sansovino would teach him to respect the difficulties of monumental sculpture which he had just illustrated in works of mark in Portugal. Granacci would remind him of the bygone days when Florentine art rose to its noblest form under the hand of Domenico Ghirlandaio. Whilst he listened to the wisdom of these older hands, his youth and similarity of taste would tempt him to join the younger frequenters of Baccio's shop; and close friendship would most naturally arise with men exactly of his own age, such as Ridolfo Ghirlandaio, whilst the fun of Bastiano da San Gallo, then apprentice to Perugino, would give him a foretaste of those ingenious artistic discussions which contributed to obtain for their originator the nickname of Aristotle.

But in the *bottega* of Baccio d' Agnolo Raphael would not meet with artists only, he might chance, and he did chance, to make acquaintances most useful in a worldly sense; he secured the patronage of Lorenzo Nasi, whose palace, now inhabited by the

family of Torregiani, had been planned by Baccio;
and he won the friendship of Taddeo Taddei, one of
the literary worthies, who patronized Michaelangelo,
and corresponded later with Bembo, and whose house
in the Via de' Ginori, now known as the Pecori-
Giraldi palace, was also built after Baccio's designs.[*]
We shall see that, in a letter written in 1508, Raphael
recommended Taddeo Taddei to Battista Ciarla, with
expressions of love and gratitude, from which it is
clear that he owed as much to that gentleman in
the years of his striving at Florence, as to any of the
more celebrated patrons, whose names pictorial annals
have preserved.[†] By other means, perhaps by the
voice of common fame, he acquired the patronage of
the Doni, whose likenesses, as we have seen, he
painted soon after his first migration from Perugia,
though not before he had learnt to become enthu-
siastic for the style of Lionardo da Vinci.

It may not be stated as an absolute fact, it can only
be gathered from a consideration of the practice which
pictures reveal, that Raphael's intercourse with Lionardo was difficult and slow. A man of such celebrity
as Da Vinci might not absolutely repel the advances of
a youth like Raphael, considering the friendship which
probably bound Lionardo to Perugino. But the magnitude of his engagements would possibly not allow
him to give up much time even to so promising an
artist. The winning manner, for which Raphael is
celebrated, and the ardent admiration of Da Vinci,

---

* Vas. ix. p. 225. | † See *postea*.

which his works for a time display, cannot have been without influence in making close the ties which evidently bound the two masters at last. The Lionardesque feeling in Raphael struck root deeply, but it struck root slowly, and it is difficult to find anything more in the first examples of Raphael's Florentine style than a general influence and grafting of the Florentine manner on the Umbrian stock.

But with what potent and irresistible force that influence was felt, is apparent already in its full effect in the "Madonna del Gran' Duca," of which we have spoken as one of the earliest examples after Raphael's first withdrawal from Perugia, yet of which we know the history too superficially to be able to say when it was finished and for whom it was ordered.

With the "Madonna del Gran' Duca" Raphael ceases altogether to be a fitter of the Umbrian ideas of the Peruginesque time. Even the sketches which precede and accompany that divine picture, have felt the breath of the Florentine air. A girl at the Uffizi, with her head more to one side than that of the "Madonna" itself, seems to have been wrought from a model foreign to the Umbrian country. She wears the veil, that protects rather than conceals the division of the hair, the forehead, and the bands of locks, that are twisted over the ears. The corners of the mouth, the melancholy eyes are just breaking, yet have not broken, into a Lionardesque smile. We turn the sheet, and the same girl appears as a mother holding the child, whose forehead is glued to her cheek. Two sides of one page thus comprise a variety of thoughts for the "Madonna del Gran' Duca" and that of Casa Tempi.* In a sheet at Oxford the Virgin, seated, holds the Babe on her knee. Half standing, half leaning, he sits on one of the Virgin's palms, whose other palm supports him under the armpits; and he lies with his hands all over her, looking at something to us unseen which also attracts his mother.† But these, and perhaps other jottings and rapid notes of things that he had seen, are garnered in Raphael's mind, and he produces first, the design of the Madonna with the infant clinging to her neck and bosom, ‡ then the picture, a more perfect rendering of the same group, and he gives to the Virgin that beauteous sentiment of love allied to absolute purity of feature, and to the child that depth of thought in the eye, which raise the master's creation at once from daily life into ideal regions.

Something may still remind us of the Peruginesque

---

* Florence. Uffizi. Frame 135. No. 497. One side contains the head first described in the text, and beneath it that of a girl with loose locks looking down. On the other side of the sheet—the same head of a girl with loose hair, to the left of it an angel partly obliterated and partly re-drawn with red chalk, and above that the group mentioned in the text. All but the angel is drawn with a pen in umber. See Pas. No. 116.

† Oxford Gall. No. 45. Pen and bistre outline. 7¼ in. h. by 5¼ in. From the Alva, West and Lawrence collections. The Virgin's head to the left, her body to the right. The Infant to the left.

‡ Florence. Uffizi. Frame 136. No. 505. Silver-point and black chalk. Oval to the knees, with a flat hanging at the Virgin's back, behind which a landscape is indicated. Rapid sketch.

Another sketch at Chatsworth, represents a group like that of the "Madonna del Gran' Duca." It is on a sheet on which a design for the Esterhazy "Madonna" is drawn. But the state of this drawing does not allow of a very safe judgment as to its genuineness.

in both Virgin and Child, and a remnant of Umbrian method survives in the cast of the drapery. But the Peruginesque is almost lost in the Florentine. With what ease the boy sits on the Virgin's hand; how prettily twisted the sash round his body. How safe he feels as he leans against his mother's bosom; what serenity and fulness of joy in the Virgin, who stands with her veiled head slightly bent, her downward glance beaming on the face of the babe. The true ideal of proportion seems obtained between mother and child; and great technical perfection is revealed in the brilliancy which overspreads the regular oval of the Virgin's face, thrown into light on the dark green ground of the panel.* The characteristic quality of this masterpiece as compared with its contemporary, the small "Madonna" of Lord Cowper, is the dignity and grandeur of the conception and the ideal beauty of its rendering in the first, and the more homely, motherly, perhaps colder sentiment in the second.

Here the Virgin sits in the open air. The sun shines out of an all but cloudless sky upon the hills and plains of a landscape, on one ridge of which a church with a dome and campanile shows its white marbled front. The Virgin's veil, striped with gold, is twisted amongst the hair, and falls from the back of the head

---

* Florence. Pitti. No. 266. Panel. 2 ft. 3½ in. h. by 1 ft. 9½ in. This picture, which belonged to Carlo Dolce (Pass. ii. 24), was sold to the Grand Duke of Tuscany, Ferdinand the IIIrd, for 300 sequins, or 3,360 lire (Gotti. Gall. di Firenze, p. 181). The flesh tints have suffered much, and parts of the Christ, and particularly the feet, have been retouched. The blue mantle is full of spots.

to the neck, whilst another, equally subtle, runs round
the bosom and shoulders. The naked Christ sits on
one hand and sets his foot on the other hand of his
mother; his arms are round her neck. The feeling
which animates the group is that of youth and strong
life combined in a familiar way. The execution,
finished as it is, has not quite the full measure which
marks the "Madonna del Gran' Duca," and this,
perhaps, with other subordinate causes, makes the
Cowper "Madonna" just inferior to its rival at
Florence.*

Raphael hitherto had confined himself to a rapid
survey of Tuscan painting. Amongst the earlier
masters, Masaccio, Filippino, and Ghirlandaio had
seemed to him especially worthy of admiration. He
showed an equal appreciation of the genius of Lionardo, Michaelangelo, and Baccio della Porta; but
after a closer study of select masterpieces, and perhaps not unbiassed by personal feelings too natural to

---

* Panshanger. Wood. 2 ft. h.
by 1 ft. 5 in. Bought by Lord
Cowper at Florence. The execution, though it recalls that of the
Tempi "Madonna," and the "Entombment" of the Borghese Palace,
is a little cold, and there is some
thinness in the pigments, yet they
still appear to have been moistened
with a fat vehicle. The treatment
of Spagna, or Timoteo Viti, by
way of help, seems to pierce here
and there. The Virgin's hand, on
which the Infant rests, is a little
rubbed down, and a finger
lengthened by restoring. A copy
of the same size, and apparently
almost contemporary with the
original, was seen by the authors
in the Lombardi collection at
Florence. It was much injured
and discoloured. It may be the
same which Passavant (ii. 26)
notices in the house of one Peruzzi
at Florence.

The sketch-drawing on pearl-
grey paper of the Infant's head
acknowledged as genuine by Passavant in the Staedel Collection at
Frankfort, does not bear the
character of a genuine work.

deserve reproof, he soon showed a preference for Da Vinci. That he should have been personally repelled rather than attracted by Michaelangelo, was a necessary consequence of a quarrel which had taken place between that artist and Perugino. Nor was it easy for Raphael, who held his master in so much reverence, not to resent the rudeness of the man who had qualified Perugino's art as antiquated and absurd. But Michaelangelo's disdain was not confined to Perugino, it extended with openness verging on brutality to Lionardo da Vinci himself. About the time when Raphael came to Florence, Lionardo and Michaelangelo had had an unpleasant encounter in the street. Lionardo had been asked some question about Dante. He met Michaelangelo, who was reputed to know more of Dante than most men of his day, and he begged him to answer the question. Michaelangelo, instead of being flattered, gruffly told Lionardo to answer the question himself, taunting him instantly after with his failure to cast the bronze of the Sforza statue.* No wonder that Lionardo's cheek should have blanched at this insult, no wonder that Raphael, if he liked Lionardo, should have kept away from the man by whom Lionardo had been insulted. Da Vinci, however, was in too great repute as a master in all branches of the arts and sciences to be materially affected by Buonarotti's want of courtesy. If Michaelangelo had distinguished himself in

---

* The anecdote is in the MS. of an Anonimo, published by G. Milanesi in the volume of the   Archivio Storico of Florence for 1872.

the "David," which all Florence saw and admired in the principal square of the city, all Florence knew that Lionardo had modelled the statue of Ludovico Sforza and painted the "Last Supper" at the Grazie of Milan. It would be for the public taste to decide which was the best man, when the cartoons for the frescos of the Town-hall were finally exhibited. Meanwhile Da Vinci's advantages over his rival were those of riper years, a longer experience, and a deeper insight into the problems which had occupied artists for two centuries. Very few people perhaps had read, most would have heard of, the precepts and laws of painting which Lionardo had written for the use of his academy. No one can read the fragments of Da Vinci's lectures even now, without the deepest admiration for the wide range of thought which they reveal and the large extent of ground which they cover. No one who has looked at them, and also studied Raphael, can fail to be convinced that Raphael had mastered them or listened to their delivery before he painted the "Madonna del Cardellino" or the portrait of Maddalena Doni.

Lionardo taught that light and shade, colour and solidity, figure and position, distance and propinquity and motion and rest were the ten matters which a painter had to care for. The first point to determine, he said, was attitude, the second relief, the third design, and the fourth colour.* Raphael paid

---

* Da Vinci, De Pittura, ed. H. Ludwig. 8vo. Wien. 1882. vol. i. pp. 78, 178, and 394.

more attention to these maxims at Florence than at Perugia. Movement and attitude, or the place to which each figure should be brought within the space of a composition, were matters which now occupied him much more than of old. In the "Madonna del Cardellino" and the "Madonna Canigiani," they are of paramount importance. Light also is distributed in these pictures altogether in accordance with Da Vinci's principles, which teach, that figures should never be painted with the sun full on them, since the result would then be shade too dark or light too strong.* "Temper the sun," says the sage, "temper it with a haze which shall interpose like a veil between the object and the luminary. You shall then have breadth of light without excess of shadow."† But Lionardo also inculcated the laws of contrast by light and shade, and Raphael displayed genius in balancing a group against the sky and landscape and figures in the group against each other. In drawing, a new and constant appeal to nature was combined with such a searching study of the parts as Lionardo recommended. "Children," Da Vinci urges, "will always be found to have narrow articulations with curved projections above and below the joints, because the sinews of these parts are not padded and flesh is banished from them entirely."‡ The characteristic exaggeration of this peculiarity in Credi and Verrocchio is almost a certain test of their style. It prevails for a moment in the Florentine work of Raphael, and

---

* Ibid. ibid. i. 144.   † Ibid. ibid. i. 182.   ‡ Ibid. ibid. i. 290.

notably in the "Madonna del Cardellino."   Again,
Lionardo says, "Avoid affected trimming and comb-
ing down of the hair about the human face. Some
people think a comb and a mirror the very best of
counsellors. It is infamous to be caught with one
hair more on one side than on the other, and a curse
attends the wind as the direst of enemies. But you,
painter, shall imagine a breeze about your figures and
let their locks float about their faces in gentle turns,
so as they be more gracefully adorned. But ornament,
too, shall be avoided, for it impedes the form and the
attitude; and when you draw the folds of a dress
see to it that they are simple, not crossed with 'projections or depressions to gather light or shade
in wrong places. Consider that drapery should be
simple, and above all that it should appear to be
inhabited."*

How quickly Raphael took these precepts to heart,
is shown in the sudden disappearance of all Umbrian
conventionalisms in gilding and ornament. Antique
simplicity replaces traditional breaks and branches in
vestment folds. Though Raphael knew much of
landscape from Perugino, he was successfully warned
by Da Vinci of certain dangers which it is clear he
invariably, perhaps unnecessarily, avoided. "Never,"
says Lionardo, "paint foliage when the sun is shining
so as to throw light through the transparence of the
leaves, for you shall then breed a confusion which an
artist ought entirely to avoid. Shun, however, the

---

* Ibid. ibid. i. 218, 394, and 396.

mistake of Botticelli, who thinks that a sponge, moistened with colours, thrown at a panel, will produce a landscape at one stroke."* So far, indeed, from thinking little of landscape, Lionardo assigned to it an enormous importance, and nothing can be more minute than his explanations of the causes of certain appearances in nature and rules for reproducing them in painting. But the precepts of Da Vinci are more marked in Raphael's portraits than in his pictures. The subtle hair is seen playing in the wind about the head of Maddalena Doni, and the light which surrounds her, is mysteriously damped in accordance with maxims, which Lionardo himself had already applied to his masterpiece of the "Mona Lisa." "If you see a figure standing in a dusky room," he says, "and look at it from outside in the line of the light, the shadow will be dark and swimming. Paint that and you will have great relief and great softness." †

To illustrate Da Vinci's precepts and their application by Raphael, we shall turn to the "Madonna del Cardellino," which, according to all probability, immediately followed in the master's painting-room the "Madonna del Gran' Duca" and the "Virgin" of Lord Cowper.

The "Madonna del Cardellino" was painted, Vasari tells us, for the wedding of Lorenzo Nasi.‡ It represents the Virgin sitting in a meadow, the Infant Christ between her knees turning from the book

---

* Ibid. ibid. i. 116.   † Ibid. ibid. i. 144.   ‡ Vasari, viii. p. 7.

which she keeps open in her left hand, to fondle the
bird which the boy Baptist presents. She presses
with her fingers the shoulder of St. John in ac-
knowledgment of his eagerness, whilst the infant
Christ with one foot on that of his mother, turns
round to pat the finch on the head. No signs of the
" Passion," no motive of serious import, no cross,
since this was a wedding picture. In the combination
of the attitudes Raphael has concentrated the subtlest
thought. The Virgin is so seated as to look down
with equal ease on the boy who stands at her knee
and the curly-pated Baptist who comes from one
side. Equal genius is shown in giving prominence
to the Virgin's face, which is at once a focus of
light and apex to the Vincian pyramid of composition.* The group is relieved equally against the
warm brownish ground and the cool distance and sky.
The children stand out clearly against the coloured
dress of the Virgin. The attitude of Christ contrasts
in statuesque and classic rest with the impulsive
movement of the Baptist, who has just arrived after
finding the bird and shows by the twitch of his eye
and puffed cheeks and open lips that he has been
running and is blown by his exertion. All the
affectation and conventional grace of the Umbrian has
vanished to make room for something better and

---

* The pyramidal form of composition was taught from the
earliest time in Florence and practised by Botticelli, Filippino,
Lionardo, and Michaelangelo. Lomazzo (Idea del Tempio, p. 40)
lays it down as a known precept:
" Esprimere il moto in forma
piramidale di foco, e fuggire gli
angoli acuti, e le linee rette come
principalmente si vede che a
osservato, il primo di tutti Michelangelo."

more refined.   Drapery sits with grand simplicity and sweep of fold.   The features of the Virgin, moulded in the finest form of Raphaelesque beauty, are not insipid but sprightly and expressive, and are full of feeling.   Correct drawing and clean articulation appear to tell of the combined study of nature and the classic.   Landscape imparts a rare charm of loveliness to the scene besides being made subordinate to the general effect by its scheme of tinting and lighting.   The flowers, chiefly white, which adorn the foreground, are all suited to the occasion on which the picture was produced.   Nor does it seem accidental that the distance should comprise Giotto's Campanile and the Dome of Santa Maria del Fiore.   The veil which should interpose between the figures and the sun, is realized in the faint clouds and haze of the sky which fades to white in the horizon of blue hills and serves as a background for the usual groups of elegant saplings.   Still the colours are bright; and the shadows are rubbed in, particularly in the infant Christ, with the swimming *sfumato* of Lionardo and Baccio della Porta.   It is possible to distinguish twenty or more pieces into which this picture was crushed when the Nasi Palace fell into ruins in 1547.   It would be difficult to praise too much the skill with which the pieces were put together, so that now, after much repair, we are enabled to admire the great, nay, extraordinary, attractions of the " Madonna del Cardellino." *

* Florence, Uffizi.   No. 1129.   Full lengths under life size.   One Panel.   3 ft. 1 in. h. by 2 ft. 5 in.   of the splits of the wood runs

Companion to this great masterpiece, inscribed with the date of 1506, and known as the "Madonna in green," we have a composition executed under similar principles and treatment for Taddeo Taddei, the second of Raphael's patrons. There is perhaps more symmetry in the arrangement than in that of the "Madonna del Cardellino," because by setting the Virgin more frankly in profile, a larger geometrical base is given to the pyramid of the contours. But a larger base was required for the two figures of the infant Baptist kneeling to offer the reed cross, and the infant Christ advancing to receive it. The Virgin again is seated on an elevation of ground in a land-

down the head of the infant Christ along the left temple. The other heads remained untouched, but there are many marks of restoring all over the picture. The Baptist wears the camel's hair shirt and carries a wooden bowl slung to his waist. A thin muslin veil covers the nakedness of the infant Christ. In the meadow behind the group, there are two tall trees to the right and one to the left. Behind the latter a stream and a bridge of one arch. In the distance to the right the city of Florence. Of this picture three copies are shown. One which some time belonged to Marquis Campana, and was exhibited in London, is said to be now in the Museum of Geneva. It is a fair picture, not by Raphael. A second, now belonging to Mr. Verity, was purchased by him in 1835 from one Laforest, and has been transferred from panel to canvas. It was exhibited about 1870, at South Kensington, but is not a genuine Raphael.

A third in the Consiglio di Stato at Florence, originally in the sacristy at Vallombrosa, is feebler than the two others.

Signor Giuseppe Cavallucci, in a dissertation on the "Madonna di Vallombrosa," which at the close of last century was considered a replica by Raphael of the "Madonna del Cardellino" (Notizie Inedite di Jacopo Cavallucci. 8vo. Firenze. 1870), quotes records which prove that a picture, which he thought to be Raphael's masterpiece, was paid for with sums acknowledged by one "Raffaello dipintore" in 1506-7 and 8. But there is now a general consent of opinion that these payments are for a "Glory of St. John Gualberto" at Vallombrosa, by a Raphael, who was not Raphael Sanzio.

scape, her frame turned to one side, her head to the other, and her arms so brought together that she holds the infant Christ on her right. With a pretty stride he catches at the cross which the Baptist offers with both hands.

Nothing sweeter can be conceived than the air, the expression, and the movements of these two children. Nothing more grateful to the eye than their brilliant lighting and balanced tonings, which stand in moderate relief against the Virgin's dress, and the wide expanse of distance receding to a far off lake edged with hills. We are inevitably reminded of Raphael's connection with the Perugian country, and recall the same landscape in earlier pictures from his easel. We remember particularly the boulder and spires of the "Vision of the Knight" at the National Gallery. The Virgin's face is perhaps more purely Lionardesque in the "Madonna in green," than in the "Madonna del Cardellino." It has less of the oblong which characterizes earlier creations, like the "St. Catherine" or "St. Margaret" of the altar-piece of Sant' Antonio. Fuller and more expanded forms are united to more powerful colour, handled with stronger substance of pigments, but the Lionardesque haze thrown over the sun damps the force of the shading, whilst it throws a glow over the whole surface of the panel. Surprising delicacy is shown in the transition of enamelled sheen to cool, grey half-tints and warm brown shadows in flesh.*

---

* Vienna Gallery.   No. 300. | the date MDV. . . I (Scil. 1506) on
Wood. M. 1·13 h. by 0·88, with | the hem of the Virgin's dress, near

"The sketching of a picture should be rapid, and the detail not too finished; but the places should be correctly given, so as the parts may then with leisure be finished.* This precept of Lionardo, of which Raphael seems to have been cognizant at an early time, is amply illustrated in his designs for the "Madonna del Cardellino" and the "Madonna in green." At Chatsworth a drawing shows the infant Christ between the Virgin's knees, one foot on hers, looking at something indistinct, which may be a finch, in his left hand. The Virgin's eye is upon him, as she holds the missal on her lap, but this is the converse of the group in the "Madonna del Cardellino," though traces may be found of outlines of the head in two different movements.† Two other versions at Oxford show the Child stretching out his fingers, not to the finch, but to the book, which

the throat. The figures all but life size. Vasari saw the picture in the house of the heirs of Taddeo Taddei (viii. p. 6). Baldinucci notes (Notizie, &c., ed. of Milan, 8vo. 1811, vol. vi. pp. 229–30) that the Taddei family sold it to Ferdinand Archduke of Austria. Till 1663 it was preserved in the palace of Innsbruck, but then it was taken to Schloss Ambras in Tyrol, from whence it passed, in 1773, into the Imperial Collection at Vienna. The drawing of the hands and feet, and the execution of the whole, show a near approach to the style of Raphael as displayed in the "Bella Giardiniera" of the Louvre. The same variety which marks the children in the

"Madonna del Cardellino" is found in the children here. St. John is curly-headed, the infant Christ has soft short hair. The preservation seems perfect.

A good old copy on canvas is in the sacristy of San Tommaso Cantuariense at Verona.

* Lionardo, De Pittura, u. s. i. p. 118.

† Chatsworth, seat of the Duke of Devonshire. Pen and ink sketch. The Infant is naked. The Virgin, turned slightly to the left, holds Christ's left elbow with her left hand, and the book on her knee with the right. The cloak on her right shoulder also covers her lap and legs.

she is reading.*   A third, also at Oxford, gives the group of three, but differs from the picture in this, that the youthful Christ raises his arm to keep the book from closing, and the Baptist stands in attentive attitude at the Virgin's side.†   More rapid and more in the nature of first thoughts are the sketches for the "Madonna in green," several of which are mere spirited lines, drawn hastily with a pen, either of the Virgin and Child, or of the Virgin and Child and Baptist.   Some are repetitions of the children in varied action, or parts of their bodies and heads.   Here the Baptist leans on the cross, or playfully withholds it. There Christ shyly looks at it, or seems to long for its possession.   In one sheet at Vienna the group of three fills one side, the two infants cover the opposite side.   Between them and the Virgin is another thought for the Baptist, a study

---

* Oxford. No. 48. Rapid pen and bistre sketch. 8½ in. h. by 5⅞. From the Antaldi and Lawrence collections. The Virgin is turned to the right, her face to the left. Christ naked between her knees, with his right arm stretching towards the book in his mother's right hand. Her left hand grasps the Infant's left arm. The drawing is rapid, and evidently from models. The bosom of the Virgin is naked, the dress merely indicated.

Oxford. No. 47. 10 in. h. by 8. From the Antaldi, Josi, and Lawrence collections. Represents the foregoing group in similar but more rapid form. To the left of it, and of much larger size, a Virgin, without drapery, sits with the Child on her lap, who chirps and clings to his mother as he sees the Baptist on the left coming forward with something in his left hand, which he holds up to view.

† Oxford. No. 49. Pen and bistre drawing. 9 in. h. by 6¼. Also from the Antaldi and Lawrence collections, more finished than the studies previously described. The Virgin is seated and turned to the right. The Infant between her knees rests one hand on his thigh, and with the right holds the leaves of the book which is in the Virgin's grasp and at which she looks down. The Baptist to the left looks on.

of a hand, and a Madonna with Christ in her arms.* A second set of sketches on the back of the first at Vienna represents the Virgin and her charge, and different forms of the Virgin and Christ.† A third in the same collection repeats the group with the standing Baptist, and six children, or fragments of children, are thrown confusedly on the paper.‡ At Chatsworth the distribution is altered, so that Jesus and John embrace each other, and different studies of boys in varied attitudes are on various parts of the leaf.§ In a different style, and quickly painted in with the point of a brush, the "Holy Family" is represented at Oxford with slight changes in movement, and above that the composition, including the head, the arms, and the body of the Virgin, is modelled in brown tinting. The upper

---

* Vienna, Albertina. Pass. No. 189. Pen and bistre sketch. In all there are three children and a fragment of a fourth in this drawing, besides the chief group of the Virgin and Child and Baptist. The two children here are close to each other, the Baptist standing and looking at Christ, whilst he holds the cross in his hands. The hand is in the upper corner to the left.

† Vienna, Albertina. Pass. No. 189. Back of the foregoing. Pen sketch in bistre, with four groups of the Virgin and Child. The centre one, including the Baptist, kneeling to the left with the cross in his arms. The sketches are all Florentine, and in Lionardesque style. In each group the infant Christ is in a different attitude.

‡ Vienna, Albertina. Pen and bistre as before. To the left the Holy Family, to the right of which two ideas for St. John, one walking, another bowing, and a third fragmentary only. Above these, also in a row of three, busts of children.

§ Chatsworth. Pen and bistre. The Virgin holding the infant Christ, who stands on the ground, and stoops to embrace the kneeling infant John. To the right of the group a standing nude child, turned to the left. Above, to the left, a boy running forwards, turned to the right, and to the right of that, the infant Christ, as if on the lap of the Virgin, looking up with an inspired look.

left hand corner of the paper includes a child's head
and some drapery in red chalk.* The complete design,
or small cartoon, from which the picture was executed,
was begun and finished in red chalk, and for a long
time adorned the Birchall and Rogers Collection—a
beautiful example of Raphael's most finished work,
with the upper part filled up by a study of the Baptist's arm and a bit of drapery, the back of the drawing comprising a naked man lying on his back.† In
most of the pen sketches the heads are mere ovals,
with rough indications of the eyes, nose, and mouth,
but in obedience to Lionardo's precepts the attitudes
are all given " with details not too finished."

Leading up to this form of Da Vincian drawings, a
series of studies are found in the Venice sketch-
book, in which naked children are worked out in
umber, heightened with white, with a delicacy of
finish and a searching of modulations unknown to the
Perugian time. One of them, inferior to the rest,
because of the shapeless form of the body, shows an
attempt to give expression of thought to a face too
young to think at all. The features and torso are
seen frontwise, but without the left leg. The left arm
and hand are raised as if to ward off a danger, and,
quaintly enough, above this, the same model is shown

* Oxford. No. 33. Shaded drawing, 8¾ in. h. by 7½. From the
Antaldi and Lawrence collections.
Here the group is like that in the
picture, but the Virgin's drapery is
closer or more scanty.

† London, Ex Birchall and
Rogers collections. Red chalk.
9 in. h. by 6¼. On the back of
the sheet is a Prometheus, lying
on his back with his elbows
thrown back, so that he rests on
his forearms.

with very marked features in profile.* More infantine and pleasing, a boy is depicted elsewhere recumbent and resting on one elbow, whilst the right hand reposes on the thigh. · Though copied from nature, this figure has almost the proportions of an antique, and is equally admirable for the purity of its shape, the beauty of its chiselling, and the simplicity of its outline.† A third represents a sleeping child,‡ a fourth, a boy held under the armpits, tottering onwards with feeble stride, one arm raised and the other thrown back like the infant Christ in the " Madonna in green."§ One marvels when scanning these leaves, either at the quick unfaltering stroke, or at the minute polish. The power of Raphael, as he runs thus skilfully up and down the scale of rapid or finished design is wonderful.

If his devotion to Lionardo in these days was apparent in the preparation of pictures, how much more so in that of portraits. Mona Lisa, whom Da Vinci had painted for her husband, del Giocondo, became at once

----

* Venice Acad. Frame XXVII. No. 3. Back of XXVII. No. 27.

† Venice Acad. Frame XXV. No. 17. Pen and umber, shaded with umber and white. The body is seen in full front recumbent, the right leg outstretched, the left bent under the right. The head is to the right and looks at three-quarters to the left.

‡ Venice Acad. Frame XXXV. No. 5. The child recumbent, with its head to the left, its feet to the right, on the lap of its mother, is fast asleep, with its arms pendent. The mother is merely in outline. Same handling as the foregoing.

§ Venice Acad. Frame XXVI. No. 20. Back of XXVI. No. 6. The child is turned to the left; its head in profile. The female who holds him has been injured and retouched, so that the eye to the right is lower than that to the left. But there are traces of the contour of another head higher up. Same execution as above.

the object of his special adoration. Maddalena Doni,
though she had not the transcendent beauty, chiselled
features, or abundant flow of locks which distinguished
the Gioconda, was a handsome woman of the Florentine
type; and when Agnolo Doni asked that her portrait
should be painted, Raphael was unable to forget
the splendid masterpiece of Lionardo with its heavenly
smile, its soft glance, and the twilight overspreading
form in a dreamy landscape of valleys and hills. He
was not as yet so fully divorced from the fashions of
the Umbrians as to sacrifice ornament and the sumptuous realism, which perhaps had a certain attraction
for the lady herself. But in the sketch contour which
he made of her before he sat down to the easel, he
drew with a few but characteristic lines a woman both
simple and young, adorned with none but nature's
charms, with hair twisted off the face in rich masses,
and a velvet look revealing happiness and mirth, if
not that wonderful contentment which Da Vinci
alone as yet had been capable of conveying. Even
the full and fleshy hands were laid across each other
in the movement of Lionardo, and the modest bodice
inclosing the muslin pleats that covered the bosom were
of that delicious simplicity which the great Florentine
described as the necessary concomitant of grace. The
only change which Raphael introduced was a clear
sky and indications of an Umbrian distance seen between the pillars of a portico.* In the picture itself he

---

* Louvre. No. 329. Pen and
bistre sketch, executed rapidly
with great boldness and grace.
m. 0·222 h. by 0·159. From the

drew Maddalena Doni in a low dress, with her hair in a net, falling thin and frizzly down her cheeks to the neck, a grand bodice of watered damask, with wide blue borders, separated from the throat by a white gathered edging, slashes, and blue damask sleeves, with patterns of a deeper blue, one ringed hand lying half closed on the other, and both reposing on the arms of a chair. Round the neck is a chain with a jewelled medallion and a pear-shaped pearl-hanging, and a larger chain falling to the waist. "You shall choose your horizon," says Lionardo, "on the level of the eyes." And so the landscape of the Mona Lisa was conceived. But Raphael preferred the light of the sky, on which a few clouds quenched the glare of the sun. The blue mountains to the right, the slopes of a hill to the left, with a slender tree waving its thin leaves in the air, are on a line with the shoulders, but every part is tempered according to Lionardo's precepts, the same breeze that gives their tremor to the leaves, sets the frizzle of Maddalena Doni's hair in motion, the light is managed according to Da Vinci's maxims, and Raphael carefully adjusts the attitude, freely balancing light and shade, and realizing a perfect harmony of colour. The smile of Lionardo is alone avoided. Devoted as he is to the great Florentine, Raphael's taste asserts itself. He does not carry out the *sfumato* of Da Vinci to its strictest expression, his modelling is

---

Jabach collection. The figure is turned to the left. The face three-quarters to the left, and the eyes look out to the right. Seen to the waist.

massive, yet sufficiently searching, the clear flesh tone admirably blends with the pearly transitions, that merge imperceptibly into warm rubbings of a greenish umber. Enamelled surface and translucent shadow and bright harmonious vestment tints are all confined within outlines of great precision and purity, and breadth is secured by a grand treatment of stuffs reminiscent of Masaccio.*

When he had finished "Maddalena," Raphael began "Agnolo Doni;" and painted a very fine likeness—a portrait of some stiffness, indeed, and not without uniformity in the depths of its complexion, but representing the man in the staid form of Domenico Ghirlandaio, and nobly dressed in the black cap and dark damask silks which the Florentines loved. He framed the head and neck in profuse fleeces of hair, relieving the sombre surfaces by white edgings at the neck and wrists, a double golden button at the seam of the doublet, and luscious red sleeves. One hand rests on the knee, another is pendent. For the rest, the same principles in execution, the same landscapes, lighting, and model-

---

* Florence, Pitti. No. 59. Maddalena Doni. Wood. Half length. Tuscan Braccio. 1·4 h. by 0·15 = 1 ft. 11½ in. h. by 1 ft. 2¼ in.

No. 61. Agnolo Doni. On the back of each panel is a scene from the fable of Deucalion and Pyrrha, by some artist of a later time than Raphael, whose sole aim appears to have been to give a priming to the panels. The surfaces have suffered from cleaning and some retouches, *ex. gr.*, in the forehead of Maddalena and the hair of Agnolo, but on the whole the pictures are fairly preserved. About 1823, these portraits were bought from the descendants of the Doni at Florence by Leopold II., for 2500 sequins, or about 28,000 Italian lire. See Gotti Gall. di Firenze, p. 182.

ling, as in the " Maddalena," but stronger contrasts of light and shade, and deeper flush of pigments.

The revolution in his own art, which Raphael thus accomplished at Florence, was rapid and excessively remarkable. His almost absolute abandonment of Umbrian for Tuscan principles was finally manifested in the " Madonna di Casa Tempi "—a masterpiece of which, as of so many others, no trace is to be found in the pictorial annals of Raphael's own time. And yet no picture more truly deserved attention for its Florentine and Vincian character, than this one. In type, mould of face, drapery, and style of drawing it is the pure Florentine that comes to be displayed, nor is it difficult to discern an approach even to the later influence of Fra Bartolommeo in dress and arrangement of headgear. The " Infant Christ " most unites the qualities of Raphael's own genius, as we find it afterwards expand in the " Madonna della Seggiola " and the " Madonna di San Sisto." How simple, yet how complex this group of two figures is, can only be realized after a prolonged contemplation. The Virgin is turned to the right, her face not quite in profile. With one hand she makes a seat for the child, whom she clasps to her bosom with the other. The boy clings to her, his legs are pendent, his arm on his mother's throat. His face is in contact with hers, and she kisses his cheek. He turns round and looks out of the picture as if at something that had suddenly come within the compass of his view. The blue mantle over the subtle veil falls behind her back, and is raised in festoons over her arms. The muslin round the boy's hips, the shawl with golden threads round the Virgin's shoulders, and her red bodice and sleeves make up a harmony of tints without any violence of contrasts, yet full of the richness produced by intense colour, moistened with abundant vehicle. Indescribable love and affection are concentrated in the action of the Virgin—her smile, her lips compressed for a kiss, her eyes half closed from sheer pleasure. Nature itself is reproduced in the movement of the child, whose look is penetrant, happy, and mirthful. The feeling, expression, and passion, combined in so small a space, recall, as the technical execution recalls, the Faith, Hope, and Charity of the later predella of the Entombment at the Vatican; but that here additional charm is imparted by flesh of transparent clearness, flushed with a healthy red in the cheeks, warm shadows, and the tenderest of pearly grey transitions between both. A loftier sentiment, perhaps, is embodied in the conception of the "Madonna del Gran' Duca;" but the "Madonna di Casa Tempi" is one of the noblest renderings of motherly love. And whereas a remnant of the Peruginesque is found lurking in the former, the latter has become and finally remains entirely Florentine.* No one

---

* Munich Gall. No. 1206. Wood. 2 ft. 4 in. h. by 1 ft. 7 in. Still in Casa Tempi at Florence in 1677 (Cinelli, Bellezze di Firenze, p. 282). Bought by King Ludwig of Bavaria in 1829, for 16,000 scudi. Well preserved. A copy was seen by Passavant in 1839, in the hands of Mr. van Hanselaer at Ghent (not seen). A copy, which may be the same as the above, was lately in possession of Monsignor Badia at Rome, of the same size as the original, with the initials R.S. and the date MDX. The style was that of the Florentine Sogliani.

would have thought that such touches of nature as we
have just described, could have come from an Umbrian, were it not that that Umbrian is the immortal
Raphael.   No one would have believed that the man
who painted the hands of so many Madonnas in the
conventional form of Perugino, would turn to idealize
nature as he did in the hand that grasps the Saviour's
waist, or that he would have formed a model so pure,
as is manifest in the shape, the limbs, and the pendent legs and feet of the babe.   And all this so
beautifully rendered, and with such brightness, in
such tempered light and vaporous atmosphere.   But
the forces of Raphael were at this time, as indeed they
long remained, so exuberant, that he seemed capable
of any effort.   And these forces are to be seen at
work not only in the final effort of the picture, but
in those which preceded it.   How he tried and tried
in sketch after sketch before he settled on the composition which ultimately came to perfection is
apparent in the drafts which are multiplied in a
dozen at least of projected groups that never go
beyond the first jet.   As he thought over the " Madonna del Gran' Duca," he already meditated over the
" Madonna di Casa Tempi ; " and we see this at once
in one of the earliest drawings, which shows the
Virgin leaning her cheek against the infant's forehead at the Uffizi.*   Even the Oxford sketch for the
" Virgin and Child," which has already been described
as a variety of the " Madonna del Cardellino," is to

------

* Uffizi. Frame 135. No. 497.

some extent a realization of the Infant Christ, as we now find him in the " Virgin of Casa Tempi." * Other and more rapid jottings at the British Museum and the Albertina show the " Tempi Madonna " side by side with attempts for those of Bridgewater House, and the " Virgin with the Pink." † Another variety which takes us back to the Madonnas with the book, is one at the Albertina, where the mother, holding the missal in her left hand, supports the infant on her lap, and bends her head to meet the caress which Christ gives with his fingers and face.‡ The cartoon at Montpellier, supposed to have served for the final rendering of the picture, is so worn and injured as to suggest some doubts of its originality. §

Whilst Raphael's activity thus took him through the scale of invention—never resting till he had found the truth after a score of trials—he never ceased to observe and to note the masterpieces of the Floren-

---

* Oxford. No. 45. See *antea*.

† British Museum. Pen and umber drawing, with four groups of the Virgin and Child. Particularly reminiscent of the " Madonna di Casa Tempi," though in reverse, is the right hand group in the upper part of this sheet, where the Virgin kisses the Infant Christ, whose cheek is pressed close to hers. We shall find the two lower groups in this drawing as preparations for the Bridgewater " Madonna." See *postea*.

Vienna, Albertina. Pen and bistre sketch of six groups of the " Virgin and Child." On the upper right hand corner of the sheet is a sketch very much the counterpart of that described above.

‡ Albertina. Pen and bistre sketch of a Madonna, with the book and a Virgin and Child, with the infant Baptist. The former shows the Infant standing on the Virgin's lap and kissing her. Group seen to the knees.

A double of this sheet (a copy) is in the Berlin print room.

§ Montpellier, Musée Fabre. Round. Much damaged.

tines in the sister arts of sculpture and of painting;
and his inquisitive mind, busy with original creation,
could still bend itself to copying and adapting forms
taken from the works of the Greeks, or those of past
and contemporary Tuscans.   What more telling of his
appreciation of the antique in any shape, than the
outline of a classic Venus, carelessly, yet with supreme
mastery thrown on the reverse of a series of projects
for the Bridgewater "Madonna" in the gallery of the
Uffizi! *   What more characteristic than the clever
sketch, which comprises in one sheet at Oxford, three
models of legionaries, with lances and shields; and
in the midst of them Donatello's St. George at Orsanmichele ! †   The bas-relief at the foot of that statue,
which represents St. George tilting at the dragon,
was, in a few months, to furnish an idea for a picture
of the same saint for the Duke of Urbino.   A stroll
into Santa Maria Novella brought him in front of
Ghirlandaio's fresco of the nativity of the Virgin, and
his copy at Chatsworth of the girl preparing the infant's
bath stands side by side with an idea for the St.

* Florence, Uffizi.   Frame 135.
No. 496.   Back, a sheet with pen
and bistre sketches of five Vir-
gins with children, and six boys.
The Venus stands on the water,
turned slightly to the right, her
head to the left, her right arm
across her bosom and the hand on
the left breast.   To the left of the
figure a female standing, and to
the right the back view of a male
torso. Passavant erroneously states
that this Venus is at the back of
the sketch of the "Madonna del
Pesce."   See Pass. Raphael, ii. No.
120.

† Oxford.   No. 46.   Pen and
bistre drawing, 11 in. h. by 8½ in.
Four figures.   The central one is
St. George, seen from the right
side.   The face at three-quarters
to the right.   The left hand on
the upper end of the shield, which
rests on the ground.

Catherine of the National Gallery.* In a noble series of studies at Oxford, which may have been made at Florence for the seated saints in the fresco of San Severo, he drew with a few pregnant lines the principal group of the " Fight for the Standard" in the cartoon of Lionardo.†

But he was not content to copy Lionardo's group. The genius with which Da Vinci represented the incidents of a cavalry skirmish fired him with something more than the wish to make a transcript. And the time now came, we may imagine, when he was able to produce those masterly designs of the Venice sketch-book, in which a naked soldier in profile marches off with the standard in front. of a horse in full career, and two naked soldiers with shields are represented defending themselves from the blows of an armed rider, who turns his charger to strike at them.‡ With what life and truth even at a comparatively early period Raphael drew figures of horses we have already had occasion to observe. His readiness in this branch of art was thought worthy of special remark by Lomazzo.§ After he had studied

---

* Chatsworth. Pen and bistre sketch. To the left the full length of St. Catherine, next that to the right the girl turned to the left, moving forward and pouring water out of a vase. Above, to the right, a bust of a girl, turned to the left, and below, between St. Catherine and the girl with the vase, a naked boy, marching from left to right with a little bucket in each hand.

† Oxford. No. 28. Silver-point, on pale greyish cream-coloured prepared paper. 8¾ in. h. by 11 in. From the Ottley, Duroveray, Dimsdale, and Lawrence collections. The group of horsemen is a very slight indication in the right-hand corner of the sheet.

‡ Venice Academy.

§ Lomazzo, Trattato, p. 71.

Lionardo, his skill in this form of creation increased, and he drew the horse with more knowledge of anatomy and with greater spirit and freedom of hand. But if his powers thus expanded in the by-paths of art, they were still more forcibly shown in his rendering of the nude of men. In some of the Venice sketches in which models are set for the searching of muscle as well as for movement, energy is allied to realism with a nobleness rarely equalled before, and with a constantly apparent desire to discover both the modelling of visible surfaces and the hidden causes of momentary action.* In the drawings which now came from his hand, the large experience which he had acquired, was applied to special purposes ; and quickness and spontaneity, as well as correctness, were combined to produce a startling effect. The standard bearer who carries off the prize with both hands marches with his head thrown forward and his chest expanded, displaying the weight of the colours on his shoulders, not only by the tension and bend of the body, but by the muscular development of the limbs

---

* See especially Venice Acad. Frame XXVII. No. 8. Pen drawing of a nude man, with his right hand on his hip, over whose head another figure, in similar attitude, holds a crown. To the right a man in profile, with his left hand resting on a stick. In the background a man in a Peruginesque helmet, and between the legs of the two figures to the left, a kneeling child. On the same lines we have another drawing. Venice Acad. Frame XXVII. No. 12. Back of XXVII. No. 15. Back view of two naked men, with a child to the right, in a walking cradle. These are highly finished studies from models, with some of the masculine strength of Signorelli in their shape and muscular developments.

in their forward stride.* The same laws find their application in the composition where three soldiers defend themselves with raised shield and ready spear from the sword of attacking horsemen.† There is evidence in the puncture of the outlines of these, and a companion drawing, also at Venice, that some one used these masterpieces for a picture of which, unhappily, we are now unable to trace the existence.‡

We thus discern a ceaseless activity and restless eagerness in acquiring, added to unequalled strength and rare qualities of assimilation, which enabled Raphael to make rapid progress towards obtaining a place amongst the jealous Florentines. We shall soon see him acknowledged as the greatest master of his time in the city which reared the best artists of the Italian Peninsula.

---

* Venice Acad. Frame XXVII. No. 22. Back of XXVII. No. 6. Pen and bistre sketch, not in the sketch-book, the paper being different. The figure marches off in profile to the left.

† Venice Acad. Frame XXVII. No. 6. Back of the foregoing. Pen sketch. The principal figure, with its back to the spectator, strides to the right and looks back, as the shield is raised, at the horse on which the man rides, who strikes at him and his companion. The water-mark on these drawings is a pair of scissors.

‡ Venice Acad. Pass. No. 99.

Pen sketch of three nudes, one to the right turned to the left. To the left of him a second, seen in front and turned to the right, both looking to the right, and holding lances in the action of defence. To the left traces of a third figure. On the back of the paper, a replica of the Standard-bearer of the Venice Acad. Frame XXVII. No. 22. Passavant thinks this drawing a copy of an original at the Albertina (Raph. ii. p. 415). But he is mistaken. The two drawings differ. The Venice sketch is punctured for use.

CHAPTER VI.

Raphael's practice at Florence and Perugia.—Guidubaldo and the Garter.—Raphael's "St. George" sent to England.—His portrait of himself and other alleged likenesses.—Stay at Urbino and Perugia. —Madonnas of Orleans and St. Petersburg.—"Madonna of the Palm."—Retrospect; his style at Perugia, and changes which it underwent at Florence.—Study of Da Vinci, Fra Bartolommeo, Michaelangelo, and the antique.—Conigiani "Madonna."—"Holy Family" at Windsor.—Studies for the "Entombment."—Varieties of that composition, and its final completion.—Influence of Perugino, Mantegna, Signorelli, Fra Bartolommeo, and Michaelangelo. —Predella of the "Entombment."—"Trinity" of San Severo, and Raphael's practice as a fresco painter.

IT is characteristic of the energy which always marked Raphael's efforts, that whilst he strove at Florence to attain the style of the Tuscans, he struggled with equal success to preserve the practice of which he had laid the foundation at Perugia and Urbino. For a considerable time Guidubaldo had been residing at Rome, where his diplomacy was seriously tried to reconcile old affection for the Venetians, with the new duties of a captain-general in the papal service. The resolute will of Julius II. to annex Bologna and Perugia to the Roman dominions, and the necessity for organizing a force for this momentous enterprise, induced Guidubaldo to visit his Duchy in the spring of 1506. But before he left the Vatican, he met an embassy from Henry VII. of England, which came to congratulate the Pope on his accession, and invest the Duke with an order. The 23rd of April was celebrated at Urbino with unusual ceremony. It was the day of St. George, the festival of England's national saint. Guidubaldo made a holiday of the occasion and went in state to assume the mantle and insignia of the Garter. He then made preparations for returning Henry the Seventh's civility, and prepared credentials for Baldassare Castiglione, whom he sent with chargers, falcons, and other noble presents to England.* Amongst these presents, there is reason to believe, was "St. George and the Dragon" by Raphael; and Raphael, we have cause to think, was asked to paint the panel between April and July, when Castiglione went to London.† The picture which was then completed, bears internal evidence of having been executed at this period. Though not mentioned by the annalists of Urbino, it was catalogued in the inventories of Henry VIII.,‡ and on the harness of the charger which St. George is riding we read the name of Raphael, and the word "Honi," which is part of every Garter since the foundation of the order.

As early as the time when he first designed the "St. George" of the Louvre, Raphael had thought of a new version of the subject, representing the Saint charging out of the foreground into the distance, instead of charging from the distance into the foreground. The sketch of this variety at Oxford shows

* Baldi, Life of Guidubaldo, ii. p. 190. † Ibid. ibid. ‡ See the Inventory of Henry VIII. for 1542-7 published by George Scharf in the Archæologia, pp. 298-323.

the horse at a gallop, seen from behind, the Saint with
his shield at his shoulder rising in the stirrup and
stooping to strike.*   The difficulty of the left-handed
stroke seems to have deterred Raphael from following
out this idea. Not till he saw the bas-relief of
Donatello at Orsanmichele, which exhibits St. George
with the lance, did it occur to him to reverse
the position of horse and man, and substitute the
lance for the sword. He now imagined the dragon
receiving the spear-wound as the knight charged past
him in full career; and the small cartoon at Florence
which he made for this composition has rarely been
excelled even in Raphael's practice for spirit and
fire.† In sketch as well as in picture a splendid
seat, great skill in the management of the steed and
weapons, cool purpose and elastic strength, characterize the figure of the saint, who has just given
spurs to his horse and urged him to charge, with his
fore-legs raised and hind-legs set on the ground.
Bending to his task, St. George lets his mantle flap
in the breeze, his handsome face seems animated and
keen for the fray, whilst the monster, rabid, and with
all his strength still in legs and loins, dies with a
helpless twist of his frame and a hideous growl from
his menacing throat. In pleasing contrast with the
strong action displayed by the saint, the attitude of

---

* Oxford Gallery. No. 35. Silver-
point drawing, heightened with
white. 10¼ in. h. by 9⅜ in. Much
worn, and cut down to the outlines;
the right hand of the saint, and
the right fore leg of the horse
being obliterated.

† Florence. Uffizi. Frame No.
148. No. 529.   10 in. h. by 8½.
Pricked for pouncing. The horse's
head is turned, with a look of
terror, towards the dragon. It
has no bridle or bit. Pen and
bistre outline and shading.

the queen in the distance to the right conveys both trust and prayer in beautiful features and a graceful kneeling posture. The wilderness which the monster haunts, the cave to the right which lies under a rock overgrown with bushes, and a pool in front of it, are well conceived. Groups of trees and underwood rise behind the queen, and lead to a vista of country enlivened by a church. The golden helmet encircled with a nimbus, the steel armour, and white charger, the harness of blue and gold, the toning of the whole picture to bring out the steed, do honour to the painter's skill, though time has had its way and spoiled his work, and the drawing with its masterly outline and shading gives a better idea of his power. Enough, however, has been spared to impress on us the exquisite delicacy of the original handling, the smooth brightness of its surface, the vigour and harmony of the broadly modelled parts, and the absolute purity of the forms. It was a royal present with which Guidubaldo, by Raphael's help, repaid the honours done to him by Henry VII.* The commission for such a

---

* Petersburg. Hermitage. No. 39. Wood. 10¼ in. h., or 0·28 h., by 8⅜ in., or 0·22. This picture is registered in Henry the VIIIth and Charles the Ist's inventories. (See George Scharf's notes in the Archæologia, p. 298–323). Vorsterman engraved it from a copy belonging to the Earl of Pembroke in 1627 (Vertue's Catalogue of Charles I.'s Collection, p. 4). At the sale of the collection of Charles I., it went for £150. Felibien saw it in the gallery of the Marquis de Sourdis in Paris (Entretiens, i. 228). Florent le Comte afterwards noted it in possession of Mr. de La Noue, who paid 500 pistoles for it. On the chest band of the horse, RAPHAEL . V. On the garter of St. George, HONI. But the surface is injured in many places by cleaning and retouching, and the picture is now on canvas. It is impossible to say whether the "St. George and the Dragon" seen by Lomazzo (Trattato, p. 48), in the

picture for so rare an occasion shows the consideration in which the artist was held by the Court of Urbino, and it may well be that he now received those orders for Madonnas which Vasari describes as having been made during one of the painter's visits to Urbino.

The portrait which Raphael finished about this time with the purpose of leaving a reminiscence of himself to his patrons or friends, hardly reveals the energy and determination which are manifested in the works that have just been described. It is the likeness of a young fellow of handsome features seen at three-quarters to the right, with a well-shaped face set on a long and graceful neck adorned by copious chestnut locks. Regular and pleasing features are a straight nose, full lips, eyebrows of faultless arching, and large eye balls protected by broad upper lids. A black felt hat with flaps, a black doublet, edged at the throat with white, form a simple yet manly attire.* What probably deprives this likeness of character, is the damage which time and retouching have done to its surface. Few pictures of the master have suffered more, and as the transparence of the flesh appears to have been very great, the flaying of the parts, by removing large fragments of colour, has probably obliterated some of

church of St. Victor at Milan, was a version of the above or of the earlier one of the Louvre.

* Florence. Uffizi. No. 288. Wood. 18 in. h. by 12½ in. Cut down at the left side. Ground, green grey. The panel is said to have remained at Urbino till 1588, when it was transferred by Fede-

rico Zuccheri to the Academy of St. Luke at Rome. The Academy sold it, with other pictures, to Cardinal Leopold dei Medici. (See Passavant's Raphael, ii. p. 49.) The abrasion of the surface and subsequent repainting not only dull the colours but alter the forms.

the subtle expressiveness which originally marked the
face. Still, it is a pleasure to possess such a repre-
sentation as this of the great master of Urbino. It
enables us, at least, to reject as portraits of Raphael
an entire series of heads, some of which may be due
to the painter's hand without reproducing his features,
whilst others are merely cartoons for pictures by other
artists.*

On his way out or home Raphael doubtless
revisited the Umbrian country, inspected the labours
which he still had to complete at Perugia, and
received the commission of Atalanta Baglioni to paint

---

* British Museum. Outline
drawing, large as life, of a boy of
twelve or fifteen, three-quarters to
the left, in a cap. The eyes are
glancing to the right out of the
picture. This is a fine and delicately modelled work, but unlike
Raphael as we see him at Florence.

Oxford Gallery. No. 26. 15 in.
h. by 10½ in. From the Wicar,
Ottley, Harman, and Woodburn
Collections. Black chalk drawing
heightened with white on pale
brown tinted paper. Portrait of
a boy of fifteen, in the same position as the last, with long hair
falling from under the cap of the
period, in a close fitting vest. The
features are regular, the eye expressive. There is some general
resemblance between the features
and those of the Duke of Mantua
in Raphael's fresco of the school
of Athens. *A fortiori* there is no
likeness to Raphael himself. The
drawing as such is a beautiful one.

Montecassino. Cartoon of the
head of a man, three-quarters to
the left, called Raphael's portrait
by himself. This is not even by
Raphael. It is the cartoon of a
portrait by Francia Bigio. No.
245A in the Gallery of Berlin.

Paris. Count Czartoriski. Portrait of a man in a black cap, long
light chestnut hair, a fur mantle
and white sleeves, seated in a
room in which there is an opening, through which a landscape is
seen. This is a good portrait. The
face is fine, the hands feeble, and
ill-drawn. The execution is dry, as
might be that of a tempera picture,
the shading red. This is neither
the portrait of Raphael nor is it
by Raphael himself. Can it be
the portrait of " Parmesano," once
assigned to Raphael, in the collection of M. Antonio Foscarini at
Venice (Morelli's Anonimo, p. 67),
or a likeness of Francesco Maria
della Rovere, by a local artist of
Urbino? It looks very like a
work of Timoteo Viti.

an "Entombment."   When he resumed his usual avocations, he seems to have divided his attention between the studies for the "Entombment," the "Virgin" of Orleans, the "Holy Family" at St. Petersburg, and the "Madonna of the Palm," the second and last of which are probably heirlooms from the Palace of Urbino.

The change which now came over Raphael's style could scarcely be more marked than it appears in the "Madonna" of Orleans.   Hitherto the master's palet had abounded in tones of great richness and the brightest intensity.   Now he sought effect by delicate gradations of more complex tints, yielding tempered melody of tone in low tertiary keys.   In the "Madonna" of Orleans the Virgin sits on a cushioned chair in a small room—a young mother in a homely habitation adorned with a shelf on its hinder walls, on which pots and vases and a straw-plaited flask are ranged.   Her yellow hair twisted with a subtle veil, her red dress cut square at the bosom, its close sleeve puckered into pleats of a vague red stuff, her green sash and blue mantle, showing its brown lining here and there, the curtain of grey red hue, all contribute by soberness of tint to the quiet scale of tones which marks the picture.   But the change in technical execution is remarkable.   The lights are so transparent that they hardly cover the ground of the panel, the shadows of such copious pigment as to produce an unusual density.   One foot on a stool, the other thrown forward on the floor, make a seat for the Infant.   Christ, who rests half-recumbent on his mother's lap, hanging on with both hands to the hem of her dress, looks round with inspired eyes at the spectator, Mary the while bending over him with a look of serene melancholy, as she supports his shoulder with one hand and holds his left foot with the other. Never was a group of " Mother and Child " more picturesquely balanced, never put together in more graceful lines. Raphael rarely imagined more lovely, chastened features. What strikes us most, is youth and tenderness, such as give charm to the " Connestabile Madonna," and besides something deeper, nay, unfathomable, a mystery as of things to come, sufferings to be endured, and supreme resignation to bear them all. Enchanting is the transparent light of the flesh parts, exquisite the glow of the whole surface.*

Hardly less beautiful, the companion picture at St. Petersburg represents the " Virgin and Child " in a palace, but in reversed position. The Virgin again bends over the Child, whose left foot she is holding. He clings with his right hand to his mother's bosom,

---

* Chantilly. Palace of the Duc d'Aumale. Half length. Wood. 11½ in. h. by 14¼ in. Once in possession of the brother of Louis the XIVth of France, then in the Orleans Gallery. Sold, 1798, to Mr. Hibbert for £500, then in the hands of Mr. Nieuwenhuis, who sold it in 1831, afterwards transferred to M. Aguado, and then sold in Paris for 24,000 francs to Mr. B. Delessert. Bought at the Delessert sale in 1869 by the Duc d'Aumale for 150,000 francs. This little picture is perfectly preserved. There is no foundation for Passavant's belief that the background was repainted in the manner of David Teniers (i. p. 45). This picture is probably one of those described by Vasari as painted for Duke Guidubaldo (Vas. viii. p. 7). It answers the description in the Urbino inventory. "Quadretto d'una Madonna con un Cristo in braccio in legno che viene da Raffaelle."

whilst he rests the other hand on her lap, and turning sharply round, looks at the melancholy form of the beardless Joseph, who stands to the left with both hands leaning on his staff.*   A more matronly shape in the Virgin, greater breadth and strength in the Saviour, remind us of the "Madonna del Cardellino," an impression enhanced by the landscape, which is seen through the arch to the right.   But the qualities of colour and execution in this little panel are similar to those of the Orleans "Madonna."   What makes the picture peculiarly interesting is the discovery that the beardless Joseph is a counterpart in features and head of that which Raphael designed for the next great work that occupied his leisure at Florence, the "Holy Family" of Lord Ellesmere, usually known as the "Madonna of the Palm."

On a larger scale, and in the shape of a round, the figures in this picture are fitted into the space with

---

* St. Petersburg.   Hermitage. No. 37.   Wood, transferred to canvas.   0·73 h. by 0·57.   Half length.   This picture cannot be that catalogued in the inventory of Urbino as Passavant thought (Raphael, ii. p. 44), because the Urbino picture was a round. (See *postea*, notes to the "Virgin with the Palm.")   We can only trace this masterpiece back to the 17th century, when it is said to have belonged to the Duc d'Angoulême in Paris.   It was sold to one Barroy, cleaned by one Vendine, and before it came to Petersburg it belonged to Mr. Crozat.   It is injured by three spots of restoring on the forehead of St. Joseph, three on the face of the Virgin, two on her throat, and two or three on the infant's legs.   It may be the second picture which Raphael painted for Taddeo Taddei. (Vas. viii. p. 6.)   A drawing of a composition like that of this piece, in the Berlin Print-room, represents Christ seated on the Virgin's lap; and St. Joseph behind to the right is beardless.   But there is something in the drawing (if it should be genuine, which is doubtful), that also recalls the "Madonna di Loretto." (See *postea*.)

unrivalled skill.   Every line is calculated to suit the
form of the panel, and the surface to be covered. The
Holy Family rests under a palm-tree during the flight
into Egypt, and it strikes one at once to inquire
whether it would ever have occurred to the master
to introduce a palm-tree into a landscape near the
Thrasymene lake.   In other respects the distance
varies but little from that of which Raphael was fond.
But this new feature in the " Madonna of the Palm "
bespeaks acquaintance with other regions and other
parts of Italy. St. Joseph, on one knee, steadies
himself with his staff, and offers a spray of flowers to
the infant Christ, who stretches out both hands to
take them.   He sits astride on the Virgin's knee, who
holds him safely by means of a veil which winds
round her shoulders and is then swathed across the
Saviour's body to be tightly held by her guiding
fingers.   She sits on a grassy rising of the ground
under the palm-tree, her right hand supporting
the infant's breast, her left holding the veil.   The
system of colouring already marked in the Orleans
" Madonna " is again illustrated by the red gown
with bright sleeves, changing from a violet tinge in
the shadows to yellow in the lights, and the purple
tunic and lemon-coloured cloak of St. Joseph. Unfortunately the harmony suffers from injury produced
by retouching, and it seems a most regrettable circumstance that the solid impast of Joseph's mantle should
appear to have been executed after the rest of the
picture by one of Raphael's assistants; pity also that
the damage done to the surface of the panel should

conceal, not only the original beauty of the handling, but some of the charms of feeling that once gave attraction to the picture.* With what care Raphael went about this work is apparent in a drawing at the Louvre, where the Virgin is represented with that winning grace and wondrous softness of look which alone give evidence of a close study of Lionardo. The Virgin and the Child both differ from those in the picture, the legs being set in a different way and apparently without regard to the necessity which afterwards arose of composing the group in a round. In the panel at Bridgewater House, St. Joseph is bearded and in profile. The drawing shows his face at three quarters to the right, beardless and aged. It is one of Raphael's happiest studies of expression, reminiscent of Da Vinci in the finish of the parts and the smile which lurks in every one of its lines. What in youth would have been dimples, is here naturally

* London. Bridgewater House. Wood, transferred to canvas. 3 ft. 4 in. in diameter. This picture has not been traced hitherto further back than the close of the 17th century. Yet it answers the description in the Urbino inventory. "Quadro uno di mano di Raffaelle con un Cristo, Madonna, S. Gioseffe, et ornamento a foggia di specchio." Before 1680 it belonged to the Countess de Chiverni in Paris, out of whose hands it passed to those of the Marquise d'Aumont, who disposed of it to Mr. de la Noue for 5000 livres, after causing a copy to be made or Port Royal by Philippe de Champagne. From the De la Noue Collection it passed, about 1680, into the hands of President Tambonneau (Felibien, Entretiens i. p. 228), and thence into the Orleans Collection, at the sale or which it was bought by the Earl of Bridgewater in 1792 for £1200. It has two vertical splits, one on the left side of the picture, one in the centre, running down the Virgin's forehead, the back of the infant's head, his body, and the Virgin's mantle. These have been necessarily restored causing repaint, on the Virgin's face, the infant's arm, Joseph's hands, and part of the Virgin's left hand.

turned into wrinkles, yet the withered face looks surprisingly happy and full of the tenderest affection. Every line, even the mechanism of the shading and the spacious planes into which shadow is thrown, are Lionardesque.* As we saw, the design which he forbore to use in the "Madonna with the Palm," was happily transferred to the "Madonna" of St. Petersburg. But before Raphael made the drawing, he had already sketched its outlines in the rapid jottings of a sheet at Lille, and side by side with the group are thoughts for the infant Christ in the "Madonna di Loretto" and the angels of the "Madonna di San Sisto," a fresh proof, if any were needed, of the ceaseless working of the painter's mind.†

Looking back into the two periods of Raphael's practice at Perugia and Florence we realise his course as he passed in succession under two influences of almost equal potency, that of Umbrian tradition as wielded by a master whose lessons gave the first impulse, that of Florentine taste, chiefly attributable to Da Vinci, which gave the second impulse to his genius. The conditions under which these forces acted were as different as the feeling of which they

---

* Louvre. No. 316. 0·226 h. by 0·154. Silver-point on yellow-tinted paper. The head on the upper left corner, the Virgin and Child below. Squared for transfer to panel, and with indications of a round. From the collections Lagoy, Dimsdale, Lawrence, and King of Holland. At the sale of the latter the drawing was bought for 1537 fr. 25 c.

† Lille Collection. No. 695. Silver-point. 0·116 h. by 0·144. The group of the Virgin and Child to the left, with a child to the right looking up, and one of the angels below looking up. To the right a similar angel, and crosswise above it a study of the child of the "Madonna di Loretto."

were the motive element. The art of Perugino, though it had been altered by Tuscan example, was after all but the highest development of that which was hastening to its decline in the Umbrian country, an art that to some extent ignored the progress originally caused at Florence by keen rivalry and competition. That of Lionardo was refined, not only by the experience of two centuries, but by his own powers of investigation. So long as Raphael remained in Umbria, his talents were partially held in abeyance. What he achieved was due to the innate taste which allowed him to impart a new grace and purity to types that were nearly worn out. For a time, indeed, a mere struggle with old customs seemed all that he would compass. His capacity for assimilation appeared unlikely to save him from the risk of constant repetition. Florence opened a new field to him in which he observed that artists were not working from set forms, but in obedience to principles and laws. He was no longer a child who had a lesson to learn, but a man with unusual acquisitive propensities, not like Bugiardini, whom Michaelangelo called happy, because he was content with the little he had learned,* but a craftsman who had acquired much, yet wished to acquire more. He saw Lionardo's masterpieces without that material craving for imitation which had beset him at Perugia. He took hold of the maxims which Da Vinci had taught, not of the very shapes, which he had painted. He made

---

* Vas. x. p. 347.

Lionardo's lessons a study, and became his disciple in a far higher sense than he had been the pupil of Perugino. The time however came when he was to lose the guidance of the master, to whose influence he had thus nobly surrendered. And just as he finished the "St. George" and the "Virgin of the Palm" in 1506, Da Vinci gave up his residence at Florence and returned to Milan preparatory to that final visit which he was to make to France. By a curious coincidence Michaelangelo, who had quarrelled with Julius II. at Rome, began to listen to the Pope's blandishments at the moment when Da Vinci yielded to the importunities of the French rulers at Milan, and towards the close of 1506 he too left the Tuscan capital for Bologna. Florence was deprived almost at one stroke of two of her most important artists, and, strangest of all, Perugino withdrew from the field of Florentine competition, and retired to end his days in the Perugian country.

But Raphael was not to be disturbed in his dream of progress, even by the departure of these valued guides. About the time when Lionardo retired from Florence, leaving his cartoon unfinished and his pledges unfulfilled, Baccio della Porta emerged from the cell in which he had been spending years of religious probation, and resumed the practice which his vows had interrupted six years before. With the reappearance of Fra Bartolommeo, a new life was given to the art of Lionardo. Raphael seized the favourable opportunity, became the intimate friend of the Dominican, and, incredible as it may seem, gave him lessons in perspective. The fruits of this intimacy were not slow in appearing. Raphael patiently continued to apply the precepts of Lionardo in the pictures which he executed; but he modified some of the elements of his manner in obedience to the lessons of the friar, and came at last to embody many of the qualities which distinguished that remarkable painter. Yet with all his admiration for Fra Bartolommeo, he was now too wary and experienced to trust to him alone. He only took what he thought suitable to his own genius, " he followed a middle course in design and in colour, and combined with these the better points of other masters in order to build up a style of his own." * The absence of Lionardo and Michaelangelo made it all the easier to compass this end, by enabling Raphael to unite, if that were possible, the maxims of both. The old dislike for Michaelangelo gradually faded from the youthful master's mind as the conviction grew upon him that no such strength had ever been developed in drawing, as he had shown in the cartoons and picture exhibited at Florence. Vasari, indeed, attributes Raphael's enormous and rapid stride as a draughtsman solely to his study of Buonarotti's works. He says that Raphael in a few months performed the labour of years, " studying the nude, testing the anatomy of living models by comparisons with flayed preparations and corpses, mastering the foreshortening of parts, the connection of bones and nerves with muscles, and the causes of the

---

* Vas. viii. p. 54

swell or projections produced by bending or stretching
a limb or a body.* But if Raphael did all this, it
was not due entirely to Michaelangelo. He studied
the antique, as we see in the copy of the red Marsyas
of the Uffizi, which is in the sketch-book at Venice.†
He reproduced, amongst others, the fine bas-relief,
which he composed into the great cartoon of St. Paul
at Lystra. He spent days in appealing to Nature and
looking at skeletons, in order to attain the perfection
of the "Entombment" and the "Canigiani Madonna."
But besides, he went back to the works of Donatello,
of whom a critic had said that his spirit passed by
transmigration into the frame of Michaelangelo,‡
and feeling that he could not equal either Buonarotti
or Lionardo in those walks in which each of them was
unapproachable, he aimed at surpassing them by
making himself universal.§ He recollected the
masterpieces of Signorelli at Urbino and Città di
Castello, and perhaps at Cortona and Orvieto, he
minutely examined the compositions of the great
Florentines, Botticelli and Filippino, which had served
to direct the later efforts of Da Vinci, and he refreshed
his early reminiscences of Mantegna, whose "Wail
over the Dead Body of Christ" he had studied in his
earlier years. One step further he went even than

---

* Vas. viii. pp. 53–4.

† Venice Acad. Frame XXVI.
No. 11. Back of XXVI. No. 5.
Pen drawing of the torso and legs
either of the "Marsyas" of the
Uffizi, No. 156, or of a preparation
in the same attitude. We shall
see this design used in the Chambers of the Vatican, *postea*.

‡ Borghini, in Vas. iii. p. 269.
" ῎Η Δωνατος βοναῤῥωτίζει. ῎Η
βοναῤῥωτὸς Δωνατίζει."

§ Vas. viii. 53.

this, he fell to admiring the methods which Michaelangelo had displayed, as to form, in the "Pietà"
at St. Peter's of Rome, as to attitude and drapery in
the "Madonna" of the Uffizi. He made Michaelangelo's system of handling his own, adapting to
his compositions the clean contour and modelling
of Buonarotti, his translucent blending of tints
and marbled smoothness of surface. Those peculiar
keys of tone, which consist in changing hues, balanced
according to the laws of harmony, he applied with
faultless precision. The force of the current which
took him into this phase of the Michaelangelesque
may be gauged by this, that he went so far as to
adopt Buonarotti's realistic rendering of hands and
feet and articulations, and his habitual contrasts and
careful adjustment of light and shade, not excepting
that chill of coldness which must invariably be the
result of a mirror-like burnish. But with what labour
and exercise of patience he compassed all this, it would
be hard to understand, if the numberless drawings had
not been preserved which preceded the actual undertaking of the altar-pieces of Domenico Canigiani
and Atalanta Baglioni. For both of these pictures
he spared no pains that an artist could expend, he
drew the models of the nudes, which he afterwards
draped, he copied the skeletons, he repeated the
figures in various movements, and even changed the
distribution in all kinds of ways. For both pieces
he made designs at the same time, as we may infer
from the sketches of the one being thrown on the back
of the sheets prepared for the other.

Domenico Canigiani was a Florentine citizen of a patrician family, whose name is more than once mentioned in Vasari's lives. He obtained from Raphael the "Holy Family," which came as a nuptial present to the electors of Düsseldorf by the marriage of Anna de' Medici, daughter of Cosimo III. to John William, Count Palatine of the Rhine. The figures which make up the composition are the Virgin and Christ, St. Joseph, St. Elizabeth, and the Baptist, arranged in a circle on the true pyramidal system. The lines of this arrangement are obtained by representing the Virgin and Elizabeth seated, whilst Joseph is placed on higher ground behind them, so as, leaning with both hands on his staff, he may look down from a vantage ground upon his companions. Raphael had probably been struck by this principle of distribution in several Florentine altar-pieces, Botticelli's "Epiphany" at Santa Maria Novella, Filippino's at San Donato, and Da Vinci's in the palace of Amerigo Benci at Florence.* The last of these was one so familiar to Raphael's mind, that he adapted some of its parts, perhaps unconsciously, to pictures of his own, and we note as derived from this source the foreground saint on the right side of the Disputa at Rome and St. Paul in the St. Cecilia of Bologna. What distinguishes Raphael in his present effort and makes him of kin with the greater Florentines is, the cleverness with which he brings the figures into focus in concentric attitudes, and

---

* Florence. Uffizi. Nos. 1286, 1257, 1252.

throws into all the faces and individuals a common
thought and action. The Virgin seated on the ground
to the right holds a missal, in the leaves of which her
forefinger is thrust; with one hand she supports the
naked frame of the Infant Christ, who rests against
her knee, one leg on her foot and another on the
ground. One sees that the divine infant has been
sitting on his mother's lap whilst she was reading;
and at sight of Elizabeth and the Baptist she closed the
book and put the babe to the ground. With the scroll
in his hand, on which the fatal words are written:
"Ecce agnus dei," he looks up innocently at the
Baptist, who stands before him, and presents it
smiling. St. John, who leans against the kneeling
Elizabeth, bends his curly head to look at the scroll.
His mother has seen the movement. She raises her
head and eyes inquiringly to St. Joseph, who stands
over her, and looks down with complacence at the
charming scene. The Virgin's head and face, with
the hair combed back over the ear and the veil twisted
through the plaits, displays the same cast of beauty as
the "Madonna" of St. Petersburg. Her dress of the
leaden red hue which characterizes certain figures in
the "Entombment," has the gloss and smoothness of
a mirror-plate. St. Elizabeth, open mouthed, in lead-
blue mantle, red gown, and white head-cloth, appears
in the realistic form familiar to the Florentines of the
new generation, prominent amongst whom was Andrea del Sarto, which shows how quickly Raphael's
intimacy with Fra Bartolommeo reacted on his style.
How vivid and lasting this impression of Florentine

art remained, is apparent in the repetition of the St. Elizabeth in the "Madonna dell' Impannata" and the "Sybil of Santa Maria della Pace" at Rome, the type of a woman, curved by age, and of those realistic features, which Lionardo was ever ready to study and reproduce. The difference of years and race between the Baptist and Christ is marked in that noble way which so eminently stamps Raphael's genius, who would naturally strive to give the Saviour a more refined air and more graceful proportions, than his companion. St. Joseph in his green tunic and yellow mantle, and hands high up on the staff on which he reposes, is one of those grand conventional figures which Raphael had now learnt to throw upon his canvas, a bald man draped in grand folds, resting his bare foot on the ground, a man with a spare, worn beard, and scant crop of grey hair on his crown and temples. A pleasing diversity of shape, of face, and of features, distinguishes each of the saints; but the landscape with its foreground of weeds and flowers, its varied strata of shaded plain stretching to a blue lake and low hills covered with buildings and churches, is lovely alike for simplicity and breadth of execution. The pure effect of the sky which sheds its light on the scene is lost to us since the hands of restorers passed over it and removed the cherubs that disported themselves in the clouds.*

---

* Munich. Pinakothek. No. 534. Wood. 4 ft. h. by 3 ft. 3½ in. Inscribed on the hem of the Virgin's dress at the bosom, "RAPHAEL VRBINAS." How the picture came into the hands of the Medici at Florence is unknown, but it is registered in the Inven-

The true distribution of this portion of the altar-piece is only to be guessed at from an early copy in the Corsini Gallery at Florence, in which there are three winged angels on the right and four on the left side of the heavens.*   In a fine pen outline of the two women and children at Vienna, the quickness with which Raphael originally conceived the subject, is manifested.   But the youthful face of St. Elizabeth tells us that the realistic idea of toothless and withered age was an afterthought which was only carried out in the picture itself.†   The nudes of the whole composition with bare contours of the head and a view of

tory of the Uffizi of 1589–1634. The panel was much injured and the upper part was painted over by one Colin, so that Inspector Krahe, at the beginning of the present century, caused them to disappear altogether.   The following parts are obviously retouched. The lights of the Virgin's mantle, and the hand with the book, the hand, shadows of the foot, head, and neck, and part of the dress of St. Elizabeth ; the hair and flesh of the Baptist, and the flesh in spots of the Infant Christ.

* Florence.   Corsini Gallery. Once in the Rinuccini Collection. Inscribed on the hem of the Virgin's dress, "RAPHAEL VRBINAS INV . SOLVTV . CADEN A MD XVII DIE XXVII MEN MAR." An Italian work so far as the figures are concerned, and the principal group better than the angels.   All by a disciple of Raphael.   But the landscape, with the tree and conical hills, differing from the

original, looks like the production of a Fleming.

† Vienna. Albertina. From the Cavaceppi Collection.   Outlined in red chalk and then rapidly with pen and bistre.   10 in. 4 h. by 9 in.   Very rapid sketch from nature, in which St. Elizabeth has a thin veil interwoven in her hair, her arms are bare and the turn of her face is towards the infant Christ.   The leg of the Virgin is bare, her hand is not in the same position as in the picture ; the Infant Christ's foot is not on that of its mother but on a stool, and the Baptist differs so far that here he is made to hold the end of the scroll which Christ presents to him.

At the Ambrosiana in Milan a drawing of the whole composition, including the angels in the sky, seems drawn after the picture.   It is, at all events, not by Raphael, any more than a copy, numbered 34, in the Oxford Gallery.

St. Joseph in profile also prove that Raphael hesitated at some particular moment as to the precise form in which he was to complete the pyramid of his composition.*

In the midst of these avocations, pressed, perhaps, by Domenico Alfani, who was manager, we should think, of his Perugian painting-room, he designed the " Holy Family " at Windsor, which, though a companion to the Canigiani "Madonna," seems never to have been executed. It perhaps too amiably represented an incident in the daily life of the Italian people. We can fancy two children in the country under the care of their mothers, the Virgin with her babe at her knee, one foot on her foot, one arm in her arm, St. Elizabeth kneeling at the Virgin's side, with her boy half on her lap, half resting on the hand under his armpits. St. John grasps at Christ's disengaged elbow, and seems to say he would like to play. Mary, in the usual attire, Elizabeth, in vest and hood, look on at the amiable struggle, but the infant Saviour resists, and prefers his rest. In the eagerness of the one, the playful indolence of the other, and the interest of the two

---

* Chantilly, seat of the Duc d'Aumale. Pen and umber outlines from the nude of the five figures of the picture. This interesting sketch is here and there very rough and hasty, and in some parts, such as the feet and hands of the two women, very careless. The attitudes of the latter are those of the Albertina drawing, and not those of the altar-piece. The nude of St. Joseph, seen from behind, but with a twist of the torso which brings the upper part of his frame in profile to the right, is very clever. St. Elizabeth is a male model.

A sketch of the Virgin and child alone is described in the Timbal Collection in Paris (not seen).

mothers, there is an almost indescribable charm, and Raphael's mastery in the execution of this beautiful pen-drawing is almost beyond belief. The reminiscences which connect it with the "Canigiani Madonna" are too striking to leave us in doubt as to the period of its conception.* We shall see that it was followed one year later by a design equally beautiful, and finished with even greater care. But Domenico Alfani, who usually received these masterpieces, was not active enough in pushing Raphael's interests at Perugia, and Raphael's practice in Umbria naturally suffered from his continued and protracted absence.

Still two great contracts remained to be completed in the "Entombment" of Atalanta Baglioni, and the fresco of San Severo. And as Raphael was bound to attend personally to the last, he now gave his energies exclusively to the first. The secret of Atalanta Baglioni's commission is unfortunately not revealed. But when it came to be executed in 1507, it represented the carriage of the dead Saviour to the sepulchre, and there is some reason to think that it was preceded in Raphael's mind by another subject, the "Wail over the Body of Christ at the Foot of the Cross."

Few themes have been more frequently and gravely pondered over than that of the Pietà. If Giotto's

---

* Windsor. Finished pen and ink sketch, with the line and effect almost of an etching. 9¼ in. h. by 5¾. The distance of lake and hills, a few trees and bushes are indicated with sketchy lines. On the foreground are grasses and weeds.

means had been equal to the realization of his thoughts, he might have furnished the model for all coming generations in the frescos of the Scrovegni chapel at Padua. His fine conception of despair and lamentation in that noble composition was only marred by inability to render the human form with all the subtlety of the masters of the later revival. Mantegna, who inherited the precepts of the Florentines from Donatello, added an intense realism to the passion of Giotto, and formed the lines of his celebrated plate on the grandest principle of pictorial distribution. Perugino illumined the scene by means of an excellent scheme of colour, and a landscape especially calculated to bring out the forms by which it was enlivened. Signorelli, with a rugged strength which alone Michaelangelo surpassed, gave prominence to muscular action, without due regard to rhythm or selection; and in spite of exceptional mastery in drawing and anatomy, he developed energy in excess, and sacrificed unity of purpose to a naturalism as marked in its way as that of Mantegna.

Raphael, whose early efforts had been mainly guided by Perugino, trusted to feeling rather than passion in the Pietà of the predella of Sant' Antonio, but when Florence opened its treasures to him he could not but observe that amiability and grace were not the sole qualities that required display in a subject of that kind, and he naturally thought of combining the precepts of Lionardo with the lessons of Fra Bartolommeo. Yet, when he drew the "Pietà," which is the theme illustrated in two splendid designs

at Paris and Oxford, it was not without effort that
he turned into the path of the Florentines, nor could
he entirely forget to make Umbrian tenderness or his
own graceful taste subordinate to the maxims of Da
Vinci.   With the greater breadth of style which
characterizes the "Pietà" of the Louvre it is easy to
discern a combination of elements not purely Tuscan,
and assuredly reminiscences of the most varied kind
were swaying him at the time.   A more philosophic
contemplation enabled him to discover qualities in
Mantegna and Signorelli to which he might previously have been blind.   Effects which might have
been produced earlier, had they not been neutralized
by Umbrian teaching, became potent enough when
that teaching was suspended.   Though Perugian habits
lingered with him still, the "Pietà" of Mantegna
came to assume an importance of which before this the
master would perhaps never have dreamt.   Pictures
by Signorelli in various cities of Umbria came back
to him with new claims to admiration.   It required a
stay in Florence to realize that there was something in
Signorelli's "Crucifixion" at Urbino which deserved to
be remembered, that numerous altar-pieces from the
same hand which we must fancy him to have seen
at Cortona, Borgo San Sepolcro and Castiglione
Aretino were to be deemed worthy of special
study.   There is not one of these masterpieces but
would seem now to have given an impulse to the
young master's thoughts.   In Mantegna's print the
Virgin sinks into the arms of her attendants, who
bend over her with intense grief, one of the Maries

kneels in despair with her hands joined in prayer, John the Evangelist erect wrings his hands and sobs convulsively. In the "Crucifixion" of Urbino the two Maries tend the Virgin in a swoon, and St. John appeals prayerfully to heaven. At Borgo San Sepolcro the Virgin, bereft of sense, lies in the arms of a woman who lifts the veil from her face. At Castiglione Aretino the Magdalen raises the feet of Christ, whilst his mother and one of the Maries keep his hand and arm from the ground. With these, Perugino's altar-piece of Santa Chiara, in which Christ is kept in a sitting posture by Nicodemus, whilst the Virgin passes her hand over his face, one of the Maries twists her fingers, and another looks down upon the group with outstretched arms.* The memory of all these works crowded together in Raphael's mind influenced him beyond conception. They set him a-thinking of the precepts of Da Vinci which told him to combine the dramatis personæ in an intertress of attitude and action dictated by a common thought of mourning. Bearing all this in mind, we cannot fail to see to whom we owe the dead Saviour of the Paris design, who lies with his legs in the Magdalen's lap, whilst she sits on the

---

* Reminiscent of Perugino, and an arrangement of his picture at Santa Chiara, is a drawing in red chalk. No. 40 at Oxford, once assigned to Raphael, but now properly classed amongst the works of a feebler artist.

No. 41, in the same gallery, is a further working out of the foregoing, comprising a study of the Saviour's torso, and the group of the Virgin with the two Marys and a standing saint; this drawing is by the same hand as No. 40. Silver-point. 8½ in. h. by 11¾ in. From the Antaldi and Lawrence Collections.

ground and powerfully grasps his limbs. The
Virgin with His head and shoulders on her knees
faints backward into the arms of an attendant.
Another female looping up her dress stoops to raise
the veil from the Virgin's face. Nicodemus in a
turban contemplates the scene, and St. John the
Evangelist to the right seems pinned to the ground
as he presses together the hands which he has raised
to his chin. It is easy to resign each of these figures
and attitudes to those in whom they originated—
to Mantegna, Signorelli, and Perugino. Fine as
Raphael's design undoubtedly is, it has something of
the conventional Umbrian still in the type and movement of the turbaned Nicodemus, in the pose and
dress of John. But the immature application of
Da Vinci's precepts betrays itself in their excess,
particularly in the girl kneeling at the Virgin's
side, who not only helps to support the Virgin's head
with her left arm but makes a pillow with her right
for that of Christ. Something inappropriate and
unfinished too is apparent in the place where the
Evangelist is made to stand. The drapery still lacks
the sweep and simplicity of the Florentines.* But
Raphael did not mean, we imagine, to present the
Louvre design as a complete composition, he drew
the nude of St. John in a sheet now at Oxford, and

---

* Paris. Louvre. No. 319.
Pen and umber drawing. 0·335
h. by 0·397. From the Mariette
Zanetti, Fries, Borduge, and Lawrence Collections. Notable in
addition to the description in the
text is, that behind the Evangelist
a profile of part of a head appears,
which reverts to us in the study of
nudes at Oxford, which follows
this.

combined with it in one group three figures of attendant men.   On the back of the drawing he made a study of a corpse, in which the body and head intended for the Saviour were more sharply in profile, and, strange to say, since we possess no picture in this form, the whole of these figures was pin-holed for use on the panel of some altar-piece.*   It occurred to Raphael in time to observe the defects of this distribution.   He put it aside and handled the same theme in a better and more appropriate shape, if not without neglectful sketchiness, in another sheet at Oxford, itself preceded by that clever but rather superficial sketch of the Magdalen, St. John, and other male spectators, now in the collection of Mr. Malcolm.†   In the last rendering of the whole com-

---

* Oxford. No. 38. Pen draw-ing in bistre. 8¼ in. h. by 13¼ in. From the Alva and Lawrence Collections.   On one side, with the head to the left, a male body on an inclined couch, with the left hand on the leg, the right hanging to the ground.   .

On the other side the three nudes described in the text, with the profile of a head behind St. John. Back and front are pinholed.

† Oxford. No. 37. Pen draw-ing in bistre. 7¼ in. h. by 8¼ in. From the Denon and Lawrence Collections.   This drawing is done from memory and without models. It is therefore of a less searching design than others. But it esta-blishes the lines of a composition of fine distribution with great freedom and nature in the attitude of each figure.

The group of John, with his three companions and the sitting Madonna, in the Malcolm Collec-tion, is in the same style as the foregoing, but consists of larger figures, drawn with the feeling and skill of which Raphael was master, but without the accuracy which he attained when he studied the model. The Magda-len with her legs drawn up, and hands closed together; her head in profile. The Evangelist in the attitude of that in No. 319 at the Louvre. Two of the other figures looking round to the left wear turbans. The drawing in pen and bistre passed from the Birchall Collection to that of Mr. Sackville Bale and was exhibited at the Grosvenor Gallery in 1878–9. It was sold, June 11, 1881, to Mr. Malcolm for 510 guineas.

position the figures were all cleverly brought into
focus. That of the Evangelist was moved to a more
appropriate place in reference to the principal
group; it was turned slightly out of profile and
received a picturesque accompaniment of followers.
The Magdalen was made to bear the Saviour's legs on
her lap, her arms were raised and her hands clasped
in grief. One of the Maries was substituted for
Nicodemus, and thus a fine and compact distribution
was attained in lines of pleasing curve without excess
of strain in any one of the personages.

Yet with all this labour expended, with this
abundance of thought, and correction, and final attainment of a fortunate result, Raphael ended with a mere
project for a picture. No altar-piece is known in
which the Oxford design was applied, nor was any
better result produced, as Raphael proceeded to vary
the subject and seized the moment, when the body of
the Saviour lying on the ground after its descent
from the cross, was about to be taken away for
removal.

The drawing which Raphael made for this incident
was of finer and riper workmanship than those which
preceded it. The system of shading outlines with
oblique cross hatching disappeared to make place for
a new system of vertical strokes woven obtusely, and
often at right angles to each other, the result being a
soft contrast of light and shade without any marked
contour of the inner features. The masterly application of this new style in a sheet at Oxford was
manifestly due to the direct effect on Raphael of the

lessons of Fra Bartolommeo. The body of Christ raised with a mighty effort from the winding sheet by a man at his head who strongly clasps both arms round his chest, the similar grasp of the legs by another kneeling figure are, as it were, an introduction to the later designs which found their final application in the "Entombment." A sketch of an arm, the shading of a hand, and four heads on the same paper further illustrate the painter's purpose. If in the full length of the lifeless Christ the model appears to have been a corpse, the head was clearly an appeal to living nature; and nothing can be more curious than to detect in the profile which Raphael made an absolute reproduction of a type familiar to the great master of San Marco. To sculptural forms of body and limb realistic accidents inseparable from the moving of a still flexible body are super-added, and the droop of the hands of the Saviour is a subtle proof of pictorial observation. The same bearded man seems to have sat for two faces in opposite views, with eyes cast down and features of mild intentness above the principal group. Next to these is a bust of the Virgin, as she swoons, with veil and mantle falling over her brow, then a fore-shortening of a male head at three-quarters to the right, with the face turned upwards;—all this thrown off with consummate ease and facility, and replete with the deep feeling and expressiveness peculiar to Raphael.*

* Oxford. No. 39. Pen and Bistre. 8¾ in. h. by 12¼ in. From the Viti, Bordage, Crozat, B. Constantine and Lawrence Collec-

In the " Entombment," which after so many trials now came to perfection, Raphael remained much under the same influences as were manifested in his early preparatory studies. A clearer reflex of the sculptural forms of Donatello and Michael Angelo may perhaps be detected, but Umbrian feeling, if transfigured, still slumbered within him and showed itself in certain movements, and occasional use of rich transparent tints in dresses and landscape contours. Michael Angelo's spirit revived in the pure Florentine shape of the body and limbs of the lifeless Christ, his compactness, and masterly application of the laws of bas-relief in the group of the " Maries attending the Swooning Virgin." Nor is it in these parts alone that we shall observe the influence of Buonarotti, not alone in the lie of the Saviour's legs, which remind us of the " Pietà " of Rome, not in the sitting attitude of the woman, who stretches her arms and twists her frame to save the Virgin from falling, which recalls the round of the Uffizi, but also in the peculiar handling of the pigments, the neutral tinting of some colours, the smooth gloss and faultless blending and the fine definition of the hands and feet in outlines of the utmost purity and elegance. From Mantegna, whose episode of the " Fainting Virgin " he had previously studied, he

tions. Though Passavant doubts the genuineness of this drawing, it is certainly original. The figure of Christ lies here with the legs to the right of the sheet, an arm is in the lower right corner, a hand in the upper left corner, the heads in a semi-circle to the right of the hand.

now derived the idea of the Saviour lifted by bearers and taken to his rest, but with ingenuity sharpened by practice, he changed the mode of carriage, and the bearers were made to move the Saviour head foremost to the sepulchre. Additional force was given to the action by supposing the tomb to be approached by steps, which it was necessary to ascend. The complicated attitudes of men, partly swinging the body on level ground, and partly straining their muscular power to raise the extra weight with a backward step, was original and purely his own. He avoided alike the pungent realism of Mantegna's expression, his passion and searching complexity of detail, and if on the whole his power as a composer fell below the level which the masterly Paduan displayed, it was only because Mantegna had produced a picture absolutely perfect in its combination and not to be surpassed on that account. That he recollected how in younger days he had copied the Paduan print, the body of Christ swathed in a winding sheet, the Virgin helping to bear the burden, the female shrieking with outstretched arms, and the porters at their task, who shall venture to deny? His first impression was to detach from Mantegna's arrangement the part of the Virgin Mary. He thought of introducing the group of the holy women as attendants of the corpse. His reliance on Perugino ceased abruptly and for ever, the utmost that he kept of his reminiscences of Signorelli was the female bending over Christ's hand. In this form he completed a very fine design, now at the British Museum, in which the two bearers are varieties of those in the picture; the three figures in rear differ. The Virgin is accompanied on the way by two females, and the third kisses the Redeemer's hand. Christ's head lies on his shoulder and presents itself frontwise, yet almost horizontally.* But a study which was made separately for the head and torso as well as for the legs of the bearer (another of the sheets at Oxford) is evidence that in the midst of this project Raphael already thought of giving to the man in backward stride that peculiar poise on the right leg and withdrawal on the left foot which came last into the picture. It is striking to observe at the same time, that whilst he is composing with ceaseless care the fragments of his mournful picture, a gayer spirit comes over him, and on the back of his paper he gives in sprightly lines a concert of antique figures, a woman with a harp, a youth playing the viol, and a satyr blowing a trumpet.†

---

* London. Brit. Mus. Pen and bistre drawing. 9¼ in. h. by 2½ in. From the Crozat, Lagoy, Dimsdale, Lawrence, and King of Holland's Collections. Bequeathed by Mr. Chambers Hall in 1853 to the British Museum. This, though executed with more freedom and rapidity than other drawings, particularly that of which we shall speak, at the Uffizi, is admirably outlined, and yet more admirably composed. The bearer to the left differs from that of the picture in the movement of the legs, which are similar to those in the Oxford study No. 42. The Virgin follows the bearers to the right, with a female on each side of her.

At the back of this drawing is a large figure of an aged and bearded man, resting on his right leg, the left leg raised. The right arm alone given, and set as if to carry a load. A tunic covers his chest and loins, and falls in three folds to his knees. Here again is a reminiscence of Mantegna's print, though the head there is turned in the opposite direction.

† Oxford. No. 43. Pen drawing in bistre. 9¼ in. h. by 7½ in. From the Ottley and Lawrence Collections. The torso and head of Christ are in the position of the foregoing. The legs of the bearer, which are naked, are similar to those in the picture; that is, the

Thinking further over the scheme of distribution which still required rounding, Raphael's next display of self-denial was the withdrawal of the group of Mary and her attendants. Under these conditions he remodelled the whole composition in a drawing at the British Museum, imagining the body just raised from the ground by the two principal bearers, and in rear between them the whole family of mourners, including the female kissing the hand, and the Virgin kneeling in silent prayer.* Something of Mantegna's spirit survived in this piece, but the arrangement, which was never carried out, offers less interest because of the skill with which it was conceived, than because of the studies which led to it. These introduce us to the

right leg on the ground, the heel of the left leg on the step, and there is evidence that the torso of Christ and the legs of the bearer were a study for this picture in the needle-holes with which they are punctured. A replica of this drawing, once in possession of Mr. de Triqueti at Paris, was not seen by the authors.

On the back of the drawing the central figure of a woman in antique drapery is seated and turned to the left, whilst her face is round to the right, to look at the youth who stands on his left leg and rests his knee on the stool. To the left is the trumpeter naked, erect, with his cheeks distended. The harp in the grasp of the female is merely indicated.

* British Museum   Pen and bistre.   8 in. h. by 12¼ in.   From the Crozat, Hibbert, Rogers, Conyngham and Birchall Collections.   In this drawing the bearer on the left is an old man, bearded, in a cap and gaberdine, who seems just raising the body of the Saviour from the ground, whilst the Magdalen stoops to look at the Saviour's face as she raises his left arm. Near her is the kneeling Virgin, and between her and the bearer, who halts after raising the feet, is the Evangelist, with his hands together at his chin. There are indications of heads of five other figures besides. There is still a reminiscence of Mantegna in the Evangelist. The bearer to the left has some affinity to that in the "Entombment," called the "Death of Adonis," No. 44 at Oxford, though here the figure is in reverse.

very life and labours of Raphael at the time and reveal
how he went about like Lionardo with sketching
materials in his hand, and visited the melancholy
resorts of death to see how corpses were taken from
their hearses and laid out in winding sheets.
In alternate position the head of one is seen to the
right, that of the next to the left as they lie in
stark attitude on the earth. Further back a robust
figure stoops with its awful load and drops it slowly
to the ground. But even in the midst of this
lugubrious operation Raphael's mind is, as it were,
protesting against thoughts of death; he sees a group
of naked children seated on a bench; one of them is
weaker than the rest, his companions have caught
him between them and laughing, yet with the cruel
playfulness which usually marks the tenderest age,
they squeeze him between them till he seems likely
to faint from the pressure.*

At last the true shape was found for the principal
part of the "Entombment," and this was consigned
to a drawing squared for use, which is now preserved
at the Uffizi. Not a trace as yet of the swooning
Mother of Christ and busy friends intent on restoring
her to life. The upper end of the shroud is in the
hands of the men that step back on the threshold of
the tomb, whilst between them St. John the Evangelist looks down. Raising the left hand in hers, the

---

* British Mus. Back of the
foregoing. The three children are
in the upper left corner, the man
stooping to put down the corpse
in the upper right corner.

Magdalen looks piteously at the death-worn face, and as she does so, another woman with raised fingers glances round in grave sympathy. The man at the feet remains unaltered.* But now came again a decisive change in the painter's thought. Either his own sense told him that the absence of the Virgin could not be accounted for, or Atalanta Baglioni demurred to the omission. A length was added to the picture. To the right of the solitary bearer the Virgin is seen falling back into the arms of her women; one fronting the spectator, half sitting, half kneeling, turns her shoulders, and raises her head and hand to keep Mary from falling, another grasps her waist from behind, a third helps at the right shoulder, casting glances at the same time to the Saviour as he passes to the grave. It is here that we discern the final appeal of Raphael to the art of Michaelangelo. Yet profoundly moving as the group in itself appears, magnificent as it is in conception, it was only introduced at a considerable sacrifice. In order to preserve the lines of the landscape it was found necessary to cancel the attendant looking at the woman kissing Christ's hand. That figure with all its loveliness became of necessity but a stop-gap. Yet it was not a complete sacrifice that Raphael here felt bound to make. He withdrew the figure of the girl at the Magdalen's side, but he presently restored her

---

* Florence. Uffizi. Frame 154. No. 538. Pen drawing, with bistre wash, hatched over in the style of Oxford drawing. No. 39. 10¾ in. h. by 11. Squared for transfer. Finished with the most minute care.

to being amongst the Virgin's attendants, and he did
so with the special purpose of uniting the final
incident of the swoon to the rest of the picture.
It was easy in studying the episode to give it a
perfectly concentric shape. The sketch which was
made of it (in the Malcolm collection), if not as
perfect or free from strain as that of the " Spasimo,"
is still a masterpiece of concentration. The Virgin's
knees have lost their strength, her arms hang powerless and her head is drooping, but the girl at her feet
raises her hands to support the waist and shoulders,
the tender arms of the two Maries are twisted round
her belt, and all express by glance and action their
grief and sympathy with the sufferer. But conceived
in this form the scene has all the character of an independent picture modelled on the round of Michaelangelo. To connect it with the rest of the " Entombment " was only possible by diverting the look of one
of the Maries from the recumbent Virgin. By an effort
of genius this object was attained by altering the
attitude and head of the girl whose first position
had been at the Magdalen's side. She was now
imagined turning her look from the melancholy scene
in which she is an actor to that in which she has no
part.

Excepting this, the sketch of the fainting Virgin,
with the busy women about her, conveys a touching
sentiment of affectionate friendship and care. The
shading and execution are realized on the system of
cross-hatching, which marks the design at the Uffizi,
and that of Oxford in which Christ is raised by two

men from the ground.* To make matters doubly sure, Raphael drew the group once more on a single sheet, belonging to Mr. Malcolm, in which the skeleton of the bones is strongly lined within the contour of the figures. Of three heads on the same paper two found a place in the picture, the third is that of the woman in rear of the Virgin, whose face and attitude were altered as we have just observed.† The studies were completed, so far as they are known to exist, by a drawing of a man carrying a load on the back of a sketch for the Canigiani " Madonna " in the Chantilly collection, and finished academies of the three bearers without drapery in the gallery of Oxford. The only divergence worthy of notice between these studies and the picture is that in the position of the legs of the man who rises backwards to the step.‡

* London. Mr. Malcolm. Pen and bistre sketch. 11¾ in. h. by 8 in. From the Antaldi, Lawrence, King of Holland and Leembrugge Collections.

The same group, seen to the knees in the Ducal Collection at Weimar, is assigned by Passavant, ii. No. 267, to Raphael (not seen).

† Same collection. Same size as foregoing. The skeleton seems to be done from memory, as the heads which accompany the figures are also.

Here might be the place to note certain studies of bones, legs, feet, arms, &c., in the collection of Berlin and Düsseldorf. But these studies are not with any certainty to be assigned to Raphael. They are—1. Berlin Print-room, a foot, a leg, and the bones of the latter, in red chalk. On the back of the sheet the head (silver-point) of a youth, three-quarters to the right, of which there is a replica in the Düsseldorf Collection. 2. Düsseldorf Academy. Pen sketch of three arms. 3. Same collection. The legs of two different figures in outline, and a shaded study of a foot. Pen and bistre. 4. Same collection. A human skull in profile to the left and a head and shoulders of a hippogriph. Pen and ink.

‡ Chantilly Collection. In this fine drawing there are two nude figures, one turned to the right, who seems to hold a musical in-

Curiously enough, as Raphael gathered up his designs and proceeded from Florence to Perugia, to take the "Entombment" in hand—for we are authorized to believe that the picture was not executed at Florence—it must have occurred to him to strike the Southerly road which led to Orvieto before he finally bent Eastward to the place of his destination. Lingering, we should think, with some satisfaction in the chapel of San Brizio, where the masterpieces of Signorelli and Angelico were displayed, we can fancy him not unmoved when, looking into one of the niches, he observed a composition which would strike him as very closely related to that which he was bent on completing. In the foreground he would find Signorelli's group of the dead Christ raised in part on the lap of the Virgin, and the Magdalen kissing the Saviour's hand, a reversal of the altar-piece of Cortona. The background would show him a classic sarcophagus with its side filled up by a relief of the "Entombment." In the grand but vehement style of the greatest of the Umbrians, he would see the body of Christ borne feet foremost by three naked men, a

strument. Lower down the sheet another carrying a load.

Oxford. No. 42. Pen and bistrè drawing. 11¼ in. h. by 9¾ in. From the Antaldi and Lawrence Collections. The figures here all close together, and the body of the Saviour indicated with red chalk, the head of the bearer on the step much disfigured by the wear and tear of the paper. But the rest is modelled from nature in cross hatching with surprising care and finish. The same figures, with the addition to the left of the bearer, who holds the legs of a woman in profile, is in the collection of the Louvre, though not exhibited. It might be by Penni, though the dolomites in the distance might suggest another hand.

fourth in front raising his arms in passionate gesture
of despair.   At the sides of the main subject Peter
Parens and Faustinus with his mill stone, the patron
saints of Orvieto.   What wonder, that seeing this,
he should suddenly think of a new form of the
"Entombment;" that he should, in a few potent
strokes, have thrown upon paper that marvellous
sketch at Oxford in which the composition of
Signorelli is reversed and Christ is carried feet foremost to the tomb with the noble addition of an all but
naked female wailing as she bends over the face and
winds one arm under that of the Redeemer in an un-
speakable agony of grief.   It might indeed be urged
that since the back of the sheet which contains this
majestic design, comprises a figure of Adam and a
fragment of a figure of Eve, which were used in one
of Marcantonio's prints, the whole page was composed
at a period subsequent to 1507, but we shall observe
that in drawings made about this time for the predella
of the "Entombment," the same power and sweep of
contour were displayed, and Raphael performed the
feat which we find so frequently repeated, of making
sketches of the utmost diversity in style for one and
the same picture.*   Yet if it struck him that a new

---

* Oxford.   No. 44.   Pen drawing in bistre.   10½ in. h. by 13 in.
From the Antaldi, Crozat, Mariette,
St. Morys, Fuseli, and Lawrence
Collections.   Bought by Mariette
from the heirs of Timoteo Viti.
This composition has been called
the "Death of Adonis," but it
may quite as well represent the

"Entombment."   The dead body
is carried feet foremost from left
to right by two bearers at the
shoulders and one at the feet.   It
is similar in position to that in
the drawings of the British
Museum and Uffizi, though reversed, excepting that the feet
here are hooked, as it were, to-

and classic energy might, if need were, be infused into his composition, he was far too forward in other preparations to alter his purpose now, and he proceeded to paint the altar-piece of Atalanta Baglioni on the lines which he had finally settled at Florence.

Eminently characteristic of the work which now rapidly came to completion is the Umbrian feeling apparent in the soft run of certain curves, whilst the Florentine element predominates in the application of the laws of bas-relief to the sway of the draperies. Raphael's chastened taste in the selection of form is shown in slenderness of shape combined with wiry strength, yet apart from the figure of Christ, whose features in their calm are perhaps surpassed for beauty by the perfection of the chiselled frame and limbs, apart also from the graceful figure of the girl who kisses the Redeemer's hand, and portions of the group of the Maries, which are realized with the noblest purity, there are not wanting signs here and there of hardness and affectation; and these would particularly apply to the somewhat rigid youth who holds the winding-sheet at the feet, the unnatural strain of the backward movement in the bearer on the step, and the lengthened stride of his more aged companion.

---

gether. The bearers are like those of the drawing of the British Museum, purchased from the Birchall Collection. To the right of the whole group we observe the head of a satyr in profile looking up.

On the back of the sheet to the left, is Adam leaning against a tree, turned to the right, and taking fruit from Eve, of whom there is but a sketchy outline of the head and arms. At the bottom of the paper to the right is a recumbent child, all drawn with a pen in bistre from models.

Sculptural immobility in some of the faces may also
be detected, though at bottom the skill of Raphael
is grandly shown in the variety with which expression
is conveyed in the glistening of an eye or mobile action
of the lips.   We may suspect the damaging influence
of Domenico Alfani in those parts which hardly exhibit to the full the delicate subtlety of the master's
hand.   A striking charm is due to the graceful trim
of hair and the light flow of gossamer stuffs in veils
and scarves.   Cleanness and precision of handling are
remarkable throughout, yet more in some places than
in others, the technical style of Michaelangelo particularly manifests itself in the group of the Maries
and the swooning Virgin.   Vasari's enthusiasm when
he called this piece divine, was not without justifica-
tion.*   It had not suffered as yet from the numerous
vertical splits and consequent patching which now
impair its beauty.   Whether we consider the
burnish and marble purity of the flesh, the neutral
shades of certain reds and pinks relieved with leaden
grey, or the wonderful intensity of certain greens,
especially those glazed with bitumen which come out
with so much richness in the dress of the youthful
bearer and his bearded comrade, there is still cause
for ample admiration of the splendid colouring of the
picture.   Umbrian in the disposition of landscape
lines, though in treatment advanced to the breadth
of the Tuscans, the distance of country and sky in
which the figures are relieved, is one of the finest that

---

* Vasari, viii. p. 11.

Raphael had as yet created. Never, certainly, had
he done anything so grand on such an important
scale. The tomb is a cave dug out of a rock rising
darkly to the left against the heavens. The sky
bounds a range of hills overlooked on the right by
Golgotha, with its crosses watched by guards. This
was the last portion of the picture to which Raphael
applied his hand, rich in details of towers, ruins, and
dwellings, and not without the characteristic tree of
slender branching which scarcely intercepts with
lightest leafing the azure of the atmosphere. An
art of less expertness appears in the formal handling
of the weeds and flowers growing in the foreground.*

Is it presuming to believe that when Raphael
finished this picture, he recollected the early time
when the corpses of the Baglioni were raised on
stretchers in the streets of Perugia, when Atalanta
pressed the hand of the dying Grifone, and the days
that followed the massacre were spent in removing
the bodies of the dead and cleansing the desecrated
churches with wine?

---

* Rome. Palazzo Borghese.
Panel, about 6 ft. square. On the
step to the left inscribed RAPHAEL
VRBINAS MDVII. Painted as we
see for Atalanta Baglioni (Vas. viii.
11). It remained in her chapel at
San Francesco till 1787 (Perug.
Raph. p. 281). In Feb., 1797, it
was carried away by the French
to Paris, from whence it was
brought back in 1815 to the
Vatican. Its present existence in
the Borghese palace is not quite
explained. It was replaced at
Perugia by a copy which in
earlier times had been made by
Arpino. A vertical split, which
runs down through the sky to the
Saviour's beard and chest, touching
the hand and foot of the bearer to
the left, and another similar split
down the figure of the bearer to
the right, and cutting the feet and
toes of Christ, three other splits at
the bottom of the panel, disfigure
the picture considerably, as the
parts have necessarily been
patched. A web of smaller splits

In contrast with other masterpieces of this age, yet in harmony with the feelings of the solitary Atalanta, the predella of the "Entombment" is filled with a series of monochromes representing Faith, Hope, and Charity, each one of which is accompanied by two appropriate figures of children. If the "Entombment" itself displays at intervals the absence of the master's touch, the predella is exclusively his own. On this occasion Raphael did the converse of that which was usual with Umbrian painters. But on that account his genius is all the more revealed in conception of the utmost grandeur, feeling of the greatest delicacy, and expression of the subtlest grace. To the sculptural form of Buonarotti ideal features and full maidenly shape are superadded, and with these, modest propriety of dress suitable to eternal youth. The softness and rounding of Lionardo combined with the freedom of Fra Bartolommeo are ennobled with incomparable tenderness and serenity.

Faith looks at the chalice, Hope prays ecstatically, with her eye rather than her face turned in profile towards heaven. They could scarcely be presented with more ideal loveliness. It can hardly be deemed probable that Raphael had seen the allegories of the Scrovegni chapel at Padua, yet he conveys with equal noblesse the feeling of the great founder of the

---

here and there may also be observed. Of copies, we know : 1. Turin Gallery. No. 122, inscribed I. F. PENN, MDXVIII. in gold letters on the step (canvas). This picture seems once to have been at Milan.—Perugia Gall. by Orazio Alfani—Perugia, S. Pietro. A very careful copy by Sassoferrato. Other copies exist besides.

Florentine school, and the art acquired in the progress of two hundred years. Charity, with her matronly look, her twins, who nestle at the breast, the child who still remembers the delights of that warm place, the first-born who courts her caress, is not without the charm of youth, though her face seems overspread with an atmosphere of profound pity and trust. The masterly arrangement of five or six beings in so small a space exemplifies anew the vividness of the impression made on Raphael by the works of Buonarotti's chisel. Winged Cupids in pretty tunics stand as the genii of the fable near these beauteous allegories. Two at the side of Faith hold tablets with appropriate inscriptions. Boys without drapery attend the figure of Charity, one of them with a vase on his shoulders, in which a fire is burning, the other raising a dish, out of which he pours a stream of pieces. They are the natural outcome of the studies so frequently repeated in the pages of the Venice sketch-book. They prefigure in their graceful rounded forms and chubby faces those perfect renderings of childhood which grace the "Madonna del Baldacchino," the Chamber of the "Disputa" at the Vatican, or the altar-pieces of Foligno and San Sisto.* It is on the back of the design for the Charity, a grand, but rapid outline sketch, of which the parts

---

* Rome. Vatican Museum. No. VII. Wood. 1 palm 6 h. by 8 palms 6 long, or 0·44 h. by 3·96. Monochromes, each of the allegorical figures in a framed round on green ground ; the genii at the sides, each in a rectangle, with a brownish ground, separated from the rounds by a yellow beading. There are five children about the figure of Charity.

were slightly altered, when the subject was transferred to the picture, that we renew acquaintance with the bold freedom of .the last drawing which Raphael conceived for the "Entombment." But here the theme is not the carriage of the Saviour, or the wail of the Virgin and saints over his remains, but the descent of the body from the cross. It would be difficult to render with fewer or more pregnant lines the power exerted by the man on the ladder, who lets the frame down with a rope, as he rests his chest on the vertical limb of the cross, the strain of the one who grasps the torso and legs, or that of the third, seen to the hips, who directs, as it were, from a second ladder the movement of the left arm. The drooping head of Christ, whose hair falls downward in pointed locks, the flexibility of the right arm and bended knees could hardly be conceived in more natural or instantaneous action.*

On the pinnacle of the "Entombment." which remained at Perugia, when the altar-piece and its predella were disposed of by the monks of San Francesco, it may be needless to dwell unless to confirm that the Eternal in the midst of angels, of which the first idea was consigned to a sketch at Lille, came to be executed by one of Raphael's disciples at Perugia.†

---

* Vienna. Albertina. Pen and bistre drawing, 13 in. h. by 9½ in., with three children. The variety here is that the Virgin's left arm is bent upwards, so that the hand shall come up to the breast, which one of the children is sucking.

The deposition on the back of the sheet is that described in the text. The drawing was in the Viti, Crozat, Mariette and Julian of Parma Collections.

† Perugia Gallery ; from San Francesco. God the Father turned

Not alone were the time and attention of Raphael taken up with more important matters than that of painting an uninteresting fragment of an altar-piece which in its principal parts had already taxed his powers to the utmost, but his efforts would naturally be diverted into another channel by the necessity of delivering the "Trinity" of San Severo. Not only was this a composition of a monumental type arranged on principles at variance with those of pictures till then designed or finished by Raphael at Florence, but it was full of novel experiences to one who had hitherto confined himself to panels and oil medium. It seems highly probable that the difficulties of fresco contributed to the slow progress of the covenanted work at San Severo and led to the numerous interruptions which caused its completion to be finally postponed. The more Raphael's intimacy with Fra Bartolommeo and the wall painters of Tuscany increased, the more he would feel that a serious task lay before him, and the sense of his responsibility in this respect would clearly weigh the heavier, as he felt that the manipulation familiar to the Florentines was not to be acquired by other means than those of

to the left, with his left hand open, his right raised in benediction, in a red mantle, strongly bearded and looking down. Ten heads of cherubs surround him. Marked outlines, brownish red flesh tints, and inharmonious draperies, show that the panel was not painted by Raphael. Yet the design was apparently his. It answers to the outline already noticed elsewhere. See *antea*. No. 607 in the Gallery of Lille. The Perugian panel is apparently not of the age of Raphael, and we must think that the original, executed in 1507, was copied by some feeble Umbrian of a later age, whose work has been preserved, whilst that from which he worked was lost.

a long and constant practice. Thinking over these matters he would naturally consult the friar who best knew the secret of the craft, and the Dominican might respond that he was welcome not only to the lessons of his experience, but to those which he might derive from studying the "Last Judgment" in the hospital of Santa Maria Nuova. If the design for the "Trinity" of San Severo had been preserved, most of the secrets of its creation would now be revealed. But the studies which have been handed down to us certainly tend to confirm that much of the preliminary work was done at Florence; and a drawing at Oxford, more closely connected than any other with Raphael's composition, contains not merely a sketch of Lionardo's cartoon, to which reference was once made in these pages, but exhibits the style which Raphael cultivated in the period of his intimacy with the friar of San Marco. Yet, as the Dominican only resumed his labours in 1506, and Raphael's acquaintance with him only began in that year, it is obvious that the fresco of San Severo was only completed after it had been left unfinished in 1505. When he returned to his duties in 1507 at Perugia, Raphael's first business was to introduce the figure of the Redeemer in benediction seated on clouds under the dove of the Holy Ghost. He then added the two winged attendants at the Saviour's sides and the bench of fathers of the Church divided into groups of three in the foreground of the heavens. In absolute contrast with the full and fleshy shapes of the cherubs near the Eternal in the apex of the lunette, the seraphs beneath them are slender and ethereal apparitions; and whilst the first distinctly recall the period of the "Madonna" of Terranuova, the second equally remind us of the later Tuscan influences which set their stamp on Raphael's mind. Of these two angels one to the left in profile to the right sets one foot on the mist and raises the other on a higher projection of cloud. His look is downward, his hands are joined in prayer. The other in a similar attitude appears in full front view. The more graceful and pleasing aspect which he presents in respect of pose and dress may indeed be accidental; possibly there was still a tendency in Raphael, surrounded as he was with assistants who cultivated the traditions of the Perugians, to relapse into Umbrian habits. But, on the whole, there can be little doubt that even these figures exhibit the qualities derived from Raphael's growing familiarity with Florentine master-pieces. The noble bend of the Saviour's head, the fine shape of his naked torso, are the more con-spicuous from the beauty of the drapery, which falls from his hips to his feet. Remarkable for purity of lineaments and a well-proportioned frame, striking for a sweet resignation and complacent expression of the features, this figure could never have been so admirably conceived unless the artist had thought profoundly over the precepts of Lionardo and the Frate. For not only is the movement natural and noble, the form select, and the face of great regu-larity, but the study of the parts, and especially that of the extremities and articulations, is finished to perfection. The foreshortenings are correct and the mantle set in the monumental fashion of the Tuscans. As he gradually advanced his personages to the verge of the picture Raphael displayed equal, if not superior strength; and though it might be said that some of the saints at each side of the fresco are not unlike each other, there are delicacies of turn and action which distinguish them all. To the left, near the Saviour, Saint Beneditus with a long beard and a bald head sits gravely looking at the Master. St. Placidus, his next companion, a young and handsome person, holds the palm of martyrdom and communes with Saint Maurus, a monk in profile who ponders over the mystery of the scene before him. To the right St. Romuald, a bearded solitary, with his head thrown back, grasps the knotted stick that usually accompanies his walk. Next him the youthful martyr Benedict sits and dreamily looks into space, his form encased in an embroidered frock. The palm is also in his hand. St. John the Martyr seen sideways on the right, displays a grand and imposing figure, from which the head has been removed by a fracture of the wall. In all these divines, in whom dignity of mien, solemnity of pose, and depth of expression are majestically combined, the common occupation is suggested by a book which rests edgewise or flat on their knees or in their hands. The mere description of them, as indeed the description of the whole fresco, suggests how vivid the impression must have been which Raphael took from the "Last Judgment" of Baccio della Porta. It shows how strongly he was affected by the splendid symmetry of that composition. Yet none can say that in working out the thoughts that filled his mind he was urged by the mere incentive of imitation. In every line and every touch he placed reliance on no one but himself; whilst he recollected the forms of the Frate's design, he also thought of those of Masaccio, and with equal skill he realized the transparence of colour, the true balance of light and shade, the graduated scale of half-tint, and the broad style of drapery, which are the principal merits of the frescos of the Carmine. Nor was Raphael's progress as a wall painter less remarkable. A novice at the outset, if such a term can apply to any part of the work at San Severo, he soon acquired experience in manipulation; and though he did not proceed with the faultless ease of Fra Bartolommeo or Del Sarto, he triumphantly conquered most of the difficulties of a method to which he had been as yet a comparative stranger. Inevitable deficiencies of modelling were corrected by hatchings, to which an aptitude for pen drawing had given him the clue. He thus applied a mixed system, combining the first tinting in liquid colours on the wet lime with subsequent retouching in distemper and a final application of shading in lines with pigments of varied depth in fine curves or strokes crossing each other at different angles. Flesh for the most part was more softened and smoothed than the rest. Coarser grain was produced by rougher plaster in the wings and dresses. Short strokes were interknit in the clouds. The high lights of stuffs were

laid in with body colour over pigment of a deeper
shade.   Illuminated or adumbrated parts were expressed by light or dark cross-hatching, whilst the
flesh of the hands was toned off with short waves
suggested by the rounding of the surfaces.*

Well as the monastery of the Camaldoles of San
Severo might be suited to furnish models for Raphael's
service, similar institutions in the Tuscan capital were
equally at his command.   Nor can we doubt that it
was there that he studied the grand and severely
dignified head in the drawing at Oxford which served
for the figure of St. Placidus or the hands of St.
Benedict and St. John the Martyr.   The Lionardesque profile on the same sheet of an aged, yet
beardless man, whose stern eye and projecting under-

---

* Perugia. San Severo. Fresco.
There is no part of this painting
which has not been injured in
some degree ; and this is due in
part to early retouchings, in part
to the "restorations" of Giuseppe
Carattoli in 1840–50, and Professor
Consoni in 1872. It was probably Carattoli who did most injury, since the fresco, though
spotted, was not dangerously
damaged before he covered them
over with smears that Professor
Consoni tried to remove. The
Perugian municipality did good
work in altering the building so
as to give it a new light and prevent the evil effects of damp. But
it is particularly unfortunate that
Professor Consoni should · have
thought fit to revive what was
entirely gone, and complete from
imagination the head of the winged
cherub to the left of the Eternal.
The fall of the "intonaco," which
carried away the greater part of
the Eternal, took away half the
other cherub, the head of the
monk on the right foreground,
and the back of the skull and
spotted nimbus of St. Benedict.
Though he left all this in blank,
Professor Consoni retraced outlines, restippled other parts, and
the result of his operations, which
would have been avoided if the
municipality had attended to the
instructions of the ministry which
forbad all retouching or stippling
with colours, is unhappily that
the whole fresco is covered over
with an opaque fog, which adum-
brates and weakens most of the
wall painting.

lip are full of ascetic character, recall those earlier studies of the Venice sketch-book in which the searching line of Da Vinci is tempered by a simpler element of nature and life.* It is not too much to say that these studies reveal a mastery in the use of the silver point equal to that which characterizes the drawings for the "Disputa." But they have more of the Vincian style in them than Raphael retained, and they seem to breathe, as the originals surely breathed, the air of Florence.†

---

* Oxford. No. 28. Silver-point drawing on pale greyish yellow prepared ground. 8¾ in. h. by 11 in. From the Ottley, Duroveray, Dimsdale and Lawrence Collections. Next to the slight sketch of the Da Vinci cartoon is the profile to the right, described in the text, and the two hands of St. Benedict and St. John on the book. At the bottom of the sheet and transverse to the profile, is the head of St. Placidus, at three-quarters to the left, the direction of the eye being here to the right, whilst in the fresco it is to the left. Two scribbles of horses' heads in the bottom right hand corner of the sheet seem late additions to the drawing.

† Other drawings there are in various collections which suggest some relation to the fresco of San Severo, ex. gr. :

Oxford. No. 31. Silver-point drawing on pale cream-coloured prepared ground. 5¾ in. h. by 8⅛ in. From the Antaldi and Woodburn collections. Study of a model with bare skull, uplifted right hand, the left on a book on the knee, the left foot on a ledge so placed as to show the sole of the shoe. It is in front view, with the head turned to the right. The style of this drawing is that of the period under notice. The drawing is squared for use, but we cannot say whether it was used for the "Eternal" or not. On the back two kneeling draped figures.

Louvre Collection, not exhibited. Pen and bistre drawing of a bearded prophet seated with one hand on his lap, the left arm resting on the edge of a folio, the feet bare, the body in a robe and mantle. The head is fine and stern and attentive. But none of the saints at S. Severo were done finally from this design.

Berlin Museum. Pen and ink drawing of drapery generally like that of the "Saviour" at San Severo, but more detailed in the Peruginesque style than that of the fresco. But there is no very abso-

Was it prospect of gain? was it the memory of the amiable disciple, whose loss prematurely struck the heart of his old master, that induced Perugino to finish in 1521 the fresco of San Severo? Assuredly whatever motive may have actuated the patriarch, he could not have produced a more instructive contrast than that revealed in the work of his old age set forth by the side of that which illustrates Raphael's manhood. But had he painted the six figures of saints which form the lower part of the "Trinity" of San Severo at the very time when Raphael left the upper part of it unfinished, he would still have remained inevitably inferior to his great and illustrious disciple.

----

lute certainty that the study is from Raphael's own hand. From the Pocetti Collection.

Paris Academy of Fine Arts. Drawing in chalk of the drapery of the "Saviour." On the back two or three pen sketches of fragments of "Madonnas," in the style of those of the "Madonna in Green" at Vienna.

CHAPTER VII.

Raphael's visit to Urbino in 1507.—His relations with the Court of Duke Guidubaldo.—Portraits of the Duke of Urbino and Pietro Bembo.—Acquaintance with Francia.—"Holy Family with the Lamb," and designs connected with it.—Lionardesque influences.— The "St. Catherine" and "Madonna with the Pink."—Bridgewater and Colonna "Madonnas," and "Adoration of the Shepherds."— Varieties of the "Virgin with the Sleeping Christ and St. John." —Cowper "Madonna," "Bella Giardiniera," and "Madonna Ester-hazy."—"Madonna del Baldacchino," and Raphael's friendship for Fra Bartolommeo.—Correspondence with Alfani at Perugia.— Raphael prepares to leave Florence.—Foundation of St. Peter at Rome, and effect of the Rebuilding of that Basilica on Julius the Second and the Artists he employed.—Raphael goes to Rome.

LITTLE as we know of Raphael's personal history before he went to Rome, the general impression reflected to us is one revealing ease in the midst of constant labour. Yet Vasari has divulged that some anxieties were caused at this period by the disorder of his affairs.* It appears from a legal document which supplies the deficiencies of Vasari's biography that Raphael stumbled into liabilities without well knowing how they had been incurred. The comparative proximity of Perugia to Urbino was probably advantageous by enabling him with rapidity and decision to settle unexpected claims upon his purse. For some consideration which has not been disclosed, possibly in return for the delivery of a picture, Raphael had bought a house at Urbino from the heirs

---

* Vas. viii. p. 7.

of Serafino Cervasi of Monte Falcone for one hundred florins, and he had obtained from the vendors a fictitious discharge in full.   Whilst the Serafini were still in expectation of the fulfilment of their bargain, they came suddenly into collision with the ecclesiastical courts for engaging to marry minors or relations within the limits of consanguinity, and being apparently unable to meet the fine, they filed a plea before a notary, and called upon Raphael to pay the debt. Taking horse and proceeding to Urbino, Raphael met the difficulty by transferring part of the fine to the treasurer of the court, promising to liquidate the rest before the following Christmas, and remitting a small balance to the Serafini.*   The absence of any allusion to the delivery of these sums into the hands of Francesco Buffi, who was then Guidubaldo's financial secretary, has not unnaturally led to the presumption that the debt to the public exchequer was paid in pictures delivered to the Duke of Urbino. The date of these transactions is the 11th of October, 1507 ; and Guidubaldo was then at home attended by the whole of his suite, including Pietro Bembo, who probably referred to this time his long acquaintance with the master of Urbino.†   Though it can hardly

---

* The original document discovered by Signor Alipio Alippi, was published in Aug., 1881, in the Roman periodical "Il Rafaello."   It has also appeared singly with Signor Alippi's commentary in an independent form. The balance to the Serafini was 12½ florins, the first payment to Francesco Buffi 50 florins, and the rest payable before Christmas, 37½ florins.

† See Bembo's correspondence ; Opere., from which it appears that he lived at Urbino, or in other cities of the Duchy from 1506 to 1509. See also his letter of Feb. 3, 1531, to Soranzo (Arch. Stor. Series of 1855, vol. ii. part i. p. 242), wherein he says he stayed

be doubted that Raphael at this period renewed his relations with the household of the duke, it is not to be presumed that he was known to the courtiers of that prince, as he afterwards became, when Baldassare Castiglione wrote in the Cortigiano of his "perfect style," and attributed to Lodovico da Canossa the opinion "that the painter's excellence was supreme." * But practically Raphael even now enjoyed the professional advantages of a high and acknowledged position, and his letter of the 21st of April, 1508, to Simone Ciarla, which seems to have been written shortly after his return to Florence, not only deplores in feeling terms the death of the duke, whom he knew, but casually refers to a picture of the "Madonna," which had been delivered to Giovanna della Rovere, and alludes to her patronage and that of her relatives as important and desirable.† It was the more desirable, as Raphael was now anxious for an introduction to Piero Soderini, who still presided over the destinies of Florence, and he had written to Rome as well as to Urbino to obtain the interest of Giovanna's son, the prefect, who had left the Vatican for Fossombrone, on hearing of Guidubaldo's illness.‡ If he painted, as Bembo gives us reason to believe, the portrait of " Guidubaldo" of Urbino, the means of ascertaining the fact has been taken from us by the

---

six years at Urbino. See also the passage in Morelli's Anonimo, in which allusion is made (p. 18) to a portrait of Bembo painted by Raphael when Bembo was at the Court of Urbino. We know nothing certain of this portrait be-

yond the Anonimo's statement.

* Cortigiano, ed. of Padua, 1766, pp. 58 and 74.

† Raphael to Ciarla, April 21, MDVIII., last reprinted in Pas. i. 497–8.

‡ Ibid. ibid.

total loss of the picture. It is still a moot question whether he did not take sittings for another extant portrait, which is described as that of a "Duke of Urbino," belonging to one of the family of Bovio at Bologna—an injured panel in the Lichtenstein Collection at Vienna, which combines some of the burnish of Francia with Raphaelesque sentiment, and details of landscape foreign to the Bolognese school. It may be necessary to recall that this portrait is a bust of a middle-aged man in a black felt hat, similar to that worn by Raphael himself, that his marked face, hooked nose, and piercing eyes are well relieved by a copious frizzle of hair, and his frame picturesquely encased in a green vest, a red coat, with a cool purple lining, and a brown mantle with red facings. The round tower, with its peaked helmet, and the castellated buildings about it, and the sweep of country on one side, in which a winding road, a tree, and a pond with swans are depicted, seems entirely Tuscan. The colours of the face are so transparent, that they hardly conceal the priming of the panel, and yet they are full of Florentine glow, at the same time feeling and expression are eminently Raphaelesque, whilst the polish of the surface equals that of Francia. It is possible that Raphael may have had it in mind to imitate the gloss of the works of the great master of Bologna.* His stay at Urbino would bring him

---

* Lichtenstein Gall. No. 67. Wood. 0·55 h. by 0.45. We say "Is it possible that Raphael here should have it in mind to imitate Francia?" The converse proposition has been taken in History of North Italian Painting, i. p. 571. It is difficult to decide. But we should, after mature consideration, favour the authorship of Raphae·

necessarily in contact with Timoteo Viti, the friend and pupil of Francia, and Viti may have helped to draw closer than they might otherwise have been such ties as already existed between Raphael and the Bolognese. That the two painters were acquainted is not to be doubted, as their intimacy is proved by an affectionate letter which Raphael wrote immediately after he came to Rome;* but it is still a question whether the friendship, which has thus been proved, began at Florence or at Bologna. In favour of Bologna, it might be urged that Raphael's patrons in that city had become as numerous as those of any other Italian capital. Apart from the " St. Cecilia " and the " Vision of Ezechiel," which were done in later years, he is said to have executed a " St. John the Baptist " for the Albergati, and a " Holy Family under an Oak Tree " for the Casali ; and he is known to have painted a " Nativity " for Giovanni Benti-voglio, a partisan of the Montefeltri, in the days when Julius II. meditated the expulsion of the Benti-voglii from the lordship of Bologna.† Yet all this,

rather than that of Francia. It is curious meanwhile to find that Giacomo Bovio, a noble of Bologna, was Senator at Rome in 1513 and 1514. Cugnoni, *u.s.* p. 54.

  * See *postea*.

  † Malvasia. Felsina Pittrice. 4to. Bologna. 1678. i. 44, 45.

  Rumohr supposes (Forschungen, iii. p. 74) that Francia's " Epiphany," No. 568A, in the Dresden Museum, may be an adaptation of Raphael's " Nativity." But this is a mere con-jecture only justified to this extent that there is something Raphael-esque in Francia's very pretty composition. As to the date of the " Nativity " we must also re-collect that Raphael, in a letter of Sept., 1508, to Francia, sends the latter the drawing of a picture which he calls a " Presepe," and of which he says that it differs somewhat from the picture made from it. (See Malvasia Fels. Pitt. i. 45.)

notwithstanding, it is not easy to decide whether
Raphael visited Francia at Bologna, or Francia
Raphael at Florence. Neither of these journeys can
be satisfactorily proved. But there is more reason to
believe that Francia travelled to Florence than that
Raphael ventured so far north of his habitual places
of residence. There is evidence in Francia's pictures
that his style was improved in the first decade of
the sixteenth century by a personal examination of
Florentine masterpieces. We shall therefore presume
that it was on Francia's coming to Florence that his
acquaintance with Raphael was made.

Returning to his usual avocations, Raphael, we saw,
became more desirous of public employment than
anxious to extend his private practice at Florence.
It was natural that having acquired repute as a
painter in the absence of Lionardo and Michaelangelo,
he should have thought that Soderini would give him
a chance of carrying out some of the great commissions which two of the best Italian craftsmen had
unaccountably neglected. Yet it would seem that
his hopes were disappointed. Their realization was
certainly so long deferred that nothing came of them
before his final departure for Rome. Meanwhile,
when writing to his uncle, Ciarla, he did not forget,
as we have seen, to do all in his power to keep up his
interest with such patrons, as he had won during his
residence at Florence. "Do honour," he says, "to
Taddeo Taddei, to whom I have the greatest obliga-
tions." Then he alludes to a picture, of which he had
completed the cartoon, and he tells how it occurred to

him that this cartoon, and the picture to be made
from it, would bring him orders from Florence and
from France worth at least three hundred ducats.*
He had, indeed, been marvellously assiduous at his
easel; and when we look at the number of pieces
which he finished, or all but finished, before the
summer was out, and the call of Bramante took him
to Rome, we are impressed again and again by the
wonderful activity of his mind and hand.

Though Raphael's contemporaries are silent as to
the history of the " Holy Family with the Lamb,"
which was discovered in our time in the wilderness
of the Escurial, it will be obvious to all who look at
the picture that the composition was suggested by
Lionardo's " St. Anne with the Virgin and Child
and the Lamb." †   It seems as if the action, inchoate
in Da Vinci, had suddenly been made consummate
by Raphael, who, seeing that Lionardo had caught
the moment when Mary helps the boy to throw his
leg over the lamb's shoulder, went a step further, and
set the Saviour astride of the animal supported by the
Virgin.   In the attitude of Christ's mother half
sitting, half kneeling on the ground, or of St. Joseph
who bends forward as he rests both hands on his staff,
a reminiscence of the Canigiani Madonna is supplied.
But the Infant Saviour riding on the lamb, and grasping its neck as he looks inquiringly upwards, is
original and life itself.   Notwithstanding the clear
derivation of the subject from Lionardo, there is less

* Raphael to Ciarla, *supra.* | † Gallery of the Louvre.

searching, and more instantaneous natural thought in the whole design than in other masterpieces of the time. St. Joseph, aged and weary of his journey, seems to court repose, whilst his fine profile is full of tender interest. The lamb cowers the better to bear the weight of the child, whose shoulders the Virgin's hands are eagerly supporting. The sacrifice of the cross is suggested by the coral scapular round the infant's neck, maternal love struggling with anxiety for the babe's safety in the full smiling features of the Virgin. Exquisite handling and careful finish are appropriately lavished on a panel of the smallest size, and the landscape is as lovely as it is minute, with its large weeds in the foreground, the lake and the road along its banks, the castle on a hill, with a church and tower in the low ground, and a flight of birds in the sky, beneath which a distant chain of blue mountains is seen. To the right of St. Joseph a sapling spreads its leaves, whilst in a distant winding of the road the ass appears unwilling to yield to the efforts of his driver.* Innumerable designs group them-

* Madrid Museum. No. 364. m. 0·29 h. by 0·21. Panel. Found in the Escurial. No trace of the date or of the way of its coming to Spain. Inscribed in gold letters on the border of the dress at the Virgin's throat : " RAPHAEL VRBINAS MDVII." The surface is slightly rubbed down, and the colours are somewhat out of harmony on that account.

A fine copy of Raphael's time, many years since in the hands of Signor Baldeschi at Rome, was sold in 1840 to Count Castelbarco of Milan, who sold his collection in Paris on the 2nd of May, 1870.

Another feebler copy, assigned to Pierino del Vaga, is in the Pembroke Collection. It seems to have remained unfinished. Other poor repetitions are : Corsini Gallery, Rome ; Cassel Museum, with the addition of John the Baptist and a rabbit, injured by restoring ; Prince Kutschubey at

selves round this little picture. In a pen and ink sketch at the Uffizi, the Virgin sits with the Infant Christ on her lap, throwing himself forward to fondle a lamb, or a dog in the arms of the young Baptist.* Much in the same action, but in reverse, a similar sheet at Vienna shows the Virgin giving the Child to St. Anne, who rests on the ground to the left.† At Oxford a turbaned Madonna holds the Babe on her hands above the recumbent John; and Christ looks archly at his companion whilst he clutches at the hem of his mother's dress.‡ A group of the same kind at the Louvre, seen from a different point, appears to realize a similar thought in varied form; and if in the lines we miss the pure contour of Raphael himself, we gather that some pupil out of his school strove to perpetuate one of his original conceptions.

St. Petersburg, on copper. Others again are noted as having belonged to Charles I.'s collection in London, the Malaspina Gallery at Pavia, Tacchinardi Collection at Florence, and Mr. Migneron in Paris. A copy, which had been sold to Count Demidoff, and suffered injury in consequence of a wreck, is now in the Gallery of Angers. (Journal des Beaux Arts, 1869, p. 184.)

* Florence. Uffizi. Frame 140. No. 515. Pen and bistre. The Virgin seated to the left turned to the right, Christ on her lap, John standing at her knee.

† Vienna. Albertina. Three Lionardesque figures. The Virgin to the right hands the infant Christ to the aged St. Anne. Full lengths. From the Ligne Collection. 5½ in. h. by 4⅞ in.

‡ Oxford. No. 77. Pen and bistre sketch. 6¾ in. h. by 5 in. From the Wicar and Lawrence Collections. The Virgin is much in the same attitude and movement as above, but the two children are of course varied, and John sits a little in the background of the colonnade, at the end of which a figure is seen. On the back of the drawing is another sketch of a "Holy Family," but without the heads of the Virgin and Saviour. A copy of this is in the Albertina at Vienna.

In every one of these compositions the precepts of Da Vinci direct the master's hand.*

It seems possible, though scarcely probable, that the cartoon of which Raphael speaks in his letter to Simone Ciarla is that which still exists at the Louvre, and represents St. Catherine with one hand pressed to her bosom, the other holding the skirt of her robe as she rests her arm on the emblem of her martyrdom. The striped sash and the gossamer veil which winds through her hair and falls across her breast and under her fingers both adorn her shape. A mantle drops from her left shoulder and comes swathed round her hips in a twist by the grasp of her right hand. The face in upward motion receives additional expression from the glance of the eye, which goes heavenward with a tender feeling of candour and trust.† To the charm of sentiment and grace which so happily commingle in the cartoon, a new charm is added in the picture by the ringing harmonics of the pearl-grey dress with its green sleeves and black or white and yellow edgings, the claret reds of the cloak and its

---

* Paris. Louvre, not numbered. The Virgin, seated and turned to the right, on the ground, with her left leg extended as in the "Madonna di Casa d'Alba," holds the infant in her arms. His arms are round her neck, and he looks at the recumbent Baptist, showing his back at the Virgin's right side. To the left two females in profile and three-quarters. To the right a child and a fragment of the head and figure of a Virgin, much in-jured. Pen sketch. From the St. Morys Collection.

† Louvre. No. 323. Cartoon in black chalk, heightened with white and pinholed for use. m. 0·587 h. by 0·437. From the Jabach Collection. The face is turned at three-quarters to the left, the body a little to the right. A rent in the paper about the wrist of the hand near the wheel has been fairly repaired.

orange lining. The eye with its four lashes and its
pupil straining towards an aurora in the sky, whence
it would seem a ray of hope descends on the head, is
as beautiful as if the apparent strain in it were not
a forcing of nature to an extreme of tension. The
cherry lips, half open, showing the teeth, are no dis-
figurement. The face, with all its beauty, has also the
mould of the best of those in the Maries of the "Entombment," or the "Faith" of the Vatican predella.
The attitude and the turn of the features and neck,
as elegant as the grasp of the drapery is powerful,
reveal the richness of the master's fancy and the
strength with which he was endowed. A dandelion
in seed, a ranunculus, and other flowering weeds,
show their leaves and blossoms above the edge or the
nearer undulations of the foreground. A pleasant
gloom overspreads the sedgy banks of the lake, on the
further shore of which homesteads appear amidst trees
in front of a low chain of hills; and over all a grey
sky is illumined by rays that issue golden from the
clouds.*

At the outset Raphael had thought of painting the
whole figure leaning cross-legged against the wheel.

---

* National Gallery. No. 168.
Wood. 2 ft. 4 in. h. by 1 ft. 9½ in.
From the Aldobrandini and
Borghese Collections. It was
bought from the latter at the close
of last century by Mr. Day, who
sold it for £2000 to Lord North-
wick. It was purchased for the
National Gallery from Mr. William
Beckford of Bath in 1839. The
surface is injured by a most unfortunate cleaning. Round the
edge of the dress there are traces
at the bosom of gold ornament
and letters, and here may have
been Raphael's name.

The copy in the Trubetzkoy
Collection at Petersburg was not
seen by the authors.

He drew the sketch on a sheet at Chatsworth, where a study of a girl pouring water from a jug is taken from Ghirlandaio's fresco. But here the head is rather sentimentally inclined than strongly foreshortened. It has the elegance, though hardly the strength, of that in the cartoon.* The figure is repeated to the knees in a drawing at Oxford with the eyes facing the spectator, but with dubious purpose in the lie of the right hand. Yet even then Raphael had resolved to create a new mould for the features, and he made a careful study of the neck, as it came at last into the picture. His next step was to turn the paper and draw the face alone, a magnificent pen and ink design, in the true shape which was afterwards preserved, but accompanied by five outlines of Cupids, copied, one might think, from some antique, yet so completely formed in the fashion of nature, as to appear reproductions from life.† Rarely have studies for one and the same masterpiece so fully revealed the daily avocations, the whirl of mind, and the current of thought that characterized the great artist in those days.

---

* Chatsworth Collection. Pen and ink sketch. See *antea*.

† Oxford. No. 52. Pen drawings in bistre. 7 in. h. by 11. From the B. West, T. Dimsdale and Lawrence Collections. On the one side the study of the neck, below which is the sketch of the whole figure. At the side an outline of a naked figure, seen to the knee. Cross-wise below a nude of a man, seen to the hips.

On the other side, the face of St. Catherine as described. To the left a Cupid, as if riding on a dolphin, with his right arm raised and looking round to the right. To the right of these four Cupids with crowns of flowers in various classic attitudes, one leaning against a plinth, another stepping down from a projection, a third resting on a curved object like a cornucopia, a fourth showing his back as he trots away.

Whilst Raphael thus expended labour on a single picture, he seems to have thought it pardonable to stock his painting-room with school-pieces which, if designed by himself and issued with the stamp of his workshop, were not always marked with the true impress of his hand. Some of these pictures were perhaps painted at Florence, others, we should think, were produced at Perugia. It has been usual to believe that where Raphaelesque Madonnas are preserved, of which no single example bears the master's true sign manual, it may be presumed that the original has perished; yet we may suppose that in many such cases Raphael never painted an original at all, but left the design exclusively to the care of his subordinates. An early specimen of this kind is the "Madonna with the Pink," a pretty group of the Virgin seated in a room, holding a blossom detached from the spray, over which the fingers of her left hand are closed, and touching with her right the hand of the Child who looks up at her. The best of these pieces in possession of Count Luigi Spada at Lucca, combines Florentine style and dress with much warmth and sweetness of tone in a rich and harmonious scale of colours, and great minuteness and purity of outline.* Yet the treatment is no longer

---

* Lucca. Count Luigi Spada. Wood. 0·285 h. by 0·227. A veil round the Virgin's head is transparent enough to show the ear under it. The dress of pearl grey in the light turns to deep red in the shadows. The close yellow under sleeve has a fall and shoulder puff of light leaden grey. On the left shoulder the blue mantle with a yellow lining, which covers the hips and limbs. The boy sits on a white cushion. The Virgin is turned to the right, the

clearly Raphael's, and it is all the more natural that replicas at Alnwick, Leipzig, Rome, and elsewhere should be less attractive since they are comparatively feebler. The nearest approach to a sketch for this group in the absence of a cartoon would be one in a sheet of five designs for the "Virgin and Child" at Vienna, where the Madonna, with alternative movements of the head, holds the Infant on her lap and allows him to play with her fingers. Thoughts for the "Madonna di Casa Tempi," and the "Madonna Colonna," which cover the same leaf, merely show what abundant materials the master had brought together, and how easy it was for him to make pictures from these materials at a moment's notice.[*]

child to the left. Through an opening in the background to the right a tower and a tree on a hill, up which a road leads. The shadows are of thicker substance of pigment than the lights. The whole panel injured by cleaning and partial retouching. The ground of the room is dark; to the left a brownish green curtain. On the back of the panel, which was separated in 1847 with a saw, are the words in characters of a later age than Raphael's. "La Ga. Maria F. . . . a ricconto F. 170. Raphael."

Alnwick. From the Camuccini Collection at Rome. Wood. Same size as the foregoing, a little inferior to it, and probably by a Florentine assistant of Raphael. The flesh is somewhat of leaden hue, but very smooth and glossy, and the draperies a little dull in tone.

Speck Sternburg Collection at Lütschena, near Leipzig. Wood. 0·350 h. by 0·227. Feebler than the two foregoing. Brescia, Tosi, careful copy, but inferior to the foregoing. Loretto Treasury. Copy of a feeble character in copper, falsely assigned to Garofolo. Earl of Pembroke's Gallery. Small and modern but curious for the inscription on the border of the Virgin's dress at the throat: "RAPHAELLO VRBINAS MDVIII." For other copies in Palazzo Torlonia at Rome, Casa Giovannino at Urbino, Fröhlich Collection at Würzburg, Duval Collection at Geneva, Bystroem Collection at Stockholm, and Haegelin Collection at Bâle, see Pass. ii. pp. 63 –4.

[*] Vienna. Albertina. Central group out of five in pen and bistre, see *postea*.

About the time when the "Madonna with the Pink" came out of Raphael's rooms he also executed the Madonnas of Bridgewater and Colonna, though in general terms it may be said that the first was a Florentine, and the second a Perugian masterpiece. Not that the spirit of Raphael was absent from either, but days had been devoted to the first, whilst hours at best had been given to the second. The Bridgewater "Madonna" was finished almost to perfection because Raphael superintended its completion himself. The Colonna remained unfinished probably because it was entrusted to Domenico Alfani.

Though it consists but of two figures, the Bridgewater "Madonna" cost Raphael as much thought as pictures of complex line and numerous personages. Its parts are set with the view to produce compactness in the highest grade on the principles of Lionardo, yet with the result of yielding something new in the method of balancing the action of mother and Child. Whilst recumbent on the Virgin's hand, the Infant Christ raises his arms and turns his cheery face to the loving features of Mary, who rests her left hand with the veil in its grasp on the boy's side. The studied attitude of the latter is that which Raphael repeated with some variety in the Amor who breasts the waves and holds the dolphin's ears in the "Galatea" at the Farnesina. The Virgin's face, of the purest Florentine cast of beauty, is but the precursor of the still more lovely "Giardiniera" at the Louvre; but here the commune of mother and Child is innate and charming as it must be, when nothing disturbs the solitude of a chamber of which the shady walls and hangings and arched alcoves are free from vulgar interruption. The Child, of that expanded shape which characterizes the last phase of Raphael's art at Florence, is modelled with surprising breadth, yet with incomparable smoothness of blending in flesh; and nothing would cloud the enjoyment which the picture creates, except the poor execution of the blue mantle which betrays the feebler treatment of one of Raphael's disciples. It was in search of the perfection which the master here attained, that so much energy and skill were expended.* He doubtless designed a cartoon which served as the groundwork for the numerous replicas due to Raphael's age and to later centuries, but on that very account, perhaps, the cartoon was bound to perish. The earliest form of the composition is a sketch half silver point, half pen and bistre, in the Albertina at Vienna, where the attitudes

---

* London. Earl of Ellesmere. Wood, transferred to canvas. 2 ft. 7¾ h. by 1 ft. 10¼ in. The Virgin seated in full front, her hand to the left. The child recumbent, with his hand to the left, looking round to the right. The veil wound round the Virgin's head is lightly strapped to the edge of her dress at the bosom. Retouched are, the hair of the Virgin, and the child's left leg. Originally in the Seignelay Collection, the picture passed into the Orleans Gallery, at the sale of which the Earl of Bridgewater bought it for £3000.

Good copies are the following:

Florence, Torrigiani Collection, a careful picture in the style of the Florentine, Michele di Ridolfo Ghirlandaio. But the background is quite plain. Naples Museum. No. 28. Careful but feebly coloured. London. National Gallery. No. 922. On poplar. 2 ft. 10 in. h. by 1 ft. 11½ in. from the Wynn Ellis Collection. On the back are the words, "Ce tableau appartient à M. le Prince Charles, May, 1722."

Gotha Museum. Modern copy on canvas, assigned to P. Battoni. 2 ft. 5½ in. h. by 1 ft. 9 in. Other copies too numerous to mention.

would be like those of the picture, but that the Child, whose legs are slightly varied, is playing with flowers in the Virgin's right hand, whilst her left holds a veil by which his waist is supported. It is on the back of this magnificent drawing that we find the rapid jottings already recorded of the Colonna, Tempi, and other Madonnas.* In other fugitive combinations for the Bridgewater panel, one at the British Museum is remarkable for establishing the presence of a new and beautiful female model in Raphael's painting-room. It also shows not only a project for the Bridgewater " Madonna " in similar attitudes to those of the Vienna design, but by its side a mother clasping her infant to her breast, who lays his hand on the Virgin's bosom, and turns to look at the spectator like the Christ of the "Madonna Colonna." Round about these principal groups are rapid scratches of a reed recalling the "Madonna del Gran' Duca," the later Virgin at Panshanger, the " Madonna di Casa Tempi," and a couple of solitary heads of children.† Companion to this sheet a pen drawing in the same style at Florence shows the action and figures of mother and Child reversed, either singly or doubly, and the Child itself more than once repeated.‡ As

---

* Vienna. Albertina. Silver-point on prepared grey paper. The upper part of the child is overrun with pen.

+ British Museum. Pen and bistre sketch, very rapid and clever. The group of the Virgin and Child which is of interest here is that on the bottom of the sheet, with a head of a boy beneath it and another to the left. Three other groups are on the upper part of the sheet.

‡ Florence. Uffizi. Frame 135. No. 496. In this cluster of rapid pen and bistre sketches, that to the left shows the Virgin, seated and turned to the left, her head

distinguishing features in all these instances we should note the picturesque trimming of the model's hair in curls with twists of veils and ribands, and her face, though indicated with but rudimentary lines, bears marks of a peculiarly sprightly loveliness, and thus differs from the mere ovals which characterize similar heads in earlier days. A couple of groups of Holy Families traceable to no finished picture fills the paper and completes the evidence which proves not only that Perugino's habit of combining studies for compositions of different periods on one and the same folio descended to Raphael, but that both kept up their practice by constant thefts from nature in varied form and fleeting moments. Nor is it without interest to note that rapid as the master's hand appears he is constrained at intervals to drop the movement to which he was attending, because, at the instant of creation, the sitter from whom he was taking his outlines changed attitude, and could or would not return to it; but even with these proofs of changing occupation we by no means exhaust the field of observation which Raphael's art presents. Turning the Florentine sheet in which so many sketches for Madonnas and Holy Families are crowded, we find

bent down and turned to the right, whilst the child, with his head to the right in the picture, raises his right hand to catch the Virgin's veil. Next this group and to the right of it, the same model, looking out of the picture, whilst the child does the same, holding on to the hem of her dress. Lower down are three different figures of children, a Virgin and child erect, a Virgin with the child, who turns away from the caress of the infant Baptist, and to the right a couple of small confused pen scratches of a Holy Family with St. Joseph.

others of a totally different kind; the model seems
to have stripped. Venus Anadyomene appears fresh
from the waves on her shell, or we see her after land-
ing on the shore hiding her limbs in drapery. Then
Venus is discarded and a man of brawny shape yields
his muscular torso to Raphael's attention. It may be
thought, as suggested in an earlier page, that these
outlines are derived from antique statues, but this
hardly excludes the belief that nature was also consulted in their production.*

Such reminiscences as may still exist of preliminary
labours for the "Madonna Colonna," establish the
predominance of Florentine habit in Raphael's style at
this period. The oldest do not date further back than
1506, but even the earliest of these is almost completely formed in the mould which the "Colonna"
displays. The first thought occurs in a sheet at the
Albertina, once described in these pages as comprising
six studies of the "Virgin and Child" at the back of
a large design for the Bridgewater "Madonna." The
infant on his mother's lap bends his left leg for a
purchase by which he can rise, and hangs on to the
edge of the Virgin's dress, turning his face as he does
so to look out of the picture. The Virgin rests her
left hand on her bosom and looks fondly on the child.†

---

* Same frame and number.
Back of the foregoing. Venus,
nude, full length, and two other
figures as described in the text.
Her body is turning to the right,
her face fronting the spectator.
The male torso, back view, is to
the right of Venus on the shell,
the other Venus is to the left of
that.

† Albertina. Pen and ink
sketches, five in number, that
which embodies the group of the
"Madonna" on the left hand
upper corner of the sheet. In a
group below that, the same mother,

The next study, coupled with one for the Bridge-water "Madonna" in the British Museum, shows more decided effort; and, but that the Virgin's fingers are shown holding the infant's foot, would be similar in line to the first.* In a third sketch at the Uffizi the turn of mother and child is preliminary, as it were, to that of the "Madonna Colonna," the Virgin's head being slightly bent to the right, one hand on her lap, the other on the waist of Christ, who sits on her knee. He seems on the point of raising his right arm and left foot to consummate the action represented in the picture. But in this graceful and masterly outline there is no more evidence than else-where of an intention to set the Virgin's left arm in the movement of holding the book.† The only sheet in which this movement is depicted, is one at Vienna, in which the infant Christ no longer corresponds to the ideal realized in the "Madonna Colonna," the child being made to stand on his mother's lap, as he presses his face against hers and caresses her cheek with his fingers. But even this is a Florentine design, on the back of which three spirited figures of soldiers

---

as regards shape and attitude, holds the infant Christ, sitting instead of recumbent. In the midst of the lines there are others showing the movements of the Virgin in reverse, and a new ver-sion of the infant.

* British Museum. Sheet of four groups of the Virgin and child. That of the "Colonna Madonna" is to the right of that for the "Bridgewater Madonna."

A very rapid and clever pen sketch, see *postea*.

† Florence. Uffizi. Frame 136. No. 503. Pen and bistre drawing. The Virgin is seen to the knees, and the whole group in a rect-angular framing, suggests remi-niscences of the Orleans as well as of the "Casa Tempi Madonnas." It is a sketch show-ing rapidity and sleight of hand.

in combat are thrown, reminiscences, as we clearly observe, of the cartoons of Da Vinci and Michael-angelo, and repetitions of similar figures, pinholed for use in the sketch-book of Venice.* The triumph of Raphael is manifested in the genius with which he forms out of such varied materials the beautiful group of the "Madonna Colonna." Is it necessary to add that this grand composition represents the infant Saviour struggling to get up as he clings to the edge of his mother's dress, and smiling at the spectator, whilst the Virgin holds the missal raised in her left hand and serenely contemplates his lively efforts to rise ? When, however, we take to examining the treatment and handling of the picture, we soon per-ceive that the work is not Florentine, but must have been left incomplete in the painting-room at Perugia. Technically weak in colour, it leaves the surface of the panel visible through a filmy varnished tinting that merely overspreads the contour. A red tinge of false transparence covers the flesh uniformly; the drapery shades are dull and undecided, and the known freedom of Raphael's touch has made way for

---

* Albertina. Pen and bistre, rapidly shaded with pen hatching. The child stepping forward on his left leg but held firmly by his mother's right, as he turns to the right to fondle the Virgin. The Virgin's bare legs are drawn over the drapery. At the side of this group is a second, unused in any picture. The Virgin seated and turned to the right with the Saviour standing on her knee, looking at the boy Baptist, seen to the breast with a bird in his hand—all in a landscape. The sheet is patched in the part above and to the left of the Virgin's head. A copy of these two groups is to be seen in the Print-room at Berlin. On the lower edge of the paper at Vienna is a study of a Virgin and Child, and a child alone. On the back the three nude figures described in the text.

the feebler manipulation of Domenico Alfani. That the same cause produced the Umbrian affectation so markedly displayed in the features and air of the Virgin's head, or the dubbing of unfinished country and trees in the distance, is hardly to be doubted. We may presume that the picture thus prepared was returned by Alfani to be finished, and that Raphael finally disdained to give it the last polish. We may regret that a thought so graceful should have remained so unfortunately incomplete. It does not seem unlikely that by dint of a little labour Raphael might have brought the noble figure of the child into better proportion with that of the Virgin. He might have thrown life into the vitrous flesh, sap into the deadened drapery colours, and atmosphere into the landscape. He might have given majesty to the Lionardesque head of the Virgin, whose attire of hair and veils combines most beautiful elements of taste and of grace. He left the picture unfinished as if hopeless of improving it, busy perhaps with more enticing occupations, or works that would better suit the fancy of the Florentines.*

---

* Berlin Museum. No. 248. Wood. 0·77½ h. by 0·56½. The picture belonged to the family of Salviati at Florence, but passed by inheritance to the Colonna. When in possession of Maria Colonna, wife of Duke Giulio Zante della Rovere at Rome, it was purchased by the Chevalier Bunsen for the Prussian Government. It is not stated in the text that the rudiments of a veil are seen surrounding the infant's foot. The Virgin's hands are much rubbed down. The infant's yellow hair, once painted over the landscape, is in part abraded, exposing the blue of a distant hill. The Virgin's head is wound about with the thin veil, which twists round her shoulders, reappears at the waist and runs to the infant's left foot. The red dress, over a muslin chemisette, is slashed to show a

A passing glance, in anticipation, at a single incident in Raphael's later life at Rome helps us at this point to throw light on a short period of the master's Florentine residence. Inclosing a design of the "Nativity" to Francia, of which he says in a letter "that it differs from the picture which Francia had been pleased to praise so highly," Raphael expresses a wish that his friend should accept it, "as a trifling testimony of friendship and love." * It would certainly be stretching licence beyond permissible limits to affirm that the composition of which Raphael thus disposed was that which is now known as the "Adoration of the Shepherds" in the Gallery of Oxford. And yet there is no reason for doubting that it might have been so. Executed with the boldness and freedom which characterized Raphael's style in the earliest days of his first stay at Rome, the drawing represents a classic ruin with some of its pillars standing, but most of its walls overthrown. The Virgin resting one knee on the ground, raises with both hands the veil which covers the infant Saviour, who sleeps on a hastily fashioned bed near the base of a column. An aged shepherd kneels devoutly to the left, whilst two of his companions admire the scene from a respectful distance. To the right St. Joseph holds a girdle with which he supports the Baptist, who moves towards the infant Christ with

---

white lining at the armpits and along the arm. The mantle, as usual, is blue. Of numerous copies the authors know but one fairly old, that once belonged to the late Mr. H. Danby Seymour, and was exhibited at Manchester (132).

* Raphael to Francia, 1508. See *antea.*

his hands joined in prayer. Behind him are two angels and three shepherds and a stretch of country between the pillars of the ruin.* The interest which this magnificent design creates is enhanced by the fact that its principal incident is one which found repeated expression in such pictures of the Roman period as the "Madonna di Loretto," and the "Virgin of the Diadem," at the Louvre. Yet it is not on these nor indeed on the drawing itself, which is an undoubted production of Raphael's Roman time, that we now presume to dwell, but on the picture of which Raphael expressly says that it had already been painted in a different form, though he does not affirm by his own hand † ;—the picture of which so many examples exist, that one is tempted to think they represent the 300 ducats which Raphael told his uncle Ciarla he would get from one cartoon.‡ All these pieces have a common subject—the Virgin kneeling in a meadow, lifting the veil from the head of the slumbering Christ in presence of the infant Baptist. The attitude of Mary is alike in every instance. Her form, as she rests on the ground with St. John in her charge, is full of grace. Seated in profile to the right, yet turning her head and shoulders to the left, she gently raises the cloth from the child's face to show him to his companion. Resting on coverlets and cushions against a rising in the ground, the Saviour's body gently reclines, one

---

* Oxford Gallery. No. 76. Pen drawing in bistre. 15½ in. h. by 10⅔ in. From the Wicar, Ottley, and Lawrence Collections. A magnificent composition of twelve figures.

† Raphael to Francia, 1508, u. s.

‡ Raphael to Ciarla, 1508, u. s.

elbow leaning on the cushion, the left arm in repose on the leg nearest to it. As she raises the veil the Virgin looks tenderly at her babe, St. John on his knees at her side is quietly pressed to her heart; full of glee, he points with his finger at the infant Saviour, and looks round with a joyful smile at the spectator. His youthful form, older than that of Christ, the touching sentiment of love in the Virgin, the quiet sleep of the Redeemer, are all contrasting elements in a beautiful composition. The country around is in the prime of spring vegetation. On one side small trees hardly conceal a range of hills beyond. A shepherd in front of a grove tends his flock, in rear of them is a stream with a low bridge. At the foot of the slopes are the towers and walls of a fortified village. On the other side broken ground, slight saplings rising to the sky, and St. Joseph trudging past with his pack on a staff, whilst a more distant female bends her steps towards the Florentine convent of San Salvi. Unfortunately the arrangement is all that remains of Raphael's work. None of the replicas in existence will bear examination as genuine productions of the master. Not even the cartoon at the Florentine Academy, though squared for use, will prove satisfactory. Yet the superior attraction of the subject is apparent from the frequency of its multiplication. If the Brocca example at Milan can claim to be the earliest and the best that we now possess, it only proves that Raphael's assistant at the time was Ridolfo Ghirlandaio, and that the whole labour of execution was confided to the ablest journeyman in his painting-room. None of the six repetitions that remain are worth a moment's attention, nor can they claim to be more than feeble echoes of the master's thoughts, though in every case the treatment is distinctly Florentine.*

If the true cause of Raphael's abandonment of the "Madonna Colonna" could be discovered, we should

* Florence Academy. Cartoon. Squared and pinholed for use, but pasted together after having been cut into fragments. Black chalk, heightened with white, so greatly injured as to leave some doubt of its genuineness. The drapery about the Virgin's head differs from that in the pictures. The face of the sleeping boy is turned to the left, whilst in the pictures it is always to the right.

Milan. Signori Brocca. Wood. 4 ft. 6 in. square. Bought at Barcelona in 1822. It is said to have been then covered with re-paints, which were subsequently removed by the painter Molteni. But certainly Molteni added retouches of his own. Though square the panel was once framed in a round, of which the track remains, cutting off the corners. It is hard to say, after the injuries which the picture underwent, who the painter was. The pigments seem moistened with a varnish medium ; the shadows are heavy, the modelling imperfect, and the colours feeble. Yet originally the treatment may have been that of Ridolfo Ghirlandaio ; and certainly there is no better example of the composition.

Pesth. Esterhazy Collection.

Round. Here the handling is that of a pupil of Raphael, and recalls Giulio Romano or Penni, without being good enough for either.

Florence. Corsini Gallery. No. 164. Square. Assigned to Mariotto Albertinelli, but by some follower of Ridolfo Ghirlandaio.

London. Grosvenor Gallery. Square. 4 ft. 3 in. h. by 3 ft. 9 in. A dark heavily tinted example of the schools of R. Ghirlandaio or Pontormo, with hard contours.

Blenheim. Square panel, with part of the landscape at the right side wanting. A brownish picture, of the Florentine school, and perhaps by one of the Allori.

Hague. Palace of the late Prince Frederick of the Netherlands. Round. Much rubbed down. From the Collection of Prince Lucien Bonaparte ; with evident traces of Florentine treatment, in the form of Pontormo and his disciples.

Petersburg. Hermitage. No. 41. Wood, transferred to canvas. Bought by Mr. de Tatistcheff in Spain. 1·25 h. by 1·09. A Florentine picture of crude tone and hard outlines.

Alnwick. Wood. Round. In the manner of the followers of Pontormo.

perhaps find a clue to the change in his art which
the "Cowper Madonna" of 1508 displays. This
masterpiece, which once belonged to a patrician family
at Florence, apparently indicates a final reaction and
protest against overwrought tenderness and Umbrian
feeling. More than any other of the works of Raphael's
middle time it illustrates the grand realism of the
school of Fra Bartolommeo. At no period of his
career had Raphael ventured on such an unconditional
appeal to the grace of nature unadorned, as in this
rendering of the Virgin and Child. He never showed
more freedom in the reproduction of form in the
strength and beauty of its ordinary daily aspects. It
was not to convey the idea of the God-like that this
picture was produced, but to manifest in the most
artistic way the care of a mother and the playful long-
ings of her child. The Saviour has outgrown the
period to which nature confines the mere nutriment of
milk. Yet his memory retains the knowledge of an old
pleasure. His mother is seated with her face almost
in profile. The rich tresses of her hair are partly
brushed in bands over her ears, or in masses off her
temples. The rest is gathered into plaits prettily
interwoven with ends of the veil which buries itself
in her dress at one shoulder. Falling from the other
shoulder, the veil winds round the waist of the infant
Saviour, who sits astride of a white cushion on the
Virgin's lap. Pleats of white muslin are just visible
above the edge of her rosy plum-coloured dress. The
wide puffs of the oversleeve cover the yellow brown of
a close undersleeve, and the knees are draped in the

pure ultramarine of the traditional cloak. The Virgin's right hand catches the striped veil as it passes round the child's body, her left lies on her bosom, and this gesture is in harmony with the fond look which falls from her large dark eye on the boy. For though he sits on her knee and looks frontwise half smiling out of the picture, and grabs with the fingers of his right hand at the cushion, as if his purpose were but half serious, yet his grasp of the hem of the Virgin's dress and the pull which he gives it, explain as clearly as the defensive movement of the Virgin that he longs for the breast, which she refuses to concede. His longing is expressed not only by action, but in a gentle bend of the head, open lips, dimples formed in the chubby cheeks by the inward tension of the corners of the mouth, raised eyebrows, and partial closing of the eyes. Feeling and form seem stolen at a glance from life. Mary, a robust young woman, whose beauty is not the less because she is gorgeously dressed and prettily attired, the child a full-shaped healthy boy, yet both without the chastened look and meaning expression which mark similar conceptions in the Orléans "Madonna" and the "Holy Family" with the bald Joseph at St. Petersburg. One almost thinks that here the mother and child, who sat for the Canigiani altar-piece, have grown apace, the first expressing tempered pleasure as of one who has tasted all the joys of her state, the second chirpy and confident, half sated with tenderness, and recalling in his look that stereotyped laugh which became conventional in the pictures of Del Sarto and Pontormo.

Raphael's superior genius gives to the group a strong pulsation of life, a realism such as he had never before attained, combining at the same time a vivid jet of light, harmonious modelling of transitions, potent transparencies of shadow, with a treatment so bold and frank as to strike us with astonishment.* No designs come down to us for this remarkable picture except the outline of a boy's face in the collection of Lille, which has the expression without the exact turn of the Saviour's head in the "Cowper Madonna."† The Virgin looking down at the laughing Christ, a masterly drawing in the British Museum, faintly displays the feeling which marked this period of Raphael's practice, but it equally recalls the "Madonna dell' Impannata," the "Madonna de' Candelabri," or the "Virgin" of Lady Garvagh, and it surely points to a moment in Raphael's life when the smiles and dimples of Lionardo merged into the gaiety and open laughter of the "Holy Families" of Andrea del Sarto.‡

---

* Panshanger, seat of Earl Cowper. Panel. About 2 ft. 3 in. h. by 1 ft. 6 in. The Virgin in half length. This picture, in which the Virgin is in profile to the left, and the child facing her, was described in Cinelli's Bellezze di Firenze in 1677, p. 409. It was purchased by Earl Cowper when H.M. Minister at Florence from the Niccolini family. The partial rubbing down which the surface has undergone has nearly obliterated the golden nimbs. The smoothness and polish of the flesh are like those of a bronze, and in this the panel resembles the "St. George" of St. Petersburg. The borders are minutely decorated with gold ornament, and on that near the throat are the words, "MD.. VIII. R. V. PIN."

Some copies of the "Cowper Madonna" have been described. They are unknown to the writers of these pages.

† Lille. No. 693. Silver-point. 0·10 h. by 0·08.

‡ British Museum. From the Wellesley Collection at Oxford. Silver-point, on coloured paper. The front face of the Virgin slightly inclined, the hair brushed off the forehead and temples, at

The moment of reaction which led Raphael to over-
leap the bounds within which he had hitherto confined his art, was short. It is evidence of the great
circumspection and command over himself which he
possessed that, feeling he had overstepped the limits,
he speedily harked back into the true path without an
effort and without regret. One of Raphael's greatest
qualities has always been that he kept a rein on his
powers which exercised the necessary check upon any
dangerous deviation, his nature in this being similar
to that of the ancient Greeks, whose aim was constantly to produce ideals perfect in form, subtle in
chiselling, and admirable for grace, or measured
proportion. It was under the sway of these laws
that he now set about finishing the "Bella Giardiniera" of the Louvre, the lovely group of the "Virgin
with the Infant Christ and Baptist," which completes
the cycle of Lionardesque compositions, begun with
the "Madonna del Cardellino" and continued in the
"Madonna in Green." It would be difficult to find
other words than those which express the excellence
of the masterpieces we have named to prize at their
true value the charms of the "Bella Giardiniera."
It is not too much to say that every part shows an
advanced refinement in construction and arrangement
of lines, elegance of attitude, purity of contour,
searching of bends and extremities, harmony of

---

her neck the head of the boy
Christ, full face, thrown back,
with an inclination to the right,
laughing open-mouthed.   This
lovely drawing, as softly modelled
as a work of Correggio, was purchased at the Wellesley sale for
£600.

colour, and loveliness of landscape. The highest principles of sublime art are united to the most minute finish in the reproduction of nature, and if ideal beauty is attained in the definition of form, we shall equally acknowledge the botanical fidelity of innumerable plants, which are part of the life that abounds in this delightful picture.

Last among the compositions of Raphael, which represents the connection of the book with the sacrifice of the cross, the "Bella Giardiniera" was originally conceived as a graceful illustration of the infancy of Christ. The first cartoon at the Louvre shows the Virgin sideways on a rustic bench, bending over the playful children at her side. Her head in front view is gently inclined to the right, and her attitude so taken that the flexible form of the infant Saviour is supported by one of her hands, whilst the other grasps his left arm. The book which she was studying, lies closed on the boy's fingers, and he, forgetting that he had just been playing with the leaves, steps from his mother's foot, on which he was standing, to look at the young Baptist, who has bound his temples with a garland of leaves, and kneels to present a struggling lamb.* But though

---

* Louvre. From the Crozat, Mariette, Revil, Lawrence, Woodburn, and King of Holland's Collections. Pen sketch, on yellowish white prepared paper. It passed, after the sale of the King of Holland's Collection in 1850, to Mr. D. J. de Arozarena, and finally into the collection of Mr. Timbal in Paris, who bequeathed it in 1881 to the State. 0·28 h. by 0·18. Squared for use. The Virgin's leg bare. The head, and particularly the nose of the Virgin, is injured.

A replica from the Lawrence Collection, long existed in the De

Raphael threw the net over this composition, and thus manifested his purpose of transforming it into a picture, he was afterwards led to change the position, as well as to alter the motive thought in each of the figures. He turned the Virgin a little out of profile, moved her head to three-quarters to the left, and confined her glance to the Saviour, instead of directing it to both children at once. Christ no longer turns to watch the lamb; his left hand stretches towards the book, which lies closed on his mother's wrist, and eagerly inquiring as he looks into the Virgin's face and opens out his fingers, he seems to ask the meaning of the missal and the cross. Not only has he been playing with the one, but he has also seen the other, on which St. John is reposing, as he kneels at the Virgin's foot. The Baptist's sidelong look at Christ, as he rests the reed symbol on his shoulders, and thrusts its point into the ground, and the repose of his left hand on his knee, are as natural, instantaneous, and true, as the attitude of Christ, who leans against his mother's lap, whilst she supports his shoulder with one hand and grasps his arm with the other. It is a pleasant vantage ground which he occupies, balancing himself with both feet on that of his mother. There is a mournful serenity in the pure lineaments of the Virgin, a longing, as if to fathom the mystery of his life in the Christ, a childish sympathy in the upturned eye and half speech of the lips of the Baptist. And

Vos Collection at Amsterdam. But the writers of these pages were unable to obtain access to it. It is not certain whether the animal in the arms of the Baptist is not a dog, rather than a lamb.

all this is so winning, the contour and features are
so lovely and so full of the rounding of health, the
expression is so charming, and the delicacy of the
hands and feet so rare, that it is hard to conceive anything more admirable. The Virgin's hair divided in
the middle, its tresses intertwined with a filmy veil
edged with black, and twisted irregularly to fall in
part on the cheek, in part on the neck, the red bodice
with its dark border relieved on a fringe of white at
the bosom, which itself is a masterpiece of anatomical
modelling, the dusky braid embroidered with golden
tracery, the greenish-yellow sleeves, the yellow sash—
all contribute to the harmony of the group, which
would be little less than perfect, but that the mantle
which Raphael had left incomplete, was ill-finished
and feebly thrown into fold by Ridolfo Ghirlandaio.
Yet the colour still serves as a foil to the grandiose
forms of the children. For brilliancy of tints, vividness of light and contrast by massive shadow, no
picture of Raphael's time approaches this, if we
except, though at a respectful distance, the " St. George
of the Hermitage " or the " Cowper Madonna." An
imposing breadth marks the balance of the surfaces
struck by the sun, and those that are thrown into
cerulean half shades, warmed here and there by com-
plementary touches of purpurine pigment. We
dwelt for an instant on the botanical accuracy of the
foreground plants. Their number is striking, including grasses, sedges, weeds, and meadow flowers. To
the horizontal and sombre undulations diversified by
Raphael's favourite trees or the line of the lake, the

banks of which are dotted with isolated towers, and the domes and spires of a city, due contrast is given by a chain of hills under a sky that deepens as it rises and holds in suspense a skim of graceful cloudlets.*

The time which elapsed between the original design for this altarpiece, and its *quasi* completion, is shown by a drawing at Oxford, which gives in a grand sweep of lines the form of the infant Christ, together with five different sketches for the lie of the left leg and foot. The back of this sheet with the skeleton of a female figure in profile to the right— a study of proportion and movement completed by a loose indication of bones—when taken in conjunction with the clever stroke of the crayon, prove that the transformation, by which the picture attained its present shape, was made about the period immediately subsequent to the completion of the "Canigiani Madonna" and the "Borghese Entombment."† The

---

* Louvre. No. 375. Wood. 1·22 h. by 0·80. Arched at top. All the figures in full length. On the edge of the Virgin's mantle, just over the foot and divided by the green limb of the cross in John's hand are the letters, "RAPHAELLO VRB.," and on the edge near the elbow, "MDVII(I)." According to the catalogues of the Louvre this picture was purchased by order of Francis I. of France, it is said from Filippo Sergardi, who had ordered it of Raphael and sent it to Sienna. Supposing this to be correct, the picture was truly

finished by Ridolfo Ghirlandaio, as appears not only from the style of the blue mantle of the Virgin but from Vasari's distinct statement (viii. p. 12) to that effect. The Virgin's mantle is raw and disagreeable in tone, besides being thrown into meaningless folds.

† Oxford Gallery. No. 50. Pen drawing in bistre. 11¾ in. h. by 7 in. From the Boehm (Vienna) and Chambers Hall Collection.

Of the sketch for the "Bella Giardiniera," which was once in the Mariette Collection with a study for the "Entombment" on the

letters MDVII, with traces of yet another I, and Raphael's name on the edge of the cloak near the Virgin's left foot, tell plainly enough when the picture ceased to be touched by the master's hand.*

Though but a satellite of a brighter star, or a pigmy by the side of the "Giardiniera," the "Madonna Esterhazy" claims to be admired for many of the qualities that distinguish its more important rival. A beautiful composition, broadly handled and grandly outlined, it seems equally remarkable for life and grace, and freedom of pictorial treatment. If Fra Bartolommeo, who now wandered in the paths of his younger friend, had once been known as Raphael's teacher, he now surrendered that position apparently without a murmur. Endowed by nature with other gifts than those which had been lavished on his Umbrian competitor, the Frate had never realized the sweetness of expression or the purity of form and

---

reverse of the sheet (Pass. ii. p. 68), nothing is known at this time. But the presence of drawings for both pictures on one paper might prove that the designs for them were begun at the same period. The cartoon at Holkham described by Pass. ii. p. 9, was not seen by the authors. A sketch for the "Virgin and Child," from the Santarelli Collection at the Uffizi, No. 8, is falsely assigned to Raphael.

* A poor copy of the "Bella Giardiniera," in a round, is at the Louvre—panel.

Another copy, once in the Mazarin Collection, was sold at the sale of the Bale Collection in 1881 to Mr. Arthur Tooth for 115 guineas.

The best copy that we have seen is that of the Townshend Collection at the Kensington Museum, which came from the Collection of the Duke of Marsa and Lord Coleraine. On the hem of the mantle above the Virgin's foot we read, "RAPHA.LO VI," and on the hem near the elbow, "MDXLV." The copy is cold and hard, but conscientious. Other copies are noted by Passavant (ii. 69–70) at Dresden, Milan, Vienna, Genoa, Avignon, and the Escurial.

feature which had always proved attractive in the
masterpieces of Perugino's disciple. When Raphael
won from the Frate all the boldness of his art and
added them to his own store, the necessary consequence was a clear superiority. Fra Bartolommeo
became dependent on his friend, though he lost not a
tittle of the grandeur or freedom which had characterized his manner from the outset. It had doubtless
been an unequal race, in which the Florentine started
with full knowledge of the ground, and an intimate
acquaintance with the windings of the course, but the
conditions under which the two competitors ran,
were similar; both had striven to develop the precepts of Da Vinci. The victory of Raphael was due to
vast powers of assimilation, which enabled him to
equal the Dominican in his own walk, and surpass
him in that which the Frate could not acquire
with equal rapidity; and thus it happened that
Raphael produced the " Esterhazy Madonna " and the
" Madonna del Baldacchino " on the lines of Fra
Bartolommeo, before it occurred to the latter to create
the Raphaelesque " Majesty " of San Romano or the
" Virgin and Saints " of San Martino at Lucca.*
But, as if to accumulate proofs of the superiority
which Raphael displayed, Fra Bartolommeo first
created the " Holy Family " of Panshanger, in which
the relations of the two masters in art were manifested, and, six years later, finished the " Holy

---

* Rumohr (Forschungen, iii. p.
71) assigns to Raphael a share in
the "Majesty" of San Romano.
But this view of the clever German cannot, in our opinion, be
seriously sustained.

Family" at the Corsini Palace in Rome, in which he
copied the pyramidal form of the "Madonna Canigiani" and the landscape of Raphael's "Holy Family
with the Lamb."

The "Esterhazy Madonna" at Pesth hardly measures
ten inches in square surface. As a composition, it
is a gem without a flaw. The Virgin kneels in the
middle of the picture at the base of a ledge of rock,
on which she holds the Babe in a sitting posture.
Turning her face to the left she looks down with a
bend of her body and a slight inclination of her
head to watch the boy Baptist, who rests on one
knee with the reed cross in his left hand and a scroll
in his right, from which he reads the words: "Ecce
agnus Dei." The infant Christ, eagerly watching
his companion, leans forward over his mother's arm
and struggles to obtain the fatal scroll. From the
recess of stones in which the scene is laid, the view
stretches over an undulating country, the hills of
which are rich in abundant vegetation. To the left
a lake is fringed with bushes, in rear of which are
Roman ruins like the temple of Vespasian; beyond,
a cliff, and above the hill to the right the cone of a
mountain rising into the sky.

But this magnificent composition proves as dis-
appointing in its execution, as it is perfect in its
arrangement. Perhaps it was one of a series of small
pieces of which Raphael traced the outlines without
finding time to paint them in, and so left them to be
finished by a pupil. The Roman distance might show
that the panel was taken in an incomplete state from

Florence and supplied with a local landscape at Rome. That in a later age the picture was sent as a present from one of the popes to an empress of Austria seems a proof that it had been brought to Rome; and this belief seems rational, because the original cartoon in the collection of the Uffizi has a different background from that which the picture displays.*   In the latter, as we saw, there are remnants of Roman architecture, in the former a view of a narrow vale, through which a stream, meandering slowly, sheds its waters over a weir, the banks being lined with alders, and two or three towers rising in front of a conical hill to the right.   Nor can we compare the cartoon and its coloured replica, which, so far as the group is concerned, are quite alike, without observing the great superiority of the former over the latter in grace of movements, or beauty of features, in the trim of the Virgin's head, the expressiveness of her eyes, the profile of Christ, or the garlanded head of the Baptist.†

---

* Esterhazy Museum at Pesth. Wood. 10 in. h. by 8 in. On a paper pasted to the back of the panel, German words are written to this effect: " This picture of a Virgin by Raphael of Urbino, with its box garnished with precious stones, was given to me as a present by the Pope Albany (Clement XI. 1700–1721).—Elizabeth K."   It seems that the Empress Elizabeth gave this picture to Kaunitz, from whom it passed to the Esterhazy family. (See Pass. ii. p. 72.) Passavant notes a copy in the Wendelstadt Collection at Frankfort-on-the-Main. A fine copy, un-finished, is in the Casa Thiene at Vicenza. Another, also unfinished, in the Ambrosiana at Milan. The " Virgin and Child," alone at the Uffizi, No. 1235, once ascribed to Fra Bartolommeo, is a very feeble production of a low class Florentine.

† Uffizi. Frame 154. No. 539. Pen and bistre sketch. 10½ in. h. by 6$\frac{5}{12}$.

A pen and bistre drawing of the whole group in the Chatsworth Collection, with a drawing of the " Madonna del Gran Duca," would require study on account of certain points in it which suggest some doubts.

All of these form a group of excessive grace, reminding us, as to the Saviour, of the "Madonna of the Palm," as to the Virgin, of the "Holy Family with the Lamb," and as to the children in general, of the boy angels in the "Madonna del Baldacchino," which we shall presently find transformed and improved in the allegories of "Poetry" and "Philosophy" in the chambers of the Vatican.

But if Raphael could compose and carry off with him to Rome a gem-like "Madonna" like that of Esterhazy, it was not so with the large altar-piece, which he had promised to execute, yet was unable to finish for a chapel in San Spirito of Florence. Looking at this picture, as we find it at the Pitti in the state to which it was brought by the painter Cassana, it is difficult to divest ourselves of the idea that the panel was due to Fra Bartolommeo, an impression which gains upon us, when we look at the monumental cast of the draperies and the grand movement of the saints in the foreground. Yet a moment's attention shows that the heads could have been done by no one but Raphael, whilst Vasari puts an end to all wavering by telling us that Raphael began the picture and left it unfinished when Bramante called him to Rome.

About the time when the "Madonna del Baldacchino" was undertaken, Fra Bartolommeo was probably preparing the studies for the "Majesty" of San Romano and the "Madonna" of Lucca. Which of the two masters preceded the other in the genesis of these graceful Lionardesque creations, it would be hard to say. It has been thought that Raphael assisted Fra Bartolommeo in the " Eternal and Saints " of San Romano; yet this theory has not found any serious support.*   We saw that there were many points in common between the two artists at this period. But the ties which underlay these points, were seemingly produced by counsel only; not a trace is to be found of Raphael's pencil at San Romano or at San Martino, nor do the drawings for the altar-piece in any way display the style of Raphael. It may be that when Raphael painted the seraphs that hover about the throne in the " Madonna del Baldac-chino," he was inspired by some earlier sketches of the Dominican friar, yet were this even so, we can easily perceive that these beings are moulded in a new shape and formed with the chosen type and pure lineaments which Raphael alone conceived. Nor, indeed, is it possible to find anything more perfectly graceful in its way, or more genuine in Raphael's manner, than these emanations of his genius during the later days of his residence at Florence. They are so perfect that when Raphael was brought face to face with the necessity of similar creations at Rome, he did little else than repeat them, as if it had not been in him to find action, movements, or outlines, that were an improvement on those. Bold as the Frate was, trained as his hand had been to all the difficulties and foreshortenings of nude, he never came near the grace, the gentleness, or elegance of

---

* Rumohr, Forschungen, iii. *u.s.*

motion, which his rival here displayed. Nor did it occur to him to compose pictures on the scantling of the "Madonna del Baldacchino" till some years after Raphael's departure from Florence, when to every-one's surprise, we may venture to believe, he produced the splendid "Marriage of St. Catherine" at the Pitti, in which the same forms of dais, of angels, and attendant saints, are brought together, as Raphael had left unfinished when he went to Rome. And yet in the natural order of things it would have been for Fra Bartolommeo to show the way to Raphael, not for Raphael to guide the movements of his older and more experienced friend.

Since the days when Raphael painted the "Coronation of the Virgin" for Maddalena degli Oddi he had never attempted anything of so much importance as regards size and number of personages, as the "Madonna del Baldacchino." No other altar-piece except the "Entombment" had more completely absorbed his attention. He began the studies for it in one of the happiest moods of his Florentine period, and if the group of Mary and Christ, of which we still possess the sketch in umber in the collection of the Louvre, exhibits some slight difference of thought in the action of the infant Saviour, it is only because he probably resolved at one time to form these figures into a whole by itself. Nothing more lovely than the shape and face of the Virgin, who sits in a landscape and supports the head of Christ, as he rests his arms on her bosom, and she presses the fingers of his left hand as if willing to induce him to resume the breast which he has left. Seated on a cushion on his mother's lap, and bending to the breast, yet looking out of the picture, his face and attitude are delightfully expressive of curiosity and pleasure.   And seldom has it been even Raphael's fortune to imagine a group more perfect in itself or more subtle in conveying expression. Though it recurs in a modified form in a cartoon at Chatsworth, where the lie of the child's arms and that of the Virgin's right hand are slightly varied, the arrangement was still better suited for a picture by itself than it was to serve as a component part of a larger altar-piece.*   In the panel as it now stands, the Virgin sits between the carved arms of an ornamented throne.   One foot is set forward in front of the other, the fingers of the left hand gracefully rest on the arm which Christ leans on her bosom, whilst the right hand catches the infant under the shoulder, as he plays with one of his feet and looks archly and openly smiling at St. Peter.   In other respects the Virgin resembles the sketch at the Louvre.   Her hair is divided and brushed over the ears, and the riband which binds her locks disappears behind her back.   The dress is gathered at the waist under a

---

* Louvre.   No. 315.   Black chalk drawing, washed with umber and heightened with white. 0·249 h. by 0·185.   From the Jabach Collection. This drawing has been greatly injured, and has been restored.   It must have been originally a very fine design of Raphaelesque Lionardesque type.

The same group, with attendant angels, a pen sketch at the Albertina of Vienna, does not deserve the name of Raphael which it bears, but seems rather a sketch by Timoteo Viti.

sash, and the mantle falls in grand folds about her knees.

The change in the setting of the "Virgin and Child" was not the only one which Raphael made after he had thrown his first thought on paper. The Chatsworth cartoon itself, though copied in its main lines into the picture, was not wholly or completely reproduced in the altar-piece. The angels lifting the curtain of the dais, the four saints at the sides differ, to some extent, in both. The only figures which correspond are the two boy angels in the foreground reading from a scroll. St. Paul in the sketch becomes St. James in the picture, yet the sketch is a fine one, drawn with the pen and washed with umber, and hatched in the lights with white on the grey tinting of the paper.*

It is interesting to observe how Umbrian reminiscences occur in the plan of the double plinth and step that make up the platform of the throne. By raising the Virgin to so high a place Raphael gives her an advantageous position above the stone-flagged floor on which the attendant saints are resting. To the left, with the gospels open on the plinth, a hooded monk of the Benedictine order stands with the book reposing on one hand, gesticulating with the other, and looking round at the profile of St. Peter near him. The spacious masses of his robes recall the broad sweep of drapery so splendidly realised in

---

* Chatsworth.   Pen and umber on tinted grey smooth paper.

the frescos of Masaccio at the Carmine.* The study
for the upper part of this figure and a separate outline
for the head without the hood is one of the finest
silver-point drawings of the Lille Collection.† St.
Peter with the book and keys, in a brown tunic and
blue mantle, faces the spectator, yet looks round at
the Benedictine. In the Chatsworth design St. Paul
to the right leans with both hands on a sword, and
we trace a distinct likeness between his bearded head
and that of St. Romualdo in the fresco of San Severo.
St. Augustin, with his scapular and Bible, turns his
face to the left. In the picture St. James and not
St. Paul attends at the Virgin's side and rests his
hands on a long staff, whilst St. Augustin in a white
jewelled mitre holds the Gospels and stretches his
right hand towards the throne, looking round at the
spectator with features pulled down by asceticism and
fasting.

Two boy angels with wings, undraped, in front
of the throne-step, are admirably presented, one,
shown frontwise, resting on his left leg and holding
in his hand the end of a scroll, part of which is

---

* Florence Carmine. Head of
a monk in the fresco of St. Peter
in Cathedra.

† Lille Collection. No. 723.
Silver-point drawing, heightened
with white, on rose-coloured paper.
0·125 h. by 0·192. To the right
the figure seen to the waist, holding a folio, in the left hand—a
model in working-day dress. To
the left the head seen at three-
quarters to the left, with a skull-

cap, and a few streams of hairs
falling on the forehead. A very
broad and massively shaded study.

In another outline drawing of
an old bald friar, seen at three-
quarters to the left, a silver-point
sketch, half size, we have a reminiscence of the Benedictine
saint in the "Madonna del Baldacchino," and of the saints in the
fresco of San Severo.

shown in the fingers of the second, who stoops in profile to read the inscription which it contains. Of this pretty couple it is not sufficient to say that the figures are pleasing and their movements natural; they seem to represent the masterly completion of the trials which began in the earliest pages of the Venice sketch-book, and lead us through many stages to the perfection of the Florentine period. If we look at all the efforts which Raphael made, we surely trace the course by which he ascended from a feeble to an exact imitation of nature, thence to the realization of ideal form, which displays itself in the genii of the Vatican predella and finds its full expansion in the beautiful boys before us. It may be that the holy children in the "Bella Giardiniera" are more lovely and more refined than the angels of the "Madonna del Baldacchino," but for appropriate arrangement and freedom of action or breadth of treatment the latter are still unsurpassed, and we feel most inevitably that we shall now be led to the nobler and yet grander emanations of the painter's genius, which are the angels of the "Madonna di Foligno" and those of the "Madonna di San Sisto." It might have occurred to Raphael to observe the pretty effect of Perugino's two boys on the step of the Virgin's throne in the altar-piece at Marseilles, or that achieved by Pinturicchio in the Baptist writing at the feet of Mary in the "Virgin" of the Minorites of Spello, but who shall say that they have not taken their ideas from Raphael, whom they had learnt to look up to as a master of consummate parts?

But if Raphael's thought in these instances appears to coincide with that of Perugino and Pinturicchio, it co-exists more palpably still with that of Fra Bartolommeo, who might have taken it home from Venice, yet who only applied it after Raphael's departure in that picture at San Romano, where the angel plays a viol on the step of the Virgin's throne, or the altar-piece of the Pitti, where two children perform a concert in a similar place.

If in the definition and treatment of form and dress we detect in all the work of Raphael, unfinished as it remained, the clear and unmistakable influence of Fra Bartolommeo—if we trace the friar's lessons in the attitudes of the figures and the solemn grandeur of their gestures and drapery, the close connection of the two masters is yet more marked in the two seraphs who look down at the Virgin, as they fly and lift the hangings of the conical dais. Never till now had Raphael ventured upon such daring foreshortenings as the bird-like being to the left, or the profiled messenger to the right display. The contrast of their flight and motion with the stillness and calm of the groups below is perfect; and the shapes have acquired a grace, a lightness, and elegance which Fra Bartolommeo was incapable of equalling, much less of surpassing. The cone of the dais with the scolloped edging that enframes it, may recall the earlier days of Raphael at Perugia, but the curve and cornice of the dome behind are a new and splendid application of scientific laws; and here it is that we discern, if at all, the probable truth of Vasari's assertion that Raphael taught Fra Bartolommeo the rules of true perspective.*

In the midst of these occupations Raphael, not unmindful of the wants of his Perugian painting-room, found time to complete and send to Domenico Alfani one of the most interesting drawings which he ever produced. In the large collection of Raphael's designs there is not one in which the lines are more perfect, the symmetry more faultless, or the combination of attitude and thought in each figure more concentrated than in this one. The Virgin reposes in profile on a natural rising of the ground in the centre of a valley. Her left foot is thrown forward to the right, and she rests her elbow on a projection of the seat, lowering her left hand at the same time to hold a sash by which she supports the body of the

---

* Florence. Pitti. No. 165. Wood. 10 ft. h. by 6 ft. Vasari tells us that this picture was commissioned by the Florentine family of the Dei for their altar at San Spirito of Florence. Raphael left it unfinished when he went to Rome. It seems not to have been delivered. It came into the hands of Baldassare Turini, who had it framed in a stone framework by Baccio d'Agnolo, and set up in the cathedral of Pescia. About 1697 it was purchased by Ferdinando de' Medici, who caused it to be enlarged by Agostino Cassana, and then placed it where it now hangs. (Vas. viii. 12–13 and ix. 228.) A copy, which the Grand Duke of Tuscany ordered Piero Dandini to paint, still adorns the altar at Pescia. The panel at the Pitti is injured by cleaning and retouchings and by spots, as well as by the patching of Cassana. The apex of the cone of the dais and all above that is new. Hence the false notion of Longhena (Quatremère's Raphael translated) that the picture was finished by Cassana. The best preserved part of the figures of St. James and St. Augustine are the heads. The whole altar-piece, notwithstanding the damage done to it, is rich, bright, and golden in tone. The two boy angels recall a group of children looking at Herodias in the dance of the daughter of Herod by Giotto at Santa Croce.

infant Christ at her side. The Saviour stands leaning over her knee, and stretches his arms across hers to reach a pomegranate, which St. Joseph is offering. One of Joseph's hands is on a pack-saddle, upon which he is seated. St. Zacharias to the right, St. Elisabeth to the left, look on with serious and sympathetic interest. The picture is completed in the left-hand corner of the foreground by the boy Baptist in his tunic, who turns his face and glance to the spectator whilst he grasps a reed cross, round which a scroll is prettily wound. In the cloudless sky above six cherubs sing or play musical instruments. But Raphael was not content with the outlines, he also gave the shading of the group, and a broad jet of shadow thrown from right to left on the figures is admirably rendered by a skilful intertress of pen strokes. It may be a moot question whether Raphael sent this sketch to Alfani in pursuance of a pre-concerted engagement or of his own accord. The subject was squared and transferred to a picture about the middle of the 16th century; and we can only presume that Raphael's scheme for keeping up double painting-rooms at Florence and Perugia fell to the ground, because Alfani was unable to dispense with the personal superintendence of his chief. The reverse of the drawing is remarkable for four lines, in which Raphael conveys directions to Alfani:

"Menecho," he says, "remember to send me the love songs of Ricciardo, which describe the affliction (*tempesta*) that befel him on one of his journeys. Tell Cesarino to send me the sermon, and remember me to him; and, it occurs to me, press Madonna Atalanta to send me the money, and see that you get it in gold. Tell Cesarino to press her in this matter, and if I can do anything for you let me know."*

We shall have occasion to observe what relations Raphael entertained with Cesare di Francesco Rosetti, more commonly known as Cesarino, with whom he had dealings at Rome in connection with Agostino Chigi.† His correspondence with Alfani cannot be traced any further, but it is clear that if Raphael at Florence had been able hitherto to support an establishment at Perugia, the utmost that he could hope to accomplish after settling at Rome, would be to preserve some of his practice in Tuscany. His communication to Alfani appears in the light of an effort to settle such claims as were still outstanding at Perugia. It has been thought indeed that Raphael penned the lines we have quoted not only with the full certainty of his selection as one of the future decorators of the Vatican, but also with the knowledge of the subjects which he was to paint in the Vatican chambers. His request for love sonnets might be referred to some passion that filled his heart at the time. The sermon might have some connection with the doctrine of the Trinity which he was about to illustrate in the "Disputa."‡ The time certainly had

---

* Lille Collection. Nos. 741 and 742. Back and front of the drawing above described. From the Fedi Collection. One side. 0·357 h. by 0·237. The other (the better) 0·072 h. by 0·245.

† See Pungileone's Raphael, p. 81.

‡ Compare Dr. Ernst Guhl's Künstlerbriefe, 8vo. Berlin, 1853, vol. i. p. 122.

come when Raphael was to leave Florence with great advantage to his fame. Bramante had taken the necessary steps to secure his kinsman's employment by Julius II.,* and it only remains to inquire when the engagement was made and how it was compassed.

On the 21st of April, 1508, Raphael, it is clear, was at Florence without a thought of a change in the life which he had hitherto been leading.† His ambition was confined to the attainment of a high position in Tuscany. Hence his letter to Ciarla, in which he described his prospects, his duties and labours at Florence, and his efforts to secure the patronage of Piero Soderini. No painter of mark had ever possessed such advantages as chance had then placed within Raphael's reach. He was the sole master of any great repute that now remained at Florence. Soderini had found it consistent with his policy to favour the wish of Julius II. that Michaelangelo should return to Rome. Sated with work, yet yearning to devote himself to sculpture, Michaelangelo had left Bologna with the firm intention of settling in Tuscany for life. Yet but a few days before Raphael wrote to Ciarla, his will had succumbed to that of Julius, and he had taken horse for Rome. But Julius had gained some considerable experience of art and its difficulties since he had first planned his tomb in the Church of St. Peter; and circumstances had occurred, which necessarily led him to alter his purpose. Early in 1506 he had laid

---

* Vas. viii. p. 13. | † Raphael to Ciarla, u.s.

the foundation of a new basilica of St. Peter. One morning, to the astonishment of all his court, he stated his intention to demolish and rebuild the church which had witnessed the enthronement of so many of his predecessors, and the coronation of so many Emperors. On the 18th of April, 1506, he caused a mass to be celebrated at the high altar of the old cathedral by Soderini, Cardinal of Volterra; he then proceeded to lay the first stone of one out of four colossal pillars, intended to sustain the weight of the choir of a new edifice. He came without the usual procession of Church dignitaries. Two acolytes carried lights, a third held the whisk with the holy water. After mass he left the altar and, passing through the Chapel of St. Petronilla on a stage made of fresh-hewn billets, he came to the mouth of the pit where numerous labourers were at work to keep down the water. For a moment he feared that the sides of the pit would fall in, and he called on those who were nearest to withdraw. But mustering heart he fearlessly descended accompanied by the architects, amongst whom no doubt Bramante was numbered. A goldsmith attended carrying twelve medals, of which two were in gold of the weight of about twenty ducats and ten of bronze, all bearing appropriate inscriptions, a portrait of Julius, and an elevation of the new building. The whole of these coins were inclosed in a vase which was sunk under a marble block about 3 feet 2 in length, 18 inches broad, and $3\frac{1}{2}$ inches high. Before the stone was lowered the Pope took off his mitre, sprinkled the

marble with holy water, and gave the pontifical benediction.   He then recited a prayer, and to the sound
of a choral sung by the choir of the Vatican, the stone
was lowered into its bed. A litany was then chaunted,
Julius knelt, more holy water was supplied by the
acolytes, and plenary indulgence was proclaimed by
the cardinal deacons in attendance.*   At the close of
the ceremony a courier was despatched to Henry VII.
of England to inform him of the founding of a new
cathedral which it was devoutly hoped would soon be
brought to perfection.   For several years St. Peter's
was crowded with workmen.   The foundation alone
engulphed a prodigious mass of materials. The money
expended on the building itself rose to an enormous
sum involving expenditure to which Pallavicini
ascribes the excess of indulgences that led to the
Reformation and the partial ruin of the supremacy
of the papacy.   But the consequences to which the
Pope's resolution led, in so far as they affected the
general body of Italian artists, though less important
than those which influenced the history of the world,
were of supreme interest to a few professional men
who practised the arts at Florence and at Rome.   One
of these consequences was that Julius abandoned the
notion of erecting his own tomb within the precincts
of St. Peter, and thus gave up the favourite plan
which had filled his mind two years before.†   When
Michaelangelo came to Rome in the spring of 1508,

---

* Paris de Grassis Diary, MS.,   † Compare Springer's Raphael
in the Library of Munich, vol. i.   and Michaelangelo, pp. 105-6.
pp. 489 to 494.

the thoughts of the pontiff were absorbed in quite a
new series of undertakings.   He planned the decoration of the ceiling of the Sixtine chapel, and that of
the vaultings and walls of the Vatican chambers.   And
whilst he called to the latter all the artists of the
peninsula in whose skill he thought he might trust,
he reserved for Michaelangelo alone the task of painting the Sixtine.*   It is honourable to Buonarotti
that he should at once have declared that he was not
fitted by nature to carry out so great an enterprise.
It is characteristic for Raphael's position as an artist
that Michaelangelo suggested his employment in preference to his own.†   Bramante had been intriguing
in secret for the purpose of obtaining the commission of the Sixtine for Raphael.   He told the Pope
that Michaelangelo would never be induced to come,
because convinced of his incapacity to decorate
the Sixtine.‡   He multiplied his friendly receptions
of the painters of the Vatican chambers, whom
he gathered and feasted at his table.   Constant
guests at his board were his old pupil Bramantino,
Perugino, Pinturicchio, Signorelli, Lotto, Peruzzi,
and Sodoma.   Not one of these masters but was employed at the time in the Vatican chambers.   But
Bramante's plans were crossed by the determination
of Julius II. to remain true to his original purpose

---

* Michaelangelo to Gio. Francesco Fattucci.   Rome, 1508, in
Heath Wilson's Michaelangelo and
his Works, 8vo, London, 1876, p.
118.

† Condivi, Vita di M. A. Buonarotti, 8vo, Pisa, 1823, p. 34.

‡ Condivi, *u.s.*, p. 33, and Pietro
Rosselli to Michaelangelo in Heath
Wilson, *u.s.*, p. 83.

and appoint Michaelangelo to the Sixtine. Then it was, we may believe, that Bramante's tactics were changed. To the probable question which the Pope would naturally put to him, as to the powers of Raphael, whose employment Michaelangelo had recommended, what more natural than that Bramante should have said: "Holiness, try him—try him at the Vatican." He probably added that Raphael was equal, nay, superior, to Perugino and the whole band of painters who then filled the chambers. The Pope sent for Raphael, and in a few months the youthful master won his heart. He superseded all his rivals, not excluding the patriarch Perugino, and we note the surprising spectacle of a youth of twenty-three suddenly elevated to the highest rank in the hierarchy of his guild, in whose favour all the oldest and best-tried craftsmen of the Italian peninsula were unceremoniously turned out and sent about their business. But by common consent of the greatest pope of any age, and the greatest sculptor of the revival, Raphael stands acknowledged as the best man in his profession that Italy had ever possessed.

END OF VOL. 1.

BRADBURY, AGNEW, & CO., PRINTERS, WHITEFRIARS.